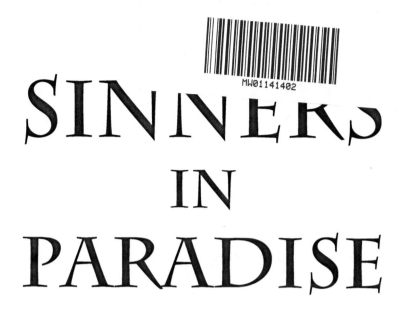

MW01141402

SINNERS IN PARADISE

ALEX Z. MODZELEWSKI

Humpback Publishing
Kailua, Hawaii

Humpback Publishing
http://www.outskirtspress.com/SinnersInParadise

ISBN: 978-0-9815183-0-5 — Paperback
ISBN: 978-0-9815183-1-2 — Hardback

PRINTED IN THE UNITED STATES OF AMERICA

To Ania, Ola and Maya,

brilliant, stubborn and wonderful Cats

"There is danger from all men. The only maxim of a free government ought to be to trust no man living with power to endanger the public liberty."

John Adams (1735—1826)

For Ania and Krzysio,

my beautiful Canadian

friends

Alex 2 Mroholosh

ACKNOWLEDGMENTS

A multitude of friends, family members and former patients speak through my characters' voices and argue their points of view in this book. Their beliefs are genuine in the sense of being evoked from my memories of real people, but all the characters appearing in this book are entirely fictional. No factual person, organization or geographic detail is described or represented in *Sinners in Paradise*.

I would like to express my special gratitude to Adam Koziol, a friend and a true blue-water sailor, who introduced me to the ruthless charms of the Pacific Ocean, and who has been an inexhaustible technical resource on sailing. He is responsible for the author's photo as well.

I wish to thank Jozef Nowak, M.D., a rehabilitation specialist as well as an old friend and colleague, who reviewed certain medical aspects of this novel.

Sinners in Paradise could never have happened without my editors: Bernice Lever—an angel of forgiveness who ploughed laboriously through the early versions of the book, and Joyce Libby who provided the finishing touches. I convey my deep appreciation to both.

Alex Modzelewski

CHAPTER 1

S teady trade winds drove clouds low above a darkened beach, but the thin sliver of a new moon broke through the cover, a pale spotlight on the empty sand below. The cloud window traveled inland, casting a dim glow over tree stumps jutting from the flattened land, then shone on a ruined house. The flat roof of a tall carport lit up as though it was floating on the pond of darkness high above the wreckage.

An irregular blot broke the shining plane, shaped like a big rag doll carelessly thrown on the roof. Her widespread arms hugging the surface twitched, then the figure crawled to the edge, raised her light-colored head and looked down. Her house had vanished. The ruins below looked like a relic of another era, long stripped of its contents and forgotten for generations. The world that Cat Milewski knew had ceased to exist on the sixth day of January 2007, hurling her brutally into an unfamiliar bleak and hostile place.

"You aren't done with me yet," she mumbled between her clenched teeth, as she crept along the roof's edge dragging her lifeless legs behind. Fifteen feet down, no rope and no ladder…. But she couldn't stay on top of her carport forever. With a disaster of this magnitude, no one might come to help for days. The neighborhood had been wiped

1

out as far as she could see. Cat grasped the waterspout that was still partly attached to the carport and lowered her body; the spout creaked and ripped off in slow motion.

* * *

Seventeen days before, with Christmas quickly approaching, Cat was sitting barefoot, dressed in shorts and a tee shirt, at her workstation trying to find and tie up any remaining loose ends. She had promised a major upload before the holidays. This was a big project, worth over a month of her work, and she could certainly use the nine thousand that the job would pay. Money aside, Cat's pride demanded that any software coming from her computer would work perfectly and be on time.

From her seat at the workstation she could see Kailua Bay. A postcard picture of Hawaii: a golden beach, blue water of the bay and a dark, gothic castle-shaped rock rising menacingly a mile off shore. The rock had an official name, but those who had any interest in it called the islet Bird Shit Rock for the white deposits that sea birds left. Seagulls liked the place because threatening white water surrounded it completely, so humans could not bother them. Waves tumbling over irregular outcroppings of basalt littering the ocean floor created whirlpools and sucking holes that could not be fully appreciated unless one rode a light boat over them. A treacherous site, definitely not a safe place to take a spill.

A man in a blue rental kayak came into Cat's view and seemed to be fishing. Lucky man, she thought, I am not going to move my butt from here for another four hours. Back to work. The next time she raised her eyes from the keyboard, he was paddling hard towards the beach. Either scared or racing, she thought watching him for a moment. The island paddlers frequently went around the rock, using it as a landmark in their practice routines. In fact, the first race of the season for *Kanaka Ikaika*, the club that she sometimes raced with, swung around Bird Shit Rock and Flat Island. This kayaker was no racer, and his blue salad bowl of a boat qualified him to play at the beach rather than in the open ocean. Ten minutes later, he was still in the same place. I need a break after all, she thought. Just as well, I'll go out to check on him.

Cat climbed into her kayak, a long and narrow surfski. Light, strong and stiff, it had all the qualities that an open-ocean craft should have, unlike rentals. She went out in her yellow boat almost every day, seeking the excitement of slipping through waves. A kayak skims through the water with little resistance, levitates the rider high on the waves so that the eyes can scan miles of the ocean, only to slide down on the other side of the wave like a long fish, a second later. Swells come and go marking the tempo of a dance between a human and the ocean. After three years, the thrill still had not worn off.

On this day, however, the water was smooth where the Koolau Mountains sheltered the beach from the western wind. Cat glided through it effortlessly, quickly closing the distance to the rock and the blue kayak. The tourist was outside of the island's shadow and had to fight the strong wind pushing him away from the coast. He had no business being there, could not control his boat and the waves smacked him repeatedly. Even worse, he decided that Bird Shit Rock was his salvation and entered the area of turbulence. He could be swimming any moment. Cat leaned on her paddle hard and reached him within five minutes; he was still hanging on. She threw a line and helped the guy paddle back to the beach. Cat felt sorry for the man. He probably felt humiliated being saved by a woman, so she cut the "thank you" scene short, and went home to finish her project.

* * *

The twentieth of December, as Jerry Roberts remembered it, was an unmitigated disaster. That morning, Jerry stood knee-deep in the warm water of Kailua Bay, which was still and smooth, reflecting white clouds above like a mirror. Weird. As a boy, he used to go to Cancun twice a year, where his parents had a timeshare, but he had never seen the sea this calm. Like my life now—warm, safe and bloody boring, he thought. Not a wrinkle. That's what I wished for, he shrugged, then went to the kayak stand on the parking lot next to the beach. Two rows of sturdy, plastic, wide-hipped craft were arranged on hot asphalt according to the color—one row blue and another yellow. He chose a blue kayak, signed a page-long liability release, took a paddle and donned a much-faded life preserver. The kayak was heavy and seemed to resist being dragged to the water's edge like a big, willful puppy. Two naked little boys wearing sun hats did not mind the hot and stagnant air as they threw sand at each other, squealing with delight. Jerry went around the kids, smiled to the moms who ogled him appreciatively, climbed into the boat and paddled slowly away. The kayak felt solid and stable.

Five minutes later, he passed over the reef extending from the small, flat island that looked like an aircraft carrier. Convoluted brown and gold shapes of brain coral silently passed under the boat's bottom, shallow enough to be touched with the paddle. The late morning sun was scorching his shoulders, just like ten years ago, in Ethiopia. The dress code more reasonable this time, he thought with mild amusement, and that bastard Murphy's not around. But again, if not for Murph, I still might be wearing boots. Funny, few lousy month . . . so many years ago . . . but never far from the surface. Hot weather, buzzing mosquitoes, some jerk cutting me off on the road—anything can send me back in a flash. Will it ever end?

Deep in his thoughts, Jerry did not notice that a light wind started causing the water to wrinkle and small waves appeared. A few minutes later, the wind increased suddenly. With certain alarm, he noted that he was more than a mile offshore, and the wind, quite stiff now, was blowing him into the open ocean. Not to worry, will fix the problem in no time, he smugly reassured himself, but the fact was, he never felt very comfortable on the open water. Run ten miles through a desert, or thrash all night through a jungle—backpack and all, no problem. But the ocean was not something he had ever trained for. He turned the bow towards the land and started paddling hard. Ten minutes of full-out effort did not bring him any closer to the beach. Jerry felt a tinge of a familiar sensation that one gets knowing that guys full of bad intentions lurk somewhere close in the darkness with their safety catches off.

Even with maximum effort, he could not make any gains against the wind. His hard but unskilled paddling produced a lot of splashing but little forward motion. A quick look around in hope of spotting a boat with a fisherman dozing off at its rudder failed to produce any prospect of assistance. The only thing that caught his eyes was that jagged black rock, perhaps a mile away, on his right side.

Bird Shit Rock. That's it, that's what the guy at the kayak rental had called it, Jerry recalled.

"It's the open ocean behind it, man. You don't want to go out there," the guy said. His lean muscular body and deeply tanned skin convinced Jerry that the man knew the bay first hand.

Damn, I am *out there*! He turned the bow towards the rock; it worked somewhat better. Now, with the wind blowing on his left bow, he started making some progress. Not towards the beach, but as long as he pointed the kayak 45 degrees to the wind, he was getting closer to that rock. Water spray was blinding his eyes and the boat rocked unnervingly. Buffeted every few seconds by large waves, Jerry knew he was out of his element. Neither the Army survival training nor kayaking experience from the Finger Lakes seemed to be of much value here. Once closer to the rock, he understood that this would not be his safe harbor; there was no way he could break through the hissing surf. Unable to land, he drifted through the turbulent water pushed by the wind away from the islet, watching the coast sliding away.

A splash of yellow appeared in his peripheral vision, on the right side. Jerry turned his head that way, fully expecting it to be just an illusion of his blurred eyes. But no, there was a long, slender kayak with a small figure in the seat. The mirage moved swiftly through the waves that appeared to part in front of the yellow bow.

"You OK?" The woman in the cockpit yelled at Jerry, zooming by on a wave within four feet of his boat. Rather risky under these conditions, he thought, but she was gone in a second, then made a tight turn, masterfully climbing water mountains and bracing against waves. She was surfing back on top of the big swell like a goddess riding a yellow horse to the rescue of a lesser creature. Her kayak passed in front of Jerry's bow and a looped line slapped against his chest. He grabbed the line, and a second later it almost tore out off his hands when the slack ran out and the momentum of the fast-moving yellow kayak got checked against his arms. He would have fallen out of the boat, but another wave mercifully slammed him from the opposite side and straightened up his kayak. Incredibly, the Goddess turned back without losing balance and smiled. She belonged to this place; she had no fear.

Jerry managed to slip the loop over his head and one shoulder and started paddling with new determination. The saving angel provided directional power that had brought the blue boat's bow under control and focused Jerry's effort; they started making progress towards the beach. Soon, the waves disappeared, the wind subsided and glassy water surrounded the kayaks again. Her light-blond ponytail was swinging rhythmically from side to side as she put in one smooth, swift stroke after another. Her back was slim but well-defined muscles rippled as she powered her way ahead. The woman turned her kayak around twenty feet from the shore. The boats almost touched each other. She smiled.

"These are Kona winds," she said. "A few times a year the trade winds stop and Kona starts blowing from the south and west, which is offshore on this side of the island. Visitors frequently think that there's no wind, and float away from the beach, but once they get out of the island's shadow, the wind picks up and—you know what happens next."

7

Jerry looked at her incredulously, his mouth half opened. The round delicate face with a small nose was deeply tanned and peppered with hundreds of freckles. But what really caught his attention was her mouth. Full lips slightly parted, she had the most beautiful, warm smile. There was no mockery or air of superiority in her smile. She is beautiful, he thought, and gracious as a swan.

"You'll be OK now?"

"Oh, yes, thank you very much. You saved me a lot of trouble. I'll be fine now, thanks again . . ."

"OK, good luck." She picked up her line, gracefully turned her kayak around, and was gone within seconds. All he could see was the swinging ponytail and the brown back crossed with pale yellow bikini straps. It had been many years since someone saved him from harm. Back then, nobody made much of it. An appreciative nod or a slap on the back was more than adequate. After all, the helper expected the favor to be returned. But what do you say to someone who saved you on a beach? A woman, and a beautiful one, too! He had no satisfactory answer, but was quite sure that his response was embarrassingly stupid. Besides, had the savior been some big local guy—that would have been humiliating enough. Being rescued by a beautiful, slim, young woman made him feel like the worst kind of a wimp. Not a feeling Jerry was used to.

Wait, wait! He wanted to shout and opened his parched mouth, but produced no sound. What could I say? Would you like to have a drink with me? I'm a better man than I am a paddler? For a moment, he thought of catching up with her, but considering her kayaking skill, he just sadly shook his head. Jerry was looking at the disappearing yellow boat with an uncustomary feeling of acute sadness. Strange emotion, he thought. Not anger, not rage, something I can hardly remember.

A racing outrigger fell with a loud slap on the water next to him, and a brown, muscular man deftly jumped into the seat. "Ho, Cat!" he yelled after the girl, and caught up with her with a few powerful strokes. It was at this moment that Jerry felt a sudden attack of rage, the reaction he was very familiar with, and a stab of jealousy, the emotion he found difficult even to identify. He directed the fury at himself.

And why should this beautiful creature want to spend a minute of her time with me? A brick-wall man unfit for human interactions. Computer models, that's what I'm supposed to stick to! He angrily pulled the kayak halfway onto the sand and collapsed in the shallow water to cool off and rest. When he returned the boat, he answered "yes" to the question if he had had a good time, then went to his room where he lay down in a bathtub full of tepid water, drank three Heinekens and fell asleep in the tub. That was the last time he could still turn around in his mind and go back to his previous life, where programs, events and people could be manipulated, arranged and controlled by a skillful operator—and he was quite skilled. Not even his enemies would deny that. The soft noise of glasses shaking in the kitchen cabinet and water ripples suddenly appearing in his bathtub did not penetrate his deep slumber.

CHAPTER 2

T wo afternoons later, Cat answered a knock on the door to find a good-looking young man holding a big bouquet of flowers. Nicely built, with a flat stomach, muscular chest and broad shoulders; he could have been one of her paddling buddies, except for the skin peeling off his pink nose giving him away as a tourist. Another thing—the golf shirt, khaki shorts and leather sandals would make him stick out from a crowd of local guys like a tomato in a pineapple field. He did not look familiar so she looked at him expectantly, waiting for some sort of introduction. The visitor had an intelligent face but was clearly dumbfounded.

"Are you ... are you Cat?"

"Yes, I am Cat," the woman smiled, "and who are you?"

"My name is Jerry Roberts," he said, then managed to close his mouth completely. "I'm the guy you helped at Bird Shit Rock. I've come to say 'Thank you'." He leaned forward and put the flowers on her lap because her hands were resting on wheels. He was, obviously, shocked to see her in a wheelchair, but recovered quickly.

Cat was used to this kind or reaction. People who knew

10

her from telephone conversations or e-mail contacts thought that she was an able-bodied, vigorous, even athletic person. In fact, that's what she was, except that her legs didn't work since the accident. At one point she accepted this limitation. *Everybody has one, right?* She learned to work around her disability; one of the ways to flout it was her kayak. As soon as she sat in her boat, she could run with the big dogs, and sometimes she did—racing kayaks. She had things under control.

"You saved my life; thank you." The man extended a muscular arm with a big grin.

"You're very welcome," Cat smiled and took the hand that was warm and firm. "But let's not be that dramatic; I don't think I saved your life."

"Well, then thank you for going easy on my self-respect," he answered, keeping her hand in his.

A sharp guy and a nice smile, she thought. He reluctantly let go of her hand and followed her as she wheeled back to the living room. Open windows were only partly shaded with roll-up blinds and a breeze pleasantly floated through the sparsely furnished room. A table with a stack of *Atlantic Monthly* magazines on top, six chairs and a small cabinet graced with a silver vessel, that was all.

Rather Spartan, Jerry thought.

Cat was done with her big data upload, and was about to hold a small celebration by herself, so when Jerry offered a glass of wine from a bottle conveniently stashed in his car, she gladly accepted his company. She removed the magazines from the table and brought two wine glasses from the kitchen.

"So, how did you find me?" she asked, throwing back her blond mane and lifting her chin for emphasis. She had a gorgeous long neck.

"Special powers," Jerry whispered slyly, squinting his brown eyes glued to Cat's face. "Frankly," he smiled, "I've just asked around, who might be the best-looking woman kayaker, and they all came up with your name."

"Right answer," she laughed. "So what do you do in your private life, advertising agency, professional schmoozer?"

"Actually, I waste my life in front of a computer trying to model the economy. Besides, someone made a terrible mistake and gave me an assistant professor's job, so I do some teaching, against my protestations."

"Really, they drafted you to the university," she mocked Jerry with fake compassion.

"Well, it looked quite interesting at first, when I was an undergrad… even later, while I was doing my Ph.D. But after that, downhill all the way: inconclusive research, lazy students, long hours at the library . . . I'd be better off painting houses." Jerry was smiling, but his complaint sounded sincere enough.

"Jerry, help me out here." Blue eyes looked at Jeremy with an expression of disbelief. "I only took one semester of Economics 101, but I understand that the economy is about people making a living, or not making it . . . How can that be boring? Greeks made timeless tragedies out of less important stuff."

He sighed. "The science of bread-winning has evolved quite far from the basic concepts. I do computer modeling and, believe me, it's hard to see actual people at work behind my numbers." He let the words flow without much thinking because his mind was focused on her full lips, which kept moving, sometimes stretching in a smile and sometimes assuming the shape meant for kissing.

"I see, but let's take a simple concept," Cat kept probing, although she became aware how thick and full was Jerry's black hair, the kind that she would like to plunge her fingers into. " . . . Unemployment, let's say. Why do we have unemployment when there is so much work to be done? You deal with that, don't you?"

"Yes, of course, we do." Jerry answered reluctantly. "We analyze it, make recommendations, etc." Jerry was impressed with Cat's interest in the economy, but his attention was leaning towards the exquisite shape of her neck, partly covered with exuberant light-blond hair, and her ample breasts stretching the tee shirt, unrestrained by a bra. The shrink who had compared his emotional landscape to a brick wall had missed an important landmark; Jerry had never lost his appreciation for female beauty.

Cat shrugged her shoulders. "Well, what you do is probably very important, but in my opinion, the answer is really quite simple: people mostly work if they have to. You take away the prospect of being hungry, and most of your workers will find more entertaining ways of spending their time."

The discussion about unemployment went on. She liked

to see his forehead furrowing and the thick eyebrows rising as he tried to absorb her points. Besides, she could not miss his efforts to look into her eyes and she enjoyed it. Even the somewhat excessive focus on her lips was rather pleasant. Jerry stayed until ten o'clock, and she was surprised how quickly time passed. She gave him the OK to call her again before returning to New York.

I've become a hermit. Human company is like an unusual treat to me, she thought, rolling to her bedroom. On the other hand, it's damn hard to find someone this intelligent to talk with.

* * *

"Pat, she is beautiful and smart as hell." Jerry moved the phone to his other ear. "I went to see her last night and we had a lovely evening. We joked about my rescue. She made it sound like it was a small, funny thing. We discussed the economics of all things. And let me tell you, the young lady has pretty formed opinions and defends them like a bobcat."

He turned off the ignition and got out of the car in front of a large yellow house; that was a really good deal, a vacation rental in a private home. Ninety dollars a night in a bright clean room only a minute walk from Kailua Beach.

"I know. I haven't been so enthusiastic about anybody or anything in a long time, if ever." Jerry had luxuriated in a blissful state of mind since last night, a feeling quite unfamiliar to him. This girl had affected him in a way no one ever did. "But, Pat, she's handicapped. I don't know what it is, but she is in a wheelchair. It's amazing how strong her upper body has to be." He sniffed the air; flowers in Hawaii are just indecent in their sensuality and the smell of jasmine was filling the backyard. A small trellis over the entrance door was covered with bright red bougainvillea that for some reason brought to him a picture of Cat's lips.

"I know, crippled people can have all kinds of emotional problems on top of their disability, but I certainly didn't see any. She is funny and confident. Well, if she weren't that sweet, I could even say slightly opinionated. Yeah, I will be careful, Sis. Talk to you later." Jerry did not call his older sister often, but after his visit with Cat, he felt an urge to tell someone about an incredible change he felt inside. Like Coke that fizzles out of a bottle once you crack the cover slightly, he could not contain his bubbling excitement. Quite remarkable for an individual with a psychopathic trait and flat affect, he thought. Murph would shit his pants if he knew that he let me off the hook before I was completely and irreversibly dead inside.

He fought the desire to see Cat again until noon. His plan to stay away at least one day, so that she would not feel pressured, was crumbling. At two, he again reached for the phone and this time did not put it back.

"Cat, I wondered . . . er . . . if you might be free later on today. Maybe you'd like to spend some time together? We haven't completely sorted out this welfare problem, you know."

She laughed. "Well, Professor, you are on vacation and I am not. I have to finish my project. But if you want to come over late afternoon, I can put you to some useful work." She sounded glad.

Jerry put the phone down with a wide grin and looked

15

at his face in a mirror. Well, my boy, you might not be over the hill yet. The Goddess will see you tonight, he remarked to himself with satisfaction. The unshaved face in the mirror was full of enthusiasm and optimism that he was not accustomed to. Something strange and exciting is happening to me, he thought, pulling his swimming trunks on, but this thought had been interrupted by the sudden noise of a vase falling of the shelf, apparently of its own volition.

CHAPTER 3

Harry Rosen sat at his desk looking through receipts. The small, shabby room was furnished with a cheap metal desk, two chairs and a scratched-up gray filing cabinet. Dim yellow light radiated from an incandescent bulb barely covered by a dirty fabric shade. Contrasting with the drab and worn-out decor of his office was a small but elegant sculpture of a naked girl curled on a pedestal. She was kneeling with her upper body submissively resting on the ground.

A local guy was coming this evening with lobsters. Rosen did not really need to wait for him; the manager could take care of it, but he wanted to see the boy. His principle was to make the acquaintance of a number of local people who could be useful in the future. You never know whom you'll need, he thought. He looked through the receipts to kill time and thought that life would be a real challenge if he had to depend on this income.

The lobster guy, Abraham, came with a sack of lobsters at nine o'clock. The big, dark boy with heavy, muscular neck and arms was handsome and friendly, but somehow intimidating. The lobsters were frisky and smelled of the ocean. That's where they were just a few hours ago, before being poached, Rosen thought. Better not to know how they got to my restaurant.

"Mr. Rosen, would you like some fresh pineapples and papayas?" Abraham pressed on with his business.

"Are you a gardener, too?" Harry asked pleasantly, although he couldn't imagine the boy digging in dirt.

"I have a friend," Abe answered, without raising his head, and brought in two extra bags smelling of wet soil. The price was very good, half of what the regular supplier would ask. He grabbed the cash and was gone in a minute, did not even count the money.

A big, strong guy with less than clean hands, thought Rosen. Could be useful for something other than lobsters one day.

Abe came back a few minutes later.

"What's up, Abe, any problems?"

"Oh no, Mr. Rosen, I just wondered if you might need a waitress. My girlfriend is looking for a job."

"Sorry, Abe, we've just hired another girl. But . . . if your girlfriend is interested in light cleaning twice a week, I might use some help at home. I don't like coming back to a dump at night, and like cleaning even less. If she's interested, tell her to come here."

Harry looked at the figurine on his desk. Some of these island girls were quite pretty—they reminded him of Consuela. That girl was a real peach, *jugosa* they said; he smiled and gently traced the outline of the figurine with his narrow, white fingers.

"Abe, what do you do for fun on this island?"

The younger man squirmed uncomfortably. "What do you mean, Mr. Rosen? You can go to the movies or to a bar . . ."

"I know about movies and bars, Abe. Is there anything else, anything special? What is the best fun you had last month, and I'm not asking about your girlfriend, he he he," Rosen cackled.

"Cockfighting, I like to go to cockfights."

"Now you're talking! Tell me about it. I've never seen a cockfight."

"Oh, we have great derbies here, sometimes five hundred cocks in one meeting. It's great fun, if you like that kind of thing." Abe relaxed and his big shoulders dropped with relief. He enjoyed talking about cockfights.

"So, I understand that chickens, oh well—roosters—try to peck each other's brains out. Is that really that exciting?" Rosen sounded dismissive, but the idea of creatures pecking each other to death held some excitement for him. He leaned forward and waved Abe towards the other chair.

"These are no roosters that you could see in any back-yard. These little devils are tough and fight like you've never seen before. They jump five, six feet in the air and fight with knives . . ."

"Knives, how can they fight with knives?" Rosen's

eyes opened wide and his hands tightly gripped the desk's edge.

"They get a small knife, like a razor, attached to the spur of the foot, and each rooster tries to jump higher than the other one. And if he gets higher, he slashes the other guy with his knife. If the cock is really good, he can finish the match in fifteen seconds. If he cuts an artery, blood squirts all over like from a water pistol."

Harry felt excitement rising. "Do they get two knives, one for each foot?"

"No, they're like people; some are right footed, others are better with their left. So a trainer figures out which is the better foot, and that's the one the cock gets his blade on."

"A trainer . . . how can you train a chicken?"

"They're all natural fighters so they know how to fight, but a trainer makes them exercise and spar. Usually, an owner will have more than one hundred young chicks, and if he lets them get together, they will fight each other like crazy. So he just watches which ones come out on top. He doesn't want them too bloodied or scared when young, so they get something like tiny boxing gloves on their spurs. This way they can jump, fight and hit but don't get hurt."

"That sounds like a lot of trouble—just to watch them fight. Is there any money to be made in it?"

"There's a lot of money to be made in it, or lost. Every time you enter a cock into a derby, and you have to enter at least five, you give five hundred bucks deposit for each one. Your opponent does the same. If you win, you get his money; if you lose, he gets yours. And, of course, the house takes its cut."

Most interesting, thought Rosen. The house . . . Of course, they're the ones that make the real money. It makes them no difference who wins or whose chicken gets slashed up. Just like any other gambling, only this one sounds like more fun. Instead of drunken idiots throwing their money away you get to see an exciting show.

Harry smiled jovially, "Well, if your chickens lose, you get a very expensive dinner."

"Not even that," Abe was animated and smiled broadly. "They're so hard that you might cook them all night and still couldn't take a bite. Besides, they are full of vitamins, steroids; God only knows what else. Believe me, you don't want to eat them."

"Doesn't surprise me at all," said Rosen thoughtfully. "If the stakes are high, obviously, the owners will do what-ever they can to help themselves a bit. Is this legal?" The legality of the practice, any practice, was important to him only as a matter of an objective fact that needed to be ad-dressed, but not necessarily obeyed. Besides, it's good to know what limitations might be placed on your opponent, Rosen believed.

"That's the problem," admitted Abe with sadness, "cockfighting is illegal. You can raise them, but if they catch you running cockfights, they could send you to jail."

"Isn't that something?" Harry commiserated, "Killing chickens is legal but letting them kill each other is illegal."

Abe shrugged, "That's certainly not going to stop cock-fighting, just makes it a bit more difficult."

"Do you think, you could take me sometime to a derby, as you call it? Who knows, maybe we could go into a little business together."

Abe's eyes brightened up. "Are you serious? I was thinking about raising cocks from good fighting bloodlines. But, you know, it takes money to make money, and I am a bit short on cash now."

"Well, we might be a good match, Abe. I might have some loose cash, but I don't have much interest in chicken farming. I might be interested in setting up a little establishment for fighting cocks. Let's see the show first and then—one way or another—we are going to make some money, Abe, me and you."

Abraham left the office with his heart filled with joy. He had found himself a business partner, a serious man, a restaurant owner. Now, Kalani would have to respect him for what he really was, a businessman.

CHAPTER 4

The house had white stucco walls and a red clay roof. First-floor ornamental ironworks and a small second-floor balcony gave it a hint of Spanish flavor. It was beautifully located on a small peninsula projecting into Kailua Bay with a canal flowing along one side. The lawn along the canal was studded with foxtail palms, beautiful trees with fronds shaped like a fox's appendage.

Jerry knocked with a heavy brass ring in the middle of the solid oak door. He could hear the lively rhythm of Spanish music. Flamenco, isn't it? The ocean creature would probably be as good a dancer as a kayaker, if she could walk, he thought.

Cat opened the door with her usual friendly smile and casually waved him in to pass in front of her wheelchair towards the living room table. Jerry could not take his eyes away from her lips, the full red lips constantly changing shape as though they had a life of their own. Her eyes were blue and pretty, more because of their warmth and intelligence than an unusual size or shape. He came up to the table, pulled the chair out and turned it towards the room, as Cat followed rolling in her wheelchair. She stopped just in front of his chair and their knees almost touched when Jerry sat down. He couldn't escape looking at her legs, clearly uncovered in shorts. Yesterday, she had them covered with a light towel. They were brown like the rest of her body, somewhat thin, but did not have the atrophic look of paralyzed limbs.

"Well, let's get it over with," she said, watching his eye movements. "I was in a car wreck four years ago, with a spinal injury. My legs are pretty useless, though I can move around on crutches a bit —prefer not to, feel much more secure in my wheelchair. Do you have a problem with that?"

"Oh, no, none whatever, I admire . . ."

"No need to admire, just treat me like anybody else," she cut off that discussion.

"Are you handy with your hands, Professor? I have a little project for you." She led him to the room facing the canal. French doors opened onto a lawn with a pathway leading rather steeply to the canal. Two shallow ruts ran along the path. Obviously, she wheeled this way to the water. A metal frame reminiscent of parallel bars stood over the bright yellow kayak at the water's edge.

That's how she gets into her kayak, Jerry thought. That's how she got on the water to help me out. Simple, ingenious—she can go kayaking any time, without anyone's help.

"Jerry, I need a little ramp and a boardwalk to take me from my home to the kayak. It gets really messy and slippery when it rains."

"Yes, Ma'm," Jerry happily snapped to attention. Quite obviously, this was not a task for one evening. Now he had a good excuse to spend time with her every night for at least a few days.

"I'll be busy for another hour or hour and a half, so pace yourself. The tools and lumber are in the shed." She looked over his broad chest barreling above the sucked-in stomach in a comical *at attention* posture, smiled with appreciation and wheeled back to her workstation.

They did not talk economics any more; she let Jerry into her world somewhat. Cat lived by herself and worked as a software systems trouble-shooter. She had developed a good business that she was able to carry out from her desk by the window. Few people that she dealt with ever met her. As a matter of fact, outside her kayaking club, she met almost no one.

Their loss, really, Jerry thought; she is so much fun.

The car accident four years ago resulted in a spinal injury, leaving her in a wheelchair. Her husband had died from his injuries in the same crash. She did not elaborate, just stated facts for the record. The house she had bought three years ago, when prices in Hawaii were not that ridiculous yet, using insurance money from the accident.

"But tell me more about your work. Tell me about yourself," she demanded.

Jerry despised his work. He had a miserable time awaiting him back in New York. In a week, the Winter break would be over, and he would return to the bored faces of his undergrads. Even worse, he would need to read their moronic attempts at economics research that was part of the curriculum. Then he would have to write some semi-intelligent critique, just to let them know that he had actually read their pitiful essays. So he gave a short and unenthusiastic account of his professional life, then escaped into stories of his childhood, family travels, Cancun vacations. At this point, he decided to leave his brief career in Army intelligence out of his resume. Supposed to remain confidential, he reminded himself, knowing well that sooner or later he would need to come clean, if this friendship was to go anywhere.

"Funny," she said, "I used to go there with my parents as well. Who knows, maybe we met at a beach in Cancun before."

"I would remember you!" he blurted out and immediately felt silly, almost blushing.

"I would remember you, too," she smiled and touched his hand.

Cat's hand set off Jerry's imagination: to take her in my arms and hold her, nothing more. I would leave New York, quit my job and just keep building the boardwalk all day, as long as I could hold her. A fine set of dating skills, polished to perfection by twenty years of romantic experience, had dropped off Jerry, leaving him vulnerable and awkward as a teenager. The professional dexterity and toughness of a human handler, acquired in the course of his intelligence career, failed to protect his poise.

"Why don't you quit your job, if you don't like teaching?" Cat asked and added with a smile, "you could pass for a carpenter, if no other opportunity comes along."

"It's a long story, which I'll tell you one day," he

added. "At one point of my life, it seemed I'd do best in front of a computer monitor. Turned out, I had a knack for abstract thinking and did well in economics research. So I kept at it and got my Ph.D. Now, it's hard to abandon the investment of time and effort that went into my degrees. Also, that would be quite a disappointment for my parents." Do you have to admit on the second date that you had been advised to stay away from people as much as possible? That you have attacks of rage with a strong urge to kill? That you can't stop treating other people like chess pawns? Jerry had convinced himself that since he was quite normal for the first twenty years of his life, his emotional problems had to be temporary, and therefore could be swept under the carpet, for the time being.

"I understand, but don't underestimate your folks' ability to see that you need to find your own way. After all, they want you to be happy, right?"

"I'm not really sure what would truly make them happier: me being happy or me being a full professor. My father is very proud of my career, more than I am. For him, quitting my academic track would be professional suicide. Parents aren't exactly happy when their kids have suicidal ideas, so we never discuss it."

Jerry wished he could end this line of questioning. He stood up, went to the kitchen and got himself a glass of water. When he returned to the living room he stood behind Cat. Her eyes were looking straight into his eyes in the wall mirror. He gently touched her blond hair. She closed her eyes and said softly, "Jerry, I'm very sensitive to touch, please, don't." The hand withdrew and rested on her shoulder, feeling the warmth radiating from her firm body. She did not shrug, just opened her eyes wide and said in a cool and clear voice, "Jerry, sit down!"

It felt like a smack with a wet towel, not intended to kill or maim, but carrying quite a bit of weight and unpleasant coldness. He returned to his chair to be rewarded with a smile and a "thank you." The rest of the evening was awkward and uncomfortable. They both pretended that nothing problematic had happened, but the conversation lost its informal lightness. Twenty minutes later, Jerry thanked her for a lovely evening and left kicking himself for spoiling the date, which had started so well. But there was hope, as the work on the boardwalk had just begun.

Jerry had to dig out a lot of dirt to level the pathway, next day. Still better than grading papers, he smiled to himself. He worked till six thirty, and then took a shower while Cat prepared a simple dinner. He liked the intimacy of taking a shower in her bathroom. He stepped out of the stall dripping wet and naked, slowly drying himself with a towel while looking at her bathrobe, a thin, pale yellow fabric. An electric toothbrush sat on the right side of the sink, a hairbrush with a cherry wood handle and a few blond hairs rested on the cabinet: all things very personal and out of a stranger's reach. He was allowed into their proximity, in her private space. He could touch the objects and smell the faint aroma of her cologne.

The following day, he made a bold move: he brought his own toothbrush and left it next to hers. Now, the significance of this action should not be underestimated. A male occupant of the house might either miss the presence of the new object altogether or wouldn't give it a second thought. "He wants to brush his teeth, so he brought his toothbrush," period. Not so with women. Women are very observant of any changes in their environment and sensitive to the emotional significance of things, far beyond most men's imagining.

Jerry had a girlfriend once who had taught him a lot about these things. It was really a relationship of convenience. Jerry was five years out of the Army and well into his brick-wall stage, unable to connect on any level beyond sex. Victoria was single and far too busy for a real romance, not to mention a family. They filled each other's need to bring "the significant other" to the school and family occasions. They also met once a week in his apartment to satisfy more intimate needs. A cold arrangement, perhaps, but based on mutual attraction and clear understanding. With their relation being so premeditated and rational, Jerry was not allowed to take any shortcuts. He was instructed on the importance of the right music, stimulating aromas, small gifts and, above all, good manners. He had the good luck of having her explain these inscrutable secrets that men hardly ever understand. So when he found his toothbrush placed in a cup next to Cat's, he took it as a sure sign of being accepted into her very personal world.

Cat had prepared fettuccini Alfredo, which they ate at the big table with candles for lighting. The whole house was dark, and there were no lights outside. A small circle of flickering, warm light carved out the intimate space from the darkness, in which the two of them existed, to the exclusion of the rest of the world. They played little games, Jerry trying to make their huge shadows, projected on the walls, touch, Cat moving away. A jasmine bush flowered outside the window filling the room with its sweet scent. An unexplained sense of safety and calm happiness slowly oozed through Jerry's jarred nervous system, soothing, a thick balm quieting the discordant din that had filled his heart for years.

Flamenco music played again in the background and she swayed her ponytail with it. "You really like flamenco, don't you?"

"I love flamenco! Maybe I have some gypsy genes, but more likely it has something to do with my legs. Have you ever seen flamenco dancers?"

"I did, years ago in Cancun."

"So you remember that there are two major elements to it. One is the footwork, all that stomping and moving around. The other is the dance of hands and upper body. I read a book about a famous Flamenco dancer in Chicago who had polio as a child. I think it was *Carmen la Coja*. Her footwork was, of course, impaired, but her hands and arms were so expressive that she was a top professional dancer for many years."

The tune was coming to its end in a fiery crescendo as Cat raised her chin proudly, extending her beautiful neck, and executed a few flamenco moves. She had a lot of grace and, quite obviously, was well practiced. The girl was animated and looked happy. She raised her glass and said, "I hope you will find your place in life. To your happy new career."

I have found my place in life—it's here, next to you, Jerry wanted to say, but the words would not come out of his mouth. It would be so much easier just to take you in my arms!

Then she put her hand on Jerry's, and he covered it with his own. She did not withdraw. They chatted happily like old friends until he reluctantly left, the sensation of uneasiness gone and forgotten.

"Would you like to go dancing?" Jerry asked casually the next day, looking over the bowl of fruit salad.

Cat looked at him unsure what to think. She frowned somewhat, suspecting that he was going to pull a less than gracious joke. "What do you mean?"

Without answering, Jerry stood up and went to the closet where he had hidden a package. "Please, open it."

Cat ripped open the glistening paper and saw a long red dress with black lace and embroidery in front. Jerry used the moment to fetch a guitar hidden in the same closet. She looked at him with an expression that caused his heart to beat faster.

"Jerry, you are a wonderful man." Her eyes were soft, and her face slightly flushed. The glorious lips trembled slightly as though she were about to cry or laugh.

Jerry strummed the guitar. "I'm not much of a guitar virtuoso; took some lessons for a year, when I was an undergrad, but I could do some rhythm thumping and try a bit of stomping for you. The rest is up to the CD and your arms."

"I will dance with you, Jerry, all night, well, that is until twelve o'clock. I am going to change now into the dress you gave me."

"Can I help you? I know from movies that ladies frequently need someone to close a zipper on the back."

"There is no zipper in this dress, Jerry. Besides, this lady does her dressing and undressing all by herself. Use the time to get re-acquainted with your guitar."

She appeared from the bathroom ten minutes later. Her long, blond hair, tightly pulled backwards, cascaded down her back. The dress fitted well; the red fabric cinched at the waist while the embroidered bodice stretched smoothly over her voluptuous breasts. With her body proudly erect and her head held in an arrogant poise, she was sitting in the chair like a queen gracing the court with her presence. She *was* Carmen, blond hair and all.

Jerry pushed the CD player's button and a dark voice trembling with passion vibrated the air. *Porque vivo a mi manera*, cried the singer against the throbbing of the impatient guitar. Jerry joined in gently thumping his guitar and stomping his feet. As he grew more confident, the stomping became louder and louder. The flamenco was heating up. Cat watched for a moment with approval, then joined in with the castanets she had brought with her. They both had a good sense of rhythm and deep sounds of guitar easily blended with the dry clicks of the castanets. Cat's hands came to life as though she were carving graceful objects in the air. The objects were getting bigger and bigger, and their surface was gently feathered with long fingers carefully dancing around imagined round shapes.

The haughty poise of her head was severely rejecting any notion of disrespectful familiarity, while her hands, arms and breasts shamelessly threw the seductive magic at

Jerry. He was happy to be charmed. With the last strum the fandango ended. Cat rolled her chair toward him and they sat facing each other, their thighs almost touching. As the music started up slowly and hesitantly, she joined in. A moment later the flamenco was in a full rage. Jerry put away his guitar so that nothing separated him from Cat. He sensed on his face the air, sliced and caressed by her hands, felt her fingertips slightly brushing his hair and neck. Jerry stopped stomping and sat with his eyes riveted to her face. Cat's mouth had fascinated him from the very beginning, and now he could watch her wet lips half open, so close he could almost touch them with his. She enjoyed their closeness and his adoration, of that he was certain. The music stopped, and Cat put her arms around his neck. "Thank you, Jerry, that was the most wonderful dancing evening of my life," and then she briefly put her lips on his.

* * *

Jerry kept delaying the completion of the project as long as he could without looking utterly incompetent. How many days could it take one to build a thirty-foot board-walk? After the first two days he had started dismantling certain sections on the pretense that they needed re-alignment. He pulled a few boards off and liberated the joists only to put them together in an almost identical position. He placed the unattached planks back and went to the restroom.

The moment he stepped back through the door, Jerry saw Cat stuck hopelessly on her wheelchair between the unfastened boards that had moved away, the joists spread apart just enough to trap the wheels. She was angrily trying to pull herself out of this predicament. Cat was facing away and Jerry stopped, hoping she could liberate herself. Knowing how proud she was of her independence, he would rather not humiliate her with his help. Unfortunately, the chair was stuck between two-by-fours as firmly as though he had designed a trap.

Jerry approached her and said softly, "May I help you, Cat?"

The woman turned her head. Her face was red under the brown tan while her eyes were burning holes into his forehead like two lasers. "You better! Hope you aren't going to build any bridges!"

Standing to the right and in front of her, Jerry grabbed the arm supports and pulled. The chair did not budge. Without thinking, he moved his right hand under her legs, the left one behind her back and lifted her. Instinctively, she put her arms around his neck to help. He stood holding her, just like in his dreams. She was not heavy, but her body had a pleasant firmness. He could hold her like that forever, her arms around his neck, but after a second, she said softly, without anger, "You can put me down next to the tree and get the chair out for me, please."

He gently lowered her next to the palm tree. Cat grabbed the trunk and was able to stand on her own. Jerry pulled the chair out and she slid into it. That was the first time he held her in his arms.

She didn't hold this incident against him; Jerry suffered no rebuke beyond the first outburst. In fact, now they were more likely to touch each other. He might briefly massage her neck when she moved away from her computer, and she ruffled his head when they watched the news on TV.

This event left him with concern about her safety.

"Cat, what would you do, if you got stuck like that, and I wasn't around?"

Cat shrugged her arms, "I would crawl uphill to the house. Done it many times."

Of course, what was I thinking? She managed on her own for three years, Jerry reprimanded himself. But, he sighed, I'd rather look out for her all the same.

She didn't leave it at that. "What would *you* do if you slipped in your New York apartment and broke your hip? I met a few people who did just that; shit happens." Cat seemed to be inflamed by the idea that she would need someone to make her safe. "You don't need to worry about me, Jerry, I have been doing on my own quite well; I don't need a keeper."

CHAPTER 5

Repeated spasms coursed through her lower body as her legs twitched in the restraining apparatus. These were not the torturous spasms they had been at first. Still, quite unpleasant. One-two-three, red lights went on when the electric current shot through electrodes attached to her legs, the muscles contracted.

Ooouch; the quads tightened and the limbs straightened out forcibly against the restraint. Five, six seconds and the spasm subsided. Two seconds break then the electrodes delivered their punch to the back of her legs. Cat's body was arching upwards as though in sexual ecstasy. Damn, that hurts! I am supposed to be numb there, for God's sake! The bloody machine could be used for third-degree interrogations. I wish we could come up with something gentler!

Cat couldn't be too bitter; she was the driving force behind building this contraption. All her time spent in the hospital provided many opportunities for her inquisitive mind.

"So, my leg muscles should be working, right?"

"Right."

"And the legs are getting thin and weak because the

muscles don't exercise. Now, they don't work out because they are not getting the stimulation from the brain. And they *would* work if they could be stimulated with a weak electrical current."

"Right."

"So, how come Rehab doesn't have a machine to stimulate them with a weak current? That doesn't look too demanding, technologically speaking."

"Well, there were trials to that effect, but they were not very successful. I can check on it for you. In any case, we don't have that kind of a stimulator."

Cat repeated this enquiry a few times; they never came back to her with their "checked on" results. Too busy. At one point she understood that it was really up to her. Why shouldn't it work? Cat wondered. The muscles were actually twitching on these weight-loss commercials on TV... but those were models, gorgeous, skinny individuals with no body fat. Maybe people are too fat, and electrodes are too far from the muscles? A few inches of fat insulation under the skin can surely make a difference! Well, I'm quite thin. Maybe people are afraid of the spasms. Maybe they don't care, thinking that they would never walk anyway. Maybe, maybe . . . I won't know unless I try.

She had called a friend who was an electrical engineer. It was a rather simple matter to design an array of electrodes imbedded into the mold taken from Cat's lower body. Each major muscle group got its own electrode. At this point, medical residents became quite useful with their knowledge of anatomy. A control box that would regulate duration and strength of the current, and the machine was ready to be built. It was the actual making of the contraption that was a challenge. Not that it was difficult in a technical sense, yet nobody would touch it with a ten-foot pole.

"Is this apparatus approved by the FDA?"

"Is it for human use?"

"What about legal liability?"

"Who is the medical doctor who will supervise its use?"

"Just forget it, it can't be done."

Unless one was determined like Cat... and had a lot of time on her hands.

The painful part came later. Cat had placed herself into the contraption, dialed the low current and pushed the button. "Holy Mackerel!" She groaned as the spasm of her butt muscles and thighs shot her out of the bed onto the floor, where she twitched and arched, stupefied by the intensity of pain in her behind. Cat had stayed on the floor for a few minutes resting before she pulled herself back onto her bed. "Holy Mackerel," she repeated, "that works, that sure works."

She had sent the control box for alterations, so that the range of current intensities started at a lower level. Then it took her a week to gather enough courage to try it again. She started on the floor this time, gingerly strapped the cast on and dialed the lowest current for the front muscles. She held her breath, closed her eyes and pressed the button. Her legs stiffened up somewhat. Since then she spent many evenings experimenting with her machine, choosing the strength of the stimuli so that they wouldn't be too painful, but strong enough to give her a good workout. She was no slacker. She knew how to clench her teeth.

That was over three years ago. Since then Cat practiced this self-punishment every night. She had learned to accept spasms the way serious athletes learn to tolerate the pain of a hard workout. The worst part was not the pain but the uncomfortable feeling of numbness mixed with pins and needles, the sensation of crawling bugs. It was always there, more or less following the crease separating her thighs from buttocks plus a few patches on her thighs, above the skin that had completely lost sensation. After her workouts, the tingling was more intense. Sometimes, it would continue for hours and prevent her from falling asleep. Those nights took her mind back to her hospital days.

One day she was a strong and beautiful girl, happily in love; the next day she was a crippled widow confined to her bed, hoping to join her husband as soon as possible. She could hardly remember the weeks following their accident. A curtain of pain killers, sleeping pills, pain and anxiety seemed to allow little light inside her memory to see the events, but her mind was neither grasping their significance nor connecting them into a sensible story.

What is sensible about Nick having gone while I'm still lying on my back, counting cracks in the ceiling? Immobilized on a frame, helpless and hopeless, she wished that one day she simply wouldn't wake up. But she did wake up, every morning, even after a whole night spent crying.

People were coming to see her. Good people, people

who wished her well. They tried to be positive, told her how lucky she was not to have a complete spinal transection. That she would surely get better and dance at their weddings. And then off they would go to their weddings, or to a beach or to play soccer while she felt she was slowly rotting away on a hospital bed. Other people were coming with important papers to sign: insurance, consent for treatment, last will. "Do you understand? Would you like to ask any questions?"

"No, no questions," she signed the papers without looking at them. Just go, people, leave me alone, she thought. There was no significance to all this activity. She decided to end her life as soon as she could, and that was the only reason she remained sane. Being immobilized, completely dependant on others, was burning her soul and driving her into howling madness.

When she was taken off the frame and allowed to sit up, she was weak, but the world certainly looked better in its customary horizontal orientation. A first hint that she might be better off than other patients came when she moved into a wheelchair. It was definitely easier for her, as she had retained a good amount of power in her buttocks and abdomen. Others had to be lifted and settled in a chair, strapped with belts, while she was able to hop from bed to chair with ease. An improvement, but almost without any significance, in the context of her loss.

That was when the nurses started watching her more carefully. There was nothing she could do on the frame; she was completely dependent. Once in a wheelchair and mobile, she could easily finish her life.

What's the point of this miserable, boring, unproductive life that awaits me? She thought every night: I'm Cat! Cat the volleyball star! I would have drooling males lined around the club's floor like puppies, when Nick and I raged in samba. That was really a Nick thing; he just had to go to one of a hundred Latino clubs in LA every week. But I was no slouch either.... It's all gone: Nick has vanished. My life has run its course. I am an old lady in a wheelchair.

She cried a lot, not only because of her loss, but also out of an indolent fury she felt at the injustice and idiocy of having her life stopped just when it was really starting. She had never made the final decision to kill herself, perhaps due to this anger, just to spite fate, to deprive the hateful providence of the satisfaction of seeing her fold in. One thing she was entirely sure of, whatever happens in the future, she would *never* allow herself to be dependant on others again. *Never!*

CHAPTER 6

K alani came to Cat's house on Mondays and Fridays, usually for three hours, but sometimes longer if there was more work or they had something particularly interesting to talk about. She cleaned, cooked a bit, took care of the lawn and hedge. Besides, she was Cat's friend. She usually came around 2 o'clock, after having finished Mrs. Oshiro's apartment. Kalani had her own key to the house and did not need to bother Cat, who worked by her window.

"Hi, Cat, how are you?" Cat waved greetings silently as she was on the phone with a client. Kalani started with dirty dishes. Soon Cat wheeled into the kitchen.

"Hi, Kalani, how are you doing? Anything new?" Kalani, a young and pretty Hawaiian woman, had a sunny disposition on most days, but not today. "What's wrong, Kalani? C'mon, tell me!" Cat pressed on for the answer.

Kalani looked up from the sink, throwing back her long, black hair, "No new problem, always same problem—not enough money." She angrily attacked the frying pan.

"But, Kalani, from what I know, you are working at least eight hours a day, six days a week, and the pay is not that bad."

42

Kalani shrugged, "Not enough money. I think I need to get a night job, maybe I could do some waiting." She was moving fast, finished the dishes and started sweeping the kitchen floor. Even cleaning the kitchen she had the graceful, fluid movements of a hula dancer. She had practically grown up in her *halau* since she was five.

"Kalani, what are you doing with the money? I don't believe you spend it all on yourself. Your mother gets a government check after your father died. Is Abe sponging off you?"

Kalani did not enjoy this conversation. She stopped sweeping, put the broom away abruptly and exploded, "You just don't understand. You live here by yourself, and no one wants anything from you. What am I supposed to do? Abe is my man, so he comes and wants money. If I don't give him money, he gets very angry. I'm scared when he gets angry, but I don't want to lose him either. Whatever I give him, he's done with it in a day or two."

"What does he do? Drinking, dope?"

"No, he bets on cocks. Now he is going to raise his own roosters with his buddy Jose, who is really bad news, so he wants me to give him more money. Good roosters are pricey, and he already promised two thousand dollars! So, if he doesn't come up with stuff, the other guys will think he is chicken shit. Now you know!" She pulled out the vacuum to clean the carpet in the living room.

"So what are you going to do?"

"I have some cash in the bank, for nursing school. I'll pull it out." Her voice cracked somewhat, and she wiped her nose.

"You can't do that! That's your future, and you're supposed to start your program in a few months!" Cat was truly exasperated.

"So I won't start in a few months! Just drop it, Cat. Since when are you such an expert on how to live with a man?" Kalani went out to trim the hedge in order to escape further conversation.

Cat looked at the door for a moment and thought, serves me right, what do I know about living with a man? I lived for a few years with a boy and even that was a century ago. But there is no question her story won't end with those two thousand bucks. Guess Kalani will have to discover it on her own. She went back to her computer.

Kalani stayed till five-thirty, picked up her money from the countertop, and left in a hurry to meet Abe. She saw a good-looking *haole* banging nails into a ramp. What d'ya know, looks like Cat maybe is getting a boyfriend, she thought, smiled at him and slipped into her old Honda.

Abe was waiting at home and jumped up from the bed the moment she pulled into the driveway. They looked good together. He, a tall and broad-shouldered man with the agility of a lightweight boxer and she, a black-eyed beauty with a fiddle-shaped figure and the elegant moves of a dancer. They used to have a good time together; Kalani's high school girlfriends stopped seeing her out of jealousy. She thought they would marry one day and have beautiful children. Boys, dark, tall and handsome like Abe and girls, slim, soft and sweet like herself.

Stupid dreams, she thought. I even had names ready for them: Maika for a boy and Lehua for a girl.

Abe laughed and joked about her dream, but did not object. He was fond of the idea of having a family, too. Besides, he liked the ending to family dreams. He would let Kalani spin her sweet story for a few minutes, then would pick her up like a soft doll and whisper in her ear, "Well, let's start making those pretty babies. Who is going to be first, Maika or Lehua?"

Kalani loved his big hard body, smooth skin and faint animal smell that she could appreciate only with her face pressed to his chest. She felt caught in a strong rip tide current, one she couldn't fight, didn't fight, because she knew that, after much pushing and pulling and twisting of her body, it would bring her to a quiet cove filled with warm and sweet water, a place of happy dreams.

Then somehow Abe had started changing. Maybe it started when his mother died or perhaps when he stopped working on the fishing boat. He smiled less and his fuse got shorter. He still could be sweet when he wanted to, but more often was irritable and snappy. He woke up about noon since he got into the habit of coming home very late. Kalani planned her day to come home at that time to fix lunch for him and herself; after all, she had to eat, too. The problem was that Abe, having slept off the last night, was by then at his best mood of the day, ready to assert his manhood. That left Kalani drained and she was hard pressed to find energy for the remaining four hours of her physical work. There was no way to persuade him to wait until the evening. He always had other plans for evenings; he wanted to meet up with his buddies.

Kalani looked into the rear mirror, placed a flower behind her ear, put on her best smile and stepped out of the car. Abe was smiling at the door of the apartment building and grabbed her for a long hug.

"Do you have it?"

"Some . . . three hundred . . . "

"A lousy three hundred?" He let go of her. "What am I supposed to do now?" His face darkened and his voice acquired a harsh quality.

"I'll have the rest tomorrow. I need to go to the bank," she added hastily.

"What time tomorrow? It better be in the morning. I'll buy some drinks for the guys tonight," he took the money from her hand, "so they will not pick on me, but tomorrow I have to have my two grand." He turned away and started walking down the gravel driveway. He stopped before turning on the street. "By the way, I got you another job. The guy who owns this new restaurant needs some help at home. You can go and see him tomorrow."

"Thank you, Abe." Kalani exhaled, her shoulders slumped, and she went home to make dinner for herself. She was glad she wasn't in a rush to make Maika and Lehua. Her future family looked less and less like a happy one. She knew all about unhappy families and would not make another one herself. Kalani went to the bathroom and took a pill from the small container hidden behind a big bottle of hydrogen peroxide. She would continue to be very careful not to miss any.

CHAPTER 7

C at sat in her hospital bed looking at the rain-streaked window, counting the ways she might kill herself with minimum pain, when a nurse came in, a middle-aged woman named Rose. Cat didn't like Rose, who was a very direct person and considered excessive nuances a waste of time.

"Cat, I know that you can't talk, not to me at least, but you probably can read."

Cat did not honor her with a look. Pushy, malevolent bitch, she thought.

"Be a sweetheart for a change and do some reading for a nice lady, who cannot do it for herself. You will like her; she is not like me."

Anything to get you out of my face, Cat thought. "Where is she, when should I go?" she asked unpleasantly, looking at the garbage can in the corner.

"She's in the chronic unit; you can see her anytime, she's not going anywhere. An orderly will take you there."

"I don't need an orderly; I can find her myself."

"Very well, find her yourself."

So Cat wheeled herself to the chronic care unit. When she opened the door, she could immediately detect the faint but unmistakable odor of urine. Unlike in her part of the hospital, here were hardwood floors and the walls were painted bright yellow. A nurse sat at the station desk, and a male orderly was pushing a bed in the corridor. Numerous patients dressed in blue robes and long hospital shirts tied at the back crowded the corridor and the lounge. Some sat in their chairs motionless; others nodded repeatedly. An older lady walked up to Cat, grabbed her sleeve with a thin, talon-like hand and kept asking anxiously about Mary, "When's she coming? When's she coming?"

That's where I will end up, Cat thought. She was ready to turn around and escape to her bed where she could relax and think how to end her miserable life, when the nurse caught sight of her.

"You must be Cat. You'll see how much better you feel when you talk to Ruth."

Better? I will feel *even better* than now? God have mercy! Cat thought, but she just mumbled, "I am supposed to read for Ruth."

The nurse pushed her chair into a room occupied by a single bed, a nightstand and two wooden chairs. An unnaturally wide head with a pale, ugly face rested on a pillow; the remainder of the body was covered with a white sheet. A pair of bright, gray eyes turned to her and the cheerful voice said, "Hi, you from the rehab unit?"

"Yes, I've come to read to you."

"Oh, how good of you, but—before you read—can you tell me some gossip from your part of the hospital? I don't get much traffic in gossip here and I miss it. Is Nurse Rose still there?"

"Yes, she told me to come and read to you."

"Quite bitchy, isn't she?" giggled Ruth. "But in fact, she takes care of her patients like nobody else. Things get done whether they want it or not. How about Doctor Yamashita, is he still trying to get a date?" An hour passed and they were still trading gossip; Cat even laughed a few times, her first since the accident.

"Cat, what kind of person were you before the accident? Happy or unhappy?"

"Well, I was a very happy person; I had all the reasons to be happy."

"That's actually not my question. Some people are happy even if screwed by life, and some are unhappy, no matter how good they get. What kind were you?"

"I must say, I was mostly happy, unless something made me unhappy."

"Then," declared Ruth confidently, "you'll be happy again. It's a scientific fact. People return to their basic predisposition after a major event, good or bad. Happy ones are happy again while depressives go to popping Prozac even if they win a million dollars."

Two hours passed before the nurse stuck her head in, "That's enough reading for now, dinner is coming."

"Do you want to come again tomorrow? We didn't even start reading yet," asked Ruth hopefully.

Cat promised to come in the morning and left the chronic care unit almost smiling. She went to see Ruth every day, until she left the hospital two weeks later, and then returned many times after her discharge. Not much reading was ever done. They had become friends rapidly and initial light gossiping changed to very personal subjects that she would never have discussed with anybody else.

Ruth suffered from progressive paralysis and had been immobilized in bed for the past six years. She seemed to have answers to any and every question a paralyzed woman might ask. Six lonely years is a long time for reflection. Obviously, she had a happy disposition before her disease struck because even now, paralyzed from her neck down, she was always full of good spirits.

"So what are the choices, Cat? You can decide to be happy no matter what, or you can allow yourself to be unhappy and, God knows, you might find a lot to be unhappy about. What do you think is better? Don't think that it will just happen. You need to make a clear decision and stick to it."

At this point Cat chose to be happy and she stuck to it. She decided that her physiotherapy sessions were not such a drag after all and she made much progress within the next ten days. Even Rose was stunned with her magical transformation. "Kid, you are ready to face the world," she declared, "and we should hire Ruth as a psychotherapist, I think."

Ruth's bloated body became invisible to Cat. Ruth lived

in her eyes. Always alert, her gray eyes seemed independent of the swollen face. Ruth explained her own concept of her body. "I often imagine that all I have is my brain floating in a pool that feeds and supports it. All this stuff that they hide under the white sheet is my pool. It cannot be too clean, as I can smell something disgusting whenever they lift the sheet. I hope never to see what exactly it is. At the end, what would I care about the pool? I live in my brain and you wouldn't believe how many things can hide in your brain. You can do things that you couldn't do in a real world. I shouldn't say real. Who knows what's real?"

Cat had probably made a dubious face because Ruth immediately asked, "Did you ever think, how do you know what is real and what's not? How do you know? How do you know that I am really talking to you? Maybe you will wake up in a moment, and find out that you just had a bad dream with the car crash in it, and then you dreamed of a freaky head talking to you. How do you know? In fact, how can *I* be sure that you are real? I could easily imagine a girl like you coming every day to entertain me, and you know what, once you give somebody shape and life in your head, they become quite independent. Sometimes they amaze me with what they say and do, although I should really know, I had created them."

"So that's what you do before I come, you daydream!" Cat exclaimed.

"Daydreaming is when you are entertaining yourself in order to kill time," Ruth's lips turned scornfully. "What I'm doing is creating reality. It may not be a reality to you, but it sure is real in my world. It's hard work and takes concentration, but it gets easier with practice. I didn't invent it.

Athletes used imagination to practice for years; it definitely improves performance. What you make up in your head can speed up your heart, raise blood pressure, change metabolism and more. There's nothing unreal about it, it's a scientific fact."

"What where you doing this morning, before I came?" asked Cat with curiosity.

"I was riding my horse. We're preparing for a jumping competition. Spartacus is a bit wall shy, so we need a lot of practice, but he will come around."

"Horse jumping, eh? Must be a pretty expensive sport..."

"It is, but I am an investment banker a few afternoons a week, so we can afford it. You should try horseback riding yourself, that would be good for you."

"Thank you, Ruth, but I would rather go skiing in Utah."

"That's fine, Cat, go skiing, but be careful, you might break your neck . . . " They both started laughing hysterically until they ran out of giggles.

"Cat, when you were married, did you enjoy sex?"

"Ruth, I was crazy about it. Sometimes, I think that's what we mainly did."

"Well then, you have a big hole in your life. You should try to enjoy it in your head."

"Are you doing it? "

"Are you kidding?" giggled Ruth, "I've had every good-looking doc in this hospital, and you wouldn't believe who visits me from Hollywood! Now go home and do some practice," and she gave her a lascivious wink. Cat felt her facing turning red as she wheeled out of the room.

CHAPTER 8

"I think this ramp cannot be any more perfect, Jerry," Cat said when he appeared on Monday afternoon. She wore a blue one-piece swimsuit that delightfully accentuated her full breasts. "Declare it finished, and we'll go out and have some fun."

Jerry was taken aback. By his book, he should fiddle with the tools at the ramp for a couple of hours, and then have a nice evening with Cat at home. These evenings were getting more and more pleasant. However, his scam was up. "What fun do you mean, Cat? I'm quite happy with things as they are!"

Of course, he lied. Since he had had Cat in his arms, Jerry's masculine animal self was turned on full blast. All he could think of during the days was the warm firmness of her body and at night . . . his dreams held no respect or restraint, as if he were fifteen again. He did not try to act on these fantasies. Much to his own surprise, he refused himself permission to fall back on his well-founded skills in manipulating a human soul. He did not try to put his fingers on invisible buttons he had been taught about. Oh, he wanted her very much, but only if she was willing; no—when she *desired* him. In any case, he had no interest in going out; he would rather stay at home and have her all for himself.

"I haven't gone kayaking for almost a week, and the ocean is calling me," she explained. "I thought you would like to come with me."

Jerry had almost managed to put away the unpleasant memories of his last kayak trip and considered that experience as the cost of meeting Cat—expensive, but worth it. He was not, however, looking forward to a repeat performance. Now, what was he supposed to answer? Say that he got scared so badly that he would never put his butt into a kayak again? So he agreed, even faked mild enthusiasm.

"Good man!" Cat exclaimed and put her arms around his neck. "I want to make sure that you don't have any fear from the last time. I love being out on the ocean, and would love it even better if you could come with me. The misadventure you had was not so much your fault, rather a lousy boat and lack of familiarity with the local waters."

God bless you, Cat, I might as well learn kayaking, Jerry thought, and he did not lose the opportunity to clasp his hands behind her back and pull her closer so that the blue swimsuit got firmly pressed against his shirt.

"I've asked one of my kayaking friends to let us use his old boat," Cat weaseled out from his embrace, "and he dropped it off this morning. Just understand, this is a racing surfski; it's very fast and very unstable. You'll tip over when you get into it, no question about it. Don't get discouraged; we all did that. Just keep climbing in and trying to paddle again. It will feel much better within a couple of hours."

Cat led him to the kayak sitting next to hers and wheeled away. She said she would be back in a couple of hours, after wrapping up her project. Then they would try a little trip together. Jerry took swimming trunks from his car and pulled the long white kayak to the large pool of calm water behind the reef. He gently tried to sit in the cockpit and transferred his weight gingerly. Suddenly his head was under water, for no apparent reason.

This is a beast! Jerry had lost any illusion that learning to ride this boat would be quick and easy. He would even doubt it could be done at all, if he had not seen Cat surfing big waves in a similar craft. The kayak was perhaps nineteen feet long and no more than a foot wide at the cockpit, just like trying to ride a pencil. Two hours later, he could sit in it. Rigid and afraid to move, he could execute tiny, short strokes with his eyes nailed to the horizon. His progress as a surfski kayaker was modest, but he did acquire great expertise in scrambling back on board.

When Cat arrived, she looked at him for a few seconds and complimented him on his excellent progress, but added, "Maybe you've had enough of kayaking for today; let's have a swim instead. You saw my swimming pool . . . it's generally quite useless because I prefer to swim in the ocean, but occasionally it comes in handy, if I want to swim at night."

Sunset was not far off, and Jerry thought that swimming in the pool was a wonderful idea. He had definitely had enough of kayaking. He started with slow, relaxing laps, waiting for Cat. The pool was rather shallow, lined with bright blue tiles, and the water was pleasantly warm. She appeared at the door a few minutes later, and wheeled to the pool's edge. Deftly, she slid out of her chair, sat on the rim of the pool, then slipped in.

They swam side by side. Cat moved through the water like a dolphin. There was little splashing when her body undulated, starting at her extended fingers through the full length of arms, torso and hips till the movements reached her knees, only her lower legs flopping somewhat behind. She took a breath every third stroke, flashing her face above the water for a second. She was a fast and elegant swimmer. If there ever were a real mermaid, Jerry was swimming with one.

He lagged slightly behind to get a better view of her body weaving smoothly through the water. They brushed and bumped against each other from time to time. He felt he was living through one of his dreams. At one turn, he extended his arm and touched the small of her back. By then, they were intimate enough for Jerry not to fear her turning around and trying to rip his head off. Instead he expected her to dive away and lead him on a joyful but hard chase that would leave them both bent over from exhaustion and gasping for breath.

What she did, he was completely unprepared for. She stopped swimming, turned around, put her arms around his neck and put her soft, wet, cold lips on his. They sank to the bottom of the pool kissing, separated there, and emerged at the edge of the pool. It was the deep end, and when they embraced again, Jerry swam to the opposite side while she never let go of his neck. They were lying in the shallow water with Cat's hands tangled in his hair and her body clinging to Jerry as his back found support on the pool's bottom.

He slowly caressed the whole length of her back until his hands came to rest on her small, round, firm buttocks. As he pressed her even tighter to his pulsating groin, Cat made a barely audible groan, pressing her face in the angle between his neck and shoulder. Short, moaning breaths sounded in his ear as he slipped the swimsuit off her shoulders. White breasts, definitely generous for a slim girl like her, glistened in the moonlight, with two dots of pink, erect nipples. The rest of her suit came off, and she helped Jerry out of his trunks.

She was looking into Jerry's eyes. Naked and vulnerable, she offered herself to the man who reclaimed her from the world of dreams and memories. "I don't really know who you are, Jerry, but I want you. I haven't been with anyone in four years; please, be gentle."

They were lying in the shallow, warm water for several minutes, then she kissed him and swam away, slowly, gently. He followed and catching up with her at the pool end he wrapped his arms around her waist whispering into her hair, "I love you, Cat, as I have never loved anyone."

She turned her face, kissed his lips and asked softly, "Are you for real, Jerry, or has Ruth sent you?"

* * *

Ruth, I am scared. For the past three years, your idea was working just fine. I got from the world what I could, and created in my mind what I couldn't. Hardly could tell the difference. I got quite good at it. No complaints. I even had a reasonable erotic life. I didn't want a lot of men, but I had Nick visiting me quite regularly. Must admit, I was cheating a bit. When we were still dating, Nick was really insistent on videotaping our lovemaking. I wasn't crazy about it, but he really wanted it, and I really wanted him, so I let him make some recordings. Who would think that it was me who would watch them? They came in a big box of personal stuff that his Mom packed for me after the accident. Hope she didn't watch them. They were sitting there for some time, but a few months after I left the hospital, I unpacked the box and found the recordings.

I put the disk into a machine and watched us making love. Didn't know whether to cry or enjoy. First I cried, then enjoyed. After all, this is what we were, a pair of kids crazy about each other and having great fun. Eventually, one scene got burned into my memory. The camera must have been on the TV stand, and what I saw was his naked body between my brown knees that were half bent, and his hard, small ass twitching and pumping. You know, he was a very athletic boy, a basketball player, and all that jumping gave him truly magnificent buns with gluts that felt like marble covered with soft, warm skin.

So, I watched this disk many times, and then didn't even need to watch. I would close my eyes, and his body would appear between my knees—always hungry, always enthusiastic, like then. I could climax if I wanted, all I needed to do was to put my hand under the sheet for a moment, but more often I would just burn slowly and go to sleep with a pleasant glow. You know, that was very helpful for the dreadful creepy-crawly feeling that I have on my thighs after my electric chair treatments.

Anyway, Jerry comes along. I like him and he uses every trick in the book to spend every evening with me. I got used to him and started looking at my watch about *three o'clock, hoping that soon he would show up at the door. We have fun together and he looks at me like a cat looks at a fish in a bowl. But that's not what I complain about.*

A few days ago, after Jerry had left, I somehow felt aroused. Did my electric torture routine, took a shower and went to bed. The crawlies were bad, I felt like a million ants were moving all over my upper legs. Well, maybe Nick would help. I closed my eyes and started thinking of Nick. I started feeling warm inside and then . . . I see Jerry kneeling on the ground, making some adjustment to my ramp, his buns lining up as if just for my eyes. He has a nice body, too. The circumstances of our meeting put him in a rather uncomfortable position; he feels like a wimp that I had to rescue. But the facts are that, though he is not very big, he has a hard, tight body, obviously takes good care of himself. Just like you, I have a special place in my imagination for male butt, and you would score him high in this department.

I opened my eyes and thought, what's this? Wrong number, for God's sake? Well, I went along with this imposition, talked to Jerry, and he was so sweet. He told me he loved me, was gentle, we kissed . . . the whole enchilada.

Now, you have to admit that Jerry had a lot of nerve to insinuate himself into my mental world and to tangle with Nick, without me ever consenting. If that's not an invasion of privacy, what is? You did mention, I remember, that characters we create in our minds start having their own ideas. Even if these ideas start somewhere in hidden places of our brains, it still comes as a surprise when our own creations start unexpectedly acting upon them. But things got worse . . .

The next day, he came early and I still had some work to finish. I was a bit edgy because I disliked his invasion of my inner life that had been so well organized. You know, Nick was much better behaved, would come only when invited, but this guy just put a foot in my soul's door and pushed in. You might not appreciate it, Ruth, after all these years that you lived in your imagination, but on the outside, you can't have that much control over others, way less than in your mind-world. They have their own ideas and do all kinds of things that you would never allow in your virtual life.

So, just to slow him down a bit, I asked him to try a surfski. I had a hell of time learning how to stay on it myself. It is very difficult at the beginning, and I knew that it would be hard on him with his recent experience off Bird Shit Rock. You might say that I was a bit sadistic, but mostly I was scared because he appeared from nowhere (actually I dragged him in myself, in a most direct way), and started moving into my life like a bulldozer. On the outside, he is a very well-behaved gentleman, but look what he did: Nick is not coming to see me any more. My days are upside down; once I could work until the morning if I wanted to, now I start getting nervous about three and almost sit waiting at the door by four. I used to kayak every day; you know the last time I was on the ocean? The day when I fished Jerry out. I am becoming dependent on him! You know damn well that's not acceptable. What if he changes his mind and goes away? Perhaps for some ski bunny with two healthy legs who had saved him from an avalanche? Should I go back to Nick? Nick seems to have left my head. Back to mind-numbing medications, booze or just crash and burn? It's scary, Ruth!

Can you imagine a dog trying to get on a wooden barrel in water? That was Jerry riding a surfski. I was watching him from the window and could not help but admire his
spirit. He kept climbing and falling and climbing again. He
gave himself no breaks, no rest, just an unrelenting struggle. I know what a struggle is, and I respect someone with a
fighting spirit. Jerry is a fighter, and giving up doesn't occur to him easily.

I digress, but it brought to my mind the observation that
Nick and I were just lucky kids. We were born good looking, smart, with natural talent for sports, also had good
parents. We had no real struggle in our lives. We danced
from one easy victory to another, maybe undeserved feat.
After the accident, I had my share of opportunities to get
hurt and fight on, get knocked down and come up again.
Nick just had left the ring. I'll never know what kind of a
fighter he would have been.

I went to see Jerry two hours later, and I was ashamed
of myself. He deserved better than what I gave him, and he
still didn't hold it against me. We went swimming in the
pool in the darkness, with only the moon shining on us.
There was something very intimate about it, and at one
point, he touched me on my lower back. You know that for
some reason, this area is very sensitive to touch, almost as
though it was compensating for my legs that feel nothing.
When he touched me there, it felt like a jet of hot but pleasant water shooting through the middle of my back all the
way to my skull. Suddenly, I wanted all of my body to be
enveloped by this jet and I did what I still may regret. I
turned to him and kissed him. Then I lost my mind. My body

took over and it wanted him so badly! I wanted to feel him with all of me. My arms and breasts and belly were gorging on the warmth of his body, my ass felt his hands pressing my hips against his. My body rebelled against my mind. All these years of good, clean fun that I used to bring about in my mind, my feeling of full control over myself and the rest of the world, it all crashed flat.

Ruth, it was very, very different from the erotic romps that we had in our heads. Remember your Ronaldo, your perfect Italian lover, who was dark, passionate and crazy? Ronaldo who snuck past your three bodyguards, and stood on a window ledge for the whole day just to spend a night with you? The point is, Ronaldo went home in the morning not to return until you had called him back. He would go home any time you willed him. He would jump through the window, if that were your desire. But I had no power over the events that were rushing over us. I was no longer a director. I was an actress, and my script was missing.

It was very scary, exciting and beautiful at the same time. It was even different from sex with Nick, when he was still around. With Nick it was like a . . . happy game of tennis finished with a wonderful victory for both of us. Perhaps because we were healthy and innocent of suffering, our encounters were so joyful and so sweet. We could do it again and again without any fear or concern or pain.

Eventually, Jerry and I slumped on the bottom of the pool. I was still feeling "aftershocks," but my hips cramped up a bit. Maybe they cramped up before, but I didn't realize it, I was shaken to my core. This experience reduced me to a level of trembling jelly that needed some time to reconstitute itself into the body I knew. I swam away to stretch my hips a bit. He followed me and said he loved me.

Ruth, I am scared to death. I cannot control what's happening to me, but I want to be with him. Am I going to be dependent again? Ruth, I wish you were here. How should I protect myself? I was doing so well.

CHAPTER 9

The restaurant's back office was small and looked like a thousand other small business offices. The only thing that caught Kalani's attention was a small sculpture of a naked young woman on the desk. It was bright white and almost glowed in the darkened room. Mr. Rosen was sitting behind the desk looking at her.

Abe has a good eye for women, Rosen thought. Perhaps twenty-three years old, pretty face, a bit too full in the hips, good waist, though. He moved forward in his chair, forced a smile, and started in a fatherly manner, "So, Abe tells me that you need some work, Kalani?"

"Yes, sir, I would like to work evenings, so I thought, I could be a waitress. But if you could use me at home in the evening, I would like to try."

Use me in the evening . . . I like the way she formulates her thoughts, smiled Rosen to himself. "I know that you clean people's homes. What do they pay you?"

"Fourteen, fifteen dollars an hour."

"I will start you at twelve and maybe you will get more, if I am happy with you. I will need you twice a week. Can you start tonight?"

"Yes, sir, thank you, Mr. Rosen."

"OK then, follow my car so I can show you my home and explain your duties."

Kalani followed Rosen's Mercedes to Lanikai until it stopped in front of a brown house, high on the hill. There were no homes on either side; deep ravines surrounded the property connected to the road by a steep driveway. The night was dark and she could see the lights of Kailua town far down below and deep blackness of the ocean in front of her. The sky was filled with millions of stars.

"Wow, you have a beautiful place here, Mr. Rosen, but it's a bit spooky to be so alone, isn't it?"

"Thank you, Kalani, but I like being alone; I don't enjoy nosy neighbors. Come in, I will show you what to do."

The girl followed Rosen. He was rather short and his age was hard to tell; his waist started expanding as it happens to middle-aged men, but he moved swiftly and lightly, like a younger person. They entered the house, an older but elegant dwelling typical for the expensive neighborhood of Lanikai. A two-story atrium led to a living and dining room, a kitchen and a guest restroom. The house was scarcely furnished; obviously, the owner had not bought new furniture yet.

This is going to be a piece of cake, Kalani thought, I could do it in an hour, and then relax a bit before going home. They went upstairs to see bedrooms. Two were practically empty unless one counted a few still unpacked boxes and packages.

"This is my master bedroom," said Rosen, opening for her the door to the third bedroom. He let her slip in front of him into a large room with expansive windows looking towards the blackness of the ocean. A large four-poster bed, covered with a carefully draped, white sheet, occupied the middle of the room. A few feet from the bed was a large, strange-looking leather chair. It had a generously padded seat, two wooden arm supports and no backrest. In addition, there were two other, more conventional-looking leather chairs and an impressive desk of cherry wood. A large sculpture sat next to the window, and Kalani immediately recognized it as a larger version of the figurine sitting on the office desk. This was a large piece, almost life size. A naked young woman was exquisitely made in white stone, kneeling with her hands and the head submissively placed on the floor in front of her. Her thin hips were elevated in a position vaguely suggestive of a sexual offering. Rosen approached the sculpture and lovingly placed his hand on the back of the naked girl.

"I want you to take special care of this young lady. It's a great piece of art made by the greatest sculptor that ever lived. I would like you to gently dust her every day. Do you like her?"

Kalani swallowed saliva and answered, unsure of herself, "Oh, she is very pretty, sir. Just . . . she doesn't look very comfortable. Why does she sit like that?"

Rosen smiled slightly, "She sits as she was told, and her comfort was not an issue...." He caught himself just in time, not to continue with the arguments why some women need to be uncomfortable, much more uncomfortable than the girl on her knees.

Kalani took the job, though the bedroom bothered her a bit, especially the sculpture. It looked like an easy job, something that would come like a reward at the end of a day, after long hours of hard work. She took a house key and drove home along the narrow, winding road leading back to town.

Harry Rosen went to the desk and, deep in thought, picked up a long, black object resting on top. It had a finely sculpted ivory handle adorned with silver inlay and a foot-long, thin leather blade. Harry absentmindedly cut through the air; the whip gave a swishing sound, and hit padded leather with a vicious thud. Rosen waited a moment anticipating a dark red welt to appear, but only living skin could do that, of course. Another hand used to wield this instrument of ultimate power and pleasure, the hand much more skilled than his. Harry, or whatever his name was then, had stolen this object and never had a quiet night's sleep since. He took elaborate steps to cover his tracks, but deep inside, he knew that his intellect was not a match for the awesome powers of the Master.

CHAPTER 10

J erry swam along Kailua Beach automatically making one crawl stroke after another, while his mind pondered a question: What's so different about this girl?

He was no naïve boy; at thirty-five, he had close to twenty years of romantic experience. Gym-hardened body, good smile, quick wit—he had no problem attracting women and slept with many, but apart from feeding his healthy sexual appetite, he felt no need for permanent female presence or affection, hadn't for many years. Jerry still could vaguely remember tender feelings for his high school girlfriend, but then he had signed up with the Army and things had changed.

"They will make a man out of you," his father said. "In any case, there is no war going on, you won't get hurt." The boot camp and the basic training did feel like they were making a man out of him, on the double. His waist got smaller, shoulders bigger... good friends, tough but quite acceptable life. The change came when Captain Murphy, an officer they hardly ever saw in the barracks, called him in for a little conversation. There was an opening at the Intelligence Unit that needed to be filled with a highly intelligent and patriotic young man.

"You, Roberts, have a chance." Murphy was good

enough in his trade to easily persuade Jerry that trading an
M16 and daily grueling training for a tape recorder and a
computer was a good deal. The Army had sent him for
some interesting courses and his lifestyle improved consid-
erably. Jerry's superiors quickly figured out that his intelligence was way above average, so he was much praised,
encouraged and offered additional training. Captain Murphy got himself a good asset. The payment for this interesting and stimulating education came due later. Once Jerry
got filled with the theory of understanding human nature,
and tutored in ways of manipulating people for the Army's
benefit, he was sent back to his unit, where Murphy
awaited him impatiently.

"Welcome home, Roberts; I've assigned you to the
team of interrogators." The captain leaned back on his
chair, coldly studying his subordinate's face. Jerry suddenly felt nauseous. "I hope nobody promised you James
Bond's job?" Murphy's thin lips curled in a contemptuous
grin. "You will be doing important work that may save
your colleagues' asses, so don't give me that hurt prima
ballerina expression."

Jerry stood in front of the desk at attention thinking: Interrogator! I am supposed to make people talk! I just can't
do that!

Captain Murphy was clearly not happy with his reaction; sat up straight in his chair and grimaced, "Don't worry,
Roberts, we don't send people away for a year to study on
the government's expense in order to use them for swinging
a bamboo stick. This talent comes cheap and needs no training. You will use your head to get what we need. Now get
out of here and report for duty tomorrow morning."

70

SINNERS IN PARADISE

Two months later Jerry found himself on a transport plane, which landed on a small strip at the desert's edge. The enemies of civilization abounded here; there was much work for interrogators, and his relation with human kind started changing rapidly.

Yellow sand of the ocean's bottom was slowly passing under his goggles, as he thought, things really changed since I've met Cat. She's definitely different, but why? She is pretty, no question about it, but so are Barbara and Camilla. She is very intelligent and argues like a pro, but it's the same with the whole debating club. Jerry noticed a small colorful reef fish grazing on a rock. Perhaps she is simply my match? Supposedly, people have a one in five hundred chance of meeting their perfect match. Maybe I just lucked out! Jerry smiled under the water.

Now, let's look at it from the other side; Jerry's analytical mind would not stop on one side of the issue. Does she think I am her perfect match? This thought made him uncomfortable. Let's face it. I'm certified damaged goods hiding in a pretty good box. I've made an ass of myself even before our relationship started and that's not even the beginning of bad news. Hope she sees in me something that I am not aware of. He sighed, blowing a big air bubble.

Later that day, Jerry and Cat cuddled on the couch in front of her TV. Colorful pictures flashed on the screen and talking heads kept nodding, smiling or grimacing. Cat turned her face up, asking, "Do you like to watch TV alone? I hardly ever turned my set on before you started coming over."

Jerry smiled, "I rarely watch TV except for news. Even

71

now I am not watching it. I'm just cuddling with you."

"Oh, maybe you would prefer to build some economy models?" Cat teased and stretched her arm to plunge her hand into Jerry's curly hair.

"The only thing I want to build right now is an extremely high wall around this room, so that nobody could get in, and no one could get out." Jeremy slipped his hand under Cat's arm until warm softness filled his palm.

She smiled with satisfaction and pressed the off button on the remote.

CHAPTER 11

Abe was happy for exactly one hour and thirty-two minutes that day. Kalani brought seventeen hundred bucks at lunch, and he still had over two hundred left from last night. That should do. He did his best to show gratitude filling his heart. Kalani came a bit late, having stopped at the bank, so she wouldn't have time to cook. Instead, she stopped at Sloppy Joe's and bought some *loco moco*, a traditional local food consisting of rice with gravy and two pieces of Spam. Abe was not a great fan of *loco moco* with Spam; he had had enough of this stuff in childhood, but rose to the occasion and ate without complaining. To the contrary, he complimented Kalani on her nice flowery dress, which she had worn day in and day out for over a year. However, Abe couldn't miss the lovely fullness of her bottom, especially when she bent over to clean the floor where gravy had spilled. Unfortunately, there was only enough time for a few kisses, with a perfunctory feeling and kneading of her round buns.

Kalani accepted the clumsy caress without protest, although she derived no pleasure from it. She knew that was her boyfriend's way of reaffirming his ownership rights. Not much different, really, from a dog raising his leg at a tree, she thought, mildly irritated. Isn't it strange what happened? My heart used to thump when he was around and I was happy all day when he touched me. And look at us now.

Abe was not too disappointed either, as he needed to meet Jose and a rooster guy at two. He thought of Rosen for a moment. He could ask him for money, but then Rosen would treat him like some sort of an employee. No, Abe should have a running chicken breeding operation, and only then invite the restaurateur and his money. That would make them real partners.

The happy part of the day ended when he met Jose and the older man. They were sitting at the edge of Kailua Swamp, a nice private place where cops had no business. The bushes were thick, covered with luxuriant dark green leaves. Hundreds of faint pathways created a labyrinth where one could come and go or simply disappear in the blink of an eye.

"There you go," Abe proudly pulled his money. "A hundred short, but I'll give you the rest in a few days."

Vincent took the money, counted it loudly and cracked his old wrinkled Filipino face in a wry grimace. "OK, that's a hundred short for chicks, but where is the money for board and feed?"

Abe's face grew dark and his shoulders rose. "You didn't say anything about board and feed."

"Oh, you want to keep the chicks in your apartment—good, good!" Vincent was laughing openly now. "I'm sure Kalani will be very happy; a woman can't have too many roosters!"

Now Jose starting laughing too, and just had to add, "Abe, Kalani and the chickens, that will be a nice family. She always wanted chicks; one will be called Lehua and another Maika!"

Abe clenched his teeth and turned to Jose, "Shut your stupid mouth or I'll shut it for you!" As for Vincent . . . someone will have to pay for his humiliation. "You try to cheat me, *makule*, old man? You let me believe that the chicks could run on your farm for free. But I will pay you for board—when I want to and how much I want to . . . And you'll take it and be very careful with my chicks because if any one of them goes bad, I will smash your face, just like I am going to do now." The young man moved closer to Vincent. With his big arms raised and head lowered, he looked like a bull terrier ready to grab a smaller dog by the neck and shake him into submission. The older man didn't move, didn't try to escape, but when Abe's face was within a foot of his, a skinny brown hand shot from his belt and instantly a razor blade appeared, almost touching the attacker's nose.

"You back off, boy!" Vincent hissed, "or your mother won't know your face tonight! I could fillet you like a fish before you knew what hit you. Keep your nose clean and don't forget my hundred dollars. And it will be another hundred for feed and board, every month. Come here tomorrow with cash or forget about your chicks. I will keep this as a deposit," he patted the pocket of his dirty shorts where the wad of bills had disappeared. Abe squinted his eyes at the blade nearly touching his lip, then at Jose. Jose was standing three steps away and gave no indication of wanting to join the fray.

75

"It's only fair, Abe, it's only fair . . ." he blurted nervously, keeping his hands in his pockets and his head lowered. The traitor just wanted a way out.

"You hear, Abe, it's only fair . . ." grinned Vincent with contempt, as he stepped backwards two steps, turned around and disappeared into the bushes.

"You brought him to me, you dirty swine," Abe turned to Jose, "and now you backed down when he took my money? You low-life chicken-shit, all you had to say was to make fun of my girlfriend?" He took a big swing with his right hand and when Jose ducked to avoid a right hook, Abe caught him with a hard, left undercut. The skinny body lifted somewhat from the blow supported by Abe's great bulk, then Jose slumped on the ground barely breathing. Abe stood over the curled body for a moment deliberating if a few kicks should be thrown in, but Jose was just groaning without moving. Abe spit on him, turned away and walked to the road. He was not quite sure where to go and what to do. At the end, he turned home.

A dark corridor of the apartment building lead to the one-bedroom apartment that he occupied with Kalani. He sat on the bed. It was a good bed with an expensive mattress. Made of dark solid wood, it had a firm but comfortable feel. They bought it three years ago, when they decided to rent an apartment together. They both had some money, Abe from fishing and Kalani from cleaning. They were doing quite well. Buying a new bed for them was like starting a new life. Kalani was so excited, and it was a good time for him, too. They also bought a table and chairs, a chest of drawers, but these were secondhand, though still good. They did not have the same meaning. The bed was new, like their life together.

Things started looking down when the skipper of his fishing boat decided he had enough of getting up at 3 AM every day. Old Nakamura had to be well over seventy, so he was getting somewhat clumsy and forgetful. Once they almost hit a rock at the harbor channel, the channel that the old guy had gone through for the past forty or fifty years. He liked Abe and wanted to sell him the boat.

"I will teach you, Abe, what you need to know. You worked with me for four years, most of it you already know." He would take the payment in installments; he trusted Abe.

Well, too late to think of it now; Nakamura's been dead for two years, Abe thought. No question, I was happier then; Kalani was happier, too. But at that time, it looked like a smart thing to do . . . take a bit of time off, sleep in, relax . . . Before he knew it, unemployment stopped coming. He took some odd jobs here and there. Help with moving, a bit of gardening, cut a tree—all of it worthless. Sometimes he could poach a few lobsters, sometimes he would visit a farmer's orchard at night . . . enough money to buy beer and cigarettes.

Heck, Kalani keeps me, he thought unhappily. Now, when I could start making some money in cock fighting, of course, something had to go wrong. Really, if I had enough money, there would be no problem. If I had just another two hundred bucks, I would be in business. The stupid bitch just couldn't come up with an extra two hundred bucks!

Dirty dishes piled in a sink; Kalani had not had time to

wash them, and this was annoying the hell out of Abe. His mother kept her house really clean. He lay on his back in bed and lit a cigarette. The ceiling was cracked and dirty. He looked at the walls, windows—all cried for a fresh coat of paint. What a dump; someone should take care of it! I'll give the landlady hell when I meet her, he thought angrily.

Kalani came home after six. She stood at the door, not sure what to make of the situation; it couldn't be anything good. "Oh, Abe, you're so early, is everything OK? How is your business?" she asked, masking anxiety with an air of concern.

"Business would be good if you gave me all the money I needed." Abe did not move from the bed, looking grimly at the ceiling.

"But I gave you two thousand, like you asked!" Her voice was rising in anger at the injustice of his implied accusation.

"You can't do business without reserves; I was two hundred short." Abe was glad to find a good excuse for his failure at the last moment. This made him feel a bit better, though at the same time, it focused his attention on the fact that Kalani was responsible for his fiasco.

Kalani turned away not to show her angry face. "I gave you all that you asked for, my money for the nursing school. And what about you? You couldn't make any by yourself? What are you, crippled or something?"

That was more than Abe could stand. Vincent, Jose, now his own girlfriend—was everybody turning on him? He harshly grabbed her by the shoulder and turned her around.

"If I need your advice, I'll ask for it," he breathed into her face. "Now, clean the bloody dishes and make dinner! I am the man of this house, and you better remember it."

Kalani shook her shoulder free and stepped back. She was furious, and forgot the sensible rule of not being too sassy with her boyfriend. "You behave like the man of the house, and I will respect you all right. So, Abe, when was the last time you did some decent work, like a man? You are just wasting your life and mine. If you prefer to hang around with this rat friend of yours, Jose, make dinner yourself."

A dry snap sounded when Abe's open hand connected with her right cheek, and Kalani landed against a wall. She was holding her burning face looking at Abe without a word. No explanations necessary—she had seen her mother standing in the same cowed posture.

Abe was almost as shocked as she was. He did not even realize when he had slapped her, never did it before. She stayed leaning against the wall, holding her face, then tried to get behind the table. She was afraid, and when he looked at her, at one hundred and twenty pounds, almost half his size, he felt a sudden surge of shame and remorse.

"I'm sorry, Kalani, I am sorry, I don't know why I did that. I was just very angry . . ."

Kalani hardly heard him. She regained her composure a bit once she got the table between him and her. "Just get out, Abe, just get out. I don't want you here. This is my apartment, and I don't want you here."

He raised both open hands in a gesture of good intentions and just to placate her said, "OK, OK, I'll go away for a few hours, so we cool off a bit, OK?"

She let him go through the door without saying anything, but once he was in the corridor, she turned the lock and yelled, "If you come back here, I'll call the police! You got that? We are through—you and me, we are *pau.*"

CHAPTER 12

The old man kept a lot of cash in his safe, so much that when Harry Rosen cleared him out, he needed a big leather bag to carry it off. Nothing frees the mind better than a good-sized hoard of large bills and golden coins—discreet, free of tax and paper trail. His financial matters were fine; what gnawed at his mind were memories of the Master. Rosen tried to suppress them ever since he had left the Nicaraguan jungle. The estate was his home ever since he had left the base in Panama, and had buried his sergeant's uniform in a deep hole. Nicaragua, those were good times, he thought, but everybody needs to advance in life, and I couldn't hope for anything else with the old man around.

Harry Rosen spared no expense and no trouble to make sure there were no tracks left behind. He was confident that Bonito, the Master's disciple, had disappeared like a ghost from the surface of the earth, and Harry Rosen began his new existence in Hawaii without any links to that past. Still, who would know better how crafty the old bastard was? He was called El Diablo for a reason. And what he would do if he ever caught up with Bonito. . . . Cold sweat broke on Rosen's back as he angrily ordered himself to stop thinking stupid thoughts.

The view from his window was incomparable to anything he knew. The deep blue of the ocean was getting
lighter in proximity of the land, and a white fringe of foam
marked the line where water touched the beach below. Two
small islands were thrown in the middle of this panorama
as though a painter had decided that more variety was
needed in his composition.

That would be too much, if not actually real, remarked
Harry to himself. Money well spent. The real reason this
property had caught his attention was its isolation. Splen-
didly situated on the summit of a volcanic rock, it had no
neighbors. There were, obviously, some houses down the
road, but the closest one was at least five hundred yards
away. Only frigates hanging in the sky could look into his
windows, and the howling of ever-present trade winds
would drown any noise coming from his bedroom. Here, at
last, he was, or rather could be, the Master.

Compare it to the view of the stinky jungle stretching
for tens of miles in every direction, he thought smugly.
Rosen liked to plan his little but absolute kingdom in great
detail, more for entertainment than for an immediate practical purpose. He knew well that hastiness could be fatal.
Most assured assumptions fail and the unanticipated problems crop up. Just look what happened to El Diablo.
Rosen's plan would be polished to perfection. Every part
would be examined many times for possible holes, and all
possible scenarios played and replayed before any action
would be initiated. All that takes time, and he had all the
time he needed. Rosen knew that sooner or later all the
pieces of the jigsaw would find their places. Still, what
wrong could come by way of a little excitement coming
from the imaginary play and handling of the things that re-

minded him of the times when he was Bonito, the Master's right hand? A hard hand that was never seen without a whip.

The black horse crop with an ivory handle gracing his desk was, certainly, not his instrument. Much too delicate for the work that Bonito did. That was a tool of an artist to be used precisely and sparingly, the instrument of the great maestro who just got too old to perform his art. Therefore, it was up to Harry Rosen to take it from the failing hand and ensure that it kept performing.

Consuela. That ungrateful bitch Consuela was the last canvas on which the crop painted its straight lines and cubistic figures. Rosen could remember nervous twitching of her muscles in anticipation of a strike. He would wait, let the anticipation grow unbearable, and just when she started thinking that maybe, this time, for whatever reason, she would get away without a whipping, a swish of a leather-bound reed cutting through the air would send her in a panicky and futile effort to move away from pain. The crop would plunge into the softness of her buttocks and a bright red line appeared immediately, slowly darkening as Rosen looked with the satisfaction of a painter who delivered a line of perfect proportion, color and composition.

She enjoyed his art. No way she could fake the volcanic passion that followed beatings. At first, when she appeared on the ranch, she was just a pretty girl scared into complete submission. The Master chose well. She came as a new teacher to a school in a village twenty miles away. When she disappeared, nobody gave it a second thought. A city girl ran away from her village post; happened all the time. The Master ordered him to take her to the inner yard every day, and Bonito was happy to do it. After the first few times, when she was just writhing and moaning until his culminating excitement made him drop the whip and penetrate her, she seemed to develop some taste for flogging and used her twisting body to seduce him into sex. Of course, that would shorten a whipping session. Soon, she was going into an erotic frenzy the moment he tied her up to the post, which might result in only one or two strikes. Could she fake it, just to escape the whip? Bonito wondered, but that did not stop him from being more and more attached to her.

At the end, it was Consuela who talked him into cleaning out the old man and running away. "I will be your slave forever, Master." That's what did him in, "Master." She certainly knew his dreams, treacherous bitch.

Rosen was examining leather straps that fit around the wooden frame of a large armchair when the doorbell rang. Amazed, he put away the straps. Who the hell might be paying me a visit? He was flabbergasted.

"Aloha, Mr. Rosen, it's my first day to work for you." Abe's girlfriend was standing in his doorway, thin dress stretching over full breasts and delightful, round hips.

"Kalani, I forgot about it, but please, come in and go ahead." Rosen followed the girl and only now understood why she seemed so familiar. She had some of Consuela's qualities. Her hips are a bit fuller, he thought, but Consuela lost some weight with my training, nothing that couldn't be fixed. Other than that— the same olive skin, black eyes, narrow waist.... Wonder what her temperament is like?

"Could you start with the bedroom upstairs? I will need to work there a bit later on."

"Sure, Mr. Rosen."

Rosen watched the girl dusting his nude sculpture and couldn't refrain from seeing her naked, tied to the armchair, with her gorgeous ass exposed and waiting for his sort of love. Just before he started, he liked to grab Consuela's black, long hair to lift her face so that he could look into it and drink in the fear pouring from her eyes. I could do it right here, without any gags. This house is just perfect, he thought as pressure was increasing in his pants. His excitement was growing as Kalani bent over to make his bed. Who would know? I would never admit that she ever showed up for cleaning. Rosen got on his feet and slowly moved towards Kalani.

Another bell rang. "Hell! What's this? Some kind of a bloody hotel?" Rosen turned to the entrance with a furious expression, opened the door, and his face rapidly changed into a warm smile. "Abe, do come in, your girlfriend is here."

"Thank you, Mr. Rosen, I just wanted to talk with Kalani for a moment."

"There is nothing to talk about," the girl was standing just behind Rosen. "I've told you, we are *pau* and don't follow me. I am working now and don't bother me anymore."

How interesting, Rosen thought. Who's the suspect when a girl disappears, if not a jilted boyfriend? Time brings opportunities. Thank you, Abe, for stopping me now. That would be most unfortunate and stupid of me to start this affair on the spur of the moment.

"Kalani, I just want to speak with you. It was such a

stupid thing I did. I will make it up to you, please." Abe was not giving up.

"Abe, if you follow me, I will tell the police that you are stalking me. I'll press charges and get you locked up for good." Kalani was in no mood for forgiveness and shook her duster at him. Abe's humble plea eased her fear and now she allowed herself to be properly outraged.

Rosen definitely didn't need the police coming to his house. He took Abe by his arm in a fatherly manner and led him down the driveway. "Listen, my boy, be patient. She is quite worked up now for whatever you did, but give it a day or two and try to see her again. Just stay away from the police; you don't need that." Then he went back inside, smiled kindly to Kalani, and started reading a newspaper that he had bought in the morning.

Abraham walked down to the end of the driveway where his bike was hidden in the bushes. He looked around and settled on the ground. The night was pleasant, no mosquitoes were buzzing around, as the wind was strong on the hill. He could wait. Kalani would have to pass by him.

* * *

"Sure, you may come over; anything wrong, Kalani?" Cat put down the phone and thought that things with Abe and Kalani were moving faster than she could predict. Kalani was upset and even more, sounded scared. Partner abuse in the islands was a significant problem, and every woman knew of a girlfriend or a wife badly beat up or murdered. That was serious. Kalani told Cat the story of her own mother being slapped around for years before she ran away with the kids from the Big Island to Oahu. The husband didn't bother to chase her down, gone too far with booze and drugs.

Kalani ran from her car to the open door, which Cat shut and locked behind her. She was wearing her usual red dress and rubber sandals. The girl was breathing fast and was obviously scared. Her right cheek was slightly bruised.

"Just sit down and tell me what has happened. Don't worry, neither Abe nor anybody else will hurt you here," Cat pulled Kalani to a table.

"But I think he followed me." Kalani slumped at the table, but wouldn't take her eyes off the door. Her face was unnaturally ashy, drops of sweat beading on her upper lip.

"No worries, I am prepared for unwelcome guests. You don't think I have no protection, living here alone?" She sounded confident and cool, but her heart was racing.

"You have protection? What do you mean?" Kalani did not quite comprehend. She knew that Cat lived by herself. Maybe this new man that she met a few times at the door . . . . He wouldn't slow down Abe, she thought. Abe was a champion wrestler in high school and got only bigger and stronger since then.

"Just believe me. So what happened?" Cat pulled out cookies and a carton of milk, hoping that Kalani would settle down.

"Well, I gave Abe two grand, actually three hundred and the rest the next day. He seemed pretty happy, even grateful, and took off. The next thing I knew, he was home when I came back at night. Very unusual, normally he would be hanging out somewhere with his buddy Jose until midnight. And he was in a really foul mood. So I asked how the business was. You know, to make him feel important. Besides, it was my two thousand bucks, for my school," she sniffed, rubbed her eyes and blew her nose. "And he really went crazy and slapped me."

"He beat you up?" Cat's eyes were sparkling with anger and her hands turned into white knuckled fists. "Has it ever happened before?"

"Not exactly beat me up, slapped me once. Never did it before. But I saw my mother being slapped, and there will be no other time. I told him to get out and never come back. We are *pau.*" Kalani's eyes welled up with tears. Finally, she could allow herself to pour out emotions that had built up for two days.

"Now I don't have a boyfriend, don't have money for school, and I am afraid to cross a parking lot to get to my car!"

Cat was sitting stiffly with her head up, eyes locked onto the black window. The trade winds were howling on the awning but nothing moved outside. The situation was new to her; she had no good and fast advice. "Whatever needs to be done, you can't go home. You are a sitting duck there. Somehow . . . I didn't get the impression that Abe was a scoundrel when I first met him, but you need to be careful. You should stay here with me until the situation clears. And Kalani, I am proud of you. You did exactly the thing that you needed to do."

"But, I am scared now and, and . . . Abe was a good man!"

The bell rang and both women shuddered. "Oh, God, it's him," Kalani whispered and shrunk in her chair. Cat wheeled to her desk and opened the drawer. Without saying a word, she removed the handgun and put it under the thin blanket that she draped over her knees. "Just stay where you are."

Kalani's eyes were closed and she looked as though she were praying. The bell sounded again and, almost immediately, once more. Cat wheeled to the door, looked through the spy hole, unlocked the door, moved the chair back two yards and put her right hand under the blanket. The doorknob turned, the door opened and the tall muscular man slowly walked over the threshold and stopped in front of Cat, who was blocking the way.

The slim woman looked up at the big man standing in front of her wheelchair, her face pale and grim. "What do you want, Abe? You should have called before coming," Cat's voice was cold and unwelcoming.

The man's eyes were fixed on Kalani frozen by the table. "Sorry about that; I just wanted to talk to Kalani."

Cat turned around and asked calmly, "Kalani, do you want to talk to him?" Kalani shook her head signaling "no," without looking up.

"Well, she doesn't want to talk to you; now just leave."

"I cannot leave without talking to her," Abe moved to get around Cat, but she spun her chair quickly to block him.

"Get out of here!" she snapped.

"Stop it, lady! All I want to do is talk to my woman. I am not going to hurt you, Kalani!" He put his large hand on the wheelchair's handle and immobilized it, then quickly moved around to make a step towards Kalani who tried to slide under the table.

Suddenly, the rage Cat knew years ago, at the hospital, came back in all its violence, but this time with a clear focus at the man who intruded into her home and did the unforgivable, tried to restrain her.

"Stop right there!" A sharp command and a loud metallic sound made him freeze. He slowly turned his head to look into the short barrel. Cat aimed at the middle of his chest, holding the small, black handgun in her extended hand, trembling with fury. The essence of her misfortune, the invisible devil she hated with all her heart for years, finally had the face and the chest that could be ripped open with a bullet.

"No!" Kalani screamed and catapulted from the table towards the man, until checked by Cat's hand grabbing her dress.

"Stay back and don't interfere! This is my house, and nobody will push me around!" she barked, but Kalani's movement interrupted Cat's blind rage. She exhaled and rested the weapon-holding hand on her knee. "You want to go out and stay with him, you are free, but he's not welcome here, and he is just leaving. Right, Abraham?" The point of the barrel vaguely waved towards the door.

"I'm leaving, I'm leaving . . . " Abe was taking slow, deliberate steps backwards. "Just wanted to tell you, Kalani, that you don't need to be afraid of me. I will never do it again. I think I was just crazy for a minute. I'll move out from our apartment so you can think about it, but if you see me again, you don't have to run. I love you."

Kalani looked in his eyes and was moving slowly towards the door as though in lockstep with the man until stopped again by Cat's hand still clutching her dress. She looked back with an expression of surprise.

"Snap out of it! You look hypnotized," Cat said. "I want to talk to you for a few minutes and then you can go if you want to. Can you do that for me?"

Abe stood at the door looking at the women, clearly hoping that Kalani would go with him.

"I will stay here, with Cat," said Kalani lowering her head," . . . but, Abe, thank you."

When the door closed the big man had tears in his eyes. She wanted to protect me, we are not *pau*, he thought. She still loves me and I can make it better. Abe walked to his bike briskly, smiling in the darkness.

"What do you think you are doing?" Cat inquired softly. "Are you ready just to go home, give him a hug and forget?"

Kalani felt somewhat ashamed, shrugged, and looking aside said, "But Abe is a good man, and I love him. And he is sorry. Don't you think he is sorry?"

Cat's heart was pounding and she felt wetness in her armpits, but she could think clearly again. Pulling a gun on anyone, that was a first for her. She could be proud of her

91

debut's dramatic impact, but neither Abe nor Kalani could guess how close to a disaster they all were. Now she was getting annoyed with Kalani.

"How many times, you think, did your father apologize after beating up your mother? Probably as many times as he beat her. That's why she stayed with him for years, always hoping he would change. Abe crossed the line, and crossing the line next time will be only easier for him."

Kalani slumped on the chair and hid her face in her hands. Now she remembered the mother hiding black eyes under big sunglasses, pussyfooting around her house at noon, because her husband might wake up in a bad mood. She remembered slapping sounds and thuds of the body slammed against the wall in that bedroom, followed by muffled whimpers so that kids would not hear. Her body started shaking, and she broke into loud sobbing.

Cat approached her and touched her dark head. "You can stay here as long as you want, Kalani, until you figure out what to do."

"But he was a good man . . ." Kalani kept sobbing.

"He was. I hardly know him, but you told me good things about him. But he is not anymore. He is a bum and abuser now."

Kalani raised her head. "You shouldn't call him that. He just had a stretch of bad luck." Now she was becoming irritated.

"Bad luck? What's his bad luck? Perhaps got hurt on the boat or got sick?" Cat's voice was rising in pitch and loudness. The evening's stress translated into a surge of adrenaline, and her face was pale despite the tan. She was breathing rapidly, nostrils flaring. "You know what his bad luck was? You, you were his bad luck!"

Kalani was sitting straight up, with eyes bulging. "Are you crazy? What are you saying? I have always loved him; I would do anything for him!"

There was no holding back now. Cat dished her opinions out. "Three years ago, when I first met you, you brought him to my house once. He was a great-looking guy, happy, cheerful and in love with you. Then you destroyed him with your love. He lost his job and could have had another within a week, but you let him just take it easy. Heroic Kalani could take care of her man! He started fooling around with his good-for-nothing friends. You were just making sure that he had enough cash for beer and cigarettes. Did you give him money for hookers as well?"

Kalani's face was purple, and she appeared ready to jump at Cat, but after a moment of hesitation she just shouted with hate: "Shut up! Just shut up! You have no mercy or understanding. You are like . . . like your computer. Just lock yourself up with the bloody machine. You are not like the rest of us . . . people!"

The silence lasted for half a minute as both women tried to get hold of themselves. Finally, Cat said softly, "I don't know the future and won't tell you what to do, but I am your friend and, I think, if you take him back now, you will end like your mother. He, indeed, was a good man and, who knows, maybe he will be as good in the future, but now he is not. If you still want him, do yourself a favor and let him straighten up his life, all by himself. Then, maybe, you will be able to pick up where you had left your good life together a few years ago. Now excuse me, but I need to go to sleep. You know where the guest room is."

She wheeled to her downstairs bedroom, and a few minutes later Kalani slowly dragged herself upstairs. Both women lay in their beds staring into the darkness until morning.

CHAPTER 13

The ramp-building ruse no longer necessary, Jerry kept coming happily in late afternoons without any excuse or invitation, but felt increasing anxiety. The Hawaii trip was inevitably coming to its end. The return trip to New York loomed, Cat being left behind. But she was not a vacation fling, not in any way. The romantic and passionate lover, who to Jerry's surprise was hiding under his skin, demanded that everything and anything be done to ensure that he could stay with this woman. What started as a lucky turn of events had to continue for a long, long time, and the time to act was now.

Jerry turned his bike into the driveway, pedaled up the pavement and leaned his ride against a white stucco wall. Having no interest in going anywhere but to Cat's house, he had given up a rental car and started riding a bike borrowed from his landlady.

Cat has her job and I have mine, she has the house in Kailua and I have the apartment in New York— six time zones apart, he thought. There is no way we can carry on like that. We need to reconcile our lives; sacrifices need to be made....

The door opened, but instead of a cheerful "Hi, Jerry" and her usual wide smile, he was met by tightly pursed lips and subdued greetings. Cat's tanned skin looked pale, and the gorgeous lips were pink rather than red. He never saw her wearing any makeup, she usually projected an air of the "fresh-out-of-water" beauty with a glowingly healthy skin, but that day Cat looked pale, thin and anxious.

She let him in, allowed his lips to brush against hers, but her usual enthusiasm and warmth were lacking. Jerry had a vaguely uncomfortable sensation he had experienced in childhood, a moment before crashing through the ice. Fortunately, they skated on a shallow pond and all he suffered was the humiliation of Pam dragging him home to change.

"What's up, Cat?" Jerry asked. "What's wrong?"

"Nothing's wrong. I just can't understand human nature and that bothers me. Apparently, I am myself like a computer devoid of human emotions," she said enigmatically.

"If you are a computer, I have to say, I love your S drive," he tried to lighten her up, falling back on their double-speak joke.

She smiled slightly in acknowledgment of his effort, but continued, "Jerry, do you know much about spousal abuse?"

He knew this was no time for joking. "Not really, I don't know anybody who has that problem."

"You might be wrong, Jerry. It's not a rare thing, and if you think that it happens only to poor, illiterate people, you are wrong. I am pretty sure there are some economists somewhere who beat their wives." She was looking through the window at Kailua Beach as though avoiding his eyes.

"Maybe, but nobody confided in me." Her irritability was spreading to Jerry. They were very empathetic, their moods tended to synchronize within a few moments.

"That's it. Women run to other women with any problem, men remain blessedly unaware. The question that bothers me is not so much: why do men do it? What puzzles me is: why do women take it? I can understand that a primitive animal and, Jerry, I am not a man hater, has a limited number of ways to communicate. So when he needs to assert his rank, he beats up on a pack member. All animals do that. Add to that poor impulse control, blah, blah, blah . . . I don't approve of it, but can understand it. But why an otherwise intelligent woman, like Kalani, puts up with it? I don't get it."

"Kalani, your cleaning lady?" Jerry remembered a good-looking girl with a great figure leaving the house on a few occasions when he was coming in. She always gave him a sweet, friendly smile.

"Well, she cleans my house because she needs money, but I think of her more as a friend than a cleaner. I shouldn't tell you about her, but soon you will be gone so why should she care?"

"About my going away . . . I thought . . ." Jeremy tried to switch the topic, but Cat continued her thought without noticing his attempt.

"First, she lets her boyfriend feed off her for a few years, then she gives him her college money for some bird-brain venture and then, even after he slaps her, she is all ready to make up. Does that make any sense to you?" She turned to him with a real interest to see if he had an answer. Jerry felt a bit like a student facing an inquisitive professor.

"Maybe she still loves him and wants to keep him?" he tried without much confidence.

"I hate to sound like Mr. Spock from the planet Vulcan, but this not logical. She fell in love with him when he was a fisherman. I met him then—charming, good-looking guy, made good money, proud of it. They were a good match. If you saw them together then you would think they were the actors from a commercial about Hawaii. But they were for real. That's the guy she fell in love with. Then he dropped out of the category of working people and has been deteriorating ever since, while she was helping him on the way down. Now, she can see that he is a bum, although won't admit it. He is not the same guy that she fell for. Do you think he can go back to being a sweet, productive man?" Cat pressed for an answer impatiently as though interrogating a suspect.

"I have no idea, Cat, I am an economist not a psychologist." Jerry had been quite prepared to disclose his past completely while riding to this date, which—he hoped— would start their life together. His work as a military interrogator, the descent into emotional stupor, the mental breakdown, the psychiatric diagnosis, his new life as a bland economist. . . . It all was supposed to be laid out in the open, to be seen, felt and probed by the only person whose opinion mattered to Jerry. At this point, however, his instinct told him to back off. This was not a moment to expose his vulnerabilities. Besides, he was getting angry himself. It looked like he was being held responsible for the fisherman slapping his girlfriend.

She examined his face rather coolly and remarked, "That's the problem with you academic people; you refuse to use your brains, to think independently. It's not in your books, therefore no need to concern yourself with it."

Jerry had enough. He had seen enough of human misery and degradation, treachery and anguish to give nightmares to a hundred nice girls living in their proper houses looking out on Kailua Beach. Even leaving that aside, having finished his Ph.D. by the age of thirty, and having written a good number of widely quoted articles, Jerry believed the accusation of him not using his brain was plain rubbish. And who was she, to imply her superiority? "Could you, please, elaborate on this particular statement?" He countered with exaggerated and cold politeness.

She knew she had taken her frustration out on the wrong person, but arrogantly muddled through, searching for rationalization. "What I mean is that you, the academics, are creating complex systems to explain simple things. Perhaps, I shouldn't complain because I make a living off these grandiose ideas."

Jerry tilted his head signaling: What do you mean?

Cat pressed on. "Businesses order custom software, and sometimes these systems don't work well. After a number of patches, corrections, new versions and so on, the program still sucks. At one point someone says to hell with it, and calls me. I find out what it is that they *really* need, go through that software package, throw out all that is not absolutely required to do the job, and I put it together again.

99

And behold, it works. Not because I am a genius; the initial project got so complex that the authors had lost themselves in it." Cat relaxed a bit talking about the subject that was her familiar territory, then ploughed into *his* field. "With your highly refined economics wisdom, what would you suggest to correct Kalani's problem? After all, it all starts with a purely economical issue: her boyfriend is not generating an income. Shall I phrase it as The Productivity Issue?" she added with unmistakable irony and leaned back, throwing her sun-bleached hair over her shoulders.

Jerry got caught up in the argument. They used to have heated discussions on the economy and politics before, but those were friendly and witty. They both enjoyed them. This was different. She challenged him, but not for a playful sparring, she wanted twelve rounds of hard boxing, winner takes all. Jerry could see now that, apart from being a usually sweet and kind person, this Cat had a hard side to her persona and could spring sharp claws like a real feline. "From the economist's point of view," he carefully staked the argument, "the core problem is that the boyfriend is not working. A secondary problem is that Kalani has no money for college now."

She was listening intently. Her bright and alert eyes were glued to his, brow slightly furrowed with concentration. She was slightly nodding her head to acknowledge the points. Still, he had a feeling that she was just watching him walk into a trap, and would pounce the very moment the jaws shut.

"The first problem could be addressed," Jerry continued, "by retraining Abe to improve his chances of employment, possibly granting him a loan for a small business. I think you have mentioned some sort of enterprise." Now he was sure that she was planning an ambush. She was smiling slightly, not with her usual warm smile, more like a fox's mouth twitching before she jumps a chicken. Still, he couldn't see the trap.

"And Kalani, how could you help Kalani?" she asked sweetly.

Jerry had a premonition that a club was being swung. "Well, Kalani could apply for a scholarship grant, get a government guaranteed loan. Since she is, probably, in a low income bracket, she might get free or discounted tuition."

He saw Cat was moving in for the kill. She leaned forward and put her hand on his. There was no warmth coming from her palm, rather the feeling of being held so that he could not escape at the last moment.

"You are very kind, Jerry. Now, as an economist, tell me who should pay for all these things that you have just granted?"

"There are funds for these expenditures set aside in federal as well as state budgets."

"And where do governments take the money from to pay for these programs, Jerry?"

"From taxes, from people who have higher incomes, like you and me. Social solidarity, you know . . . " Every corporate citizen, all productive individuals, had a sacred duty, he was taught throughout his youth, to help alleviate poverty, level the playing field, and reduce social tensions.

It never occurred to him to question this principle.

Her hand tightened as if she were restraining her victim before the final blow. "But Jerry, you know very well that the tax revenue doesn't cover the government's budgets, by a long shot. So the money you have just distributed must be coming from other places." The trap shut with a loud *clank*, Jerry's foot firmly in the iron jaws. "Do you think it is possible that the government will just print new money for Abe and Kalani? Would you happen to know what the current M3 is?"

Now she was just gloating and dancing on his grave. M3 is a statistical measure of money in circulation, and reflects the amount of new currency printed by the federal government. Obviously, she knew more about economics than Jerry suspected. The government stopped publishing this index in 2006, raising the suspicion that its true intention was to conceal the torrent of newly printed money flooding the country. Now, that was a debatable hypothesis, but before Jerry could start building any resistance, she pushed even harder.

"Jerry, would you agree that printing money in excess of the economy's growth causes inflation?"

"Heck, this is a much more complicated issue than that! For God's sake, my boss Schumacher spent his life trying to clarify this relationship!"

"That's where we disagree, Jerry. It is, actually, quite simple. You, the academics just make it look like it is complicated. Imagine that I have a chicken farm that produces two thousand eggs a day. You have a restaurant that needs one thousand."

Jerry had a fleeting thought that this might be a solution to the problem of consolidating their lives.

Cat continued, "I charge you a dime for each egg, which is good enough to keep your restaurant profitable, and gives me sufficient revenue to buy chicken feed and keep some profit for myself. My other customers get an egg for a dime as well. We can go with this price forever, no inflation. Now, you've become really smart, smart like . . . government. You set up a printing shop in your basement and start printing money. Having extra cash you come to me and buy twelve hundred eggs, but my chickens still lay only two thousand eggs. The rest of my customers are two hundred eggs short. As you well know, demand will drive the price up. Now everybody gets stiffed with expensive eggs. That's what we call inflation, my friend, and it's caused by excessive creation of paper money, from thin air. Nothing particularly mysterious about it."

Now she was leaning back with her arms smugly crossed in front of her lovely breasts. No need to hold his hand any more, blood mixed with brain flowing from his cracked head.

Jerry lost his temper. He did not have the bloodthirsty rage that was his hallmark reaction to frustration; he would never want to harm his blond opponent. A suffocating sensation of being tied up in face of the outrageous provocation had overcome the indignation of being railroaded into this very simplistic argument. A great body of knowledge, some very sophisticated computer modeling, the work of many bright people had been contradicted by this blundering amateur, a naïve computer geek, someone who just learned a few terms! He remained seated at the table in front of her, though pacing the room was what he would rather do. "Well, your one-dimensional example does reflect inflation but there is so much more to it!"

"Thank you, Professor," she interrupted rather rudely. "I am glad we can agree that printing money causes inflation, one way or another. Going back to our example, what would you care that eggs are twelve cents at present? You can always print more paper. On the other hand, Abe and Kalani have to earn their living. They will pay full price, and it will hurt them badly because they need every cent. Worse, even if they have managed to put a few bucks away, inflation will eat that, too. So that's what you call assistance? Giving them free money by way of your programs, and then pulling cash discreetly from their pockets?" She was looking at him with cool satisfaction and an arrogance he never guessed she possessed.

Jerry was sitting still, his eyes glaring; he could almost hear his teeth gnashing, unable to formulate a reasonable argument. Why is she blaming me? I am not the government. What does it have to do with *me*?

Apparently, she was reading his thoughts because she added, "Of course, you are not to be blamed, Jerry. You just teach your numbskull students who later go on to work in the financial institutions that are robbing us all."

Fanatic! Nihilist! He had to have a piece of her or his brain would blow up. Jerry jumped to his feet, violently pushing his chair away from the table. "Oh, look who is talking! You mean you never benefited from the largesse of this corrupt government, Miss Righteous? Just a contributor and a benefactor?"

"Damn right, Jerry!" Cat met him head on. "My parents were immigrants and didn't have this notion that someone should pay for their way or their children's education. I never got any grants and never applied for one. That is except for my family loan. You see, my old folks had this funny idea that since their parents educated them for free, they owed the same to their child, a kind of intergenerational loan. Now it's my obligation to pay for my kids, if I ever have any. And you can be damn sure that I will pay every red cent, with interest."

"At the very least, you could show some social solidarity, maybe a token gratitude for the nation that took your family in," Jerry was reaching for arguments that made him feel uncomfortable.

Cat was sitting up stiffly, thought for a moment, then slowly uttered through teeth almost clenched, "I am a part of this nation, Jerry. And don't you think that I am any less than you are, with your Mayflower ancestors. As a matter of fact, I don't have much respect for people who hide behind the achievements of others, relatives or not. Your pride should be based on what *you* represent: *your* effort, *your* intelligence, *your* courage. In my humble opinion, people who wrap themselves into a national flag are losers who have no personal achievements to show. Being a Mongolian doesn't make one Genghis Khan. And shaking an American flag doesn't make you a patriot either, just a hypocrite hiding behind other people's glory."

Jerry stood across the table as stiff as a soldier on guard, glaring at her, clutching the chair and waiting for her tirade to end. He opened his mouth to respond but she raised her hand.

"One more thing, Jerry. I care very much for people like Kalani or even this bum Abraham, but not for your theoretical notion of the nation. What they need is the freedom to work and the security to keep the fruits of their work. They don't need to have their money stolen—by inflation, taxation or anything else that *your* government is good at. And what they certainly do not need is the demoralization of being offered subsidies and free lunches. You know as well as I do that there is no such thing as a free lunch. So why don't you teach that to your students?"

The great declaration of hostilities was coming to an end, and Cat looked as though she was ready to roll away toward the window waiting for Jerry's counterattack, when she suddenly changed her mind and returned to the battlefield. "I also would like to make a recommendation how you could expand your professional expertise, Professor. When you get back to New York, google the name Bakunin. It will come together with the word 'anarchism', but don't be scared. Take a drink or pop a pill and read it anyway. You may find it interesting that some people believe that the State (and I presume that would include the United States) is an organization dedicated to oppressing its people. There is little good or benevolent about it—mostly buttons, guns and coercion to make sure that the herd moves in the right direction. As for the idea of a nation, with all its flags, hymns, holy patrons, and national days— these are the tools of propaganda to keep the flock nicely bunched up. It's better this way as the need for sheep dogs is less. Besides, isn't it more fun when the herd sings?"

Cat wouldn't wait for his response, and Jerry hardly had a coherent riposte, his thinking process encumbered by fierce anger as well as difficulty wrapping his mind around

the ideas so extreme and contradictory to his patriotic up-
bringing.

"And about my family being admitted onto this continent . . . They were young, healthy and well educated—
perfect new subjects. As a matter of fact, that's what the
immigration officer told them. If you believe that was an
act of compassion, you have to ask yourself a question:
why is it that poor peasants from Guatemala or Honduras,
or anywhere else, have to risk their lives sneaking through
deserts in order to scrape a few bucks together while being
hunted like vermin?"

Jerry had nothing lucid to say. He could cross rapiers
with any sophisticated opponent who understood the nuances of economics and the parameters of the discussion,
but this aggressive thug in a beautiful body wielded a thick
and rough stick. If there were rules to the duel she pro-
voked, they were not known in his current society. He
knew the world where arguments could be met with a
sneer, a boot and handcuffs, but he loathed that world, and
broke out of it at a grave personal cost many years ago. No
amount of provocation could push him back. The daydreams of the last few days seemed plainly ridiculous. She
was a self-righteous, arrogant bitch hiding behind a sweet
face.

Jerry stiffly thanked her for her hospitality before he silently walked out. The next day he took a plane from
Honolulu to Los Angeles. No one came to see him off, and
as he was watching clouds over Diamond Head, he already
knew that something tragically stupid had happened, something that would be bitterly regretted.

ALEX Z. MODZELEWSKI

* * *

Hi, Ruth, it's me again. I am not thinking clearly, I've hardly slept for two nights. I think this time I am done. I've chased away the man I love, demolished the only friendship I had. I am a damn destructive fanatic, can't control my belligerence; I don't deserve to be happy. She took a pill and fell into deep, coma-like sleep that would not be interrupted by the loud bangs of boulders crashing down the steep hill behind her house.

CHAPTER 14

Jerry was thoroughly depressed by the time he landed in Newark. He tried to persuade himself that this was a natural consequence of the long flight and jet lag, but he knew that leaving Cat was the real cause. They had connected so fast and so deeply that parting ways after one disagreement over such a theoretical issue was just . . . unreasonable. But, there he was, six time zones and five thousand miles away. He tried to divert his attention by reading the *New York Times*, but his eyes scanned over the pictures of war ships deployed in the Middle East without understanding a word of the commentary. Having experienced the warmth and happiness of being with Cat, he desperately did not want to go back behind his brick wall, but that's where he was heading.

Jerry was almost looking forward to starting classes, as it guaranteed that his mind would be occupied and unwelcome thoughts chased out. He was not disappointed. Eleven-thirty on Thursday morning, he had finished his lecture, and there was Miss Ambitious standing in front of his office. I can just kiss my lunch break good-bye, he thought, resigning himself to the conversation leading from nowhere to futility. This was a sad case of diligence and ambition mismatched to a limited power of abstract thinking. Amanda attended all lectures sitting in the first row—eyes alert, never bored; no teacher could dislike her. Her assignments were always delivered on time, neat and nicely bound. It was just that she could not grasp the ideas that required abstract thinking. She would do fine as long as the problems were solvable with arithmetic, Jerry thought. But throw her a bit of more complicated abstract theory, and she is lost, lost, lost. How had she made it so far? This is her third year, and in another year or so, Amanda could be a proud Bachelor of Economics. Probably no one had the heart to stop her, just like me.

"Professor Roberts, thank you for seeing me during your lunch break," she started timidly.

Rather skinny, but with a nice round butt under tight jeans, pleasant face, dyed blond hair tied in a ponytail—not a bad-looking girl, Jerry thought. Shouldn't have any trouble getting her a decent boyfriend. So what's she doing at the library, every time I go to do some research at night? But I am wasting my nights, just the same.

"No problem, Amanda, I am not hungry at all," he lied smoothly and smiled with encouragement.

"About my research paper, how did I do?" Her voice was thin, without a trace of confidence, and her eyes locked on the backside of the photograph sitting in the middle of Jerry's desk. "The Dean said that if I don't do well in your class, I would have to rethink my major."

Aw shit, now it's up to me to screw the kid over, the one student in my class making any effort to study. Is it her fault she was born without the gift for abstract thinking? Actually, someone blundered a few years ago; she should have been shoved into a subject that relies on more concrete reasoning. She'd be a good administrator, so why does she need to do the esoteric theories in economy? Looking at her with sympathy, he replied, "Well, you did get confused a bit in your paper."

Amanda's head dropped even lower. Jerry really hated this hatchet job.

"Amanda, can you tell me, why do you insist on graduating with an economics major? Why not business administration? You know that you don't have a knack for esoteric theories. At the same time, you are really good with numbers; you are well organized. Why don't you switch to something that better suits your personality?"

"My father would be very disappointed; he is an economist."

Now Jerry remembered: of course, her father teaches economics in Chicago. There are more Nobel laureates walking the corridors in his department than many countries had in their history. This Assistant Professor's input might not be appreciated, but who's going to help out this lost soul? "Amanda, your father is a great economist, but you don't have to be your father. You can't be your father, whatever you do. I think the Dean might be right. Your paper is really not any worse than the average for your class," he felt charitable, "but you should think about redirecting your studies to something that you will enjoy more."

She thanked him and left, no spring in her step and her head bowed.

Good advice, Professor, how about you? Cat's ironic voice sounded in his head so clearly that it startled him. It amused him rather than upset.

You don't give up easily, Cat, do you? Hearing her voice lifted his spirits for a moment, then the gnawing feeling was back.

He called his sister Pam. They lived about an hour's drive from each other, but met perhaps twice a year, mostly on Thanksgiving or Christmas. There was ten years difference between them, and with an age difference that big, there was little chance for friendship. Now, suddenly, Jerry felt a need to talk to her. If Pam were surprised, she didn't show it, and they made a date for dinner on Saturday.

He still had Friday to be filled, or spent alone. Jerry did not feel like seeing anyone, but knew that another evening by himself meant long hours of the heart-breaking memories of Cat, and self-recriminations. So he pulled his little black book out of a drawer and went through a few pages. A prospect of any romantic encounters felt, actually, horrible, but something had to be done to break his bondage. Jeremy went through a few numbers.

Kelly, a good-looking if somewhat overweight girl, had divorced a few months ago and was still quite angry about it. She was a pleasant companion and fun to be with most of the time, but turned into a viper after the second drink. And she really liked to have the second drink. Jerry moved on.

Camilla, slightly built, quiet, a bit mousy, but attractive. Could be fine, as long as animal abuse and dog rescue operations were kept out of the conversation. Jerry dialed the number only to be informed that she was engaged now, smug satisfaction palpable. One name

112

scratched from the book.

Virginia, a fellow post-grad student, a woman of great intelligence and remarkable figure. Her face would be pretty but for the nose that was way too prominent for her small face; would be fine on a large person with a long face, for Virginia it was just too large. She frequently looked into a mirror wondering how she would look with a smaller nose. Should she consider a nose job? Regardless of the operation's hefty price, she would never have time to do it. The boss drove them hard. Virginia and Jerry understood each other well and had compatible temperaments. They had unpretentious private meetings in his apartment, without great passion and without obligations. Just good, solid sex that left both satisfied and content. No promises were made and no plans for the life together spun. Call Virginia? Jerry imagined her comfortably reclining on his bed, naked and beckoning for him to come. He would sit next to her, gently run his hand starting on her brown hair, over her cheek, slide down the neck, round the breasts, linger over the stomach and submerge fingers into her curly hair. She was a good buddy and they had good times together in the past, but now, after Cat . . . anybody who was a real person seemed inappropriate. Once, these numbers and faces behind them brought comfort to his life; now they seemed to spell "t-r-a-i-t-o-r." Jerry cursed and threw the book back into the drawer.

Oh, heck. Why not toss the worries to the winds, and submit to the dictates of providence? He tried to break his depressed mood with a lighter thought. Go to a bar and see what happens. There was one nearby that he used to patronize often while writing his Ph.D. dissertation. He had no time to cultivate anything more demanding than a potted plant then, and didn't feel any need for a complicated love affair either. The bar worked very well; in addition it had the great advantage of being close to his apartment. No need to take a cab; a romantic but reasonably short walk was appreciated by most of his new "friends."

Jerry walked down from the street level and entered a large, warm room distinctly smelling of beer and chicken wings. It was still early so he had no trouble getting a strategic place at the bar. He hung his coat on the rack and sat sideways, back to the wall, left side to the bar and right side open to the room with its small dance floor. Jerry ordered a Boston lager and was ready. The lighting was dim except for frequent flashes of a strobe light from the dance floor, which he found rather annoying. The bar filled up rapidly, and the noise rose to the level that forced people to yell into each other's ears.

Not much chance of a conversation, intelligent or otherwise, he thought. Jerry kept an alert eye on the crowd. Most of the girls were young, hardly of drinking age. The guy at the gate can't be a very suspicious person. The fake blond sitting next to him could not be twenty-one. There were a few women in their late twenties who would be more suitable to strike up a conversation with, but they looked rather unattractive. The one that he might consider had an eager man on each side, both probably ten years younger than he was. What the hell am I doing here? He asked himself angrily. What did I expect, a beer commercial scene? A row of gorgeous models flashing their whitened teeth at me, just drooling at the thought that I might give them my phone number? What would a good-looking, intelligent woman be doing in here, especially if she was of an age that wouldn't get me arrested? He gave it another

ten minutes, just in case Humphrey Bogart showed up behind the bar and asked, "So what are you up to, kid?"
Since Bogart didn't appear, Jerry finished his beer, paid
and got up. Two men standing next to the wall raced to
grab his place at the bar.

The fact was, he could not fill the weekend. People—
read women— who might be available, he did not want to
see them anymore. Places that he used to like had lost their
appeal. He ended up watching the tube with a bottle of
Marquis de Villard brandy within easy reach. Serves you
right, old fool; he had no mercy on himself. After thirty-five
years you found someone who made you happy. No! A divine intervention was necessary to bring her into your life,
an act of God, nothing less. And what did you do? You
blew it, for the sake of an economics theory, causation of inflation. Well, wait for another miracle, but even Jesus was
not known to bring Lazarus from his deathbed twice. By ten
o'clock, Cat was everywhere. He spoke to her, she responded, then he had her in his arms and she put her hands
in his hair, as she liked to do. He got drunk as a skunk and
woke up on Saturday about eleven with a jackhammer in his
head.

At last, his mind cleared. He knew he had to get her
back. Despite a headache, he felt much better. It took him
a few hours to figure out what to say, so that he wouldn't
sound like he was begging for forgiveness. She's a reasonable girl and she likes me. I'll make a step, she'll make a
step, and we'll meet in the middle, he thought. Life held
some promise again. After a considerable amount of finger cracking, neck stretching and straightening books on
the table—all the things he habitually did when nervous—
Jerry dialed Cat's number. Her phone kept ringing, but

nobody picked it up, and there was no answering machine. Jerry tried calling a few more times, then went to dinner with his sister's family. Maybe Pam will have something intelligent to say on how to deal with this situation, Jerry hoped.

Pam was quite different from Jerry. One might wonder how it was even possible for them to be children of the same couple and grow up with the same parents. Jeremy remembered that as a child he was afraid of his sister. Not because she could beat him up, though she certainly could and on some occasions did. No, he was scared of her withering comments and sarcastic smiles. She was not a person to pamper her little brother with affection. It is true that he enjoyed a certain amount of immunity at the schoolyard due to their blood ties, but he suspected that the potential bully's assumption that she would defend her little brother was mistaken. Still, he needed Pam to notice him and was desperate for her approval. Both were hard to achieve.

Pam had left the family home early, and the last eight or ten years of Jerry's childhood, he enjoyed the status of an only child. Now he was knocking on her door with the old sense of anxiety. Pam opened the door and let him in. In her mid forties, she was slim, strong and full of energy. She ran marathons, competed in triathlons and it showed. It was always a mystery to Jeremy how she could raise three kids, work and put two hours a day into her fitness mania.

"I sleep on Sundays," she would offer as an explanation, "and the kids have a choice: keep their noses clean or go with me for a marathon. They don't like long distance running, so my motherly duties are not that grave."

"Hmm, I see . . . "

"Good to see you, Jerry, tell me everything's fine, or is there a problem? You don't have a habit of dropping in on me just for a little gossip." She hadn't changed that much; the interrogation started before they got to the table. This time, however, it was Jeremy's initiative. In fact, this time he wanted her opinion *exactly* because he knew it would be given to him clear and unsweetened.

It will hurt, thought Jerry, but I need advice made of stainless steel, and dear Pam will give it to me without reservations or misplaced empathy. "Where are the kids and Henry?" he asked politely.

"Kids are gone to the basketball match. Isn't it great that I don't have to drive them any more? Henry grabbed the opportunity to go play chess. I personally can't understand how he can sit on a chair for three or four hours, staring at a chess board but I am not Henry. So, it's just you and me. Spill it, kid...."

"Remember when I called you about my little ocean adventure and about my Saving Grace?"

"Sure do, you sounded like you'd fallen in love. As a matter of fact, I think that would be a very good idea. At your age . . . it had crossed my mind that you might be gay. Are you, Jerry?"

"No, Pam, I'm not gay, and I have been enjoying a fulfilling heterosexual life."

"Oh, good. A heterosexual, and fell in love with a woman. So what's the problem?"

"The problem is that we had a huge fight. You won't believe it, but we argued about economics. She was stubborn and pigheaded. which made me so mad that I used stupid arguments, even putting down her immigrant family. Pam, most of the time she is the sweetest person on earth, but so strong-headed and her worldview comes directly from Genghis Khan."

The aroma of coffee wafted from the kitchen counter and Pam turned off the percolator absentmindedly. "You know, people get together for many different reasons, sometimes very stupid ones. Physical attraction and good sex to start with. I have nothing against it. In fact, I see no point wasting time on a relationship where sex is anything less than very good. It won't last. But it seems that this is not an issue between the two of you." Jerry just nodded his head.

"After that, a very good reason to stay together is that you need someone to trust, a friend. But how do you know if someone is trustworthy? You really can't know that ahead of time, but chances are good if your partner has a tough inner core."

Pam is onto something, Jerry thought and listened without interrupting.

"Take, for example, Henry, a nice man with an easy smile and a soft belly. Many people look at him and think that he is weak, an easy prey. They get hurt badly. Inside, Henry is tough as a railroad nail, and he plays a game of chess in his life that his opponents hardly ever survive. People look at us thinking, 'How can this athletic woman live with that round, fatherly Santa Claus?' The truth is that

118

in our family, he is the hard point of a spear. Do I suffer because of his inner hardness? Am I afraid of him? No and no. He is a great partner."

Jeremy noticed that Pam had developed crow's feet around her eyes. She kept her figure, but time did not stop for her. "So how does it work, Pam? You don't quarrel like most people do, you just take orders?"

"We argue. We don't quarrel, we argue. You can't quarrel with a chess player. If I want him to do something, I better be well prepared. He listens intently, says little and sometimes asks a question. If your argument is not clear, he will lead you to strangle yourself in your tangled thought process. At one point, you'll feel like saying: sorry for taking your time, forget my idea. But he will never back off from a well-reasoned argument, and will not pretend that there is no point where there is one. And, Jerry, when Henry agrees, I don't have to look over my shoulder. I know he is right behind me, ready and able to push or shove or stab, if necessary."

Jerry shifted in his chair uneasily. "That's what Cat does; she is a great listener, but punches right back with her counter arguments."

"What did you argue about?" Pam abandoned her plans to pour coffee.

"I'm not sure how we started. Basically, she said that people who happen to be in a state of misfortune—I remember now, her friend's boyfriend didn't work and was taking money from the girl—should overcome their problems on their own, and that government assistance actually harms them. Rather unfeeling, don't you think?"

"I would rather say rather American, if we look back to times when America was a real power. Know the saying about pulling oneself up by one's bootstraps?"

"Pam, you can't be serious. You are not saying that unemployed people don't deserve some help by retraining or some assistance with living expenses?"

"Well, I would first ask why are they unemployed, and how come they don't have the necessary skills. What's wrong with this unemployed boyfriend? Is he sick or what?"

"I'm not sure."

"Then why do you assume he needs government help? I would say that this should be the last thing he needs." Pam was looking at her brother with a strange expression. "I like this girl more and more, and I suspect that an excess of theoretical science has damaged your brain center for common sense."

Jerry felt surrounded; the people closest to him kept contradicting the very foundation of his professional beliefs. "Pam, you were always hard on me and nothing has changed. Now you're siding with her just to put me down."

Pam did not answer for a long time, looking at him until her blue eyes lost their hardness. "Jerry, I might have been tough on you when you were small. I thought I should harden you up. When you first came to school, you had this air of a two-day-old duckling: a soft, fuzzy, yellow ball, a perfect target for anyone with a beak. I saved you quite a lot of pecking, but I wanted you to grow and to learn how to take care of yourself. But I always loved you, my little bro, and I love you now."

Jerry found himself holding her and feeling her tears on his neck. This was a moment he had longed for all his childhood. But Pam wouldn't be Pam if she tolerated it for more than ten seconds.

"Back to the subject—that's all? That's all your disagreement?"

"Well, she has a strange hostility towards the government. You should hear her accusing the government of stealing money from poor people. Sounded like Che Guevara or some other kind of anarchistic rebel."

Pam started giggling, "I don't think you remember grandfather Vito. He was not a stupid man, also a good businessman. Grandpa used to say that there was only one Mafia. Some families are mostly into gambling, others into prostitution and still others into government. And they all do the same thing, run a racket for profit. And he never failed to add that New York is no different from Palermo. So, I think your little friend will fit into this family very well."

Jeremy must have smiled at the idea of Cat fitting into their family because Pam got serious and sighed.

"But you have a nasty problem on your hands, brother. I don't think 'I am sorry' will bring her back into your arms. From your description, she looks deeper than you think. If she came to believe that you are an opinionated, semi-demented academic running away from her argument, if she thinks that you are a brainwashed dummy unable to think on your own, and—more than anything else—if she thinks you are a Boston cream donut inside your nicely toned body—you are toast, my friend! I don't know what you need to do, but I am quite sure that if you really want her back, it is not going to be 'I am sorry, but I love you' over a telephone line."

Jerry felt a quiet desperation because he knew that Cat could have grounds for exactly these same conclusions.

"Now, I'd like you to do a manly job, Jerry. Take the mallet and pound these six cutlets into submission. Henry and the kids should be back in half an hour."

Jerry liked Henry, who—indeed—impressed him as a rather mellow character. Now, after his sister's disclosure, Jerry looked at him in a different light. They had never had an argument as they met only twice a year at the family gatherings, but Henry never showed any interest in drawing Jerry into a serious discussion. The society seemed full of amateur economists, but Henry was apparently not one of them, despite being a chief executive officer of a major company. The man frequently dealt with highly placed government officials on account of his company's armament contracts, but seemed oblivious to Jerry's background. Is it possible that he just ignores me, his brother-in-law, as a harmless idiot, free of any useful knowledge? Jerry wondered.

"Henry, in your line of business, are there any signs that the economy is on the mend?"

Henry looked at him thoughtfully, swallowing a piece of the meat that Jerry had pounded half an hour earlier, then answered, "That depends on which economy you're referring to. Government contracts have never been better. I guess our electronics don't last very long on a battlefield. Mind you, they are pretty sturdy, almost indestructible when we test them. But they clearly can be blown up." He was slowly and methodically loading peas onto the piece of meat already backed up with a chunk of potato.

"How about the other, non-governmental side of business, Henry?"

Henry looked at him with even more attention, chewed his mouthful slowly, swallowed, took a sip of wine and asked politely, "What non-government business are you asking about, Jerry? We make electronic components. Have you seen any electronic consumer goods made in the U.S.A, recently? TV sets, boom boxes, DVD players? You might catch some products of American-sounding companies, but I assure you, they don't buy their components from us or from our domestic competitors."

"But don't we sell a lot of electronic goods abroad?" Jerry knew that the U.S. had a positive trade balance in high tech goods.

"Yes, Jerry, we sell a lot of weapon systems, planes, warships, but, to the best of my knowledge, not much more. Even our telecommunications equipment, which had practically no serious competition ten years ago, doesn't find that many buyers these days."

"This is not a healthy situation," Jeremy remarked. "Weapon sales may turn on a dime with a change in global politics. How are we going to pay for all these imports?"

"I hoped you could tell me that, Jerry. You are an

economist. What do you tell your students?"

Check mate. Henry finished him in three moves, never losing his benevolent smile and never missing the tempo while cleaning his plate. There was no point to make believe that Jerry might have a reasonable answer. Maybe he should simply try to learn something new.

"Henry, we deal in theory. What I would like to know is how things are in the real world."

"That is really pretty simple," shrugged Henry.

Simple? Didn't someone else recently tell me that the economy was a simple matter? Jerry thought, and was determined to learn more about this "simple" explanation.

"What do you need to make anything?" Henry asked rhetorically and answered himself, "Money. Money to buy raw materials or components, money to pay your workers, sales force, etc. Where can you get it? From the banks. And the banks? From people who save money and put their savings into banks. The problem is that our fellow countrymen decided they didn't need savings. Somehow they manage to spend more than they earn. How this is possible I don't know; maybe someone at your university could do a research paper on the subject, and perhaps invent an antigravity principle while at it. That would be very helpful for our economy. But, back to our subject, banks shouldn't have much money to lend, but they do. Ever heard of the fractional reserve?"

Jeremy used to teach central banking to his undergrads, but mustered all the humility that was hiding in his heart and declined to answer the question.

"Well, banks are allowed to lend more money than they have from deposits, but still have to keep a fraction in ready reserve, in case there are a lot of customers lining up in branches demanding their cash. What's the reserve? Who knows? Supposed to be about ten percent, but a lot of smart folks think it's far less than that. At the end, who cares? It is so low that it makes no difference. Would you care if someone put four or six bullets in your head?"

The metaphor of multiple bullets in one's head put into new perspective Jerry's professional inclination to require very detailed data for analysis.

"That means," Henry continued, "that almost all money they pump into the economy comes from nowhere. Nobody needed to make or sell anything to generate it. It was created from thin air, like by an act of God. Remember '*fiat lux*' meaning 'let there be light?' Same with money, so some people call it 'fiat money'."

The children started shifting in their chairs. Really good kids, Jerry thought, obviously getting bored to death. He felt sorry for them but, at the same time, had to know Henry's conclusions. They would be dramatically different from the prevailing wisdom of his Department of Economics, Jerry was sure of that. Henry also noted the rebellion brewing at the table and started speeding to the conclusion.

"People who we are doing business with are no less intelligent than we are. They take our money and extend us new loans, pretending to be great believers in our ability to pay bills. I know that you and your sister went to regular, public schools, so you must know a schoolyard racket, where the nastiest kid in the yard provides candies to the selection of weakest youngsters. Of course, they have to pay through the nose, but that buys them the friendship of the meanest bully. They pretend to enjoy the trade, and so avoid the schoolyard's unpleasant aspects, like having their noses bloodied or being thrown over a fence. Quite an acceptable arrangement, really, if you have a bit of free cash. Did you ever know this scheme?"

"I don't think so," Pam broke in. "I used to come from my high school on the opposite side of the street to kick some ass from time to time."

The kids started enjoying themselves. "Mom, could you come and kick some asses at our school, too? Mr. Gallant, for example?" said Cecilia, the oldest one.

"And Mrs. Ferraro! And Mr. Sobick!" younger children were suggesting enthusiastically, until Henry sent them a look saying, "That's enough for now."

"Our partners and neighbors do the same. But now imagine that the bully starts losing weight, sweats easily and coughs up blood. For some time, the racket keeps going. Nobody knows what's going on, and the consequences of bad judgment might be very unpleasant. But at one point, the truth breaks out: the big guy has tuberculosis. What do you think happens to the candy trade? But to answer your question, they are still buying our candies."

That was a new way of thinking for Jerry. He felt his education had progressed for the first time in a long time, but it gave him a dreadful sensation of having wasted away the best years of his life.

Jerry went home, and tried to call Cat again, still no response. It's hard to throw away years of hard work and the security of a well-organized life, but reasons for him to stay in New York were growing very weak, he felt. Jerry pictured himself on a tropical beach, working with a hammer, and fell asleep smiling.

CHAPTER 15

"**C**at, Cat, CAAT!" Kalani kept shaking the limp body until the eyes opened up and hands clumsily pushed her away.

"What are you doing? Why don't you leave me alone? What time it is? What day is it?" Cat was slowly regaining consciousness. Kalani let go of her shoulders.

"You've been sleeping for almost twenty-four hours. You were sleeping when I was leaving in the morning, and you were still asleep when I came back. It's seven o'clock in the evening. Are you OK? I thought that something happened to you!"

Cat sat up and let her legs dangle down. "The fact is, I feel somewhat confused but much better. I guess I needed this snooze. I took some Halcyon, and it really did a number on me. So what are you up to? Back from work?"

Kalani was wearing her "good" white and green dress that Abe had bought her a few months ago in a sudden surge of romantic feelings. He suddenly came into some money although Kalani was not aware of him getting any job. Sometimes it's better not to ask. She also spread a faint aroma of perfume. Obviously, she was doing something more than cleaning Ms. Oshiro's apartment.

"Have you had any problems with Abe?"

"No, not at all. Want some coffee?" Kalani looked rather perky, definitely not the way a woman would be expected to look two days after a dramatic separation from the man she loved.

"Thank you, Kalani, that might help. I should check my e-mail and see how my customers are doing." Secretly, she hoped there might be some other, personal mail, but there was none. The events of the last few days came back in all their sadness, but she was better prepared to face them after a good rest. She worked for a few hours on her software and went to sleep again. She dreamed of being safely cuddled, her head moving slowly as Jerry's muscular chest rose and fell, until the screeching brakes and the sick thud of the car collision reverberated from her past and woke her up to the fact that she had crashed again.

For the next few days, she sat barefoot in front of the computer and grimly banged away at the keyboard. The work was helping. She couldn't think of software bugs and a broken heart at the same time. But below the smooth flow of logical, conscious thought there was an ugly, dark and dangerous rock, causing hardly a ripple on the surface, but ready to crush the thin walls of her resistance without warning. She glided over this menace knowing that it was only a question of time and random events lining up before the rock would tear into her mind and plunge her into a dark and murky depression, one in which even breathing becomes an effort almost too big to undertake.

On Saturday, she finished a few minutes after five o'clock, and wheeled herself onto the ramp to the kayak launch. The boards were cut and fitted together with surgical precision, hardly any spaces left between them; bright red oil paint almost completely bridged the small gaps, giving the ramp the look of a shiny metal bridge leading to the ocean.

Jerry certainly spared no effort to smooth my way; she smiled getting over the spot where she had gotten stuck, where Jerry had rescued her like a knight in shining armor. That was a long time ago; she would donate this memory to her Museum of Real Life Happenings, so that later she could spin her imaginary adventures around it. The smile faded. His arms were strong when he cuddled her like a baby. She liked the smell of his body, even though he had worked for several hours in the sun. She could feel the texture of his thick hair in both her hands. Tears started burning her eyes, and she commanded herself: stop this melodrama, right now!

Suddenly, the ground under her wheelchair bucked, as if kicked from the inside by a giant foot, and Cat was thrown onto the grass. Deep, grinding noises came from the earth's center and kept coming, mixing with the dry cracking of boards and two-by-fours twisted by unimaginable power. Heavy thuds of large objects falling on the ground and the screech of steel frames torn apart joined into the hellish symphony.

She was lying on her side, grasping in panic at the short grass in an effort to stay in one spot. The terrifying thought of being crushed seized her throat, but a quick glimpse showed only blue sky above, nothing heavy to fall and squash her into the grass. The undulating ground made her slip and roll like an empty bucket on the bottom of a wave-tossed boat. With unbelieving eyes, she saw red shingles falling off her house; first one by one, then the whole sheet surged down to crash next to the wall in a cloud of red dust. A second later the whole roof collapsed. Through the shattered window she saw her desk, with the computer still on it, bucking like a frightened horse until the monitor bounced to the floor. A large segment of the second-floor wall had disintegrated in a big white cloud of stucco putting into view the upstairs bedroom, an unmade bed shamelessly exposed, Kalani's red dress and colorful contents of the closet spilling to the floor. Water ran down from the broken pipes in the bathroom, dripping from the ragged edge onto a pile of shingles mixed with broken furniture, underwear, computer components and other objects, all of which, until a moment ago, constituted most of Cat's material world. It took her a moment to identify the source of the heavy, pounding sound—her own blood racing through the arteries like a terrified herd ruled by only one desire—escape.

A fountain shot up where PVC pipes of the sprinkler system had snapped, but quickly subsided as the water lost its pressure. A short, bright flash illuminated the house's shaded interior but no fire followed.

The ground stopped shaking, but a deep, low frequency growl went on. Cat crawled closer to the canal edge and looked down. Where there had been water on which she used to launch her kayak, there was only brown mud and rocks. A small fish was thrashing around, suddenly out of its element. The ocean had withdrawn. She knew it would be back very soon; a tsunami was coming. She had learned about the dangers of a murderous wave during her first year in Hawaii. Forty years ago, a wall of water slammed into the Big Island. First, the ocean disappeared at the beaches, leaving the exposed bottom littered with fish, sea cucumbers and other creatures one would never see without diving. A teacher had let the kids out of school, so that they could go down and see the ocean floor for themselves, maybe catch some fish. A few minutes later, a huge wave came to crush and drown all those in its way. Many people died that day. Cat knew that a destructive wave would be much quicker this time since the epicenter of the earthquake seemed to be somewhere very close. The wave would come within seconds, no more than a couple of minutes. The water would follow paths of the least resistance, so canals and streams would be first.

She rolled away from the canal and started crawling feverishly toward her home. The wheelchair was nowhere to be seen, thrown by the force of the violent earth. Cat clawed her fingers into grass and soft dirt, pulling her lower body behind like a caterpillar in an effort to reach safety. There was no question of her escaping to the safe higher ground. The hills of Lanikai were no more than three miles away, but with the tsunami coming fast, they might as well be on the other side of the moon. All she could do was to try and reach a point as high as she could on her house.

The roar of approaching destruction reached her less than a minute later, when she was crawling up a flight of stairs leading to the second floor. The house trembled as though an earthquake had hit again, and the deep, vibrating noise covered all other sounds. The big wave raced up the channel, then instantly flooded her lawn and crashed into the house. The stonewalls of the lower floor resisted the water's brutal power; instead, tons of brown muddy liquid gushed through the blown-in windows and doors, flooding the building. The currents of water swirled through her dining room and kitchen, slamming and slowing somewhat in their circular motion. By the time water reached the narrow stairway she was in, it had lost some of its smashing violence. The water level kept rising rapidly, and Cat found herself suddenly submerged, but a moment later she was shot up the narrow passage like a human cannon ball. Blinded by the brown water and disoriented, she held her breath until an unyielding wooden beam brutally met her back and halted further motion.

Her head popped out of the water and a loud gasp relieved her bursting lungs. The roof had disintegrated minutes ago, but left behind a few beams randomly spanned by sheets of plywood. Cat grabbed onto exposed wood, but water kept pushing her up until she pivoted around the beam and found herself precariously perched on the sheet of trembling, wet plywood. From her perch, she could see the cascade of coffee-colored liquid raging through the roof rafters. Cat forced herself to break her eyes away from the torrent and looked around. She was sitting on the top of her slanted roof that ended at the attached carport. The house had been built on the slope of a small hill, with the concrete carport situated higher up, its roof designed to be an upward extension of the building.

Cat took a deep breath and crawled away from her life-saving plywood towards the carport. She had her upper body on a cement support when the house finally gave in with a final tremor and disappeared under brown water. The roar of the torrent did not allow any sound of the dying building to intrude on its own fury. Cat clung desperately to the solid structure, then pulled herself up, aided by the still rising water, until she reached the carport's top.

The wave was on its way out. She was looking down with horror as boats, cars, uprooted trees and human bodies tumbled past her vantage point, down the channel into Kailua Bay. The muddy water hissed with profuse foam; it bore no likeness to the blue and friendly element that she once loved and had made friends with. Still, it was this ugly and violent cousin that gave Cat the final push, so she could reach the point where she could live a few moments longer.

Cat stayed on her carport for three hours, knowing that the great wave might return. By nine, she had abandoned the safety of her perch; her intense shivering became unbearable. As she looked down, she knew that life in this New Year would be very different from anything she had known before.

CHAPTER 16

The waterspout ripped off the carport in slow motion, landing Cat on her bottom, no damage done. The ground was covered with brown, slick mud hiding splintered wood, twisted metal and broken glass. Not the kind of terrain she would like to crawl through.

Slowly, she made her way towards the remains of the house, getting around the neighbor's motorcycle half buried in mud and a big portion of a roof that must have floated from another part of town, as she could not recognize the blue-glazed shingle still attached. She managed to crawl to her kitchen with only minor cuts on her hands. The door had been blown off, but the stove was stuck sideways in the doorway, blocking an escape route for the fridge and a few cabinets. She crawled over the oven, then squeezed herself inside the kitchen between the fridge and the doorframe. Not much was left there except a thick layer of wet mud. She pushed the fridge and opened the door. A miracle, despite all this violent upheaval, food was still in it. Cat removed a carton of milk, a small package of smoked turkey, cream cheese and bread. She sat among the ruins and ate as much as she could, all that would be spoiled by tomorrow. This was not the time for dieting; food would be scarce in days to come.

At least she had time to think now. Her situation was more than disturbing. Her wheelchair was probably somewhere on the reef, and the car had disappeared. There was no movement or sound in her close neighborhood; she might be the only survivor. Cat could not think of any positive action to take. She scraped part of the kitchen floor clear of mud and put herself to sleep thinking of Jerry carrying her in his arms.

I never thought you could be such a violent individual, Cat. Ruth was flabbergasted. *The mayhem you have created.... Can't see the purpose of this all.... Why don't you take up parachuting or hang-gliding if you need all this extreme excitement? I am kind of stuck with you, but will tell you honestly, I don't like these scenes at all. Besides, they are so realistic that I have this irrational feeling that they might belong to the real world. And that makes me really uncomfortable.*

* * *

Residents of Kailua emerged from the night of terror bloodied, exhausted and stunned. Thick smoke bellowing from burning houses mixed with the pungent odor of a plastic fence smoldering around a burnt-out gas station. The town resounded with cries for help, wails of despair and shrieks of frightened children. Only the waterfront was silent. The tsunami had erased most of the houses together with their occupants on the east side of Kalaheo Street. The Beachside neighborhood, the pride of Kailua and dream of many aspiring millionaires was no more. Single houses remained scattered along miles of Kailua Beach; most had been shredded and dragged to the bowels of a hungry ocean.

The mud around the house was baked into a hard, broken surface by ten AM; that was some improvement, as far as traveling was concerned. Cat looked around for anything that she could use to help her move, but the ground was swept clean by the wave. A washing machine and the cadaver of a Harley-Davidson projected from the muddy crust, but the waves had left behind no object light enough for her to handle.

She was increasingly thirsty and waiting for help appeared to her a loosing strategy. Besides, once before, she had decided to take care of herself without looking for anybody's assistance; this would be another test of her resolve. Cat slowly crawled out from the shade of her house and was immediately blinded by the sun. She squinted and started creeping towards the street. Soon her hands and elbows were bleeding, her lower body coated with a layer of mixed brown and red matter drying quickly into hard scabs, except for the spots where fresh blood kept the mixture moist. She stared at the small rocks imbedded into the broken asphalt ten inches from her face, then a painful forward surge of her body moved the gravel fifteen inches back, only to be replaced by another small stretch of the fractured pavement. Cat dragged herself forward with stubborn determination knowing that soon she would be defeated.

A ringing bell sounded out of nowhere. Cat raised her eyes and looked at a wheel in front of her. The wheel was attached to a rickshaw, and on the rickshaw sat Abe. "Need a taxi, Ma'm?" Abe was grinning from one ear to the other. "Kalani told me to find you." Abe got off the rickshaw and picked Cat up off the ground, placed her in the seat and carefully extended the canvas roof to shield her from the sun. Looking at her with horror, he hesitantly reached for a canteen hanging on a leather strap on his side. "I drank from it, but . . . probably you'd be better off to have some."

Cat brought the open flask to her lips with two trembling hands and drank greedily, spilling water. She got in control of herself in a moment and stretched out her hand. "I'm sorry, Abe, you need water, too."

"Oh no, we have a lot of water at home; that's where we're going right now. Kalani will be so happy!" He jumped on the rickshaw and started pedaling towards Oneawa Street to their apartment. Cat slumped in the back, closed her eyes and allowed herself not to think at all. She put her life in Abe's hands and this dependence came to her almost naturally.

CHAPTER 17

The blaring TV tore through the steady noise of the busy street below Jerry's apartment. It was only six o'clock in the morning, and Jerry wanted to sleep another thirty minutes. That's what hearing aids are for, Jerry thought, annoyed, but got up, went to the bathroom and turned his set on.

"A seven-point-nine earthquake has occurred in Hawaii, at five-fifteen PM local time, followed shortly thereafter by a tsunami," reported the anchor solemnly. "Casualties are not known at this time, but are expected to be high, as many buildings in Honolulu collapsed. All means of communication with Hawaii have been disrupted, except for satellite links. All airports are closed. Military observers report major damage to roads and tunnels." Jerry froze with a toothbrush in his hand.

Cat, how is Cat? He whispered in panic. The footage from a Katrina-ravaged New Orleans replayed in front of his eyes: handicapped people struggling and dying, trapped in a mass of able-bodied neighbors frightened into an unthinking, stampeding herd. He could imagine Cat struggling in her chair against the rushing water, stuck between some boards, like in the ramp he had built. His need to protect Cat returned with a force displacing all his other feelings and priorities. Without thinking, he reached for the phone and called a travel agency.

"Sorry, sir, no flights are available to Hawaii, and we have no idea when they will be. Please, try again later." He put the phone away.

The TV anchor was reporting on blizzards in the mid-West. Jerry switched through a few news channels; nobody knew anything else. There was no up-to-date footage, apparently TV stations had no reporters in Hawaii or could not get through to them. Whom to call? Henry. Maybe he'd have some connections to put me on a relief plane or a military flight or whatever.

Henry was sympathetic; apparently Pam had briefed him on the new developments in the family. But the best he could do was to put Jerry in touch with a colonel in some West Coast military air transportation establishment. Jerry called his department head to tell him he was leaving.

"Jerry, you must be kidding. You've just come back from vacation. We have a whole semester ahead of us and we're short of people. You can't go now."

"I am truly sorry, Professor, but this is a family emergency. I cannot stay; I am taking a plane tonight." It came to him very naturally to say "family emergency." Cat *was* his family, even if she didn't know it yet.

"It, it ttt . . . is a very immature attitude, it . . . it's just stupid," Schumacher started stuttering as he usually did when upset. Jerry was apologetic because his boss was a decent, fair man. He drove them like dogs at work, but gave them the recognition and took care that the university promoted his staff as quickly as possible. But Jerry did not waiver for a moment.

"Sorry, Professor, I really cannot stay."

"You are close to tenure; you can forget it if you leave now!"

Tenure, the ultimate academic recognition, an unassailable guarantee of employment for life, was a carrot dangled in front of all junior professors. "I understand. I will have to quit my academic career." That's it, a first step in my new life. I'm coming, Cat, no matter what! Jerry felt worried about her, but serene about his future. A bridge to his old life had been burnt; the only open way was leading forward.

The colonel was located at the Edwards Air Force Base, near Los Angeles. Jerry managed to get a ticket for a red-eye flight to LAX. He arrived at six in the morning, quite tired but in high spirits. He rented a white Neon and drove to Edwards. The radio carried repetitive news and commentary about Hawaii, but no fresh assessments were available. An hour beyond Los Angeles, the earthquake news was pushed aside by reports of military activities around Iran. Merchant ships had been boarded by U.S. troops in the Strait of Hormuz; Iranians protested, then shots were fired. As he was driving on the plateau towards the base, he saw big planes landing and taking off every couple of minutes. It seemed to be a large airlift.

Colonel Kowal was a tall and somewhat stooped man of nearly his father's age. The officer looked like he had not slept since yesterday, but was polite and friendly.

"What can I do for you, my friend?"

"I need to get to Hawaii," Jerry stated shortly, out of respect for the colonel's time.

Kowal raised his eyebrows with curiosity. "Right now, we would love to have the means of moving people out of Hawaii, not in. Why do you need to go there?"

"I have to take care of a family member in Hawaii," Jerry said, referring again to Cat as his family.

"Out of the question," Colonel Kowal said, shrugging his shoulders. "There are close to a million people on Oahu alone. They will need everything, I mean, everything. Whatever supplies they have will run out in a few days. There is no way we are going to ferry two hundred pounds of you when we might carry four bags of rice or a water-making machine. What's your profession? Can you honestly fit into any rescue worker category?"

"I am an economist, sir."

"Son, I suggest you go home and wait for further information; there is nothing I can do for you. As a matter of fact, we have very few planes available for an airlift to Hawaii, we have been given a different priority now."

"A different priority? What can be a higher priority than relief for Hawaii, now?"

"Do you listen to the radio or watch TV at all?"

"You mean," Jerry erupted, "that killing Iranians has a higher priority than saving Americans in Hawaii?"

Kowal stood up, stretched and said without anger, "You should go now. And you need to control your emotions better. In these difficult times, you should keep certain thoughts to yourself."

"Thank you for your time," Jerry said coldly and put his hand on the doorknob.

"Jerry," Kowal knew his first name. "There will be a transport ship leaving from Coronado for Hawaii tomorrow, but I just cannot see how you could sneak on board with your story."

He was right. Jerry made it all the way up to a lowly lieutenant who practically laughed at him and threw him out of his office. "If you really, really need to get to Hawaii, the only way I can imagine that happening is by sailboat. And don't forget to take a lot of provisions, the last thing they need right now is another hungry mouth to feed." Then he yelled at his assistant; a load of water purification chemical had not yet been loaded on the ship that was due to sail in a few hours. The audience ended abruptly and Jerry walked away towards downtown San Diego.

His new life had come to a sudden stop. He sat at a restaurant's window watching the waterfront. This would be his first meal of the day. He was very hungry, but the thought of a million people running out of food was very disturbing. Anybody who saw TV reports of Hurricane Katrina knew that desperate people do nasty things to each other. Now Cat was in the middle of a big crowd, which would turn very desperate in a few days. His fish and chips kept getting stuck in his throat.

There was no question of fast relief. Kowal was right, Jerry thought. Harbors and airports are in shambles; there is no easy way to supply the million people on the island. There *will* be hunger, disease and a crime wave. Only the military can do anything about it, except they seem to have different priorities. I have to be there to take care of Cat.

A white sailboat motored along the waterfront, its skipper nonchalantly holding the wheel with one hand, talking with two blond girls. One might expect Michelle Pfeiffer to look back from the yacht, smiling for a camera, or a pencil boat roaring along pursued by James Bond in a small plane. Quite a different set up from January in New York, still, a certain similarity was striking. People were laughing, having lunch, drinking beer, apparently without any concern for fellow Americans in Hawaii or even for the war breaking out in Iran. The waitress returned to ask if everything was OK. She was young, blond and had an intelligent face. "Would you like anything else?"

"I'm fine," Jerry said. "It's a terrible thing that happened in Hawaii, have you heard?"

"Awful," she agreed with a smile. "Would you like another beer?"

People don't give a damn about other people, unless they are very close, Jerry thought. Social solidarity! Perhaps in a small village, but across the continent or the ocean . . . a nice propaganda tool, that's all.

He paid his tab and started walking along the waterfront until he came to a marina with a forest of masts. He had no sailing experience to mention, but—he wondered—how difficult could it be to sail to Hawaii? Navigation shouldn't be a problem; GPS would take care of that. Sure, there's the risk of heavy weather . . . He was prepared to take a lot of risk in order to find Cat. Jerry walked along a dock with boats tied up on both sides. Mostly, there were no people on board, sails neatly rolled and covered, hatches closed, decks empty. He stopped in front of a boat with an occupant on it. The boat with a dark blue hull, paint moderately scratched up and peeling in some places, had one mast and a radar unit at the back. That was about how much Jerry could tell.

The man could be sixty-five or more, but it would be difficult to guess because his face was thin and wrinkled. He wore a thick turtleneck sweater, woolen cap and shorts. The old sailor was half reclining on a cockpit bench reading a newspaper. Caustic smoke drifted from his cigarette. An open bottle of beer was placed within his easy reach on the bench. The boat seemed fairly messy: a bicycle leaning against the railing, laundry drying on lines in front of the mast, remnants of food on the small table in the cockpit. Unlike other boats in this marina, this boat served as a home.

Jerry stood in front of the yacht looking at the man who, after a moment, raised his head, looked over his reading glasses and said, "Yes? What's the problem?" He was not very gracious, but not aggressive either, mildly annoyed, perhaps, at this interruption of his reading.

"Sorry to bother you, sir. I was just wondering how difficult it would be to cross the Pacific to get to Hawaii."

The man looked at Jerry for two seconds and shrugged, "Difficult enough if you don't know what you're doing," and returned to his paper.

"I wonder how long it would take, of course providing that you knew what you were doing."

The old sailor sighed, put the paper down and sat up. "I sense that you definitely need to talk to me, don't you? The least you could do is bring some beer, as my supplies have just run out."

Jerry quickly walked to a little grocery store at the marina and bought a six-pack of Sam Adams. A moment later, he was back to buy some chips and peanuts. This might be an interesting conversation. The old-timer extended a blue awning over the cockpit so they could sit in the shade. Jerry handed over the six-pack and immediately regretted not buying a twelve-pack. The older man opened two bottles with a bottle opener attached by a string to the steering wheel's base. He handed Jerry a bottle and then introduced himself.

"John Browser, skipper of *Lady Luck*," and gestured around him, indicating the boat.

"I'm Jerry Roberts, pleased to meet you, John. I just wonder if you could tell me about a hypothetical trip to Hawaii. Are you familiar with long ocean passages?"

"I wasted most of my life making ocean passages," grimaced John, "so you could say I'm familiar with it. I was a seaman and an officer on a dozen freighters until I gave it all up a few years ago. What is it that you want to know about your hypothetical trip to Hawaii, buddy?"

He had developed an interest in Jerry and studied him

146

with keen eyes partly hidden by heavy eyelid bags. He was probably closer to seventy.

Not knowing the right questions to ask is the first problem when trying to learn any new subject. "Could you just tell me, how would you go about sailing there?" Jeremy asked awkwardly.

John took a long sip of bear. "You're not a sailor, are you?"

Jerry shook his head for "no."

"Then I would start by finding myself a skipper, a captain who does not need to ask too many questions."

"Then, John, would you be interested in a job?"

John Browser looked at him with even more interest, but frowned, "Jerry, you scare me. What makes you believe that I am a competent skipper, enough to put your life in my hands, even if I were to agree?" He was genuinely exasperated. "Would you put a thousand dollars in my hand if you met me on a street? If not, how could you put your life in my hands? Isn't it worth more than a thousand bucks?" After a moment, a flash of understanding showed on his face. "You work for the government, don't you, Jerry? If that's your real name."

"Oh no, I don't work for anyone, in fact, I was a university professor, until yesterday. I can show you my school I.D."

The skipper waved his hand, dismissing further explanations meaning, "If you are a spook, couldn't you have a fake I.D.?"

Jerry pressed on. "Good comparison with the thousand bucks, except that on a busy street you could take the money and disappear in the crowd. Once we are on the water you couldn't vanish. My only risk would be that you are, indeed, not up to the job. But then we would both share in the trouble."

John considered it for a moment. "True, but let's reverse the situation. Convince me that you are not crazy. How do I know that you won't jump off the boat in the middle of the ocean, leaving me by myself, or cut my throat when I am asleep? What mentally stable person would want to sail to Hawaii in January, when the chance of very nasty weather is excellent? Besides, what's the attraction of the Islands just after a major earthquake? They must be ruined. Surely you're not planning a vacation?"

He lit another exceptionally stinky cigarette, and Jerry had a few moments to decide on further strategy. How could he provide proof of mental stability? A lot of people, including the military shrink, Professor Schumacher and the lieutenant from Coronado might vouch to the contrary. There was no other way; he would have to tell the truth, strange as it sounded.

"John, my wife, I mean my future wife, lives on Oahu. She is handicapped and I will do anything to get to her." He kept catching himself referring to Cat as his wife, even though they were not particularly friendly when he left a week ago.

John slowly opened another bottle and offered it to Jerry who declined; Browser did not insist. He took a large gulp and stated with an air of objectivity, "Temporary in-sanity, then. You are a pup in love. That's not too bad. That would guarantee that you don't try to kill yourself or me, at least until we get to Honolulu."

CHAPTER 18

Reuters: *Middle East is rocked with violent demonstrations in response to the U.S.—Iran conflict. Russian ambassador expresses concern about escalation of fighting in the Persian Gulf.*

For the first few days, people kept busy trying to dig out their or the neighbors' relatives. Cries for help and moaning under the rubble were growing weaker every hour, and after two days few victims had been pulled out alive. Stunned survivors lifted their eyes and contemplated the damage around them. A short walk through Kailua brought the realization that the destruction had affected the town very unevenly. The neighborhood of Beachside, a row of expensive homes facing the ocean, was almost completely flattened and washed away by the tidal waves. Dried mud covered foundations and broken tree trunks. No living creature disturbed the peace; even rats that used to live in canopies of coconut trees abandoned the zone reclaimed by the ocean. Only waves resumed their easy and pleasant pattern, sweetly washing the wounded shore and bringing fresh golden sand.

Further inland, where the killing water did not reach, the destruction was patchy and without any apparent pattern or sense of justice. Some buildings crumbled into heaps of rubble while houses next door survived without major damage. Only the loss of utilities was egalitarian; no service that required conduits survived. Violent shaking of the earth had broken water mains, shuttered sewage pipes and ripped electrical wires. The roads were broken, wide fissures gaping in the pavement in some places, and folds of asphalt mounting surrealistically in others. Emergency vehicles crept slowly through the fractured streets hauling wounded and dead. The last fires died out the previous night when the rain fell, typically heavy at this time of year. What struck people harshly at this point was the complete loss of communication. Landline phones and the Internet were dead. Local radio and TV stations lost their transmitters and so did the cellular services. Few residents had any information about areas further away than a few city blocks. A few ham radio operators, who had battery backup, broadcast their news, but their voices were going silent one by one as the circuits went dead.

Those who had battery-operated shortwave radios turned their dials in disbelief. The radio waves were filled with music as usual. News broadcast from somewhere far away mentioned the earthquake in Hawaii and went back to the top twenty. Radio hosts argued the merits of attacking Iran, which had apparently already happened. There were no specifics about Hawaii. The islands seemed forgotten, left to themselves.

The windward side of Oahu, where Kailua lies, is separated from the rest of the island by the tall, steep Koolau Mountains. For centuries, one could travel to Windward either by boat, around Makapu'u rock or by the narrow and dangerous mountain passes. In modern times, tunnels were built for highways H1 and H3, cutting the travel time to

Honolulu to an easy twenty to thirty minutes. In addition, there was a road hacked into the slope of the mountain rising from the ocean, creating a picturesque though precariously winding route half way between the surf and the mountaintop. People who left Kailua in an attempt to reach Honolulu on the day of the earthquake came back a few hours later with disturbing news. Both tunnels had collapsed and were filled with rubble. A rockslide had closed the road along the ocean. A fit and brave person could climb over the mountains, but mass transportation was out of the question.

Most Hawaiian households kept a few days of food and water supply in case of a hurricane, but these were rapidly running out. Stores were looted first, then empty houses. On the fourth day, robbers figured out that there was no force to oppose them, so gangs started openly roaming the streets. The terrified people of Kailua were locking themselves in their houses at night, but that was a pathetic defense. The thugs did not wait for night; day was just as convenient. As for the locks, very few doors would not give in to a good kick. Home invasions became common as predators picked their prey at leisure. Police stayed on the job, but few in numbers and unable to move quickly through the wrecked roads, they were overwhelmed by rapidly multiplying looters striking at random.

Cat sat in the wheelchair requisitioned by Abe from a broken health supplies store. "It's everybody for himself," she said. "If this continues, the only people who survive will be thieves and gangsters. We have to help. There is nothing we can do until some degree of public safety is restored. Mike, how many people do you have now?"

Sergeant Yoshida cleared his voice, "We have fourteen guys who can do full duties, two female dispatchers and a few walking wounded. There is no way we can respond to all the crime. First, we don't know what's happening because people have no phones to call us. But even if we knew, we're out of gas for patrol cars." The man who always felt he could handle any situation was bitterly discouraged. One doesn't become a police sergeant if helplessness is part of his mental makeup; Yoshida did not accept defeat easily, but he could see no way out now. "In any case, most of the roads are badly broken up, so it is really back to foot patrols," the sergeant added.

"Is your communication equipment working?"

"Well, we have a backup generator to run our station's radio, but as I said, we're out of gas. We've kept a few gallons for the generator, but that won't last long. We still have battery-operated radios, but if we use them routinely, we'll soon be out of any communication all together."

Cat looked around the long table used for meals by Kailua cops. Mike Yoshida, short, perhaps forty years old man of Japanese ancestry, was presently the highest-ranking member of the Kailua police force. Next to him was Sharon Lim, a slender, older woman who was the medical director of Castle Hospital. Carol Nakamoto, a Kailua politician and a ranking member of the Democratic Party, was sitting on the opposite side. There were a few other people Cat had never met before. No one was volunteering any response.

"How about if we deputize some people? We could make twelve or thirteen patrols—each led by a cop, with

Mike and his deputy at headquarters. They could cover a lot of territory."

Nakamoto shifted uncomfortably, "That smells like a lot of legal problems. The deputies can get hurt; untrained staff will break laws. I think we should wait for instructions from Honolulu."

"Carol, have you had any instructions from Honolulu, Washington or anywhere else over the past few days?"

"No, but I'm sure someone is working on it right now. All we need to do is wait."

"Dr. Lim, do you have everything you need to treat the injured? Can they wait?"

The doctor shrugged her shoulders, "We're out of all IV antibiotics and scratching the bottom on any medical supplies altogether. All the dressing material is gone. We saw over a thousand people going through the Emergency Room, and we've sent almost all of them home. A good portion of those will be back with infections. People are dying, and there is little we can do. This isn't a situation where we can wait."

"Mike, did you have any murder reports?"

"Two likely killings on the first night, five the next night, and today I had reports of three stabbings and two gun-wound deaths, and it's only seven PM!"

"Carol, can we afford to wait any more?"

Nakamoto hated to be put on the spot like that, and all

her legal training was telling her, "Stay away from this mess, there will be consequences." She lowered her head, pretending to take notes on her yellow pad, and mumbled something difficult to interpret. Yoshida looked at Cat and nodded.

"Well, we cannot force anybody to join, but those who are tired of locking themselves in their bathroom and hoping that the robbers miss them, should be able to defend themselves." Cat was looking at Yoshida, who seemed to be in agreement. "I suggest that everybody present here gets in touch with their friends and family and send volunteers here to the police station. We'll prepare some fliers, and they need to be distributed by hand. That's a lot of leg work; we need a lot of people."

CHAPTER 19

J erry and John chatted for a few hours, during which
time the skipper slowly finished off the beer. He was a
slow but steady guzzler; however, alcohol did not seem
to affect him. The sun was setting now and the water wrinkled into tiny wavelets raised by a slight wind. People
started showing up on the boats, and a few barbeques were
fired up. The smell of meat started spreading throughout
the marina. Jerry was getting hungry again, so he invited
John for dinner in the nearby restaurant where he had had
lunch.

As they walked, John offered his life story. He had a
son who lived with his mother while the father plied the
oceans. There was very little contact between them when
the boy was young. John did not give himself much credit
for being a father or husband, though he didn't feel he was
any worse than his shipmates. Eventually, his wife found
her own way to happiness, thus he had lost contact with the
boy. What made him unhappy was the story of the last two
years.

He had retired in poor financial shape, no savings, basically lived off a social security check supplemented with
occasional jobs. His son found him and included John into
his life. He was doing well himself, running a small but

prospering used-car lot. He offered his father a job, and John turned out to have a gift for selling. The old mariner was used to living on a really low budget and his needs were few. Beer, cheap cigarettes, a bit of food and a place to sleep, that's all he needed. He was saving money for the first time in his life. After two years, he had saved enough money to realize his dream; he bought the boat, *Lady Luck*. He put the money in escrow; the next day his world fell apart. Two men knocked on his door at six o'clock in the morning and arrested him on charges of money laundering and aiding a terror organization.

"You wouldn't believe it, Jerry, they were actually wearing dark suits, like the 'Men in Black'. Only they weren't so funny. They handcuffed me and took me to a lockup in some unmarked building. The next few days, I spent answering again and again: what was my name and what was my religion? Jerry, they did not like that I didn't subscribe to any holy church. Could I speak Arabic? Yes, I could: *shukram, afwan, masalama*, thank you, you are welcome, good-bye. For God's sake, I was a sailor! Apparently, I had sold some cars that the F.B.I., or some other government organization whose acronyms you wouldn't even know, had traced to some terror suspects. Their money had touched my hands so I had become a suspect myself."

He had been held for a few days, and then was released with a warning to remain in the San Diego vicinity. What he was not warned about was that his bank accounts were frozen. He had been left on the street with twenty dollars in his wallet. Fortunately, he had already paid for the boat, so *Lady Luck* became his home. Any inquiries as to why his accounts had been frozen caused fifteen minutes of confusion, whispers in a backroom and invocations of the Patriot Act.

"When can I have my money back?" The banker's eyes had rolled up in expression of helpless ignorance.

"That wasn't the worst, Jerry," John was getting agitated. "My son's accounts had been frozen as well. Other salesmen were interrogated and harassed, again and again. The money ran out; even the secretary bailed. The car lot went bankrupt within a few weeks. My son never blamed me openly, but stopped asking me to drop in." The old man was again a lonely, poor guy, albeit living on a boat of his own.

Jerry and John felt comfortable with each other, and the skipper did not consider Jerry crazy for his travel plans. Jerry decided he had found himself a way to get to Hawaii.

"John, I'd like to buy your boat, and hire you as a captain to skipper us to Hawaii. Will you consider it? We really don't know each other, but I have no time for extensive investigations. If you want, we can spend the whole night talking, but by morning I need your answer."

Jerry had finished his grilled mahi-mahi, and John had been done with his steak for the past ten minutes; now he was shifting impatiently in his chair, dying to have a cigarette. Jerry signaled the waitress for the tab, and they left. John lit a cigarette, inhaled slowly and kept the smoke in for a few seconds. "First, you will not find anyone crazy enough to sail to Hawaii in January, especially knowing that the Islands are probably in ruins, no matter what money you offer. So, it is either I, or you start taking sailing classes and—if you are a hard worker—you might be ready in a year." The skipper stuck the cigarette butt into a sand-filled ashtray and immediately lit another. "What would you offer for my boat and what would you pay me?" He asked somewhat embarrassed, as though selling *Lady Luck* was a shameful act. "I don't need this money for myself, but I would like to repay my son, somehow."

"I have no idea what the value of your boat is, John, but I will offer you this—I have an apartment in New York, nothing fancy, but it should fetch over half a million dollars. I will swap it for your boat and your services. If you agree, we'll go to a notary in the morning, and I will sign papers transferring ownership to you or your son."

"That's a lot more than my boat is worth," John said, "although it's a good boat," he added with certain haste. "You sure you want to do it?"

Jerry shrugged, "As you said, you and your boat are the only game in town, and I am desperate. The swap is a good value to me. Besides, I won't need a New York apartment any more."

"Well, then," Browser said with some hesitation, "I will gladly take the shirt off your back, but you need to know certain facts. First, this is the storm season, and we may get into weather that will make you wish you had never left dry land. In simple terms, we may die. Secondly, I am an alcoholic. I function just fine, but if you try to limit my drinking, you may have to tie me up. I wouldn't like that, neither would you. Can you put up with an old drunk for a few weeks?"

"You look to me like a very reasonable drunk, John. I won't interfere with your intake."

"As you noted, I also smoke, well over a pack a day."

"And they are a pretty stinky kind, but as long as you smoke outside, I won't complain."

"Then it's a deal. And let me tell you, Jerry, when we pull into the Honolulu harbor you'll be a real sailor. I'll make sure."

"John, the Men in Black, didn't they tell you to stay in San Diego? They might be unhappy . . ."

"If I can make them unhappy, Jerry, that would just be frosting on the cake. I would love to stick it to them. In any case, there was no court order. Besides, once we get fifty miles off shore, they might just as well go to hell. They have no power over the open ocean, Jerry, it's the last place where you're truly free."

They stayed up till dawn making lists of provisions and supplies. The skipper made no special demands for food. Probably he wouldn't object to dog food, if it were necessary. He did insist that they needed a gallon of drinking water per day for each of them and recommended that, in the great tradition of the British Navy, a good portion of it could come in the form of beer. "Safe, healthy and keeps the crew in sweet disposition," declared the captain.

Jerry suspected that this recommendation was not entirely unbiased, but did not object. Forty cases of Heineken were added to the list, with a few bottles of Tequila "for emergency." *Lady Luck* was a forty-two-foot-long sloop and could carry a six-man crew, with supplies. With Jerry and John as the only occupants, they could take on some cargo. Jerry kept in mind the lieutenant's words: "The last thing they need is another hungry mouth to feed." Apart from food, Jerry wanted to take something that would be useful in Hawaii, something that they would definitely need. Didn't I hear about a missing load of water purification tablets? Did they manage to slip it onto the ship at the last moment?

"Skipper, where could we buy water purification chemicals?"

"Bleach, it's nothing but bleach. You can have a ton of it for a few bucks. Just keep in mind that the heavier the boat, the slower we'll move."

Jerry was ready to set sail in the morning, but John was not. "I need to repair a head sail and service the motor," he said.

"How long is it going to take, Skip?"

"You've got yourself a skipper *and* a mechanic, sir. I can do the engine myself, if I can find replacement parts. The sail, the shop guys should be able to fix and re-enforce it within a few hours, if you pay a bit extra."

"I'm fine with extra money, but would hate to wait for engine parts. Is it feasible to go without the motor job?"

John lighted another stinker, puffed and said, "Jerry, you don't fuck with the ocean. You start cutting corners and then the next thing you know, your lungs are full of water. If you want to do some good in Hawaii, first you have to get your ass over there, while it is still warm. We're taking enough risks already sailing in the winter."

ALEX Z. MODZELEWSKI

And that was it. The skipper took the sail in Jerry's rental car and was gone. A few bottles of beer went with him as well. Jerry went straight to the lawyer he had found in the Yellow Pages. He gave his sister power of attorney, signed papers that transferred ownership of his apartment to John's son, and with a heavy heart dialed the number to Pam.

"Pam, it's Jerry."

"Jerry, what are you doing?" Pam was not waiting to exchange civil greetings.

"There is nothing I can do here in California, so I am going to Hawaii by sailboat."

All he could hear was irregular breathing, as if she was fighting to control sobbing. He gave her a few seconds for a question, but none was coming, so he continued. "I've found a good boat and an experienced skipper who will take me there. Don't worry, thousands of people have done it before without any problems." He did not mention that the vast majority of them did not try to cross in winter. He forgot to mention John's drinking problem as well. As to a "good boat," he might be right; they would know soon.

Pam's breathing became more regular. "You've quit your job as well," she sighed.

Jerry had almost forgotten about his teaching job; it seemed a long, long time ago. "Pam, I want to ask you for a favor, there is some unfinished business...."

She easily agreed to take over all his financial affairs, and didn't object to his real estate deal. Before they disconnected, she cried briefly and said, "You know, Jerry, you grew up to be the man I hoped you would. I am worried sick about you, but I am so proud of you as well. I hope you pull it off and bring Cat to New York. I love you." Jerry had tears in his eyes as well; now he was ready.

He returned to the boat with some Chinese take-out for John. There was no smell of tobacco on the deck, and he had a moment of terror thinking the skipper might have pulled a fast one on him; a moment later, he was ashamed of himself. The captain was lying on his belly, head in the diesel compartment, struggling to unscrew some mechanical device and breathing loudly with effort.

"Hey, John, there's some food up here for you. And it sounds like you need fresh air for a moment."

"Be out in a few minutes," growled the skipper from the diesel, "but not before this little fuck gives in."

He emerged ten minutes later disdainfully displaying the old part; it reminded Jerry of nothing that he had ever seen. "The motor should be ready in three hours. You can pick up the sail from repair at five o'clock."

"Great," Jerry could not control his excitement. "Then I'll bring our supplies in the evening, we load the boat and we're ready to sail!"

John looked at him with a silent question.

"I went to the lawyer and made the real estate transaction; my sister will finish the deal." Jerry showed him copies of the documents. "You should mail them to your son tonight and perhaps you might write him a letter?"

"What's there I can tell him? I wanted to speak with him after our defenders of freedom let me out. But he didn't want to see me. Never said so, but I knew. I called his house, his wife answered. When I asked to speak with him, she covered the phone for a few seconds, and then said he wasn't home. But he *was* home. I was calling from the street, just outside his house. I hoped he would say: 'Dad, just come in, we'll talk.' Instead, I saw him sitting at the kitchen table, waving 'no' to his wife. I used to sit at that table, play with the kids, and have a beer with him. When he gets the apartment, maybe he'll see that I am not an old, worthless piece of garbage." John pulled out a cigarette and cracked open a beer.

Jerry didn't have anything comforting to say, so he just put his hand on John's thin shoulder. They completed their last land activities at 11:30 PM, started the motor at 11:35 and slipped away twenty minutes before midnight. The forecast called for winds ten to fifteen knots and likely showers.

CHAPTER 20

The meeting at the police station was over, but the participants lingered, talking in small groups. Kalani tugged Cat's tee shirt. "Remember, there are kids living on the streets with no one to care for them. Something has to be done. They are all hungry, filthy and scared to death."

"You're right, Kalani, something has to be done. You're the one to do it. Hereby, I pronounce you the chief of public welfare," Cat declared ceremoniously.

"You must be kidding!" Carol Nakamoto couldn't resist. "That's impersonation of a public official; it could be criminal."

Cat had had enough of the politician. "So where is your public official? There is no official but there are hungry children. Hmm, what to do, what to do? Let's take a poll and see what the people desire. Carol, if you don't want to help—go to hell, but do not intimidate people who might want to do some good!"

Carol withdrew silently with lips pursed. Mike Yoshida watched with pleasure. Nakamoto was part of the Police Board and she had made him cringe more than once in the past. He was happy that someone finally rubbed her nose in the dirt. "Cat, would you like to join the police force?" He broke into a wide smile.

"Where am I supposed to get food for the kids? Where do I put them up?" Kalani, who apparently accepted her new public responsibility, moaned. "My apartment is too small to take them all in."

"Good point," remarked Cat. "We need a house to put up the kids. Oh, I know a house on Kailua Road. It's one of those on the Beachside that survived the disaster. It's empty. I know the owners; they're on the mainland. Decent people; won't mind if we use it. At least nobody will break in. As to food, until we get some kind of supplies, you'll have to resort to guerilla tactics. Desperate times call for desperate measures. Get some volunteers and comb over the groceries. The looters must have missed something; after all, they worked under pressure. Mike, are you willing to look the other way?"

"We're very short on staff, as you know," the sergeant replied with a smile. "I don't think we'll be able to cover Foodland and Safeway tonight."

* * *

Kalani pushed Cat's wheelchair, trying to avoid cracks and holes. They approached a large, dark house. It had a strange outline, one end having a distinctly round shape.

"The Round House," exclaimed Kalani. "I always wanted to see how it looked inside!"

The metal gate and solid concrete wall surrounding the house had held back the torrent of water and debris, already slowed down by two rows of buildings standing between this home and the ocean. The front yard was covered with caked mud, but the sturdy oak door was intact.

Kalani looked into the dark windows, "Wow, it's huge, and there is not much damage." She removed pieces of broken glass from the window frame and carefully let herself in. A moment later, the front door opened, and Cat wheeled into a very large room. It was dark, but the moon was bright enough to illuminate the interior through the windows. The room was two stories high and the ceiling seemed intact. A marble floor was covered with fragments of sculptures and shards of pottery, but there were no apparent large cracks. A carpeted stairway led to a higher floor and, apart from the water damage, it all looked sound.

"This is good," whispered Kalani, impressed with the size and elegance of the hall. She ran upstairs to check the bedrooms. There were three, all without any major damage, except for the shattered windows and a TV set crashed on the floor. An assortment of household items was scattered around, and the carpet displayed a huge stain where water had leaked from the broken pipes, but two large beds and a sofa were ready for use.

"I can put eight or nine kids right here, on real beds," enthused Kalani. The kitchen pantry was stocked with hurricane supplies.

"There you go," Cat smiled. "You can start your public career without looting. We'll see how long you can last."

The house was big enough for their orphanage upstairs, and the grand hall downstairs could double up as a community meeting place, much larger than the cramped police station. They would certainly need it, if any volunteers did show up.

"Kalani, can you go back to Mike Yoshida and tell him about our discovery? Tell him to send all the volunteers here, and then you can go trolling for your homeless children. I'll stay here and start preparing assignments for volunteers." Cat set up her command post at the big, dark oak table.

Two hours after the first bunch of leaflets had been dispatched, the first volunteers showed up. Silent, depressed and exhausted people were greeted with a cup of hot soup or coffee. A camping propane burner in the back yard kept delivering a new pot of hot liquid every few minutes. People sat against the wall nursing a cup, possibly their first in a few days, then were given a small but definite job to do.

"Your name is John, right? John, you'll be in charge of lighting. We need a few lamps or at least a bunch of candles. Can you try to get them?"

"Leila, what did you do before the shake? Senior at Kailua High? Excellent! You'll be our printer-in-chief. Get some kids together and you'll be handwriting notes to the public. Just remember—neat, big letters so that people can read them without glasses."

Cat was looking at the pale faces, blood-soaked bandages and dirty clothes, thinking—how much can people take? We are all scared, tired, injured and hungry. As people were offered a chance to help themselves, she saw backs straightening. We're tougher than one could have imagined three days ago, she thought.

The list of needs seemed to have no end. Sweep the town looking for people, or more likely, bodies still trapped under the wreckage; provide care for orphaned children; remove dead bodies and store them in the empty warehouse looking over the swamp. Could we bring one radio station on air for public address? Support the Police Department. There was more than enough work to occupy the dozens of volunteers filing in and out.

What volunteers could not provide was food, fuel and medications. The hospital was out of all supplies. It remained open, but apart from minor surgical procedures, all they could offer was advice and consolation. No patients were being admitted. A large number of Kailua's inhabitants had suffered injuries during the quake. Now, a few days later, infections became the main worry. Septic shock claimed older people and diabetics first, but that was only the beginning. People healthy just a week before saw their wounds opening, skin getting hot and red, then purple. They filled the Emergency Room, families begging for treatment, but there was little treatment the exhausted doctors could offer. A deadly mixture of germs found excellent breeding grounds in deep, ragged wounds inflicted by splintered wood, concrete debris and broken glass. The pile of bodies in the warehouse was growing rapidly.

The aggressive patrolling somewhat kept down the rampant crime. Yoshida, despite his big smile, had a firm hand. A curfew had been ordered for ten PM, and permits for moving around at night were issued on an individual basis. The instructions for patrolmen were simple: "No one's allowed to get away unchecked; shoot if you need to." A few shots had been fired on the first night of the curfew, but none on the second. The criminals understood force better than anything else.

"Why is no help coming from Honolulu or even the mainland?" Everybody was asking, but there was no logical answer.

"Probably Honolulu's been hit just as badly as we have, but they couldn't just disappear under water like the mythical Atlantis. We keep sending radio messages on our emergency transmitter, which they confirm, but nothing of substance comes back," Yoshida was baffled.

"They must have emergency warehouses; they were supposed to keep supplies for us," Carol Nakamoto added. "How about the military? How about the marines in Kaneohe?"

"That's the strangest part," Cat tried to explain. "We've sent a delegation asking for help, and they didn't even let them past the gate. A Major Stevens, their public relations officer, came to explain that they were on the highest alert, and there would be no one leaving or entering the base. They have also refused to share any food rations or fuel with the town. Basically, they told us to get lost, and don't bother them because they have other problems. Looks like they might be off to Iran shortly. Eventually, after much pleading, they agreed to provide a phone link to their headquarters. There it is, sitting on that glass table, if any of you would like to talk to Major Stevens."

"At the same time, they are flying choppers over the island, wasting fuel," remarked Yoshida gloomily.

Candles were almost completely burned in their jam jars. The meeting participants sat around Cat's table, nobody talking. They were just staring ahead, as people do when extreme tiredness overtakes the mind, no matter what the consequences, eyes partly open but nobody's home.

"We're just wasting time sitting here; let's get some rest." Yoshida stood up, took two steps towards the wall, removed a heavy volume from a bookcase, lay down with the book for a pillow and fell asleep almost immediately. Cat closed her eyes and was about to doze off when Kalani shook her shoulder.

"You can't sleep sitting, Cat, you know that...." She knew, with no sensation in her lower body and infrequent moves, she could develop necrotic skin ulcers.

"Thanks, Kalani." She let the girl wheel her to a small side office, which she appropriated as her living quarters. She got out of the chair and rested on a small day bed. Sleep went away. "So, how did it happen that you're with Abe again?"

Kalani felt a bit defensive, "Actually, we are not to-gether. I love him and want him sooo bad, but we can't go on as we were. We decided to start again from the begin-ning; maybe we'll get it better the second time around. I'm not afraid of him any more. What happened is something he doesn't understand, and neither do I. But I am sure he'll never do it again. I met him the next day after that scene at your house. He was waiting for me on the street. I was a bit afraid, but he was very sweet and wanted me to come back to our apartment. I said 'no'— not because I was afraid of him, but I was afraid of myself. I knew that if he hugged me and touched me, we would be in bed in no time, and then we would be back to the same old game. No, we start

from scratch. We live apart and we're dating. It's fun...."
She giggled like a teenager.

"You smart woman," mumbled Cat, "and I like this bum of yours." She fell into a heavy sleep filled with nightmares. Her face was thin and pale with a greenish tinge, hands and arms covered with bloody crusts, blond hair matted into a semblance of dreadlocks, dirty and sticky. She was the face of the town that had been delivered a double mortal blow but refused to die.

The morning was no better. The burning sun was up and exhausted people tried to find some rest in the shade of their ruined homes. By now, personal food stores were running low. Fortunately, it rained every night and clean water could be collected from roofs and flat surfaces. The hospital reported that critical patients with infections were piling up.

Priorities:

1. antibiotics and surgical supplies
2. food
3. fuel

Cat wrote on a piece of paper, and underlined "antibiotics." She was scribbling thinking: There must be emergency supplies on the island. Someone has to have them. They're sitting on the provisions and using them, but won't share with us. She wrote:

Suspects: the military and the state

Cat made a frame around the world military. If we don't make them, they won't share—it's that simple, she thought. Is there anything that they might want from us?

Do we have any leverage? Doesn't look like they're going to be shamed into cooperation.

She threw a tennis ball in the direction of a girl sleeping on the floor. The ball bounced and fell on the slumped body. Leila raised her head, looking towards the table. "Leila, sorry to wake you up. Can you try to find someone from the Department of Water Management or the City Manager's office?"

Leila got up without a word, got on her bike and left. An hour later, a short man arrived. He used to be quite overweight; now his pants were loosely hanging on his belt.

"Lee Kurohara, Town Hall, what can I do for you?"

Cat was continually surprised to see other people taking orders from her. After all, she was not a manager or chairman or director of anything. She was just an upstart who told people to do things, that's all. However, she would continue as long as they were willing to listen. "Lee, can you tell me how the water supply works in Kailua? We have no big problems now because it keeps raining at night, but if it stops raining, would we have water?"

"Well, we do have water in the reservoir; it's actually full. But we can't pump it because we have no power. Then, if we start pumping, it will all escape through broken pipes. The whole system is shattered. It would take a lot of time to repair, even if we had power and materials."

"Fair enough. Would you be able to reconstruct one or two lines to some sort of central location? You know, a public watering hole so that people might come and get it if needed."

"I'm sure we could, good idea," agreed Kurohara. "But we would have to pump it manually. You would have to provide some muscle power."

"No problem, Lee." Cat did not want to think now how much manpower that would require. Definitely, a lot of exercise for these starved men. "One more thing—is there anybody else pumping water from our reservoir? After all, nobody gets as much rain as we do."

"There is a big pipeline to the leeward side, but it's broken and we've shut it down. And, there is a small pipeline to the Marine base, which somehow survived the shake without big damage. They've fixed it; it's operational. They have pumps on their side, and they use them."

"Thank you, Lee. I'll be in touch with you, probably in the next few hours."

Cat wheeled herself to the table and sat there for a few minutes, tapping her broken fingernails on the glass top. What's there to lose? She sighed and reached for a telephone. "Major Stevens, please."

A few minutes later, an energetic voice sounded from the other end of the line. "Major Stevens, whom am I talking to?"

"Major Stevens, my name is Cat. I am calling from Kailua. You spoke with our delegation yesterday."

"I'm sorry, Ma'm, I know you have a big problem on your hands, but we can't help you."

"Major, I am not calling about our problem. I am calling about *your* problem. Your water supply will be interrupted in thirty minutes. We have to shut it down for repairs, indefinitely."

"What kind of joke is this? And who are you?"

"As I said, my name is Cat Milewski, and I am just one of those people you refused to help. This is not a joke; your last drops are running in right now. However, we could try to help you, if you help us."

"Lady, if you are trying to blackmail the Marine Corps, you are in deep trouble!" The voice sounded somewhat flustered, but not actually angry. The situation was too absurd to call for anger.

Cat wiped a speck of dust off the table in front of her. "So what are you going to do? Drop some napalm on Kailua? You just don't understand how big our problem is, Major. We are desperate people. We are dying by dozens every day, and your threat is quite empty to us. We're not looking for any additional trouble, but your outfit has all that we desperately need. If you don't help us, we will keep dying, so spare yourself huffing at me. Either you help us or we'll do our best to make the world notice us."

The silence on the other end of the line lasted a full twenty seconds, while Stevens tried to absorb the implications of this conversation.

"Can I call you back? I need to speak with the commanding officer."

"May I suggest," Cat answered calmly, "that you come here in person and see for yourself. I can see your choppers flying, so obviously you do have fuel. I'm in the house at the corner of Kalaheo and Kailua Road." She put down the phone and stretched the rigid muscles of her arms.

They'll come, either to talk or to arrest me. Most likely I'd be better off in their dungeon, she smiled tensely.

Kalani's success had become her nightmare. She collected nine kids and brought them to the Round House. A baby, maybe a year old, pulled from the wreckage, parents confirmed dead; a ten-year-old girl named Ashley whose parents and a brother had disappeared, probably under the waves of the Pacific; and seven others, between the ages of two and six, who seemingly belonged to nobody. They took residence upstairs, under Kalani's watchful eye. The hungry mouths cleaned out the house pantry by day four, despite meager rations. From that time on, the only food available was what Kalani could beg or steal.

Both she and Cat lived on a few bites a day of whatever was available. For the most part, Abe kept them alive, making long trips into the fields of central Oahu. He climbed over the Koolau Mountains, walked many miles and hid from gangs preying on foragers like him, to get a few pineapples, guavas or papayas. The big man lost much of his imposing bulk; likely he ate what was still available after he had filled his sack for Kalani. But Abe had never been happier in his life, except maybe for those few months when he first met Kalani. He was in love and could show it in a way that men had shown their affection for thousands of years. He fed and protected his mate, despite all the difficulties that fate piled in his way.

Kalani left Ashley in charge and came down for a chat

with Cat. "What's up? Any food coming from anywhere?"

"Working on it." Cat smiled mysteriously. "We can expect some military vehicles soon, carrying either supplies or MPs to get us rebels under lock and key. I hope your young delinquents will qualify for a military jail. Can you imagine all the food they would feed us?"

"Food is good . . . but what have you done exactly?"

"Oh, I've just told the Marines that we're going to cut off their water line. And, if they don't show up here in an hour, I will do just that. They must have a reserve, but there are a lot of people living on the base; they can't ignore us for long. They'll be here the moment their toilets stop flushing."

Kalani's mouth opened, "You're crazy, Cat!"

Thirty-five minutes later, a military Hummer rumbled along the broken pavement of Kailua Road and stopped in front of the Round House. An officer got out from the passenger side, and two soldiers jumped out of the back. The officer put his hat on and marched through the open gate into the big yard.

Hearing them, Kalani looked through the broken window. "They're here."

"Do they have 'MP' on their helmets?" Cat could not hide her anxiety.

"Only one is coming, and he has no helmet, no 'MP'."

A broad-shouldered, tall man in battle fatigues stood in

the doorway. "I am Major Stevens. I'm looking for Cat Milewski."

"I am Cat. Do you come with gifts or napalm, Major?"

Stevens stood for a moment while his eyes adapted to the darkness of the room. He saw a painfully thin figure sitting in a wheelchair. How old is she, for God's sake, sixteen? Like a sixteen-year-old who ran away from home, he thought, surprised.

"You are Cat? The person who threatened the Marine Corps?" Stevens just could not carry out his intended plan to submit the offender to maximum pressure and abuse, and only when she was completely shattered, to offer some modest help. He needed to regroup in mid-mission. "You certainly have guts . . . " He could not hide his admiration for the audacity of his opponent. "Look, Cat—we are a military establishment. We operate by orders and we can't just decide to give Government Issue supplies because we would like to."

"Just a moment, Major. Could I ask you to go upstairs for a moment with my friend, and then we'll continue our conversation?"

Stevens went up and Kalani introduced him to the kids, with their sunken eyes and sore-covered skin, bunching behind a big bed, afraid of the stranger. They reminded him of a litter of homeless puppies cowering in the darkness. Downstairs, he again faced the skinny person in a wheelchair, who looked like she herself should be in child protective custody.

"Do you have any children, Major?"

He nodded: "Two."

"Do they look anything like that bunch upstairs?"

He could not say "yes" and averted his eyes.

"Do you think they deserve some protection from their government? Isn't there anything in your officer's code of conduct that says that the children of this country will get the most basic assistance when in dire need? I know you have the Iran problem, but that means nothing to those guys upstairs, they'll be dead before you sort out your latest adventure."

The officer raised a hand to stop her. "Look, there's no need for any more of that. The commander has agreed to provide you with a small amount of medical supplies and food. It will come unauthorized from our standard provisions, and he can get into a lot of trouble for that. I hope it'll get you over the hump, until FEMA wakes up. And, if we hear anything more about water supply interruption, your town will be crawling with uniformed and very unfriendly men."

He could not resist a smile in response to the big grin on Cat's face.

"Thank you, Major Stevens. What's your first name?"

"It's Gary," Stevens seemed embarrassed.

"Thank you, Gary, and please convey our gratitude to your commander."

Two soldiers brought ten boxes of food rations, five

bags of rice and five boxes marked with the Red Cross logo.

"On your way back, would you please drop it all off at the hospital, except for one box of food rations and one bag of rice?"

"No problem, Ma'm."

"Gary, can we count on some more help in the future?" She was looking straight into the major's eyes, willing him to say "yes."

"You are a remarkable woman, Cat, but short of a mutiny, the commander won't be able to give anything else without permission. But he is working on that." The Hummer rolled away.

Kalani watched from upstairs. "Well, we've dodged another; we should be OK for a few days. Maybe we'll make it until they send us something from Honolulu. Anyway, I hoped that they would arrest us all." She grinned and went back to her kids.

Two days later another military vehicle stopped in front of the house, and two young men in brown and beige fatigues jumped out. They hurriedly unloaded a few duffel bags, dumped them in the middle of the room and were ready to leave when Cat stopped them.

"Wait, wait—what's in the bags and who sent them?"

"That's from Major Stevens, Ma'm. He bought out the whole cafeteria and told us to bring it here. But we have to go . . ."

"Where is Major Stevens?"

"He's gone, Ma'm, and we have to go, too. Bye." And they were gone.

"Chocolate, chips, candies, fruit bars. . . . Kids will go ape," Kalani was digging through the bags.

"He spent his own money to get this stuff for us." Cat was gazing into space. "Good, decent man. And yet, tell me, Kalani, why would an intelligent, honest person voluntarily give up his free will and his own judgment to anyone higher up? I don't know about you, but to me, to accept orders without questioning them is a fallback to slavery; and it's immoral, especially if you're in the business of killing people."

"Well, when you're in the military, you do what they tell you," Kalani shrugged.

"That's why I think you'd have to be either brain-dead, in which case you need to be told what to do, or be immoral, then it makes no difference to you what you do. Gary Stevens is none of the above."

"Cat, I need to hide these bags before Ashley comes back with the children. Can we put them in your room? It's just like the night after Halloween. My mother always hid our loot bags, and we would find treats only from time to time. We felt she was robbing us!" The duffel bags went under Cat's bed.

CHAPTER 21

We've got a radio conference with the Governor, tomorrow, eight o'clock. You need to come to the station," Yoshida looked around. The usual crowd: Cat, Kalani, Lee Kurohara, Carol, Dr. Lim and a few others who would occasionally come if they had business to attend to. This was not a democratically elected government of Kailua, rather people who took the responsibilities because nobody else wanted them. Some were town employees, like Lee. Carol was a career politician and some, like Cat and Kalani, were citizens so private that hardly anybody knew them until a week ago.

"Someone needs to speak for us; the Governor prefers an elected official. I guess that would be you, Carol? You are here frequently enough to know our problems." The sergeant looked at her with a query.

"That's fine, I'll be glad to if everyone agrees." Nobody objected and the meeting moved on to the next item.

"Good news," a large man with a braid of thin, gray hair announced. "We've fixed our radio transmitter so KLBY can go back on the air. Obviously, we have no power and have to rely on a generator, so we'll broadcast only as long as someone gives us a few gallons of gas."

"That's terrific!" Carol almost clapped her hands. "People need local information almost as badly as food. We have a new panic every day, and there is no way to respond. Yesterday, there was the story of rats attacking sleeping children, but we had no such reports from the Emergency Room. Today, I heard that water collected from the roofs was contaminated with radioactive fallout. Where this fallout would be coming from and who spreads these lies, I have no idea, but people are ready to believe anything now. Someone should give a daily, short service of local news."

Nobody moved. A few long seconds later Cat sighed, "OK, I'll do it." And so Cat became the voice of the lost world of Kailua. Every morning at 10 o'clock, after dealing with the first round of problems that had accumulated overnight, she would ride towards a small building a few blocks away, which housed KLBY, the local radio station.

The sun-filled streets felt like a different world after she emerged from the cavernous hall of the Round House. Broken pavement and collapsed houses did not heal, but Nature was not holding off. New grass and weeds grew boldly out of the cracks and bougainvilleas assertively displayed huge red and purple bunches of flowers, taking advantage of the rainy season. A thin black cat jumped out of a bush, hoping for a handout. Things just go on, Cat thought, trying to get her wheelchair over a foot-wide break in the asphalt. Whatever happens to you, it happens just to you. Everything and everybody minds their own business—animals, plants, and as far as people go . . . some care, but only if they are very close to each other.

"Friends, this is your neighbor Cat speaking. I used to

live by the canal, in Kaimalino." She went on with a long list of reports about water, prospects for getting fuel, diseases seen at the Emergency Room. She shared what she knew about orphaned children, about hunger—a lengthy list of evils that had been forgotten during the fat years of prosperity, but re-emerged when the cataclysm hit. "And, since it is Friday today, I'd like to beseech you not to commit the sin of gluttony."

A wave of belly laughter and giggling rolled over the island. That's too much, too rich—overeating in Hawaii was certainly not a problem in January 2007. People needed a joke to release the tension, frustration and pain of the last days; they loved the person who gave it to them.

A group of Kailua citizens squeezed into the Police Department's lunchroom next morning; the speaker—crudely patched from the communications center—whistled somewhat, but the governor aide's voice came in clearly. After a brief exchange of greetings, it said, "Please stand by for the Governor." Carol shifted in her chair and brought the microphone closer to her lips.

"Good morning, everyone, this is Nancy Brown," the Governor spoke with the confidence of authority, her voice rich in low, warm, reassuring tones. "I am so glad that we, at last, have an opportunity to talk and share our experiences during these trying times. It is terrible that the windward side of Oahu is cut off from Honolulu so completely. We are very worried about you. Can you please give me a short assessment of your situation?"

"Good morning, Madame Governor," started Carol in a smooth, nicely modulated voice. "Thank you so much for taking the time to speak with us. We know how busy you must be. These terrible events, both the natural calamities and geo-political challenges that our country has to meet, call for the utmost in our resolve and courage. We are certainly trying to cope."

Cat and Yoshida exchanged stupefied glances; Kalani leaned to the next person at the table and quietly whispered something.

"Yes, yes," said the Governor, "I am so glad that you understand the enormous difficulty of our position. Our resources are hardly sufficient for the population of Honolulu alone, and the relief effort from the federal government is seriously hampered by military activities in the Middle East. By the way, whom am I talking to?"

"Oh, this is Carol Nakamoto . . . I'm sorry I didn't introduce myself. My apologies . . . " Carol was smiling her best smile and almost giggled.

"What the hell are you talking about?" Cat's shrill and unrestrained voice cut into the very civil conversation like a horsewhip. She snatched the microphone from the hands of shocked Carol. "Governor! We came to this conversation to find out how you can help us. We have been left to ourselves for a week. We are completely out of food now; there are no emergency supplies here. We are almost completely out of fuel, even to run generators for the hospital and the police station. We have no medical supplies; people are dying every day from simple infections. *What are you going to do about it?* We cannot cope by ourselves any more!"

The silence on the air stretched for many seconds before a question came. "Who is this?"

"My name is Cat Milewski. I coordinate most of the work we're doing in Kailua. And what's the importance of my name? I would like to know why we haven't received any emergency supplies yet. I know that the roads are closed, but how about airdrops? How about supplies by boat? To the best of my knowledge, the sky didn't fall and Kailua Beach is still open!"

Brown recovered somewhat, and answered in a stern but not unfriendly voice, "Cat, I understand that you are desperate, but so are we. I don't have any helicopters or transport planes at my disposal, and we are running on the last drops of fuel ourselves. We do have some food reserves, but I also have close to a million people to feed. The truth is, I cannot promise you any significant relief."

"How about the National Guard, aren't they supposed to help in these circumstances? How about the military? We see them flying over our heads, wasting fuel. What's with the federal government, the rest of the country? A week is not enough to send some help?"

"The National Guard had been committed somewhere else. The military cannot provide any assistance because of the Middle East events. I can assure you that the helicopters that you see flying do so for very good reasons. We do receive some relief from the federal government, but the port facilities are mostly ruined."

"Does that mean that you are going to leave us here to die because our government is too busy? That we keep all these military bases in Hawaii for someone else's benefit? Hell, what's the use of being a part of the glorious Union—

maybe we should start looking for new tenants for Pearl Harbor!"

"Cat, you are talking treason now. I suggest that you calm down and give the microphone back to Carol!" The voice was cold, containing an unveiled threat.

"Just one more thing, Governor! I want you and your buddies in Washington to know that some of us *will* survive, and this conversation will be remembered. If you abandon us now, don't expect our loyalty in the future. We are not traitors; you are! Our loyalty will be to our families and neighbors, people who helped us as we helped them. Today, we've found out that promises you made are empty. You can go to hell!"

Cat threw the microphone on Carol's lap, backed away from the table and wheeled out, followed by Kalani.

New York Times: Cat to Governor, "Go to Hell!"

International Tribune: "Hawaii to U.S.—Traitors"

London Times: "Your promises are empty, our loyalty is not for you."

Conversation secretly recorded in a Washington restaurant:

Voice 1: *The whole conversation was over open airways. Anybody with a scanner could hear and record it. And, believe me, there are a lot of scanners in and around Hawaii. Reuters made the transcripts available through their feeds within two hours. I'm sure there were transcripts with TOP SECRET stamped all over them on some very important desks within a few hours.*

Voice 2: *So what can they do about it?*

Voice 1: *Basically, two choices—either have this Cat person arrested, and hide her under a rug or make her a Very Important Person in a Very Important Government Office.*

Voice 2: *They can't hide her now; she is already a celebrity. That would cause an unending open season on the Prez. She would come up at every press conference.*

Voice 1: *Then she has to be promoted until she shuts her face up.*

CHAPTER 22

B y dawn, they were about forty miles off the coast of California. They both had very little sleep during the past couple of days, but John was happy and wide wake. The old buzzard felt like singing. He turned on the wind vane, a wind-driven autopilot, and the gizmo was doing all the steering. The skipper went down to make coffee and eggs for breakfast, humming and banging rhythmically on the stove.

"What's with you, John? Are you on drugs now? I didn't know you were such a happy-go-lucky devil." Jerry, on the other hand, felt queasy and the smell of fried eggs coming from below made him turn his head away.

"Ho, ho, there is no happier moment for a sailor than the first morning on the sea. Well, perhaps, except for the first morning after landfall. Are you feeling sick, Jerry?"

"Maybe not exactly sick, but I surely don't feel like eating anything, least of all the greasy eggs you've made. I forgot to take Dramamine."

"I have news for you, my boy. You'll get worse if we pick up more wind, then you will get better. And forget all this Dramamine nonsense. Do you know that Admiral Nelson got seasick every time they left port? Nobody saw him on the deck first day, probably puking in his cabin. And look how well he did afterwards! As for Dramamine, it's good for nothing. Maybe if you were on a cruise ship, but even then you would have to be careful with booze, so what's the point? On a boat like ours, you can get drowsy, fall overboard and that's the end of your trip. Better get used to it. But you have to eat, very important . . . "

Jerry waved his eggs away, but had some black coffee and felt marginally better. The skipper was right; two days later Jerry was his former self and John started the sailing instructions. Points of sailing, tack, jibe—Jerry had no problem with basic concepts, but then the captain introduced an unending string of hypothetical situations that required decision making. He had a personal anecdote for all of them, apparently lived through a thousand close calls to be eventually grounded by the Men in Black. Jerry cleaned the fuel filter, tied knots and trimmed the sails, feeling like a young cadet on a man o' war. The skipper kept annoying him with his attachment to the old technologies. With two GPS receivers on board, Jerry had to take sextant readings every time the sun showed its face.

"Do you have any guarantee the GPS will be on the next time you want to check your position? What if some space junk blows the satellites off? What if the US government decides to turn them off, just to piss off the Iranians? What . . ."

"What if we get struck by a meteorite, John?" Jerry interrupted, annoyed because his measurements indicated their position was off the coast of Oregon.

The old man looked at the figures and remarked

snidely, "Good progress, my boy. Yesterday, I was concerned about the shoals off Alaska. Now, we—I mean you—have to check if the wind vane works properly."

"I know, Skipper, you can't fuck with the ocean."

"Right on."

They had been doing about a hundred and thirty miles a day for the past three days and considered themselves lucky, as the winds were blowing steadily at twenty knots and they had only transient rains. That was about to change. The barometer kept falling and gusts of wind increasingly pressed the boat on its side, causing the books Jerry left on the table to fall off. They were moving into a low-pressure system.

The storm came at night, during Jerry's watch. The wind singing in the shrouds became louder, and big waves kept coming from the darkness like black mountains, visible only a moment before slamming the boat. *Lady Luck* started heeling excessively, her railing disappearing under the waves momentarily. They plowed through the water, leaving behind a wake like a motorboat. Jerry yelled for John to wake up, and moments later the old man climbed on deck wearing his yellow rough-weather suit and a fisherman's hat.

"Fuck, we're carrying too much sail. You should have woken me up a long time ago. We have to take down the jib."

"OK, Skipper," Jerry started scrambling out of the cockpit.

ALEX Z. MODZELEWSKI

"Get down here and hold the wheel; I'll do it." The yellow-clad figure impatiently waved at Jerry. Waves that seemed taller than the mast kept coming every six or eight seconds, breaking on the hull and flooding the board. The boat shuddered and vibrated as though she was falling apart. The jib had to be taken down or they might capsize.

Water hissed like a boiling pot of water, as the deck was tilting up steeply, and patches of foam flew through the air—a trip to the bow would be risky for anyone, more so for the old man. "John I'll . . ."

"Just shut up, and hold the wheel! It's no time . . ."

"I know, . . . fuck with the ocean," Jerry muttered.

Overruled by the skipper, he watched through sheets of rain as the yellow figure crawled along the railing, and then lurched to get a grip on the mast. Once John undid the halyard, the big white sheet of stiff fabric came down and instantly blew over the railing. The deck's tilt decreased immediately. John fought the rebellious sail for ten minutes, until he wrestled it down completely and tied it to the railing. Then he inched his way back, and slid into the cockpit. He was smiling widely. "That's the life for us, Jerry, isn't it?"

Jerry looked at him with a newly found respect. This was no fragile old-timer at sea; he was Captain Hook. The boat still heeled, but the railing stayed above the water. Winds diminished at dawn, and only then could Jerry appreciate the ocean's condition. *Lady Luck* was surrounded by thousands of big waves, all crowned with angry-looking white caps. Streaks of water mixing with air flew with the wind, and the surface between waves was marked by long patterns of low wrinkles whipped up by the gusts.

"What do you think the wind speed is?" The meter had quit working on the second day at sea.

"Forty knots maybe," answered John without much excitement.

"What do we do if the wind picks up to fifty knots?" Jerry wanted to know.

"We'd drop all the sails and deploy a sea anchor."

"And what if it's even stronger?"

"Then, Jerry, we could start 'Hail Mary', or open this Tequila bottle that you bought. I'm for the bottle."

Though still windy, the rest of the day was nice, an opportunity to dry their wet clothes. Fortunately, it was getting warmer, and the winds stabilized at twenty knots; they had entered the trade winds zone.

* * *

AP: *A Panama-flagged tanker carrying 80,000 tons of crude oil has been attacked with a land-to-ship missile in the Straits of Hormuz and sunk. The crew of 21 is missing.*

Reuters: *U.S. ships attacked Iranian coastal missile installations with cruise missiles and carrier-based warplanes. The installations have been completely destroyed.*

Once at sea, there was no question who the boss was, but John treated the younger man more like his son than a crewmember or even an employer. He never missed an opportunity to teach Jerry something about sailing. The stinking smoke of his cigarettes was kept outside of the cabin, even if it rained, and beer flowed at a rate that ensured a happy combination of a good mood and an alert mind. The man had visited every rotten hole on the planet, as long as it had a harbor. "But at the end," he concluded, "they are all alike. Your crew gets drunk, all that local women want is your money and the police treat you like shit. You are really better off out there at sea, but then, after a week or two, you want to see the land anyway."

"John, I have a confession to make...." Jerry felt distinctly uncomfortable holding back revelations of his past. "The Men in Black—for a short while in my life I was their colleague, only I was wearing a uniform."

The skipper looked at Jerry without a smile, "You know, I had this feeling when we first met, and you said you didn't work for the government." John looked at the younger man sharply, with no hint of good humor.

"I didn't lie," Jerry met his eyes. "I was indeed with the university for over ten years. But before that, I had a stint with Army intelligence, which ended in a rather unpleasant way. So, you might say I was a failure as a Man in Black, or if you prefer, a spook redeemed."

"Tell me about it, Jerry." John relaxed somewhat, pulled a cigarette out of a box. "I would like to hear about the failed spook. Ah, sit on the starboard bench; you should have the sun shining in your eyes," he smiled slightly.

"I wasn't even twenty and was green as a cucumber when I signed up with the Army. They decided I could be better used collecting information rather than blasting enemies to hell." Jerry accepted the offer of beer and they both gulped in silence. "You realize that every army needs to collect information. So that's what I was trained to do."

John watched Jerry keenly, without interruptions.

"People think you basically beat information out of the prisoners, and I am not saying that it never happens, though I was never a part of it. But what you can squeeze from your captive in that way is really very limited, simple information: an address, a name, a phone number—yes, but those things change very rapidly and your information becomes worthless. What you really need is to get your subject to cooperate, to volunteer more permanent and meaningful information. In a sense, you want him to help you for reasons of his own. If he believes that your success is to his advantage, you got yourself a well that never dries up. Even if he has really nothing more to tell, he can still help you understand scraps of info that you get from other sources. The art of interrogation lies in giving him these reasons."

"Sounds pretty benign so far," John remarked, "almost hard to believe."

"Well, it's not benign, John. It's easy with common criminals; public prosecutors cut deals of this nature all the time. It's a completely different story with extremists, terrorists, rebels and whomever else the army needs to deal with. Those are committed people; they actually believe in their causes. No matter how mistaken they are, they are strong believers, otherwise they wouldn't be there in the first place."

John nodded as he raised his hand to stop Jerry, then he turned a winch to adjust the main sail, which had started wrinkling and fluttering. "You were saying . . ."

" I was saying that in order to bring these people over to your side, you have to destroy their beliefs, honor and self respect. You have to kill their soul. It can be done, not always, but even an occasional success is a big breakthrough. They are exposed to relentless pressure, anxiety, fear and sleep deprivation until they crack and turn into stinky, shaking goo, whose only desire is to be left alone. Once they start talking, they have no way back. Their every attempt to resist is countered by the threat that their earlier deeds of cooperation could be leaked to those who were their former comrades."

"*A soul killer*, congratulations, Jerry. You better tell me how you failed in your work or I might be tempted to take the dinghy and go my own way."

"The problem with this business, John, is that soul killing is a very dangerous job. Every time the screw tightens on your client, it does something strange to you, too. In effect, it kills you both—at least—if you were a normal person to start with. There are people who seem to be particularly well suited for this line of work, but you wouldn't like them in your preferred circle of friends. In fact, some of them like this work so much that they get kicked out on grounds of committing torture crimes. My unit had a guy who deserted some years ago in Panama the day the investigation had been launched into his methods. More often the interrogators just break down, like I did."

"I'm glad to hear you broke down, Jerry." John's eyes

lost their hard look. "How did you get out of this mess?"

"We were in Somalia. I had inherited a turncoat Arab, who used to be an officer with insurgents, a tall, handsome man who had started giving some valuable insights a few weeks earlier. His handler had to be sent home and I'd gotten the guy. I did a terrible thing, John; I developed some sympathy for him. This man bounced back from the bottom and started having second thoughts—not very coherent, he was anything but a rational human being, but he knew that his only escape from the nightmare was to die. My job was to put a jackhammer to this newly found self-respect and remorse. I tried, John, and I failed miserably. His chance to go back to his previous life had been irrevocably annihilated by his treason, but he begged for the opportunity just to stop his existence."

"What did you do, Jerry?" The skipper held his breath.

"I couldn't let him go, I couldn't let him touch my weapon, the only thing I could do for him was to shoot him myself. That day, he knew I was going to kill him; he looked into my eyes with deep gratitude, love almost. Well, I failed even at that. The interpreter who was in the room knocked me down the moment I reached for my side arm. Apparently, Captain Murphy, my commander, had some suspicions about me, and ordered the interpreter to knock me on the head the moment I might reach for my weapon."

"And they let you get away with it?" John clearly was not convinced.

"Well, just lucky coincidence," Jerry shrugged. "I was under arrest, awaiting my superior's decision what to do with me. You know, court martial or whatever he might come up with, and he was not a nice man. No belt, no shoelaces—standard procedure. Then, the commanding general appeared suddenly for an unannounced inspection. When I heard the general was visiting, I thought he might want to see the rotten bottom of the barrel as well, the miscreants under arrest. You have to understand, John, I was pretty crazy then, just a notch above my Somali. I had no hopes for a normal life. Heck, I'd lost the concept of normal life, living there at the edge of the desert—sleeping, interrogating, writing reports and getting drunk so I could sleep.

"No laces—no shoes, no belt—no pants, I thought. When the general entered my cell I was standing at attention in my jacket and nothing else. The old man looked at me for a moment, said nothing to me, then turned to Murphy who was standing behind him. 'I see why your reports read like someone crazy wrote them, Murphy. I want this man sent back home immediately'."

"So they just sent you back to the U.S.?"

"I was on a plane next day, but that was certainly not the end of it. The shrink on the base talked to me a few times and, eventually, I got discharged on the grounds of being unfit to serve. I did exaggerate my mental problems a bit, of course. But the fact was, John, that I was really screwed up big time."

"I can't blame you," John shrugged. " I'd be disappointed if you weren't."

"The shrink wrote a report that got me off the hook. He said that I had a psychopathic trait, and had the emotional capacity of a brick wall, although I was quite normal until my overseas adventure. Whatever. It did the trick; they discharged me. I think that Murphy wanted to get rid of me with minimal damage to his career, and added his own little insight about my mental fitness."

"So what happened next?" John was fascinated, like he was watching a spy movie. "Did you go back to your family, your old place?"

" I tried, John, but it didn't work out. I felt that my father had given me bad advice that screwed up my life. I still do, though I realize he meant well. I agreed with the psychiatrist that in my new occupation I should stay away from the public as much as I could. I had lost the ability to treat people as persons. We had been trained to see humans as objects, to be intimidated, manipulated and exploited. I hated this new personality of mine, but couldn't shake it off. I was a very lonely man after the discharge. Even women—they wanted me, a lot, but my turnover was mind-boggling. They often didn't understand what the problem was; there was a lot of crying, but in the end nobody could connect with me. In a way I *was* a brick wall; no roots could penetrate beneath the stucco. It was worse with men: I had these attacks of aggression, was close to killing a few guys over really minor stuff."

"And you say you were a professor, you taught kids?" John turned his head, amazed.

"The army knows how to keep their secrets, John. I don't think my professor ever got his hands on my medical file. In any case, I enrolled into Economics, and found out that I could find peace working in front of the computer monitor. I breezed through my undergrad years and did a Ph.D. in econometrics. I was good at it and had more time on my hands than other guys. You see, I knew all the buttons that needed to be pushed to get sex, and I didn't want or need anything else from the girls. So, I spent a lot of nights at the library, while my fellow postgraduates entertained their girlfriends. Not that it made me happy, but I've learned it just didn't matter. I was simply not interested in them as people, and they would figure that out sooner rather than later."

"So what the hell are we doing here, in the middle of the Pacific?" John demanded. "I thought you were a puppy in love. Now what, a squid in love?" He was perplexed and growing impatient.

"A miracle happened, John." Jerry took his sunglasses off. "I've met a girl in Hawaii who simply tugged on my old, stiff, uncomfortable hide and it fell off, like a snake shedding its skin."

"Hallelujah! I hoped there would be a happy end to this story, Jerry." The skipper went downstairs to bring up a new beer pack.

* * *

Reuters: *In view of oil delivery interruption, prices of crude rapidly rose to 112 dollars a barrel today. The Department of Energy announced that strategic reserves are being mobilized to counteract any shortages.*

John was not optimistic about Hawaii; he did not hold humankind in high esteem. "People look after themselves, Jerry. When there is a lot of food and the weather is fine, you can see a lot of nice folks, charity and so on. Take food away or a disaster of some sort strikes—then watch out. There are no nice folks any more, just crowds of guys ready to steal your last piece of bread or kill you for it. I saw it in Ethiopia, saw it in Sudan, I am sure you saw it in Somalia. I don't think we would be any different in the U.S. It's just that nobody was really hungry in America for a long time, so we forgot how it feels. We better be very careful when we get to Hawaii. A boat like this, with supplies, would be a great target for anyone who can get to her."

On the morning of the thirteenth day after departure from San Diego, a mountain appeared on the horizon. "Mauna Kea on the Big Island, or maybe Haleakala on Maui," declared the skipper. John had been to the Big Island a few times when he worked on a cruise ship. They were still not getting any Hawaii radio stations, but picked up scraps of conversations that sounded like a police or fire department.

"If you want to see a place where people get along fairly well, and the skin color or shape of a face are not that important, this is it. You'll see it tomorrow. That's how God meant for people to behave."

This piqued Jerry's interest because, as a New Yorker, he always believed that the Big Apple was a model (maybe an imperfect one) of interracial integration. Wave after wave of immigrants speaking hundreds of languages descended on the city and somehow sank into its big body, although they differed in appearance, just as much as Collies and Dobermans.

John just waved his hand dismissively. "That's your

upper-middle class experience talking, Jerry. Yes, if you have enough money, you can have nice black or brown or yellow neighbors in your expensive condominium, who also have some serious moollah. But if you were challenged in the cash department, you would find out that your waves of immigrants didn't peacefully dissolve into the big body. I like your metaphor though; New York is like a big, fat whore, and you can sink in and get lost in her. Africans, Mexicans, Puerto Ricans, they all stick to their own and hate all others. Even small nations—take El Salvadorians— make their own gangs and try to beat the brains out of the other guys. No, Jerry, there is no brotherly love and understanding on the streets of New York, perhaps except at a few addresses where folks like you live."

A large mountain appeared on the portside, black at the top, turning to green in its lower portion, with a yellow and brown transition zone. Jet-black rivers of frozen lava cut deep into the green slopes as the red sun was diving behind the volcano's western slope.

The skipper was back to his musings on racial integration in Hawaii. "Hilo is a completely different story. There is no big money there; heck—there isn't much medium-size money there. So these guys cannot buy a cocoon around them. Maybe there are some gated communities there, but I've never heard of any. They actually learned to tolerate each other. Sure, they aren't blind—they can see your skin color and know which way your eyes are slanting. They tease each other, but where it counts, they don't seem to care much for all these superficial differences. Tomorrow in Hilo, you'll see so many interracial couples you'll believe me. Youngsters try to get into each other's pants, no matter what the color of the ass is, and then they have kids.

Let me tell you, Jerry, you can't hate your grandchildren. In fact, most of them on the islands are so racially mixed up that you could never guess what's in the mix. They say this attitude goes back to ancient Hawaiians, a spirit of Aloha. I believe them because I've never seen anything like it anywhere else."

According to the pilot book, Hilo had a large harbor protected by a reef and a wave break. The skipper planned to stop there to find out what the situation in the islands was. By the time they approached the harbor's entrance, the sun was down. The sky was overcast and the night was dark. They could not see any buoys marking the course. Not willing to risk the boat, John guided *Lady Luck,* crawling inch-by-inch just behind the head of the breaker, while Jerry continuously read the depth gauge.

"That's good enough, we're protected from the wind and waves. We'll sleep now. At daybreak, we'll sail to the harbor office and find out about Oahu." They opened a bottle of Tequila, the first one of the passage, raised a toast to Neptune and went to sleep.

CHAPTER 23

Reuters: *A Chinese Navy battle group has left the mainland and is steaming towards Taiwan. The U.S. State Department has requested an urgent meeting with the Chinese ambassador. Highly placed officials in Beijing insist that their Navy has started routine exercises scheduled over six months ago.*

Harry Rosen sat in his restaurant with all the doors locked. The windows were broken, but they wouldn't be any obstacle to looters anyway. That's why he was sitting there, his gun on the table beside him. The building had been mostly spared, except for broken glass covering the floor. Rosen found it useful, though—no one could sneak by him without a lot of crunching noise.

He was tired from lack of sleep, but otherwise quite comfortable. The restaurant storage room was full of canned goods so even though the refrigerated food had spoiled, he did not fear hunger. The thought of selling food for a very nice profit occurred to him for a moment, but he realized that it would bring crowds to his door, impossible to control. Better wait. For now, survival is all that counts. He fell asleep sitting in a comfortable armchair in a dark corner, away from the window.

A piece of glass broke under someone's foot, and even

before Rosen's eyes opened, his right hand closed on the gun's handle. A slim figure was standing just inside the window. The thief stood motionless, frightened by the crack of glass. Rosen grinned slightly; that must be the fifth today. He would see the intruder flying through the broken window in a second. The figure turned sideways, and the silhouette of female breasts came into view. Rosen held his breath. A situation you wait for eventually happens, and when it happens, you have to be prepared to grab it. He raised the gun and said sternly:

"Over here, come over here with your hands on your head." The startled intruder jumped, then came two steps closer with hands obediently placed on her head.

"Kalani! Are you a looter now?" Rosen was most amused—the situation was getting even better than he could have planned. He lowered the gun.

Kalani lowered her hands. "Mr. Rosen, it's not what you think. I take care of nine kids, and we're completely out of food. I though I might borrow some from you until we get relief."

"Borrow, eh? But Kalani, I'd be happy to share my food with you. I understand how difficult it must be to survive these days. Look, I have a lot of good stuff; it would be only fair if I gave some to you and your kids." Rosen put away the gun and opened his arms as though he was going to hug the girl.

"Oh, Mr. Rosen, you're such a wonderful man. God will bless you. We're in such a terrible situation, and you're like an angel sent to deliver us from starvation." She was ready to cry; that really did not fit into Harry's plans.

"Now, now, have courage. We must be strong. What I ask of you is that you help me take a load of food from here to my place first, and then you can take as much as you need. I have all kinds of cans, salami, cheese, Spam—things that will never go bad, even without a fridge."

Kalani was ready to start packing immediately, but Harry thought it prudent to wait until dark. The streets were mostly empty, but one never knew who was watching from behind dark windows. After sunset, with no streetlights working, they could move through the town like ghosts. There was enough time before curfew.

Rosen felt rising excitement and the warm, pleasant sensation in his pelvis. He felt confident; he certainly could wait for his plan to develop, to achieve the high standards dictated by his imagination. It would be the feast he had waited for a long time; a bit of delay would just help his appetite.

"Come on, Kalani, we're not going to do all this heavy hauling hungry. Let's have a little supper before we go." He opened a big can of ham, slowly cut thin slices of bread and buttered them carefully while Kalani watched, swallowing saliva. Rosen placed thick slices of ham on the bread, slowly cut thin wedges of pickle and pushed the sandwich towards her; "There you go." She swallowed it in five seconds, hardly chewing. Harry watched her with a smile. She had lost a lot of weight; now she looked more and more like Consuela. The same big, black eyes, thin waist, still with nice hips.

"Would you like another one, dear?"

"Yes, please." He enjoyed the hungry expression in her

eyes watching his every move.

She'll be a gem, a gem I'll polish to perfection. Rosen taunted Kalani, creating the second sandwich even more slowly before allowing her to snap it up. He was enjoying the game already. Little appetizers before the main course, he thought, already feeling the delicious power of being the Master.

After dark, they packed a big suitcase on wheels and a rolling duffel bag, in addition to two backpacks. "That's going to be quite a trip up to my house," he sighed. Kalani was a bit anxious about getting home late, but the prospect of bringing all these supplies she saw in the storeroom made her feel very, very happy.

It took an hour trudging through empty, dark streets just to get to the bottom of the hill on which Rosen's house stood. Cracked pavement and large holes made pulling their luggage exhausting. Thirty minutes later, they went through the heavy entrance doors of Rosen's residence, and he locked them securely.

"You can leave the bags here, in the kitchen, but come with me upstairs. I'd like to give you something for the kids," Rosen said, after they stopped panting. He let her walk in front of him in a gentlemanly fashion, directed her into his bedroom and lit a kerosene lamp. Rosen led Kalani towards his bed, pretending there was something in the nightstand that would be his gift. When she stopped in front of the bed, a forceful shove threw her forwards. The girl stretched her arms instinctively in front to protect her face as Rosen jumped at her back and slammed the handcuffs on her wrists with the expertise acquired by the thousands of dry runs he had lived through, waiting for this moment.

That's it. She's my property. There's nothing that she can do! Rosen was triumphant. It had been even easier than in his daydreams. He skillfully clipped the handcuffs to a chain that ran through a block over the bed and pulled it tight. Kalani was sitting now with her arms stretched up and terror in her eyes. She did not scream or talk, just her breathing increased to a fast whine. Rosen looked into her fear-crazed eyes, listened to her high-pitched whimpers while he sat comfortably in the armchair by the bed. Consuela had had the same wild expression when he was taking her to the courtyard. But this time he was no longer Bonito, an instrument of the Master. He *was* the Master.

That's how intelligence, courage, diligence and patience bring dreams to fruition, he congratulated himself. The timing was perfect; the whole town was in disarray. Nobody had any idea that she might be in his house; no one would come here disturbing him. He had ample supplies of food, and he could stay at home for many days, living his daydreams and enjoying the fruits of his clever scheme.

He picked up his black crop with the ivory handle, looked at her fear for a moment with great satisfaction and started the introduction."From now on you are my slave, Kalani, and I am your master. You don't understand this relationship yet, how could you? You've never been instructed. But I will spare no effort to educate you." He slowly brushed her face and neck with the crop. She retreated with terror.

"This is a tool. I like to use it, but it's only a tool. The goal is for you to submit the last little bit of your free will to me. You will do what I tell you; you will guess what I would like you to do, without questioning, without any resistance. And it will make you happy. It will take us a long time and a lot of discipline to get there, but I am more than willing to contribute. Are you, my little darling?"

Kalani's body, suspended at the end of the chain, trembled; she closed her eyes and did not answer.

"Well, you refuse to answer. Disobedience in the very first moment of our relationship! We'll try to remedy that right away." He released the chain and her hands fell down. Rosen pushed the girl on her face, put his knee across her shoulder blades and raised the crop. A loud swish was followed by a thud as the blade cut across her buttocks covered with thin fabric. Kalani screamed, and her body tensed, only to fall limp a moment later.

Rosen controlled his desire to see the effects of the whip on her skin. The time will come; I will proceed slowly, enjoying every moment, he persuaded himself. For now, he was giving instructions, speaking slowly like a teacher to a dim-witted student. "That was just to get your attention. I am going to let you up, and you will undress and put your clothes neatly on the side. Then you'll have a good look at my sculpture, and you'll assume a position exactly like hers. You'll remain in this position until I tell you otherwise. Her name is Anaïd; she is your role model. Learn from her and that may spare you a lot of pain. Now, get moving."

He removed his knee from her back. Harry walked out of the room, leaving Kalani handcuffed, at the end of the long, loose chain. He watched her through the open door as

she moved slowly from the bed. Obviously, she was smart-
ing badly. "That must be quite a cut," he chuckled to himself. We'll see later.

Kalani slowly took off her clothes and put them neatly
away. She went up to Anaïd, studied her for a moment,
then kneeled on the floor with her hips raised and lowered
her face to the floor, somewhat turned to the left side. She
became motionless.

This girl is a canvas worthy of the great masters,
thought Rosen, watching the naked girl on the floor with
admiration. Let's have her wait for me a bit and contem-
plate her situation. Harry Rosen went to the kitchen to
make himself a roast beef sandwich, richly garnished with
lettuce, pickles and baby artichokes. After a moment of de-
liberation, he added a few slices of Swiss cheese and a
small red paprika. Perfect. He chewed slowly and washed
the food down with a glass of Castillo del Diablo. Not a
bad wine by itself, he thought, but he really got his kicks
from its name. Then he went slowly upstairs to continue the
first lesson of submission.

He was pleased when he entered the room. Kalani knelt
with her face to the floor, without movement, exactly like
Anaïd. He looked at the sculpture, then again at Kalani.
Well, Monsieur Rodin, or shall I call you Auguste? I like
my creation even better than yours, he chortled with delight. He was exuberant. Even from the doorway, he could
see a bright red line crossing the tops of both buttocks.
What a beautiful start for the piece of fine art I am going to
create today; he felt inspired.

Rosen came closer and Kalani raised her hips in a gesture of sexual offering that any male mammal would understand. Just like Consuela, only you figured it out faster, he thought, amused. But he himself had learned quite a bit since then. He put his right hand on the girl's arched back, and slowly moved it into the crease between her buttocks, following it down and forward. Little cheat, he chuckled. She was not aroused at all. That didn't bother him. It was not her pleasure that he sought. In fact, he figured out years ago, had she enjoyed whipping, what would be the point of it? The slave should be scared out of her mind, again and again, until she lost any mental resistance. Only then could she be considered a real slave, and this, certainly, wouldn't happen overnight.

Rosen squeezed the buttock hard until the skin became pale, except for the red line of the whip mark. She did not move, which annoyed him slightly. It was supposed to hurt! He desired to see pain in her eyes. Harry walked to the front, grabbed her black hair close to the scalp and harshly raised her head. Kalani's dark and large eyes were not filled with the fear he expected; they oozed hatred. He appreciated the fact too late. Two hands, joined together and wrapped with the metal chain, shot from below and hit him in the middle of his face. His head bounced back and his eyes filled with tears, which almost blinded him. A second later another blow came, to his right temple, then, before he fell, yet another on top of his head. He fell, still conscious, but pretending to be knocked out. Rosen liked to beat but had no taste for being beaten. He felt a hand searching his pockets and finding the key to the handcuffs. A moment later, Kalani grabbed her clothes and was flying down a steep, dark road to Kailua.

She ran into the Round House and stood panting in the

doorway. Cat was talking with Mike Yoshida, his deputy and a town manager. Leila and her crew were at the main table copying yet another proclamation. Abe dozed sitting on the floor with his back against the wall, waiting for Kalani. Everybody turned to the door and conversations stopped. Kalani was pale as a ghost, and her bare feet were bleeding.

"What happened to you"? Cat exclaimed.

"I was kidnapped . . ." and she related the events of the day.

Yoshida and his deputy looked on with strange expressions. "You don't believe me, do you? The crazy girl invented a story to get attention! Well, how about this?" Kalani turned around and lifted her dress for everyone to see the red line crossing her bottom. "You think I did it myself?" She was indignant and enraged.

Yoshida gave a whistle. "Sorry, Kalani, I've never seen anything like that. Have you, Ben?" He turned to his deputy. Ben had not. "This crazy bastard is going to kill someone; you were very lucky. No, it's not luck; you were too damn gutsy for him. In any case, I don't think you killed him. We better pick him up before he has a chance to do more... to you or someone else. Knowing that his cover is blown, he won't hold back now."

"He has a gun; you better take someone else with you." Kalani looked around. "Where's Abe? He was sitting here a moment ago." Abe was gone. "He went to kill Rosen, and Rosen has a gun! He's going to shoot Abe . . . " Now Kalani started crying. "Mike, please hurry! Help him!"

The policemen ran out. When they reached Rosen's house twenty minutes later, Abe was sitting on the stairs. "He's gone, just a pool of blood left in the bedroom. The bastard ran away, but he won't run for long. I'll finish what Kalani started."

CHAPTER 24

A quiet, rhythmic banging penetrated the thick cover of unconsciousness and Jerry opened his eyes. The cabin was dark as the sun was not up yet, but the black of night was changing into gray light of dawn. He climbed the companionway and, sticking his head above the deck, noticed a long blue outrigger gently bouncing at the starboard side. So, that's what's banging; we have company, he thought. Suddenly, a hand clasped his mouth and a sharp metallic object firmly nudged into his neck. Jerry shuddered in panic; the hand pressed his head against a muscular chest and the pressure on his neck increased.

"Don't move or you die," he heard a whisper and stopped struggling. His captor led him up the last few steps of the stairway, then to the aft end of the cockpit where he pushed Jerry onto the bench. Jerry noted two more men standing on the foredeck, not visible from the stairs. One was a young man, less than thirty, a tall and powerfully built individual with heavy arms and the big chest of a paddler. The other intruder, older by perhaps ten years, was short and wiry.

Seeing Jerry immobilized, they silently moved barefoot towards the cabin's entrance. Before they could look in, John's balding head appeared and, almost simultaneously, a fishing spear shot from the companionway striking the man holding a knife to Jerry's neck. The projectile slid under the raised left arm, and entered the prowler's chest. The knife fell, and the palm of the intruder's other hand slid from Jerry's mouth. The pirate stumbled backwards and crashed on the bench, the shaft of the metal spear jutting out five inches below his armpit. He burst into a spasm of violent coughing, spewing copious blood from his mouth.

The other two men jumped to the stairway. The skinny one reached it first, crashed into John, then they both went tumbling down the stairs. The second attacker could not get into the narrow space; he hesitated, waiting for the stairway to clear. He had just put both feet into the companionway, when Jerry leaped over the body flailing in the cockpit, and grabbed a boat hook that the skipper kept on deck. This was not a modern, light aluminum hook; John kept a six-foot-long, heavy wooden tool with a solid piece of hardware at the end. Jerry's big swing ended with the brass hitting just below the base of the invader's skull, crushing the neck. He crumpled like a rag doll and slid down the companionway, his head bouncing on the wooden steps.

Jerry dropped the boat hook and rushed down the stairs. There was little movement in the cabin, just soft groaning and gurgling sounds mixed with harsh respiration. The body of the intruder Jerry had hit rested on top of the pile, his head grotesquely twisted to the side. Jerry pulled him away by the belt, and saw John's face protruding from under the unconscious, older prowler. A jet of blood spurted rhythmically from the robber's neck wound, and a mass of pink froth swelled with his every breath.

The skipper's eyes were open and his lips moved a few

times, but made no sound. When Jerry pulled the insensible body of the intruder aside, a small puncture wound above Browser's left nipple came into view, discharging a thin stream of bright, red blood. His face paper-white, John tried to smile, squeezed Jerry's hand, moved his lips again, but a few seconds later his eyes rolled and his head drooped. He was dead. The gurgling behind Jerry was becoming less and less frequent and soon stopped.

Four men dead in the span of a minute; Jerry had lost a friend and a mentor. "Welcome to Paradise," an absurd thought came to his head.

He had to leave this place; his future on the Big Island held only promise of either jail or never-ending explanations. Neither was acceptable—his mission was to find Cat, and he would not allow anything to prevent that. The diesel started on the first crank. Jerry stepped on the winch button and weighed anchor. The grayness of the dawn was quickly changing into the bright light of a new day; he could clearly see the full length of the breakwater and the town of Hilo on the opposite side of the harbor. There were no boats on the water, but a few brightly colored outriggers set on the black beach. He still could not see a buoy, but the harbor's exit was obvious. Jerry engaged the motor and slowly moved out into the open ocean. He set course to the northwest, and turned on the autopilot.

John's death seemed so absurd that Jerry could barely absorb it. The old guy was snoring next to him only an hour ago, and then he was gone. He had been right again; human kind was not to be trusted. Hungry people do desperate things, except . . . the pirates did not look emaciated; they were well nourished— thriving among desperate people, at others' expense.

Jerry threw the intruders' bodies into the water some twenty miles off shore. The physical act of removing heavy bodies from the cabin through the narrow and steep companionway was a challenge. Eventually, he rigged a block and hoisted them one by one with a rope tied under their arms; three cadavers fell with big splashes overboard. Jerry watched them floating side by side surrounded by a cloud of blood. The boat moved fast and they disappeared among waves within two minutes. I hope sharks get you, he thought.

John was a slightly built man and could be carried up in Jerry's arms. He put the body on the blood-splattered cockpit bench, where the old man used to lounge with his newspaper. You kept your word, Skipper, he thought. You brought me to Hawaii. He watched over the body for a few minutes and let the truth sink in: John was no more. Jerry slipped the body gently overboard and did not look back.

Jerry washed pools of blood from the cabin floor and wiped the cockpit benches, then hoisted the sails, turned off the motor and engaged the wind vane. He was the captain and the crew now. There was nobody to give him a hand, offer advice or just keep him company. He graduated from the Skipper John's sailing school earlier than intended, but there was no way back.

Trade winds blew steadily, and a few hours later *Lady Luck* entered the Alenuihaha Channel, the body of water separating the Big Island from Maui. The channel, having a reputation for violent weather, was much feared by sailors, but for Jerry it produced just a fresh breeze. It gave the beginner a chance.

AP: *Nationwide, temporary rationing of fuel is in effect immediately. The Administration assures us that unrestricted supplies will resume shortly.*

Jerry dozed off in the cockpit, raising his head and checking the horizon every ten or fifteen minutes. He tried not to go into the cabin; the smell of blood hung in the air. At daybreak, the Koko Head volcano, and soon after that Diamond Head, came into view. He was within a couple hours of sailing into Honolulu. VHF radio was still silent. The regular stereo picked some music and transmissions in foreign languages. Eventually, he found English-language news. A real, shooting war in Iran, casualties in Iraq, movements of the Chinese Navy . . . nothing about Hawaii.

Jerry was almost shocked to see the lighthouse on Makapu'u Point flashing, and then there was a buoy off Diamond Head. Finally, someone was alive and doing his job! Jerry knew the Honolulu waterfront from land. He had never been a great fan of Waikiki, but walked the beat a few times. Now looking from the offshore perspective, the landmarks were difficult to identify. A line of white breakers clearly marked the reef; as long as he stayed well outside the surf, he should be safe.

A large pink hotel on the beach looked undamaged, not counting broken and blackened windows. The towers— reflecting the glory of a Hawaiian afternoon in their gold-colored glass when he was leaving—were still standing, but on this day of his return, they appeared like dead bodies in a horror movie, cadavers that had lost their skin. The acres of gleaming sheets were fractured and splintered, exposing big patches of gray, bleak flanks marred by irregular jagged holes, twisted metal and broken windows.

Finally, he got the Honolulu Coast Guard on Channel 16. "Wrecks are completely blocking the entrance to the Ala Wai Marina," he was told. The commercial Honolulu port was off limits, except by special permit, which he, certainly, would not obtain.

"How about Pearl Harbor?"

"I hope you are joking, sir."

"So, where can I go? I have been at sea for two weeks."

"Sir, your best bet is Keehi small boat harbor, which is only three miles west of the Ala Wai. You still have two hours of daylight, and you are strongly advised against attempting to enter the harbor at night. There are major navigational hazards right at the mouth of the channel."

"Do you think they'll have space available for me; can I call them?"

"There's no one to call there; the harbor master's office is gone, but I wouldn't be worried about berths. There are very few boats in Hawaii that have survived."

As *Lady Luck* continued along the south shore of Oahu, Jerry for the first time noted some human activity. He could see one yellow crane moving, a few others were twisted or broken in half. They must be unloading supplies; some emergency stuff has reached Hawaii, he thought with relief.

A large ship hung on the reef, listing towards the land

and immobile. A few hundred yards short of it, Jerry noticed a tangled mass of sunken boats, right at the mouth of the port channel. Bows and sterns protruding from the water, masts sticking out in all directions, the jam occupied the middle of the channel. Probably these were the boats that had been moored in the lagoon when the tsunami hit. Dislodged from their anchorage, they were overturned by the tsunami flooding the lagoon, then sucked out by the enormous current of water leaving the basin. Whatever was movable had been snatched by the gigantic vacuum cleaner only to be dumped in the deeper water. Jerry aimed into the narrow space between this menacing mass of projecting points and the brown reef covered with two feet of water. *Lady Luck* slowly passed the wreckage.

The lagoon turned out to be a large body of water that normally could be home to hundreds of small boats. Indeed, a lot of boats were moored there at one point; their wrecked bodies were now submerged, heaped one on top of another, forming patches of impenetrable thickets along the land side and smaller clumps of twisted plastic and metal on the reef side. Not a single boat looked usable. The harbor had returned to the state of wilderness, rimmed by a surrealistic jungle of steel, aluminum and fiberglass.

Since Hilo, Jerry was acutely aware of his precarious security situation. He knew that a working boat would be a great trophy for any gang, both for its supplies and the craft itself. He could not defend it. He had to sleep and had to go ashore in order to look for Cat. *Lady Luck* had to be hidden.

Jerry motored slowly along the convoluted outer rim of the lagoon. He passed coves overgrown with mangrove trees and deep blue channels cutting into the reef's brown

body. Finally, he came upon a tangle of three boats blocking access to the narrow but clear channel leading into a
mangrove-lined dead end. There seemed to be twelve feet
of space between the keel of the dead boat resting on its
side and the branches.

He let his yacht touch the submerged boat, stopped the
motor and jumped on the wreck with a bowline in his hand.
For the next few hours, he pulled, pushed and cajoled *Lady
Luck* into the cove in order to hide her behind the mass of
overturned hulls. The wrecks were already stripped of their
ropes, instruments and anything that held any value. The
looters considered this area already done with, he hoped.
Eventually, he was hidden from the world and felt almost
safe. The cabin still smelled of blood, so he dropped exhausted on the cockpit bench and fell asleep.

CHAPTER 25

J erry's jaw dropped when he heard the closing sentences
of the broadcast. A woman's voice on the radio had
told people to avoid gluttony. He was not sure at first if
that was Cat's voice, though it had her low timbre and the
characteristic inflection, leaving listeners wondering if she
was making a statement, asking a question or making a dis-
guised joke. But, certainly, it was her wicked sense of humor. That was *his* crazy Cat. He was done with masking
the boat; lines removed, sails taken down under the deck,
large pieces of broken metal and fiberglass heaped on the
deck—*Lady Luck* looked like the rest of them: broken,
rusty and unworthy of a second look. But she held a treasure: enough food to last a few weeks, if used sparingly, the
remaining fifteen gallons of diesel fuel, fishing gear and
some other useful stuff, including bleach.

Jerry lowered the dinghy and rowed towards the shore,
meandering along the reef, taking cover behind obstruc-
tions, in case someone was spying from the shore. Once on
the beach, he dragged a large piece of half-rotten plywood
to cover the dinghy, and threw a few pieces of deadwood
on top to complete the masquerade.

The wooden slips of the marina were completely ripped
out; only the concrete foundation slab marked the site of a

building, which had to be the harbormaster's office. A distinct chemical smell permeated the air despite a breeze. Jerry walked inland following an asphalt road behind the harbor. The broken pavement was covered with a thick slick of oil slowly leaking from the large storage tank that was still upright. Two other tanks were knocked off their foundations, and lay on their sides as the tidal waves had left them, the contents long gone.

A middle-aged, thin man passed him on a bike. He kept a ten-foot distance when Jerry stopped him, but provided useful information. One could walk east, to Honolulu where food was being distributed, but hundreds of thousands of people waited in lines and fought over it. Going west would take a traveler to Leeward, where there was hardly any government presence, but the locals seemed to cope by themselves well enough. The man was from Makaha. As far as Kailua was concerned, the town was almost completely cut off, but some guys from Leeward were crossing to Windward, along the H3 highway, over the mountains.

Jerry went west. Carrying a small backpack with food for a day, a few fishing hooks for trading and a box of bleach, he trudged along the blistering highway. He passed by the sprawling complex of the Pearl Harbor naval base, shut off by high fences and armed sentries. A few hours later, he stopped in front of a white house, hoping to get a drink of water. He was dry as a leaf in November, and his water bottle had been long empty. He had not urinated for a few hours, and the last time he did, his pee was the color of orange juice.

The yard was overgrown with weeds and an old, blue

pickup was parked in the driveway. A man working on a ladder was covering broken windows with plywood. Jerry asked for water, but the man shrugged his shoulders without even looking at him. Jerry was not in a condition to allow himself to be ignored.

"C'mon, man, you're not going to refuse me a drink of water!"

The man on the ladder stopped nailing, and looked at the unwelcome visitor, weighing the hammer in his hand. "Just move along, buddy. You know I don't have any good water to share with you. It's either you, or me and my family. You want water, help yourself," he pointed his hammer towards a puddle filled with murky fluid. "Fresh, there was a bit of rain last night; it'll be gone by evening."

Jeremy went to the puddle, plunged in his hand and brought wet fingers to his lips. At least the water was not salty. It tasted fresh, even though it was brown with dirt. He took out his water bottle, put a bit of bleach in and topped it with water. Then he came back to the house and sat in the shade shaking the bottle. A few minutes later, he had drunk it all. The water smelled like a swimming pool, but it felt wonderful in his parched throat.

The worker watched with interest. "You think you'll be all right? People get pretty sick drinking that water, you know."

"Oh, I'll be fine." Jeremy answered with great confidence. "This is good water—as long as you have proper purification chemicals."

The man put his hammer away and sat beside him.

"You have purification stuff?"

"A lot. I could make a lot of clean water . . . but I could use some help myself."

Ed lived with his wife and two kids in the white house. Someone had tried to break in early that morning, so Ed had decided to board the lower windows. People were getting desperate about water. It rained little on the leeward side, even though January is a rainy month. One could not count on rainwater. Ed had built a small water still from a garbage can, but it produced just a few glasses of brackish water a day, hardly enough for his family. Some people drank water from a stream in the mountains, but that was clearly polluted, as a lot of them got sick. Particularly, young children were falling ill in large numbers. A remaining option was to trek ten or fifteen miles to Honolulu.

"How many cans of water can you carry?" Ed complained. Jerry didn't blame him for refusing a drink of water to a stranger. They lived on food scraps: remnants of taro or pineapples found in the fields, fish caught in the ocean and an occasional feral pig that one of the neighbors shot in the bush. The locals shared their food and no one seemed to be better off than the others—all hungry but alive. The big issue was the shortage of clean water.

Ed led Jerry down the village road to meet an older man named Kawika, an individual of imposing size and dignity. The elder listened intently to the visitor's boast about his water purification chemicals, and then asked a few pointed questions.

"How much water can you treat? Where do you get the chemicals? How do we know it's good?" His dark eyes expressed a keen interest as well as a hint of a threat, in case the *haole* was less than sincere.

Jerry could not disclose *Lady Luck*'s existence. She was his only asset in this dealing. "I have a warehouse where my chemicals are stored, and I will provide them as necessary. Are they good? You'll see by tomorrow. Ed saw me drinking a whole bottle of muddy water that I treated with my stuff." The witness enthusiastically nodded. He felt that credit was due to him for finding Jerry and his bleach. "You need to find a large tank or a reservoir where I could treat water in large quantities; that would be more economical," Jerry added with the confidence of a water-treatment plant manager.

Kawika thought for a moment. "A swimming pool. I know a guy who has a small swimming pool in his backyard. It might be cracked, but that can be fixed. I'll have people fill it with the water from streams and ponds; there must still be some that haven't dried up. It should be ready by tomorrow. You'll stay with me; I want to keep an eye on you. If you are OK in the morning, you treat the water, and we'll give it a try."

Jerry was usually indifferent about religion, but that afternoon, when he got cramps, he was begging for divine intervention. Apparently it helped, he did not get sick, though he continued to drink his concoction mixed again in Kawika's presence.

The small, empty pool among tall weeds had been patched up with concrete, and at daybreak people started filing along a pathway carrying buckets, canisters and jars of water. Jerry had fashioned a makeshift filter out of a sand-filled bucket; every drop of water falling into the pool had to come through the drainage holes at the bucket's bottom. The pool was half full at ten o'clock when Kawika proudly and ceremoniously brought Jerry to it. The biological tests went well—Jerry was alive and apparently healthy. To his joy, the house owner had a kit for testing pool water. Jerry figured that if he kept the water within a range appropriate for swimming, that should be safe enough to drink and nobody would get his guts burned by concentrated chlorine. He poured the bleach, mixed, tested, poured some more, mixed some more, tested, giving a great show for an hour or so. People stood around looking with interest, waiting in the full sun without a sound of protest. Eventually, he turned away and left for an hour. When he came back, people were still there, waiting. Jerry filled the water bottle, looked at it under the sun. The water appeared clean and he greedily drank it all. It was noon and he was thirsty.

All heads turned to Kawika who gave a solemn go-ahead nod, triggering a rush to the pool. People drank their first fill and went back to refill their containers. The silent crowd suddenly turned into a block party, kids running and screaming, women filling their water carriers, while men carefully tasted from glasses and cups as though they had a new and exotic beer to savor. Jerry's chest swelled with pride as it had never before.

Kawika beckoned. "You did a great service to us; what can we do for *you*?" He listened to Jerry's story without interruption, then leaned towards him, "I would like to have a friend like you. We'll give you a hand." As the Hawaiian turned away, searching for someone in the crowd, Jerry knew that his chances of finding Cat were improving.

"This lady friend of yours . . ." the older man faced him again. "You say you heard her on the radio yesterday? If she's the one broadcasting from Kailua, you got yourself a famous woman. The whole island listens to her. She is a spunky girl and funny, too. She'll take good care of you, ha ha ha," he roared, smacking Jerry on the back. Two guides were appointed to take Jerry over the mountains to Kailua. He biked back to Keehi the same afternoon accompanied by one of his escorts, bringing back large backpacks filled with more bleach and food.

The trek to Kailua was to begin the next morning, but at dawn a breathless young man barged into Kawika's house. "Whales, whales are close to the beach!" Within minutes, the whole neighborhood ran to the shore, carrying paddles and an amazing number of firearms. Handguns, pump shotguns, snub-barreled shotguns, hunting rifles, assault rifles; these people were prepared for a war. Once they reached the shore, where three outriggers rested on the sand, the whales came into view half a mile offshore, spouting fountains of water and breaching.

The boats were quickly pushed onto the water, and filled with the firearm-carrying paddlers. The canoes moved swiftly, paddles rhythmically plunging into the water on both sides of the hulls. Every five or six strokes they changed sides without any splashing, loss of rhythm or speed. The boats split up and started approaching the large black shape from two sides. With paddles drawn in, the canoes were closing on the whale, moving with the momentum, all arms pointed and ready. There was not a movement or sound among the crowd on the shore. The canoes were about eighty yards from the prey when the whale moved as in preparation for a dive. A single shot sounded, followed by a cannonade carrying on for at least fifteen seconds. A submachine gun rattled a lengthy staccato as numerous small red explosions erupted on the giant's head.

The whale submerged the front of its body, but that was as much as it could do, its head exploded by hundreds of bullets. The crowd broke into a great jubilant noise, and a bunch of kids jumped into the water, swimming to the whale and the canoes. They attached ropes to the humpback's tail, and the canoes slowly, with great effort, towed the carcass to the beach, a great trail of blood extending behind. The size of the beast was staggering; there was a lot of meat for all. Jerry knew that his trek would not start that day. He'd be lucky to go the next day.

A lot of people gathered in front of Kawika's house. Large pieces of whale meat were roasted over a fire, boiled or smoked, as nobody knew how to prepare it properly; experimentation was the answer. Long after dark, people on the beach kept butchering the unusual game. "What are you going to do with all this meat, Kawika?" Jerry asked. "It is not going to keep long."

"We'll try to smoke some, we'll try to salt some, but— in the end—you're right, most of it will go bad. I've sent word to our people on this side to come and get as much as they can use."

"You might send some to Honolulu, even sell it, or trade it. Maybe you could get some gas for your car."

"You don't understand, Jerry. Sure, they're as hungry in Honolulu as we are. But if we let them know we have food, they will come here by the thousands. They'll take our food, burn our homes. It happened before; we don't trust them. Let them catch their own whale."

Even though he did not feel it was right, Jeremy could not disagree with the Hawaiian's reasoning. It had happened before.

Fires on the beach burned till morning as the party went on, augmented by new arrivals from the western part of the island. While Leeward celebrated its big catch, east of the Koolau Mountains hungry people slept fitfully, fearing the morning when they would have to look into their children's hungry eyes.

CHAPTER 26

Despite Jerry's fears of delay, they set out to Kailua the next day, at five AM. Alika, his companion on the recent supply trip to the boat, brought a younger fellow named Kekoa who stayed by Jerry while Alika led the expedition, frequently out of sight. Jerry understood perhaps half of the heavily accented and grammatically inventive talk, but he was not expected to contribute a lot to the conversation.

They started out on bicycles and covered almost twenty miles on a broken but passable pavement, before it ended where an elevated segment of the highway had collapsed. Leaving the bikes with Alika's friends, they climbed from the highway to the slope of the mountain. From there the hike continued up, treading over the unsteady gravel of eroding volcanic rock. Every step could instantly change into a slide down the steep slope, with feet desperately searching for solid ground.

Jerry carried a heavy backpack filled with dry food from his boat supplies; his guides carried packs brimming with whale blubber, a gift from Kawika and his clan. A distinct odor emanated from their burden, fortunately not the stench of spoiling meat but the more tolerable smell of fish oil.

In the scorching heat of noon, they followed a faint pathway between boulders up to the mountain pass. Jerry trudged along trying to keep up with his younger companions, swaying under his big backpack, until they all collapsed at the summit. Slumped in front of a big rock, they turned their faces to the cool breeze rising up along the mountain's slope from the ocean. Jerry watched the drama of deep green valleys separated by ragged steep cliffs, set against the background of the placid blue ocean in the distance. A speck, a mere rock surrounded by millions of square miles of empty water, Jerry thought, looking from the mountaintop. One of the most spectacular places on earth had become a prison, well guarded by its isolation.

Walking downhill was no easier. Mostly they slid down on their backsides, desperately trying to slow down, grasping weeds, bushes and branches, until the steep slope changed into the less inclined foothill. A fifteen-minute rest in a grove of wild guava trees, probably an orchard many years ago, turned into a greedy hunt for the small fruits packing amazingly aromatic, pink juice; perfect to satisfy their cravings for energy and water.

Alika disappeared ahead while Jerry followed a narrow pathway meandering between high bushes, his eyes lowered to the ground. The plants were dramatically different on the windward side. Once they had crossed over the mountain's crest, the brown and dry shrubs of the leeward side gave way to green exuberant grasses, succulent bushes and leafy trees. The pathway took a right turn when he suddenly heard a command:

"Drop da pack!"

Jerry looked up and faced a short, thin, older man wearing shorts, a dirty gray tee shirt and rubber flip-flops. He held a cut-off shotgun, but was not aiming at Jerry. There was no need. His victim carried no apparent weapon, and the robber could finish the contest within a split second. His brown and weathered face was not particularly threatening; it was simply saying: I need your pack, so drop it and go away, no need to get hurt. Jerry stopped, then heard Kekoa stopping behind him and moving to his side.

"Eh, he's with us, so beat it, *brah!*"

The mugger looked alarmed and raised his shotgun without saying a word.

"You touch him, and we hunt you down and kill like one pig," continued Kekoa, in an almost friendly tone. This time Jerry understood every word and admired the succinct clarity of the pidgin dialect. The man stood there for another second, then suddenly jumped among the bushes and disappeared.

"You did good, *brah*," they heard Alika's voice from the undergrowth just behind the spot where the gunman had been standing a moment ago. He sheathed a ten-inch long hunting knife and returned to the lead. The old man would never know how close he had been to his own end.

Kailua was completely dark by the time they entered the town. Walking between damaged but inhabited homes they arrived at the area where the tsunami had reached. Ruined houses, abandoned cars, garbage—all evidence of human presence had been replaced by a brown surface of dried mud broken into a million small patches. Jerry found Cat's home with considerable difficulty by following the

233

canal, until they came upon the concrete walls of the first floor sticking out from the mud. The second floor was completely gone, only the carport absurdly stuck up high above the house's remains. Most of the contents had been taken by water, which left behind a thick layer of sand and mud where Jerry and Cat used to have romantic dinners.

Climbing over the fridge wedged into the kitchen doorway, Jerry saw a metallic object underneath. It was a richly ornamented contraption designed for making tea, much more elaborate than a simple teapot. It had a burner, and a container for water as well as a little faucet for filling a teacup. The vessel was made of silver and engraved. Jerry recognized it at once because he had seen it many times in Cat's hands.

She did not make tea; this thing was her treasured heirloom of high sentimental value. Perhaps she felt in touch with her parents or grandparents when she handled it. She liked to polish it, and indeed, the silver required a lot of polishing to maintain its shine in Hawaii's climate. Jerry saw Cat slowly gliding her gloved hand over the shiny curves, her eyes unfocused, as though she were talking to someone far away. He did not interfere with these moments; a few minutes later, she would put it away and return to his world.

Jeremy dug it out from the mud, then they hobbled towards the town center. There were no lights, except for candles and little lamps flickering behind broken windows, but many people scurried about. Then they disappeared, all at once. The travelers shuffled along the dark and empty street until stopped by two firearm-carrying men. One was wearing a torn and dirty police uniform, the other was a ci-

vilian, but carried a rifle. They wanted to know what Jerry
and his companions were doing out after the curfew.

"A curfew?" Jerry gasped. That would explain why
people had suddenly disappeared. "We've just crossed from
the leeward side; sorry, we didn't know about the curfew."

"What's your business here? What are you looking
for?" The policeman asked with suspicion, stepping back to
avoid the odor drifting from the suspects.

"I'm looking for Cat, a young woman who used to live
by the canal in Kaimalino."

The policeman looked at his partner who shrugged his
shoulders, "Let's take them to Cat; they are in no shape to
give us any trouble."

Flickering lights broke the darkness at the far end of a
large hall, revealing a group of people sitting around a long
table. They stopped talking and looked at the commotion at
the door, raising sharp, thin faces with dark shadows
around sunken eyes. They could only see outlines, as the
newcomers were standing in the dark part of the room.

"These guys were walking on Kailua Street after curfew. They claim to have come from the lee side, over the
mountains," the policeman reported.

Jerry saw Cat sitting in her wheelchair. The face, round
and freckled just a few weeks ago, was almost white with
indrawn cheeks accentuating the impossibly high cheek-
bones. Her full lips had changed into ribbons of pale skin as
though they were simply meant to mark her mouth opening.
Only the eyes.... The eyes became big, blue windows shin-

ing with quiet power, dominating her image, shutting out the emaciated body, wheelchair, matted hair and ragged clothes.

"What's that smell?" Yoshida asked, sniffing the air. "Have you guys really come over the mountains? And what for?"

"Blubber, whale blubber," said Alika. "We've got a whale, and thought you might want some. But we came here because of him," and he pointed a finger at Jerry.

Jerry stepped forward into the lighted area and dropped his pack. He had not shaved since San Diego and had a few strenuous weeks behind him, so although he was not starving, he had lost a lot of weight and looked ten years older. He was looking at Cat, and she was looking back, not sure if this shabby man was really Jerry.

Jerry cleared his voice and found himself at a loss for words, just like when they first met. "Hello, Cat. I . . . I came to be with you." His words sounded just silly, and his embarrassment spread to his guides who almost cringed. But it was the truth.

"Jerry? Jerry, what the hell are you doing here?" She did not sound happy, rather shocked and, possibly, somewhat annoyed or embarrassed.

Kalani was looking at him with wide-open eyes, and slowly, almost inaudibly said, "It's love, it's love."

Carol started giggling and rolling her eyes until Yoshida stopped them all saying, "I see you've brought something . . ."

The change of subject to a practical issue brought Jerry relief. "I thought you might use some food, so I've brought a few supplies. Also, Kawika from Kalaeloa sends you pieces of the whale that they hunted down." From the first moment, he knew he would not be able to take Cat away. She was in the middle of this crisis, and she would not quit until the drama was over. The best he could hope for was to be re-admitted into her world, and that was what he planned to do.

Alika and Kekoa happily lay down on the cool marble floor, their feet elevated on the blubber packs. Jerry was also very tired, and he was not going to stay on his feet a second longer than necessary. He pulled himself a chair up to the table and sat in front of Cat.

"Yes, I've come to be with you. I see that the landscape has re-arranged itself, so I would like to help until some relief arrives."

Cat recovered from her shock, and her face softened with a smile bringing a hint of better times. "Then you may have to stay quite a while. We spoke with the governor and no relief is coming anytime soon. We are grateful for the supplies you brought, but how exactly do you propose to help us, teach us economics?"

As much as he liked her smiling again, that remark annoyed Jerry. After all, he had made quite a few major changes in his life, and it took no small effort to come back, so a bit of appreciation was what he expected.

"First, I wouldn't mind a drink of water for my friends and myself. Secondly, I quit teaching economics a few weeks ago, and now consider myself more of a sailor, a handyman, a smuggler and a pack mule, as well as a bit of a diesel mechanic. Ah, I was also offered a carpenter's job a few weeks ago."

Cat's face was warming up; now she was looking at him with pleasure and a sparkle of humor. "All that! I am sure we'll find something usable in this mountain of qualifications. Mike, what do you think, maybe we could use a smuggler?"

The policeman picked up on the joke, "I prefer that he fixes my squad cars, so they don't need no gas." They were an easygoing bunch, even though the six of them together could not weigh six hundred pounds.

"So what's in the pack?" Kalani asked. Between her orphanage, herself and Cat, the supplies that came from Rosen's home were used up. She firmly believed that she had the right to his food, as Rosen never came back to change his offer. But, all that was gone. She could have more had she gone back to the restaurant sooner. Unfortunately, someone beat her to the food store. The kids were again crying from hunger and she was getting desperate.

"A gallon of olive oil, a big box of cubed sugar, ten-pound sack of rice, another ten pounds of flour, vitamins and powdered milk...." Kalani's smile was getting wider and wider. "Jerry, if Cat doesn't want you, I might consider. Just kidding—nobody tell Abe."

"Hey, *sistah*, how about us, would you consider us?" Kekoa was grinning from his spot on the floor, waiting for recognition.

"All this blubber!" enthused Kalani. "I certainly would

consider, except that good-looking guys like you must have their steady women on the lee side."

"They don't smell too good, either," sniped Lee.

None of them did after this long day of climbing and marching. Jerry decided to cool off and wash in the ocean, a two-minute walk from the house. He hoped Cat might go with him, so that they could speak privately. She agreed so willingly that he started to believe that coming to Kailua had not been in vain.

Jerry pushed the wheelchair as far as the broken asphalt allowed, then picked her up, carrying her in his arms to the water's edge. She clung to him like a sleepy child and weighed just as much. Her body had lost the firmness that his hands remembered. He laid Cat on the sand and slowly helped her take her clothes off. With her full breasts shriveled, the belly sunken and the hipbones protruding she was an icon of abandonment. Jerry undressed himself quickly, picked her up and walked into the water.

They floated for a moment, then started swimming slowly along the beach. The bright moon shimmered on the black water, glittered on small waves spilling onto the sand, and brought into relief the gray dunes stretching all the way to the motionless black ironwoods. Cat was weak, so a few minutes later they beached themselves at the water's edge. They were lying in the foot-deep warm water holding each other, just as they had in her swimming pool, a lifetime ago. She pulled herself onto Jerry's chest, looked into his eyes and gently kissed him. "Even if you are an apparition, I will make you stay with me for ever."

His hands felt her wet head, her spine, vertebrae sharply

sticking through the skin, the thin hard ribs and her tiny buttocks shining white in the moonlight. "I want to stay with you forever, but I need a condition, a privilege. You will have to grant me the right to take care of you. To carry you, to feed you and do whatever you need—even if you don't know what it might be." Jerry knew that, for this fiercely independent person, granting such a privilege was the consent to take her.

"I do," she said, "and I want the same from you."

"I do, too," he said and that was their proposal and marriage ceremony.

They returned to the Round House where Kalani opened a can of tuna and pulled out three crackers for their wedding party. Jerry went with Cat to her office room where they slept on her narrow bed, too small for two grown people but perfect for two scarecrows in love. He felt the warmth of her body in his arms, caressed her hair and thought, "I've won her back, Pam; she is mine."

CHAPTER 27

Surveillance transcript, Washington, D.C.

Speaker 1: *What are they going to do with this Hawaii mess? It looks worse and worse by the hour. Now foreign relief has been prevented by the Navy's exclusion zone around the islands.*

Speaker 2: *Yeah, they're concerned that the Chinese might take advantage of the situation and try to establish some presence. You know, an NGO relief post today, foreign government office tomorrow. Meanwhile, they might support local opposition, independent Hawaii movements and so on. The strategic value of Hawaii is just too high to take this kind of a risk.*

Speaker 1: *How about the population? There's hardly any relief effort. All our transportation assets are directed at the Middle East.*

Speaker 2: *Quite unfortunate, indeed. We don't have enough of the long-range transport capacity, so first things have to go first. But, the Prez got really pissed about the governor's intercepted conversation. You have to agree that won't look good at the exhibit in the Presidential Library. So he ordered a few transport planes to be sent to Hawaii. They can land at the Marine base or the Air Force base—it seems that we have quite a few operational assets in Hawaii. That should shut the press up for a few days. Then they'll come up with some other solution. There is not much that can be done until you can send big cargo ships, but the ports are quite damaged.*

Speaker 1: *You mean, we don't have landing craft to transfer stuff from the ocean-going ships to the beaches? After all, there are beaches in Hawaii!*

Speaker 2: *Don't be ridiculous, of course we have amphibious craft—even in Hawaii, but they have to stay on stand by, in case we need them for something else or somewhere else.*

* * *

"Be quiet, mice, or Cat will get you!" Kalani threatened.

"Cat, Cat, get us! Get us," yelled the kids happily.

Cat was listening from her place beside Jerry smiling. "I should go; Kalani needs my help," she whispered, sitting up. She dressed quickly, pulled herself into the wheelchair and rolled to the main room. She looked better that morning—some color had returned to her lips and cheeks.

Jerry came out a few minutes later to see a toddler sitting on Cat's knees and two others trying to climb her legs to get on her lap. Kalani was distributing soup into bowls. She was happy to have some food in store; it might last, perhaps, three or four days, but—certainly—she would not ignore the blubber. A propane stove was hissing, brewing something that might be called soup for lack of a better name. She had thoughtfully placed the burner and the pot downwind from the house so that the smell was not too bad.

"Kalani, you think somebody will actually want to eat your soup?"

The girl smiled with mischief and declared, "First, I put a little ginger into the soup. That'll make it muuuch better. Second, nobody gets *nothin* until they've had my soup. That includes the two of you, too. We'll see." Much to Jerry's surprise, the children ate their blubber soup without a word of protest. Hunger is a great chef. Then everybody was given one guava, a multivitamin tablet from *Lady Luck* supplies and a spoonful of rice. That was all.

Kalani turned her eyes to Cat and said sternly, "I'm watching you." By way of explanation for Jerry, she added, "It is a strange situation when the mice," she pointed at her little herd, "eat the cat," and she pointed at Cat. "She gives them her food, and at some point, she'll just drop dead. But they need her; we all need her, more than a miserable spoonful of rice." Cat began eating humbly.

Abe came down from the bedroom where he slept next to Kalani. He had come in last night from a long foraging trip along the shores to the north, past Kaneohe. He had brought some guava fruit, a few coconuts and pineapples, a small heap of mussels, but the biggest prize was a foot-long fish that he had killed with a stick in a tidal pool. He looked worn out from a lack of food and the long marches. The men shook hands before Abe sat next to Jerry.

"Not much stuff for all the looking," he said half in complaint, half excuse.

"Lots of guys are looking," Jerry said.

"That's it," Abe sighed.

"Have you tried to fish? I know you're a fisherman by trade."

"Everybody tries to get fish in the bay," Abe shrugged. "There are more men in the water than fish. It's easier to get poked with a spear than to see a fish. You would have to go a few miles out to catch a real fish, but I don't think there's a boat left on the island. In any case, there's no fuel, so I'll just keep beating the dirt. God, I hate walking!"

How could I miss this? Jerry thought and almost slapped himself in the forehead. Deep-sea fishing! I have a boat. A boat that needs no fuel is sitting uselessly in Keehi, pretending to be a dead piece of scrap. What a waste!

"Abe, what would you say if I got you a boat that could go all the way to the mainland and needs no fuel?"

"I'd say that you need a doctor, but what's the use of a doctor if there are no medicines. I told you; there are no boats on Oahu."

"Jerry," Cat sat up, "how did you get here from the West Coast?"

With all the things they had talked about, no one had asked about his miraculous re-appearance in Hawaii. "In a sailboat, and the boat is sitting hidden in Keehi Lagoon. I figure, if we make one last long trek to Keehi, we won't have to walk any more. What do you say, Abe?"

"I'm ready to start right now," Abe's smile had the qualities of a carved pumpkin, wide beyond nature's design and lasting till the first frost.

"You took a lot of risk and trouble to be with me, Jerry," Cat said softly.

Jerry would never forget the scene of the whale hunt, but what particularly stuck in his memory was the dilemma after the hunt. What do you do with a mass of food that spoils fast? Fish must be even worse than a whale carcass. "Folks, we need to start some sort of market economy here. The way you live now is about thirty thousand years old. Hunter-gatherers, that's what we are. If we, indeed, catch a few decent fish, that would be too much for us to eat, and there is no refrigeration. We should swap the fish for something else useful. We need a market."

"We could give it to the neighbors; that's what we did every time we had more than enough for ourselves," Kalani said.

"Giving is nice, but it doesn't encourage work," Cat remarked thoughtfully. "We have fewer volunteers now than we had at the beginning, and nobody seems to do anything productive. Jerry's right; we need a functioning economy so everybody will get off his or her butt. But what would we sell it for? Who needs dollars? You can't eat greenbacks."

"We can start with barter. How would you like an electric lamp here or a radio? There must be an electronics guy in town who can take a wind generator off a wrecked boat and fix it. Maybe he already has it, for himself. Now, in exchange for a mahi-mahi, he could do it for us. How about starting home repairs in town, your home? Building materials are there—on the ground, free for the taking. Yet I wouldn't say there is a building boom around here. This better start soon, since nobody's rushing to help from the outside. Someone must be growing fresh vegetables as we speak, and might want to swap them for fish. As for money," he continued, "trust the free market. People will find something they want to keep. I'd bet that a few weeks from now, gold, for example, will buy a lot of things."

"Gold is good." Abe interjected. "My grandpa told me that in the thirties, when food was hard to come by, people who had a few gold coins ate well when everybody else was starving. He even got a gold piece once, when they landed a big marlin."

"What happened to it?" Kalani wanted to know.

"He bought himself a woman," Abe answered with a straight face. "But she left him after a week, because they found out that the coin was a fake. But, grandpa said, this week was worth his marlin," and he broke into loud, boisterous laughter while Kalani pretended to be offended.

Jerry and Abe set off that afternoon, hoping to make it to the mountain pass by nightfall, sleep in the bushes and start going down at sunrise. Once on the ocean, they could try the fishing lines he had on board. Hopefully, they would be carrying a few mahi-mahi or *ahi* by the time they returned to Kailua. Climbing was remarkably easy without backpacks; they carried only bags for water bottles, and a small packet of cooked rice. They reached the pass with the last rays of sun. The windward side was already in dark shadow, valleys completely black. The lee side displayed a majestic panorama of golden foothills flooded with the warm glow of the sunset. The yellow hue of the mountaintops was greening closer to the ocean, where the deep blue of the Pacific merged with the sky overpowering the palette of colors. The temperature began falling, but hot rocks baked by the day's exposure to the full power of the sun were slow to cool. They hid behind a big boulder, collected dry wood with the last minutes of daylight and made a small fire. Abe was very much at home on the mountain, a confident and skillful man here, happy with his life despite all the deprivation he had suffered.

Jerry was cold in the night and woke up blanketed by the black sky studded with millions of stars. Above, below, around his mountaintop perch, countless brilliant points congregated in swirls and patterns that fed the imagination of every race on the earth. He had seen some beautiful night skies during his cross-Pacific sail, but the sky above the Koolau Mountains was incomparable. The air clarity, the darkness encompassing the island below, brought the heavenly lights into relief so sharp that he felt an almost religious awe. He woke again at dawn, deeply chilled, with stiff limbs. As he slowly and painfully got up, a familiar sarcastic voice asked, "Where's your backpack? You shouldn't be here by yourself."

It was *him* again, the old man with the shotgun. This time he was more personal and disagreeable. Perhaps, he felt embarrassed about the failed ambush two days ago. The barrel aimed at Jerry's belly; the mugger had a small, cold smile that meant no good intentions.

"No backpack, I'm coming back with nothing." Jerry desperately hoped Abe would come to his rescue. Obviously, the gunman did not realize there was a companion.

"Take your shoes and clothes off," the old guy commanded. Jerry sat on the ground fiddling with his shoelaces, trying to distract the scoundrel, so that Abe would have a better chance of sneaking up on him. The robber was getting annoyed and brutally shoved the gun's barrel into Jerry's stomach. Curled on the ground, Jerry missed the sudden movement behind the gunman. Hearing a sudden thump, he raised his head to see the mugger tumbling sideways as though hit by a car. The shotgun went off and a load of lead missed Jerry's chest by inches. Pellets splattered against the rock behind him as the shooter's body rolled down the slope, until his blindly clutching hands grasped a clump of dry grass. He stopped falling, but was hanging at the point where the steep slope became a nearly vertical cliff.

The brown face looked up. "Help me, please!"

Abe took a few steps down the slope. "What is it, Vincent? You ate all your cocks? You ate my chicks as well? You turned to robbing people! Well, it's nothing new for you."

The mugger knew that his fate was sealed and said nothing else, just held onto the grass. As the roots broke out of the red dirt, Vincent uttered a long moan, then plummeted down still grasping the dry tufts. They lost sight of him as soon as the body cleared the cliff's edge, but heard the heavy thud as it hit a rock. There was no moaning after that.

At one point, Jerry had a reflexive urge to look for a stick to extend to the old man hanging above the precipice, but Abe grabbed his arm without a word and held it. He was right; there was no other justice for people like Vincent. The basic law of the struggling town was: you take care of yourself the best you can, and we won't bother you with small stuff. But if you cross the line, we will not tolerate you among us. Vincent had crossed the line.

Kawika was happy to see Jerry again. The number of diarrhea and bellyache cases had decreased dramatically since people started using the treated water. Daily treks to Honolulu stopped. The food shortage was, at least temporarily, alleviated with the whale meat. Life in the community started to normalize.

Lady Luck waited in her hiding place. Kawika's people unloaded the remaining bleach and took it to the village, then returned to fill the boat's tanks. Perhaps fifteen gallons of diesel left, Jerry calculated. That will be my reserve; the sails are fine; they will take us to Kailua. They caught a few hours of sleep, then pushed *Lady Luck* out of the mangrove cove at five the next morning.

The sky was still black, but starting to turn gray in the east. They moved through the lagoon with extreme caution. Jerry did not dare to hoist any sails, though the winds were favorable. The harbor was littered with dozens of submerged boats, pathetic bows or sterns jutting out of the water. Some boats had sunk upright, with a mast projecting upwards like a tree growing from the lagoon's bottom. Shreds of steel rigging hid just under the surface, the flailing arms of a zombie boat, ready to snag the keel of a vessel that was still alive.

Jerry had devised a technique based on kedging, an ancient way of moving tall ships in tight ports long before motors were invented. Abe rowed the dinghy slowly between wrecks searching for a clear path for *Lady Luck*. He carried an anchor in the dinghy, and once he had made the length of the eighty-foot line, he dropped the hook overboard. Jerry, standing aboard his yacht, weighed the boat's second anchor at this point, and started taking in the line attached to the anchor that Abe had just dropped. This way *Lady Luck* was pulled forwards slowly but safely. They reached the harbor channel as the red rim of the sun touched the city towers in the east. A few weeks ago the sunrise would have flooded downtown Honolulu with orange and yellow light reflected in thousands of gold and silver panels. Now, the buildings were throwing long dark shadows showing off their scarred bodies. Jerry raised the jib sail and their hard labor ended, as the wind gently pushed the boat out through the channel. They hoisted the main sail and the boat turned her bow to southeast, taking fifteen-knot wind on her port beam as they sailed towards the Penguin Banks. Abe had worked the Banks, the well-established fishing grounds, long enough to be confident he could catch fish there that they would not be ashamed to trade.

With Jerry at the helm, Abe worked on the fishing tackle, assembling the bits and pieces he found on the boat into functioning fishing gear. Soon, four lines trailed from the stern. Two hours later, as the wind increased and the boat heeled, Jerry turned the bow north on a course that would take them past Makapu'u Rock. Once past the point, they would turn left and run with the wind along the east coast of Oahu to Kailua.

The first fish struck Abe's line about one PM, just when

they had finished a can of stew from the boat supplies. Jerry had not eaten a decent meal for a few days and was hungry, but Abe . . . Abe had not eaten above starvation level for a few weeks! Whatever food he could find, he kept bringing to Kalani, where it disappeared almost instantly into the hungry mouths of her orphans. Abe had a feast. Just when he was ready to relax and digest it, one of the rods bowed and its float disappeared under the water. There was nothing subtle or ambivalent about it. A beast had taken the bait and planted the hook solidly in its mouth. The shaft bent immediately, and Abe let out some line.

High stakes politics in action, Jerry thought, looking at the contest between Abe and the fish. Whenever the creature tried to dash for freedom, the fisherman released some line, fearing it could break. Between the attacks, the line was relentlessly rolled in. The tired fish allowed these calm periods to last longer and longer, and finally the rainbow-colored dorsal fin of a large mahi-mahi broke the surface. Soon, a blunt head appeared next to the boat, and Jerry swiped the fish into a net on a long handle. The mahi-mahi was much too big for his net, but they pulled Abe's prey onboard by grabbing its fins and gills. Abe hit it on the head with a beer bottle from John's cache, and the fight was over.

An interesting morality tale with forceful conclusions, Jerry thought. Don't take a free meal—it could be bait. Once you take a hook—try to break away hard, but you've probably lost by then. Finally, you won't see the guy who's holding the line until it's time to get a blow at the back of your head.

Abe had started filleting the fish, but the second rod

bowed, and before he had time to bring the second fish in, the third floater went under water. It was time for Jerry's budding fishing skills to be called upon; he pulled in a small tuna after a brief struggle.

They had over sixty pounds of fish by late afternoon, and were happy to see the Makapu'u lighthouse passing on their left. Jerry started rounding the course to the west, and the ride became quite comfortable when the wind shifted towards the stern.

"Beats walking, eh?"

Abe raised his head from the fish he was filleting and grinned widely. "For sure, I forgot how good it is to be on the ocean. I was stupid not to take old Kumashiro's boat. We both would have been so much better off." Obviously, he was referring to Kalani.

"So, what will you do now, Abe? Looks like things are good and happy between you and Kalani."

"Oh, we're fine now. You know, I sometimes have this crazy idea that all these terrible things happened so that I could come to my senses. Then I feel somehow guilty, like other people had to pay the price for my stupidity."

"Other people had their own reasons to go through this. We are all sinners, Abe, and we all had to go through purgatory. Maybe the kids had nothing to pay for, but they will forget it all. The rest of us, we all did enough shit to deserve some major whipping. The important thing is, we have a second chance and some folks, like yourself, will take it, and others will screw it up again."

Abe considered for a moment. "I didn't know you were religious. Cat never mentioned that. I like it. We got whipped like naughty kids, but maybe we'll survive. And if we do, we will be much better people."

"I'm not a religious guy, Abe, and this has nothing to do with religion. Don't call any shepherds on this sheep; I like to graze by myself. It just came to my mind because they call this place Paradise. Some Paradise! But again, maybe it's us who don't fit into Paradise. You can't have a Paradise full of sinners, can you?"

Abe finished filleting. They had a large heap of beautiful pink flesh lying in the middle of the cockpit. Without refrigeration or ice, the fish would not stay this good for long. They packed it into buckets filled with salt water and hoped to make it to Kailua in a few hours. Meantime, they enjoyed *ahi poke*, fresh tuna cut into cubes and consumed raw.

Jerry thought that Skipper John would have ordered him to share his beer with Abe. They looked different, had unlike backgrounds, but were made from the same piece of cloth. Both were strong characters making their living at sea, but loosing their way on the shoals of domestic life. Abe had the good fortune to be knocked back to his private Paradise early in life; John was the lost soul who wasted his life away, and when he had a chance to get a new though late start, it was taken away from him. Jerry opened a bottle of Heineken for each, and they savored the beer under skies full of stars.

CHAPTER 28

The person who was once called Harry Rosen lowered himself slowly and carefully from the ledge to the bottom of the rock. The blackness of night was turning into gray, and the sun would be up within thirty or forty minutes. It was the time when even human predators were abandoning their hunt and decent folks still clung to their pillows. For exactly these reasons Rosen has chosen this time of day to travel. He had good reason to fear the authorities: who knows how widely his unfortunate affair with Kalani had been circulated? His swollen face and off-kilter nose would attract unwanted attention. On the other hand, the island was full of people with swollen faces, broken body parts and worse. So maybe he was too cautious. But the incredible failure of acquiring Kalani as a slave proved that there was no such thing as being too careful.

Harry could not think of it without rage. He had everything; everything was going for him and still he had landed on the floor with his nose broken, while his prize flew off like a flushed quail. Frankly, it could have ended worse; she could have whacked him with some heavy object right then. He would have to forgive himself and just learn from the experience. Yes, learning experience, that had a fine sound to it, helping to drown the bad memory.

On the other hand, I did show remarkable foresight, he was quick to remind himself. There was a plan B—prepared and executed ahead of the need. That's why he was not very worried about the future. A small apartment in downtown Honolulu was waiting for him; where he could hide and plan for the future. His modest one-bedroom place with ample provisions, a small cache of emergency money, a new passport and a new identity were his safe haven—once he got there safely.

Rosen had run out of his house in Lanikai ten minutes after watching Kalani rushing down the steep driveway. He thought he would have at least thirty minutes to get out of his lair, but was not willing to test this hypothesis. His personal treasure bag containing most of El Diablo's assets had been pushed into the backpack with a bit of food, and a handgun thrown in on top. He ran down the driveway and along the road to Kailua. Once outside Lanikai, he chose to walk on pathways protected by trees and bushes along the beach.

Sneaking through deserted streets, Rosen carefully picked his way towards Waimanalo, a small beach town closer to Honolulu. There, he jumped a chain link fence and found himself in a well-protected corner behind a huge banyan tree. He had a lot of time to mull over the events of the last night. He slept and ate some food from his back-pack. At dawn, Rosen made a wild dash across Waimanalo and followed along the coastal road leading as far as the landslide.

Black, unstable rubble spread all the way from the eroded volcanic mountain onto the beach and into the ocean. Millions of rock fragments, ranging from a fraction of an inch to a few yards in diameter, looked ready to roll if someone set foot on the slope. This was not the time to be bold. He could make out a faint pathway; someone had already walked this way and more than once.

Rosen found himself a place in weeds nearby and patiently waited. The sun was already heating his hideout harshly when two men carrying empty backpacks approached the path. Harry assumed they would try to cross the landslide in an attempt to get some supplies in Honolulu. They would know the way and, possibly, could protect him from muggers. They might try to rob him themselves, of course, but probably not before reaching Honolulu. Why shoot a mule before the end of the trek? Rosen thought. I will be prepared for that moment before they are.

He approached the men, humbly asking if they could help him to get across, to Honolulu. The shorter, older man, who seemed to be in charge, looked him over, his eyes lingering on the bulging backpack. His younger companion, an obnoxious-looking boy with Japanese letters tattooed on his chest and Polynesian patterns on his naked shoulders and arms, turned his head to the leader with a silent query. The somewhat rotund, pink-faced *haole* looked like an easy prey.

"*Vot's in da pack*? Why you go to Honolulu?" The older man asked sharply.

Harry declared himself a tourist stranded in Kailua, trying to get to Honolulu to grab the first plane leaving the island. "The backpack? Just a few personal things, and some food. Of course, I'd be happy to share it with you!"

The guy struggled with himself for a moment, but did

not reach to feel the pack; there would be lots of time for that. He shrugged and without saying much agreed to let Harry tag along with them. The older man led, followed by the youngster and Rosen, who was commanded to stay twenty feet behind. Afraid to trigger a new landslide and distributing weight—smart, Rosen thought.

Walking uphill on a shifting mass of small rocks was hard, and they kept sliding back. Fortunately, none of these slips resulted in an avalanche. Harry was wearing solid hiking boots, which made the climb somewhat easier, but his guides had only rubber sandals. Despite that, they were moving rapidly up like mountain goats with Rosen falling behind more and more. He lost sight of them when the trek turned from the loose, gravel-like pathway into an almost indistinguishable trail among large, black boulders. Now he had to climb ledges, jump over wide fissures, guided only by faint and uncertain marks of recently acquired wear on the rock's face. He walked with desperate determination and suddenly came upon his guides sprawled in the shade of a large boulder.

"Lunch time. What you have to eat?" the older man asked unceremoniously. Rosen dutifully pulled out a piece of bread, cheese and a can of beer. The guides were truly impressed, swallowed the food greedily and opened the beer. The foam of the warm and shaken beer spilled out of the can to yells of joy. They shared it between themselves without offering any to Harry.

"Good," said the boss, "now we go. We were waiting for you forever."

"How much longer is it to Honolulu?" asked Harry. He

257

was already exhausted.

"Hour over the rockslide, then fifteen miles to Honolulu. Way you walk, you'll make it by tomorrow," and both started laughing loudly and disrespectfully. Harry said nothing, but it was not his plan to walk another fifteen miles that day.

They disappeared between towering rocks within a few minutes and Rosen followed them at a slower pace, knowing they would wait for him somewhere, probably at the end of the rockslide. The trail led him now on the exposed ocean side of the mountain, and he could clearly see Rabbit Island a few hundred feet below. The black finger of rubble extended from the mountain, across the beach, pointing at the small rocky islet ringed by white surf. Beyond, the blue Pacific waters were unmarred except for the white wake of a small boat speeding south to Honolulu.

Wonder who has gas to motor to Honolulu, Rosen thought wistfully. He sat leaning against a warm rock, exposing his hot face to the ocean breeze. He was quite certain what he had to do. Regardless of their intentions, it would be extremely imprudent to leave two witnesses to his relocation. His broken face was easy to remember, and whoever was looking for him might easily meet these two men.

As he expected, they were sitting and smoking under the first tree that survived the landslide. The tree was sparsely covered with leaves and offered meager shade. Yellow and brown grass thinly blanketed the rocky soil. They were definitely off the windward side; rain was an infrequent visitor in this neighborhood.

Harry approached them with a tired smile, stopped six feet in front of them and took his backpack off. He reached inside and pulled out two chocolate bars—soft, bent and leaking brown beads. He held the chocolate out for the hungry men to see and desire. He knew that the high-energy food would be irresistible to the men who were starving and tired. They both rose from a slump, and then Rosen threw the chocolate on the ground in front of them. They looked down and reached for the bars, disregarding for a moment his disrespectful gesture.

Harry put his hand into the pack again and removed a short-barreled pistol. Before they looked up, one shot delivered to the top of the older man's head splashed his brain onto the drying grass. A few droplets of blood and yellow fatty substance landed on Rosen's pants. The boy struggled to get to his feet, but another bullet tore into the middle of his chest while his knees were still touching the ground. Rosen looked for a moment at the two bodies; the youngster was still twitching and moving. He stepped back to avoid additional soiling of his clothes, then another crack of the gun sent a bullet into the boy's temple, stopping all movement. One can't be too cautious.

Rosen picked up his chocolate and placed the bars back in the pack. There was nothing of value in the guides' pockets. They were just the mules that would take goods on one side of the rockslide and deliver on the other. Cigarettes were of no interest to Harry—a filthy and unhealthy habit. He took their almost empty bottles, poured the water into his own container and went looking for a suitable place to spend the night.

He knew of a golf course in this area, which might offer

a reasonable hide out. Indeed, thirty minutes down the road, there was a sign pointing to the Windward Golf Club. Rosen used his last bit of energy to walk to the empty lodge. The interior was fairly dark and pleasantly cool. He climbed through a broken window and sprawled himself on the polished concrete floor with great relief. Things were gradually looking up.

* * *

The small apartment building on Kalakaua Avenue had a backyard entrance. The house seemed undamaged; even windows were intact, except for the shattered corridor pane. The landlord was an old man who lived somewhere else, and this fact was just another small element of the elaborate plan of concealment that Rosen had orchestrated. Old men have bad eyes and poor memories; therefore, his landlord would be very unlikely to recognize Rosen whom he had met only once, when the lease had been signed. The rental checks were sent by mail, always on time. There was never any noise or disturbance; Harry Rosen was a perfect tenant, one whom the landlord would not remember.

Rosen positioned himself on the opposite side of the street in the shadow of a fern tree; he sat down like a tired traveler. He was tired, of course, but that was not the reason to sit under the tree. Inside his apartment, he could lie down, eat and drink. The reason he stayed outside was to allow himself the time and opportunity to look for any suspicious signs. No one knew of his safe house, but being security-conscious is a mindset. He went through the proper routines every single time, otherwise—he knew—someone would surprise him sooner or later. And he hated surprises.

CHAPTER 29

With the wind blowing at the stern, the weather appeared milder, and the boat's movements became gentler. Long smudges of fluorescence streaked in the wake, and sounds of the ocean decreased to be hardly noticeable.

"I know my sins, stupidity—mostly," Abe was coming back to their somewhat spiritual discussion. "Do you think stupidity is a sin? What are you guilty of?"

Jerry was not surprised by this question; he had been asking himself for weeks: why did I screw up so badly the first time I met Cat? The mental problems were not an excuse; the brick-wall man ceased to exist after their first evening together. What were my biggest faults?

"Laziness and stupidity, I think." Jerry reasoned aloud. "I was so accustomed to my way of living and thinking, that I couldn't make myself throw them off. I heard the arguments, but stuck to my old ideas like a bug to a windshield. It took a disaster to kick me out of my rut and—look at me—I took quite a bit of kicking, but I am a hundred times happier."

Abe nodded his head. "Same here. I think that stupidity is a major sin, whatever the pastor says on Sunday. If you think clearly, you don't do all these things, you know: stealing, killing and screwing around . . . Why would I steal if I could spend a fine day on the ocean, catch fish and make money? Killing? You must be drunk or high, otherwise it's such an obviously losing proposition. Adultery? If you're smart, you pick a woman that you really, really like—then what is the point of running after another?"

Jerry agreed. "Stupidity is the root of most evil," he declared. "Not so much because people lack brains, but more often they just don't want to use them. Guys who don't have enough horsepower in their skulls are rarely a problem. They do whatever it is that they can do, and often shine, in their uncomplicated ways. Decisions that we make in our lives are not that hard, most of the time."

Abe watched him, sprawled on the cockpit bench where Browser used to lounge.

"No, it's the folks with good brains who have problems. They're lazy and happily take someone else's opinion as their personal convictions. Why work the gray cells? It's easier to believe. Not only is it less tiring, but to fall into a fold is so much more sociable. The herd gives warmth and companionship, even if it's walking to the slaughterhouse. Politicos, market gurus, reverends provide all the answers, so why bother thinking on your own? Funny thing how many holy men enjoy a good life telling believers how to please God, as if it would be hard to figure out."

The wind was picking up and clouds covered the sky, making the skipper anxious—there was no harbor anywhere close to Kailua. Jerry's plan was to pick their way through a reef break, then come to the beach as close as they could, watching the depth gauge. But he feared two problems. First, you can't see the reef at night. He remembered from his kayaking an opening in the reef just to the right side of Flat Island, but to see the actual reef would be most reassuring. The second problem had no solution: the bay offered some protection from waves, but none against the wind. Jerry had to rely on luck, hoping that no storm would catch them, causing *Lady Luck* to drag her anchors and get stranded on the beach. His plan was to stay anchored for a few hours only—just enough to unpack the supplies, move out the fish and spend a bit of time with Cat. Then they would get out of Kailua Bay into the open ocean, far out into the ocean, where they would be safe from rocks, reefs and shoals—sailors' curses.

A dense layer of clouds covered the sky, reducing the shoreline to vaguely marked outlines. Not until midnight, when a cloud break allowed the moon to illuminate the shore, did Jerry realize to his horror, that they had overshot Flat Island; they were already downwind from it. Not far, perhaps a mile or two, but for a sailboat to be downwind from its mark is no small thing. They would have to turn far, a few miles at least, into the ocean, trying to gain distance upwind before aiming at Flat Island again. The wind was increasing, white water swirled around the boat, and they were extremely tired. They had slept only six, perhaps seven, hours over the past three days. Jerry could clearly see Flat Island now, a low-lying small patch of land. He could make out the spot inside the reef where they should have dropped the anchor, but to get there was not an easy task.

Skipper Browser would probably say: "We turn around and tack against the wind. We come in again in an hour or two." But Jerry was not Captain Browser, he was not a tough, old mariner with experience long enough to match his will. Jerry had forgotten: "You don't fuck with the ocean, Jerry."

"We turn the motor on, make a turn and come in motor-sailing. We'll be there in no time." The diesel came to life and *Lady Luck* stirred, vibrating and throwing white foam behind her stern. Jerry saw Bird Shit Island on his left, the place of the defeat that had transformed his life. He might never have met Cat if the islet had not brought him to his knees. Jerry might have had romantic notions about the Rock, but he was dead wrong to consider it a safe place for him. Bird Shit Rock did not care about his love life; it wanted to complete the job started a few weeks ago, finish him off.

The boat made a right turn, and carried on into the wind, seeking a course as parallel to the beach as possible. The bow crossed the wind-line and the headsail started fluttering anxiously on the right side. Jerry would never allow himself to do that with sails alone. The Rock was a very dangerous presence, and any mistake during the maneuver could land the boat in the boiling water, then on the rocky bottom. But he was running the motor, the reliable fifty-horsepower Yanmar. Jerry felt safe with the diesel to fall back on.

A sudden gust of wind leaned the boat to its right, and quickly increased their downwind drift. Jerry watched in horror as distance between the boat and the Rock was rapidly shrinking. He threw the throttle into full power, and the motor roared over the noise of crashing waves and whistle of the wind. *Lady Luck* accelerated slightly, but with the wind gust pressing even harder, a few seconds later a loud thud announced that the keel had struck the bottom. It was not the bone-crushing shock of a boat running into a rock; it felt as though the boat was pushed on the rocks sideways, her drifting keel prevented from moving further by the hard resistance.

The helmsman jerked the main sheet to release the sail, too slow. The wind attacked again with a great fury, but *Lady Luck* could not move aside any more, she was against the wall. They heard a loud crack above, and the sails came tumbling down. Standing behind the steering wheel, the skipper was outside of the area covered with the white fabric and had a full, terrifying view of the consequences that his unfortunate decision had brought.

The mast had broken off six feet above the deck and flew over the right railing, as far as the steel rigging allowed. Its tip was submerged in the water, but not deep enough to act as an anchor that might stop the boat right there, at Bird Shit Rock. The faithful motor kept roaring and pushing the crippled craft away from the islet. The boat straightened up once the mast fell, and in a moment the horrible thumping noise had stopped. They were off the rock and moving forwards.

The white mass of the sail moved in front of the cockpit, and a few seconds later Abe's head appeared from under the fabric's edge. He was not injured, just badly shaken. "What the fuck!" He looked up and did not need any further explanations. They tied the mast to the hull and gathered the sails as best they could.

Flat Island appeared ahead a few minutes later, and they

passed the reef's breach without problems. *Lady Luck* floated gently towards the beach where they dropped two anchors in twenty feet of water. That would have been perfect, if they still had the mast. John would not be happy with his student, but they were alive and home. The Rock had missed him again.

Kalani and Cat made an official party in honor of their men, but the *Lady Luck*'s crew and skipper fell asleep with their mouths full of fish. Kalani's herd had a great time and stuffed themselves for the first time in a month.

* * *

Jerry woke up before noon the next day, alone. He went to the beach to see his boat. There she was, gently rocking on her anchors, a broken mast sticking up, crying to the heavens about his poor seamanship. Jerry swam to her, dove outside, climbed aboard—there was a nasty scar on the right side of her keel but no punctures, and she was not taking water. There was a chance for him to remain her captain.

The aluminum mast had broken off six and a half feet above the deck. Jerry thought he might extend it by inserting a smaller-diameter pole into the remaining stump. That would give him a bit of sailing power. Sure, not enough to cross the Pacific, but maybe just enough to sail a few miles out and catch some fish.

He went looking for Cat and the rest of them; it couldn't be too difficult to find Kalani and her kids. Jerry was surprised to see a lot of people on Kainalu Street, all heading in the same direction. Following them, he soon found a good-size crowd at the recreational center, mostly on the tennis courts. When he came closer, he saw a rudimentary market in full bloom.

At least twenty people stood or sat behind tables removed from the recreation center, hawking their goods. Jerry could only marvel at the variety of offerings in this devastated town that had been cut off from the rest of the world for close to a month. Despite widespread hunger, there were some food items. An elderly Japanese man was showing off holdovers from better times: a few cans of sardines and tuna. He had a lot of potential customers for his food, but the old guy did not see anything that he would like or need. He held out for a better offer. The concept of money had not entered this economy yet.

A Filipino family put a few bunches of bananas on the table, as well as a small bucket of guavas and herbs that Jerry did not know. They were in the process of haggling over an ancient manual drill, which in this society, without electrical power and an unimaginable need for repairs, suddenly had become an object of desire. The man lost his trader's cool and, despite his wife's not so subtle hints, was rapidly throwing additional guavas in to close the deal.

Cat and Kalani had already sold their fish, trading it for Government Issue packages of Meal-Ready-To-Eat food that had found their way to Windward under mysterious circumstances. A few papayas and some chives neatly put away into their basket, they were currently haggling over a solar panel coupled to a battery and an inverter. The fish was commanding a good price.

A large portion of the crowd were just onlookers, but trade was brisk. In the morning, Kalani had sent word that there would be fish for sale, and after a slow start the number of traders increased steadily. It appeared that everybody had something they could live without, as long as they could find an item they needed. Barter was the mode of exchange, but Jerry the Economist was sure that money, whatever its form, would appear soon. One thing he did not expect at the market was paper money. One doesn't trade things of value for a piece of paper, no matter what the number on it is.

Many people had no business to conduct at the market, but they lingered, drawn by the palpable excitement. The mere act of trading made them feel like logic had returned to the overturned world. In a place where apathy, depression and deprivation ruled, people suddenly found an outlet for their energy, a reason to make an effort. Choices had to be made, intelligence exercised, plans made for the future. The crowd was noisy and happy. Laughter, laughter that was so rarely heard, broke out like a rainbow after a very long rain.

Kalani's charges were running in circles through the crowd, happily contributing to the din and hum of the large, outdoor party. At one point, one by one, they returned to their protector and stood next to her, holding onto the flowery fabric of her tattered dress. Not one said a thing; they all looked in one direction with painful desire in their eyes. The adults followed their gaze and there, next to the door leading to court number three, stood the first manufacturer of post-cataclysmic Kailua.

A short woman, with loose folds of skin on her arms, was holding a pole crowned with a red ball. Multiple five-inch-long sticks projected out of the ball, each with a lump of colored sugar stuck to its end.

"That must be Mrs. Hewlett, the lady who owned the dry cleaning," whispered Kalani. "Hard to recognize, she's lost so much weight."

Mrs. Hewlett seductively waved the candies towards the children who responded with a simultaneous movement of their heads, as if hypnotized. The kids, who had been close to death from starvation a few days ago, who had eaten blubber soup without complaint yesterday, now fell under the spell of the primitive candies.

"Good morning, Mrs. Hewlett," Kalani greeted her politely. "Your candies look very tempting."

"What do you have?" the older woman was inspecting Kalani, then the rest of the group.

"The fact is," Kalani sighted, "that we have nothing to trade now. We had fish, but it's all gone."

The candy lady was disappointed. Seeing nine kids mesmerized by her wares, she had been ready to make a killing. She shrugged and said mildly, "Well, then . . . Maybe tomorrow . . . "

"Tomorrow" has all the qualities of "never," "forget it," "maybe some other time"—in children's minds. Nine faces fell; the mouths turned down, eyes blinking to hide tears, but even so clear drops trickled down their cheeks.

"How about a pound of fresh fish for nine candies?" They heard Abe's confident voice coming from behind. He knew she could not refuse a few lumps of sugar for a pound of fish.

Kalani looked around, "But we're out of fish, Abe. We have none left, even for us."

"Well, a pound of fish—but not today: tomorrow or day after. We will go out fishing today, right, Skipper?" And so Abe initiated a futures market in commodities.

Jerry's heart, though he still considered himself anything but an economist, sang at this marvelous display of chaos organizing itself into a living, breathing free market economy. All in the span of one morning, Adam Smith would have been proud of the people of Kailua.

* * *

Neighbors and friends, this is Cat again. I want to share great news with you. Today, we can mark as a day when our community started moving forward again. Oh, we are still in rough shape. Lots of us are sick, and nobody had enough to eat today. But, we've made the first step to make Kailua a thriving town again. We have restarted its economy. The market opened at the recreation center today, and it was a great success. People who came had few things to trade, but you can't overestimate the impact of this event on our lives.

We have rediscovered reasons to work and produce. We need everything, and people among us will produce most of it. Today, we were selling fish, enough to put sushi on a lot of family tables tonight. We sold papayas, guavas—all the things that grow abundantly in our loving Hawaiian soil. Tomorrow, we will be selling furniture, bicycles, and wheelbarrows. The day after that, you will see electronics, you will have power in your homes. We will make it happen. Just remember, we did it ourselves. There were no knights in shining armor showing up at the rec center, no Santa dropping packages from the skies. It was you and I, and all our friends who got up off the floor like a boxer still punch-drunk, but we are back on our feet. We are on our feet and fighting back. So when someone comes telling us how lucky we were, and what they could do for us—just ask them, "Where were you, when we were dying?"

If there is any silver lining to this thunderstorm that has shattered our lives, it must be this lesson: in order to survive one must rely on himself or herself, family and neighbors. Far-away people, organizations and governments have their own problems and agendas. The welfare of Kailua is so low on their list that, I believe, someone must have stepped on this part of their paper, and that's why nobody has noticed us starving.

We want to have the right and means to protect ourselves when another disaster strikes. Food warehouses in Honolulu and the uniformed men commanded from the Mainland did us no good, even though we paid for them with our taxes. The power and resources have to remain here, where we can control them.

Cat did not feel well and wanted to finish quickly—she felt a wave of nausea coming. "That will be all for tonight, folks. Have a good rest; there is a lot of work for you, to-morrow."

Jerry stood behind the glass pane looking at her talking, gesticulating and waving her hands. She was a powerful orator and had the instincts of a leader. Cat finished and slumped in her chair. The on-air light went off and he entered the studio. Her eyes were closed, her breathing fast and shallow. She felt hot to touch.

"Are you OK, Cat? You feel warm," he was worried.

"No, no, Jerry, I'm fine. It's from excitement, and I am really worn out. Let's go home, OK?"

They traveled along the dark streets, meeting people who greeted her like an old friend. Maybe it was just an illusion, but Jerry thought the people were moving in a more purposeful way, keeping their heads higher. Cat was right; Kailua was on its way to recovery.

No matter how much he wanted to stay with Cat, *Lady Luck* needed to go out into the ocean; concern of her being stranded did not leave him. They were lucky so far; the wind had been no more than twenty knots, and the anchors held, but that could change in a very short time. Besides, the market was waiting for fish.

Abe had spent the last few hours trying to restore the mast. They discovered that it was not easy to find a pole long, strong and light enough. As in the old joke, they could have any two features, but not all three. Eventually, three windsurf masts wrapped together with duct tape and thin line, then stuck into the stump, provided an additional ten feet of height, while being remarkably light. The new mast was supported with ropes and the sails wrapped around it. There was no way to know how much this rig would allow sailing upwind, but downwind, they should have some sail power.

Cat did not look well. Her cheeks were flushed rather than pale, but that did not give her a healthy appearance. Her breathing was fast, and she slumped anytime she thought Jerry was not watching her. He could worry, but he could not stay.

The night was clear when Jerry and Abe slowly motored by Flat Island. Starting out that early, late at night actually, they hoped to be back before sunset of the next day. In view of their recent trading success, they wanted to deliver a truly commercial load of fish this time.

They motored upwind for fifteen minutes, then started unwrapping the main sail. Lashed to the boom, it rapidly filled with wind and, though misshapen and stubby, it could be called a sail again. The jib followed and the boat heeled slightly. The improvisation worked! The boat would not tack to the wind at more than seventy degrees, but, Jerry thought, neither would Columbus's Santa Maria!

The long and shallow tacks slowly gained them distance to the east; that was all they needed—with the fishing lines trailing behind they were in no hurry. In the afternoon, they would turn west and swoop into Kailua like a Spanish galleon carrying a treasure of fish.

The ocean had a great influence on Abe. On land, he was a shy and withdrawn man; only among friends could the full extent of his personality and wit be revealed. On the water, Abe displayed not only an amazing physical strength and agility, but also an intellectual curiosity that Jerry had not suspected.

"What Cat was saying about us having to rely on ourselves, do you think it can be done?"

"Don't see why not," Jerry answered curtly—the stress and anxiety of taking the crippled boat to the ocean was only slowly dissipating.

"But, you know, they will never give up on us, I mean, the Americans." Saying this, Abe remembered that Jerry was an American as well, and started fumbling with a fishing rod.

Jerry shrugged, "Abe, what you are saying is that the American *government* would not allow that, right? I can assure you that the average American wouldn't care whether Hawaii has a governor, a king or a president." He remembered that waitress in San Diego.

Abe put the rod away and returned to the topic, "I don't know; they did this thing to Queen Liliuokalani, just locked her up."

Jerry didn't think it was Hawaii independence that Cat meant in her speech, but the subject was interesting and the fishing lines remained undisturbed. "We have to ask the question: what is it that the American government wants from Hawaii? I don't think they are after your pineapples or fish. They want their military bases. If you try to evict them from Pearl Harbor, yeah—that looks like a major problem. They won't allow that as long as they can breathe. But, if you would give them, say, a long-term lease, they might be open to discussion. Not willingly, mind you, but if you produce enough stink, at one point someone might say: 'To hell with it, all these problems and bad press—we can just as well keep our bases and let them run their bloody islands into muck, if that's what they want'."

Abe smiled and asked, "You think we would run Hawaii into muck?"

"I don't know, buddy. Do you think you have enough people who know how to run the country?"

Abe checked the fishing lines, which were still not attracting any bites. "We could hire people; Cat, for example, she seems to know what to do. Perhaps, even you...." He smiled provocatively.

"What makes you believe, Abe, that I could be hired for a government job? I'm a free spirit now, don't you see?"

Abe's white teeth shone in the light of the oil lamp. "If Cat agrees to work for Hawaii, you might need a job here." He had a point, but Jerry would rather stay clear of any government employment; there had to be a more productive way to spend one's life.

The dawn colored the sky pink in the east. Now all the vital elements— light, wind and waves—were coming from the same direction, as though someone had made a hole in the great black canopy covering the earth, allowing new and exciting things to stream through this opening into a world that was dark, solid and static.

Something moved at the periphery. Five or six torpedo-shaped creatures shot up from the water, spinning along their long axis. Silver bodies shone for a moment in the early morning light only to splash back into the dark water. Spinner dolphins, smaller than their more commonly seen bottlenose cousins, seemed to perform their unusual tricks just for entertainment. They stayed around for a few minutes and disappeared under the waves.

Abe was back to the theory of redemption taking place in Paradise. "So what do you think Cat's problem is? She's certainly not stupid."

Jerry had secretly pondered this question for the past few days. Cat was just, just too perfect! Not stupid . . . not lazy . . . What was the sin that she was paying for?

"Bitchy?" Abe proposed without further elaboration, looking the other way.

Jerry raised his head, somewhat offended, but Abe's remark did direct his thoughts to the fact that Cat could be quite an arrogant, opinionated and unsympathetic individual. The image of the last day of his Hawaiian vacation came to his mind. Jeremy smiled. "You might be on to something, Abe, though I would prefer to use a different word. She is . . . let's say uncompromising and forceful in her opinions. The other thing, Cat has only recently learned to trust other people—not that many, as a matter of fact. Like the rest of us sinners, she's only slowly struggling towards sainthood."

A rod suddenly bowed into the letter "U" and the float disappeared under the water. "Wow," uttered Abe. "That's a big one!" They had hoped for a large fish, and Abe had loaded rolls of hundred-pound rated fishing line, but for this monster it might not be enough. Abe positioned himself at the stern, holding the rod. This would be a long fight with no certain outcome.

"You better haul him in," Jerry yelled, "Mrs. Hewlett is waiting for her fish."

Abe only smiled excitedly; there was no room for distractions at this moment. He did what he loved, and he did it well. Jerry thought they did not need to worry about food anymore. The fish was running deep, taking a lot of line. Every time Abe tried to slow the reel, the rod was bending sharply, so he hastily backed off. More than an hour passed and only a little line was left on the drum. Abe was desperately trying to rig an extension when the fish changed its tactics, allowing Abe to start reeling line in as well as let it out.

Jerry's head snapped forward when a loud flapping noise resounded in front of the boat. The headsail had worked its way out of the improvised point that tied it to the bow and started fluttering wildly in the wind. The fabric might get shredded in no time. Jerry lashed the wheel to the pulpit and leaped to the bow. He took his position just out of the flailing sail's range, and lunged when its wild thrashing subsided for a moment. He wrestled it down and retied it. This would have to do for now; *Lady Luck* stopped, the bow pointing straight into the wind, the boom swinging from one side to another, within a foot or two of Abe's head. He could get knocked out at any moment, as he was facing the stern, unaware of the heavy object flying behind him.

As Jerry brought the yacht on course, the duel between Abe and the fish continued. It was another hour before the marlin was brought within a few feet of the boat. They were ready for him. He could be lost if they tried to pull him in with the boathook; he was much too big to even consider their pickup net. Loosing this fish was not something they could afford; this was not a sporting event, they needed the beast for its body. Beautiful or not, noble or not—it was much-needed food. Jerry had no scruples; he shot the marlin with his spear gun the moment it was close enough. The sharp point plunged behind the head, and the harpoon's metal butterfly opened up, fastening the fish solidly to the gun by means of five feet of braided nylon line. The prize was theirs.

The fishing trip was already a success, no matter if anything else took the hook, but they did catch more. By two o'clock, they also had a good-size mahi-mahi, a small tuna and a barracuda. It was a good day. They looked at each other; they were ready to return to the Round House. *Lady Luck* turned her back to the wind, the bizarre sails hanging from the squat mast bellowed and she started her sedate journey home. The triumphant crew filled the air with boisterous laughter as Jerry and Abe egged each other on to ever more outrageous stories and discussions. They felt like warriors coming back from an expedition successful beyond their dreams. They had proved to themselves to be individuals of wisdom and power; very shortly their women would see that as well.

Flat Island came into view, the reef passed harmlessly on the side and the boat came to rest in her previous spot. Abe took the marlin on his back and proudly carried it to the Round House while the skipper cleared the deck. He was back ten minutes later looking very worried. "You better leave the boat, Jerry. Come home; Cat is sick."

CHAPTER 30

Honolulu was much hotter than the trade-wind-cooled Kailua. Rosen was getting increasingly hot and uncomfortable. He had no more water. After forty-five minutes, he got up with a great effort and walked across black, soft asphalt. There were no pedestrians on the streets; whoever could hide from the sun did so.

The corridor was quite dusty, just as he remembered it, but otherwise unremarkable. The walls were moderately dirty but without graffiti; no teenagers, who would deface the walls or be nosy about their neighbors, lived in this building. The other three tenants of this quadruplex were two elderly couples and an old woman with a small dog, seemingly even older than she.

"Juan Gomez" announced his little brass plate. He had a weakness for Spanish sounding names, sweet memories of Nicaragua, probably. The lock looked fine, and his key turned twice, unlocking the door. Rosen opened the door and strode straight to the refrigerator where there should be an ample supply of Gatorade. It wouldn't be cold, but he was dehydrated and craved the slightly salty drink. He reached for the refrigerator's handle.

"Senor Gomez, will you please close the door?"

A cruel, hard hand seemed to grasp Harry's guts and twist them mercilessly. He turned his head slowly, already knowing the inevitable. In the corner next to the door sat an old man. Of all things and people on earth, there was nothing and nobody that Rosen feared more than this man. Without thinking, he sank to his knees and prostrated himself before El Diablo.

"The door, Bonito, the door," reminded the voice benignly. "You kept me waiting a long time." Rosen obediently rose to his feet and slowly closed the apartment door, which felt like a heavy steel gate of a bank vault closing on his life. The thought of bolting out did not even occur to him. El Diablo made no mistakes, except once: when he left the hacienda in Bonito's hands. No gun, Rosen thought, but certainly, it's there . . . somewhere, aimed into my belly, perhaps under the hat covering his right hand.

"The handcuffs, on the table, put them on."

Bonito took a pair of metal handcuffs, put them on his wrists and tightened them carefully. He knew the routine. It was a victim's duty to apply restraints. Any resistance or negligence was watched for carefully and punished extra severely to indoctrinate absolute obedience.

"Same for the legs, Bonito." Harry applied leg irons. The old man had come fully prepared. Rosen had no right to have any hope. What he had done was punishable only by death, and not just any death. He could be sure that the Master had prepared something extra painful and extra long for him. Something that would make him hope for death and await it eagerly. At the same time, the instinct of self-preservation would not let him rebel and invite a quick end.

Bonito returned to his prostrate position.

"Bonito, your worst crime is causing me severe embarrassment. I was embarrassed in front of myself by having placed my trust in hands as unworthy as yours. The mental discomfort you caused me was just increasing as I followed you. Your stupidity and clumsiness were so acute that I repeatedly had to question my own judgment. Having all the means that you stole from me, having the benefit of my tutelage for a few years, you still made the most miserable effort to hide your pathetic person."

Rosen remained on his knees waiting for the pronouncement of the verdict. Am I going to die here, or will he take me to some remote place to enjoy my cries, moans and begging for days? He wondered, as his terror mixed with morbid excitement.

Carlos, the warehouse attendant on the hacienda, the stupid man who had tried to steal food and escape . . . he had been brought back. In fact, Bonito had brought him back himself; made him run barefoot behind a slow-moving truck. It had taken them four hours driving in low gear to get over the twenty miles that Carlos had managed to cover during his escape. By the time they entered the compound, Carlos's feet were leaving bloody tracks with every step. Then he was hanged by his hands from a branch of the big tree, right in front of the Master's studio, close enough to be clearly seen whenever El Diablo wished to have a moment of relaxation, but far enough to avoid the smell of the decomposing body. Nobody knew when exactly he died. After a week, his body had simply fallen off, probably helped by vultures. Bonito ordered him buried in a hole dug in the jungle.

"First things first," continued the old man. "Let's start with you returning my stolen assets. They wouldn't be in this backpack, would they? That would be awfully thoughtful of you. Empty the pack!"

Rosen crawled on his knees towards the pack.

"You really let yourself go, my former disciple." The Master looked at him with contempt. "Just looking at you makes me sick. A fat, ugly monkey without a spark of intelligence. How could I tolerate you around me for so long? That's what bothers me, the extent of my unforgivable misjudgment. You are one of those people who can't live and prosper without a master providing structure and discipline. You are a slave, in other words, not a master's trainee. You need pain and degradation, just as much as you need food and air, perhaps more."

Bonito's humiliation and fear mixed into a paralyzing cocktail. He pulled out remnants of bread and chocolate, then noted the handle of the pistol buried among plastic bags containing wads of hundred-dollar bills. A sudden bolt of hope sprung him into action. He took the handle and was about to pull the gun out in a desperate attempt to win his life back, when—perhaps he moved too fast—the hat on El Diablo's hand jumped and a shot reverberated through the small room. Rosen felt as though someone had kicked him in the stomach. He fell on his side, clutching his abdomen; his hand turned red. He couldn't move his legs.

"So, actually, in the end, you showed a tiny bit of character; you've reached for a gun," noted the old man with grudging approval. "Just as well. I had other plans for you, but you've forced my hand, congratulations! In any case, with a belly wound, it will take you a few hours to die, so we have a bit of time to talk."

Rosen looked up from the worn-out carpet. To his surprise, the pain was not that severe. Surely, Carlos had it worse, or Consuela, he thought.

"The second reason I felt offended was Consuela. I trained that girl to become a fine instrument of pleasure, and you stole her and then destroyed her. That was the act of an oafish peasant, not the way of an artist I hoped you would become one day. Shame on you, Bonito! She was probably just too smart for you to control her, but not smart enough for her to control you. Not like this other girl, in Hawaii! She really did a job on you, didn't she! I was laughing my head off."

"You were in my house in Kailua?" Bonito asked in shock, forgetting for a moment about his wound. Intense shame and humiliation overcame his physical pain. This was the last man on earth he would have liked to witness his defeat. The master of the dark art of torture observed his incompetence and laughed. Rosen used to enjoy thinking of himself as someone akin to a grand chess master, planning his actions with inexorable logic, executing the moves for reasons so far ahead in the future that other humans could not possibly guess their significance. Now he had suddenly become the subject of ridicule. The person who truly knew the beauty of deadly intrigue and a cunning mind looked down at him with contempt.

The old man chuckled happily, seeing Rosen's pride shattered in the last hours of his life. "A nice house you bought with my money, well situated, too. It's the interior decoration that was rather unfortunate. Anaïd . . . a beautiful piece, it's true, but so predictable. I thought you might want one in your bedroom so I called around to see if any marble-sculpting studio might have had a recent order for a reproduction. When I found that one piece—and that was a big one, a full size figure— was shipped from Pietrasanta, Italy to Hawaii, I just had to come and see it. It looked really impressive, and when I saw your girl dusting her . . . Well, old man that I am, I was more than touched. I just wish you had outfitted this apartment better. I had to wait for you here almost twenty-four hours."

Harry shivered and could not feel his lower body. A pool of blood was slowly enlarging around him, dark clots forming at the edges. The Anaïd, he thought, she betrayed me, like all the women in my life. There was no way I could keep them, even with handcuffs and leg irons. Consuela, the one who promised to remain my slave forever, escaped too, killed herself. El Diablo is right; I could never become the master, I am too weak.

"Well, Bonito, I would like to stay longer to entertain you in your last moments, but I should not repeat your mistakes. Who knows, maybe someone else is following your clumsy steps? I must go. I am going to shoot you once more in the belly, to make sure you won't survive, then I'll be on my way."

He raised the handgun and aimed between the chained-man's eyes; Rosen instinctively raised his hands to protect his face. The old man dropped the barrel quickly, almost touching Harry's upper abdomen, then another shot shook the apartment.

"I told you I would shoot you in the belly, you stupid oaf," the old man chuckled again. "You don't get it, even when told. Well, with your liver shot up you are as good as dead. Enjoy!" He stood up, put the gun into his pocket, took the backpack and slowly walked out. He kindly held the outside door open for the old lady coming in with a small dog and walked away with short steps, the way old men walk.

Harry felt very cold. Then darkness came over his eyes until, in a moment of terror, he saw the face of his old Master. Harry Rosen was dead.

CHAPTER 31

C at lay on her back, staring passively at the ceiling, but turned her eyes to the door and smiled weakly when Jerry entered the room. It was a very sad smile. Jerry knew Cat being happy and had seen her angry, but never experienced the dejected look of Cat vanquished. Her face was flushed and a thick blanket covered her up to her chin, despite the afternoon sun heating the house.

"You were right, Professor; I must be quite sick. There is nothing I can do, can't even think. But I'm happy to have you back. You know, Ruth was right. I can bring you back if I really, really want you. I brought you from New York and now from the ocean. We may not have much time together, so I'm really happy you're back."

Jerry listened to her, feeling his scalp tingling. "No!" He did not mean it to sound that sharp. "We are going to have a lot of time together, and I won't let you slip away again!" He turned around and bumped into Kalani. "We're going to the hospital!"

"Jerry, Dr. Lim was already here, and she will be back in twenty minutes. She said there is nothing they could do for her. It's an infection and they have no antibiotics."

Dr. Lim was a pleasant, older woman whom Jerry had

met once. She was apologetic, but could not help. Cat had a urinary tract infection, which would have been a minor, common thing under normal circumstances, but these were not normal circumstances. Cat had been starving for weeks, and her body's ability to fight infection was gravely compromised. She could be saved with an antibiotic costing only a few dollars, but there was none left in Kailua.

"Jerry, I can't tell you how sorry I am. She was our soul and our brain in the darkest hours we ever had. But now she is on the way to developing sepsis, blood poisoning; then the organs will shut down, and she will die. She needs antibiotics to survive. There are none here; I know that. Believe me, I have seen a lot of people dying from infections over the past month. The families would have dug medications from under the ground, if any could be found there, but there are just no drugs here anymore. They might have some in Honolulu. I've heard they had a few transport ships unloaded, but she doesn't have much time. I can't tell you exactly how much, but anything over twelve hours would be pushing her luck."

There is a chance then! Jerry's mind raced. Twelve hours—how can I get to Honolulu over the mountains and be back in twelve hours? Even Abe couldn't do that. How about getting Cat to Honolulu? That would halve the time. We could sail with her to Honolulu on *Lady Luck*. A few gallons of diesel left . . . if that just lasted to Makapu'u— once we clear the point, it's a straight sail downwind to Honolulu. The boat is Cat's last chance!

Fifteen minutes later, the fish were off the boat and Cat bundled into the cockpit. She wanted to stay close to Jerry and he agreed; the cabin was—at least in his mind—still reeking of blood. She nestled on a bed of pillows, covered with warm blankets. Cat was smiling and seemed comfortable. Reassuring vibrations shook the boat with a turn of the key and push of the button. A group of silent well-wishers looked on from the beach as they moved past Flat Island. Jerry kept his course just outside but parallel to the reef, hoping to shorten the distance; they were running on fumes. The fuel gauge was hanging over "empty."

The wind's direction had been changing; it was coming from the northeast now. If they had to rely on sail power, Jerry would have to tack very far into the ocean. *Lady Luck* being crippled, her ability to gain mileage upwind was very poor. It would take much more than twelve hours just to reach the Makapu'u point. Their only chance was *Iron Jenny*, the motor.

"Give us just another ten miles," he prayed, "ten miles." Abe stood at the bow, looking for rocks that might lurk under the water as they skimmed the reef. Cat was quiet, not complaining, not moving, following Jerry with her eyes. Perhaps she was losing her sense of reality. Her eyes would remain still for long periods of time as though she was asleep with her eyes open, and then she would emerge, look at him with understanding and sink back again. There was nothing more Jerry could do, but hope and keep his mind focused on sailing.

Makapu'u lighthouse was blinking closer and closer as Jerry recited his mantra, "Don't quit yet, don't quit yet," his white knuckles on the steering wheel. It was completely dark when *Lady Luck*'s bow protruded beyond the blackness of the rock and the vista of the Molokai Channel opened to the south. At this point, Jerry could take a right turn, and the wind, which by now was coming almost directly from the north, would propel them to Honolulu. They had a straight shot. The old friend Yanmar was still purring when they turned around the point, closer than prudence would dictate, and spread their jury-rigged sails. The wind in the channel picked up and hissing white caps appeared all around.

Jerry's soul soared, even when the diesel coughed and quit a few minutes later. It had delivered, brought them as far as he had begged. Now the sails would do their part, and they should be in Honolulu in a couple of hours where, he was certain, there had to be a functioning hospital with basic supplies.

The sky was overcast and visibility was poor, but they could distinguish the dark shapes of Koko Head volcano and the irregular outlines of Hawai Kai town passing on the right side. The ridged mass of Diamond Head was coming into view, illuminated by moonlight flowing through a break in the clouds. Moments later the gap between the clouds closed, and Jerry could not see the buoy, which should be somewhere nearby. He kept close to shore, suspecting that *Lady Luck* would maneuver poorly in the strong channel wind; he dreaded overshooting Honolulu port as he had done landing at Kailua Beach the first time. He wanted to sail as straight a course to Honolulu Harbor as possible.

A month ago, he had sailed the same way, saw the same landmarks, but now he felt that the man who crossed the Pacific must have been someone else. Jerry, the person holding the steering wheel now, was born in Hawaii; all the events of his life that had some meaning had happened on this island.

The boat crashed without any warning. The sudden jolt threw Jerry against the steering wheel, the only reason he stayed upright. Abe, who had been standing at the bow, was thrown overboard, but with his great strength he held onto the railing and pulled himself back in. The impact felt very different from drifting onto Bird Shit Rock. It felt as if *Lady Luck* had been hit by a runaway locomotive. The explosion of the crash penetrated every fiber of their bodies as the boat came to a standstill with a slight list to the starboard side. The waves ran by, kept crashing against her hull, but the boat was not going anywhere. They were stuck on a rock.

Cat slid along the bench like on a shuffleboard, but stopped on the pillows bunched up at the end of the seat. She opened her eyes and looked at Jerry, but did not look alarmed. She smiled and quietly asked, "Are you OK, Jerry? You look really good." She was gone, not aware of the world around her.

Jerry could see the halogen lights of the Honolulu port; they were probably unloading another ship. They had supplies, and Cat was dying within reach of her salvation. In better days, on her kayak, she could have gotten there within thirty minutes.

Abe came back from the cabin. "No water's coming in."

Thank God for that; we are not sinking, but that won't save Cat. What would John do? Jerry thought in desperation. Help me, old friend, what else I can do?

His eyes fell on a dinghy lashed to the deck. Dinghy! There was no gas for the motor, of course, but maybe he could row ashore. The distance to the crashing waves marking the shore was not more than a mile. On the other hand, rowing a rubber dinghy in the channel, with winds accelerating up to thirty knots, was just impossible. The wind blowing on the tall sides of a rubber craft would overpower the strongest man. With no keel, a little rubber boat would slide like a dried leaf driven by capricious winds. But again, what other options were there—sitting and watching Cat die?

"Abe, help me put the dinghy in the water."

"Jerry, you can't make it. You'll both die."

"Put the bloody boat in the water!" They wrestled the dinghy down against the wind trying to yank it out of their hands or turn it upside down. They threw the oars in, and Jerry jumped into it. Abe lowered Cat in, who obediently wrapped her arms around Jerry's neck. He put her on the floor, and Cat seemed somewhat disappointed when told to let go, but snuggled against his legs on the rubber bottom. The oars in place, Jerry looked up and nodded. Abe nodded back, "Good luck, *brah*, you deserve each other," and threw the line into the dinghy.

The rubber boat was immediately seized by a gust that drove them away from *Lady Luck*. Jerry plunged the oars in, trying to give direction to their movement. He knew it would be futile to fight the wind, but hoped that floating with the wind and waves he could nudge the boat slowly until they touched the shore. No matter where, he could carry Cat from there. They were still a couple of miles up-

291

wind from the harbor and, although the dinghy moved fast with the wind, he had perhaps thirty to forty minutes to close the distance that separated them from the land.

Thirty minutes of furious work produced little result. They came a bit closer when the wind slackened, only to be blown away a few minutes later, when a swirling gust turned the dingy around and pushed them in a different direction. His heart pounding and his body at the breaking point, he was not making any progress. The bright lights of the port appeared close by now, and he saw a freighter being unloaded by a crane. The last murderous try as they floated by had failed, and then they entered the darkness of night below the port. There were no other lights down the shore. He was defeated.

Old Man Ocean has won. "He always does," John said. "It's just that often he doesn't mind us playing on his lap. Sometimes he feels like a grandpa; allows us to take his fish, smiles when we sail our little ships. But when he gets angry, you better take your tail between your legs and get out of the way. He always wins."

I know, John, you don't fuck with the ocean, Jerry almost smiled. I am totally spent. The game is over. He slumped next to Cat and took her in his arms. She was warm and seemed quite content. They lay on the rubber floor of the boat that was sliding on the waves—forward, backward and sideways. All they felt was the rocking movement, made gentler by the rubber craft's elastic walls. The sky above them swirled and jumped. The water splashing their bodies was warm, and they were protected from the wind. It did not feel like a disagreeable way to end their existence.

Cat's alertness was fluctuating. Sometimes she tightened her arms around him or touched his face, and then she would go limp as though in a deep sleep. He knew they were passing Keehi Lagoon, where *Lady Luck* had been hiding, then Barber's Point with its single red light on the refinery chimney; after that, there was the open ocean. Two or three thousand miles of open water to the Cook Islands, though the current would more likely float them towards Japan. We're crossing the river Styx into Hades in our own rubber boat, Jerry thought.

He slept somewhat during the night, and when the first light started breaking over the horizon, he felt some energy coming back. A look over the dinghy's sides showed only water, 360 degrees around. No land, no ships, just miles and miles of water. Surprisingly, he felt no anxiety.

What's there to complain about? I've lived through enough excitement for three lives. I have Cat in my arms; we are not in acute pain. . . . Yes, it would be good to live with her for another fifty years, see our children and grow old together. But would I swap this moment, as it is, for a lifetime of existence as it was before Cat? No, certainly not. I've found my place. It's here, in this dinghy because that's where Cat is.

He found a plastic bottle of water on the floor and a signaling kit. Probably, Abe threw those in at the last moment. He gave a sip to Cat every now and then. He did not drink himself, did not want to outlive her. There was no way he could throw her overboard as he had done with John and the pirates. This was a fitting way for them to go, together. In fact, although his mouth was very dry, and he felt thirsty, it did not cause him any great discomfort; dehydration is not a painful death.

The sun was up and beat on their heads mercilessly. Cat opened her eyes. She was not talking but appeared more aware. He gave her the last drink and filled the bottle with ocean water; soaking their heads brought relief. So many things he could tell her, but really, there was no need. Her blond head was resting on his lap; they felt each other's presence and it was as good as they could have it, under the circumstances.

Transcript of a conversation, Washington D.C.

Speaker 1: *This woman in Hawaii has crossed the line. What are they going to do?*

Speaker 2: *Well, she definitely has nerve. There is no way to interpret her radio speech other than a call to separate Hawaii from the old U.S. of A. Not that they will not try to spin it another way. The Prez was quite irked. The last thing he needs now is to have a new trouble, a new front to fight. Much depends on what she does next. If she appears at a press conference in Washington and says that all she wants is to fight an inefficient bureaucracy and corrupt officials, they will make her the new governor of Hawaii or something along that line. If, on the other hand, she's serious, I don't know, she better watch her back.*

Speaker 1: *So, did they order her arrest?*

Speaker 2: *Arrest, shmarrest. Why call things ugly names? Let's say that the Prez would like to speak with her personally, pronto. The Secret Service will take care of that. Meantime, the relief operation will start in ten hours, as soon as the President gets to Hawaii.*

SINNERS IN PARADISE

Speaker 1: *You mean they have goodies on the ground and will hold off until the Big Man arrives?*

Speaker 2: *Of course. How could he miss such a photo-op? They waited a month, so they can wait another ten hours. Can you imagine a marine landing craft touching the beach in Kailua? This footage will be all over the world, and you will see it again and again until the next disaster strikes somewhere else.*

CHAPTER 32

Abe watched the dinghy dancing among the waves
until it disappeared. Big seas ran along the sides of
Lady Luck and crashed on her stern; she shuddered
with every blow but did not budge in any direction. She
was solidly grounded. Abe went back to the cabin. Books,
tackle, glass from a broken lamp covered the floor; every
object that was not nailed, screwed or clamped to the walls
and bulkheads had left its place, and they all met in a heap
on the floor. Abe pushed the junk roughly aside and removed wood panels covering the bilge. The faint smell of
mold, stagnant water and wet wood drifted out—quite
normal for a sailboat that crossed the ocean. But there was
no water sloshing around, just a bit of wetness from con-
densation on the hull's surface. Obviously, she took the hit
on her keel; with this magnitude of impact the thin fiberglass sidewall would be crushed like a cardboard box under
a truck's wheel.

Abe was not particularly concerned about his personal
safety. The shore seemed so close that he could not imagine
drowning. He used to surf and was a strong swimmer; he
could battle the waves for hours, and eventually reach land.
Cat and Jerry, on the other hand, were—most likely—lost.
A man in the water would not be affected by the wind that
much; if strong enough, a swimmer could power across the

waves towards the shore. A dinghy, however, was a play-
thing for the winds. Two pitiful oars were no match for the
channel's winds and current. His friends' destiny was to be
lost in the Pacific, never to be seen again. They were *haole*,
people foreign to the Hawaiian Islands, but Abe had experienced the sweet Aloha they had for friends and saw
their bravery in a fight. They were equals to his Polynesian
warrior ancestors; they were friends Abe always wanted,
and now had lost, so soon after Fate brought them together.

He removed the sails and sat dejected on the bow looking south, where the ocean had swallowed Jerry and Cat.
The morning did not bring any apparent changes to his
situation. The boat was fixed on the rock like a stuffed bird
on its perch nailed to the wall. She was upright, which
meant that the keel had to be wedged in the rock at a depth
similar to the boat's draft, six feet. Her stern was rhythmically coming up and down as the waves running from behind lifted it, but the bow seemed to be gripped in a vice.
This movement had to generate enormous tension on the
hull; it was bound to crack sooner or later.

Abe lowered himself to the surface on the line hanging
from the bow, took a big breath and dove. The waves
sweeping along the hull tried to carry him away, but he
held onto the bow's leading edge. Following the bow
down, he reached the rock straddling the keel. Good! It's
coral! Coral, made of calcium-based skeletons is much
softer than volcanic basalt. That might explain why *Lady
Luck* was spared instant destruction upon impact. The leading edge of the keel had crushed through the one-foot thick
obstacle, split it open and had been trapped in the fissure,
flanked by solid chunks of the reef.

In addition, he discovered that the good luck that had allowed them to motor from Kailua to Makapu'u was really Fate's joke. The coral barrier they had run into was only six or seven feet long. Pure bad luck coming on top of more bad luck, he thought. Had we sailed a few feet to the left or to the right, we would have missed this thing altogether; we would have never known it was there. If Cat were not so sick, we could have waited till morning, after the crash. If gods want you to die, you die.

Abe surfaced, hung onto his line and when his breathing quieted down, dove again. The keel was seemingly still well attached to the hull. It's crazy, he thought. If only the wind would push the boat from the side, the soft coral would have to break out, it's not that thick. Either that, or the keel might get torn out. One way or the other, *Lady Luck* remained captive only because the wind blew at the stern, pushing her at a right angle to the obstacle.

The distraction of diving helped to suppress Abe's depressing thoughts. The only thing he could do was to take care of the yacht and go back to Kalani who needed him. If he could only twist the boat a bit in relation to the wind, the waves would work on her like a big hammer pounding on a lever every few seconds until something would give— the coral or the keel. The chance had to be taken, if she was to be free again.

Having no dinghy to tow the boat's stern or to take an anchor out, Abe tried to use the wind by winching out the boom with the sail, until it was at a right angle to the hull. The boat did not move and he had no more ideas, so he sat dejected in the cockpit.

"Eh, anyone on board?" A black curly head appeared just above the deck's edge. Abe jumped. There was a six-man canoe alongside *Lady Luck*. The front man stood on a bench looking inside the boat.

"Hey, *braddah*, *kokua*! I need some help here!"

"Got stuck on the reef, eh? You alone?"

"Yeah, my buddy tried to get ashore in a dinghy last night; must be lost."

"Could swim ashore, you never know. What do you want us to do?" The outrigger crew was willing, but had no idea how to help.

"I'll throw you a line from the stern; tie it to your canoe and try to tow me that way." Abe waved his hand at a right angle, towards the coast that was now brightly lit by the morning sun.

"Can do." A stern line attached to the canoe's last bench, six powerful bodies leaned on their paddles, with no effect. They tried a few more times; eventually the helmsman waved at Abe, "Eh, *bro—no can do*. Maybe we'll bring some more guys later on. We have to catch some fish now."

Abe had lost his hope, too, but asked, "Can you try just once more, but from a flying start? Get some speed on the left side, come across the stern as close as you can, and keep paddling hard until you give it the last good jerk. *Kokua*; can you do it for me?"

The leader talked to his men and the outrigger slowly

pulled to the left side of the boat, as far as the line allowed, eighty feet. The crew positioned themselves, ready for a canoe sprint. "Go!" Six muscular bodies threw their weight into the paddles and the outrigger jumped like a spooked fish. It was accelerating rapidly, whizzed three feet past the stern with the paddlers giving powerful, short strokes until the line ran out. It seemed to stretch somewhat, but in an instant it brought the canoe to a sudden stop. The paddlers fell to the front of the canoe laughing and cursing, while *Lady Luck* moved slightly and exposed her left flank.

The wind blew the sail and waves started hammering the boat's side. The canoe crew picked themselves up to their seats and watched with interest the slow process of the yacht breaking out from her confinement. Ten minutes later Abe felt an underwater crack transmitted by the boat's fiberglass, and she started drifting with the wind. He prayed that the breaking noise came from the rock rather than the boat, but did not have time to investigate the bilge. The boat had caught the wind and was slowly accelerating. He trimmed the mainsail and found that she could be steered, even though responses to the wheel came with nightmarish slowness. The canoe moved along, the crew in festive mood. They forgot about fishing.

Abe pulled into the mouth of the channel leading to the Ala Wai small boat harbor escorted by the outrigger, and tied *Lady Luck* to the tangle of wrecks in the middle of the channel. The mass of sunken boats formed an island, well rooted into the ocean's floor, held together by metal spars deeply embedded into sunken hulls, fiberglass bodies entangled together by vines of spliced steel. It looked solid.

Abe invited his rescuers onboard for beer and that expression of gratitude was very much appreciated. Beer had not been seen in this town for a few weeks. John's supply came to an end, and he would have been glad to know how well it was spent.

The next order of things was to find someone who could inspect the boat for damage and fix it. Despite his recent success, Abe did not consider himself a sailing expert, not enough to take on this job. Right on the beach, a large catamaran rested on the sand, a crew of five men patching her hulls. She had her mast removed, probably broken, but her rudders looked undamaged.

"Not too bad, eh?" remarked Abe, by way of introducing himself.

The closest worker raised his head, "Yeah, another day and we'll put in the stick. Then she'll go out to catch us some fish."

"You the boss?"

"Nah, the boss will be here in a while, went to fetch the mast from repair."

Abe was impressed. Things are working here, people busting their butts to get back on their feet.

The boss was busy but open to new business. "Sure, I'll go to the Ala Wai and take a look. How much you can pay?"

Abe had no money. "A bottle of Tequila?"

"Yeah, a bottle of Tequila will do." The middle-aged

man, his skin almost black from years of working the boats, was looking forward to a pleasant night on the beach with a bottle of Tequila and a few well-chosen friends.

Old *Lady Luck* was tougher than the rock, it appeared. She had clearly chipped the front edge of her keel, but the screws were holding securely and her hull was intact. Abe was getting cocky. "How about fixing the mast?"

The boss shrugged his shoulders, "Find yourself a half decent mast," he pointed towards the tangle of boats, "and I will rig it in a day."

Abe spent the balance of the day climbing dead hulls, diving to inspect submerged masts and went to sleep with the knowledge that a fairly straight aluminum pole could be retrieved if he had a few people to help.

The mast he had chosen was shorter than the original one and slightly bent at the top, but by late afternoon next day, *Lady Luck* had the new spar stepped and rigged. Abe paid three good fishing rods, lots of lures and other fishing tackle for help. That's a lot, he thought, but what good is having fishing gear without a boat?

CHAPTER 33

*C*at . . . *Cat* . . . *Catherine! Listen up, it's me, Ruth. You may play dead for the whole world, but I know you can hear me. You are pushing this thing too far. To have a bit of fun and adventure is one thing, but what you are doing is extreme. Maybe I didn't tell you, but if you knock someone off, if you kick him off your world—you can't bring him back. You can create someone who looks the same, and has the same name, but the person inside is gone. I did it to my second husband, Erwin. I was quite happy with him, but then I sent him off on an extramarital affair. Maybe I was a bit bored and wanted to spice things up. In any case, when I saw him banging this stupid blond (and I called her Lola) that I created for him, that pissed me off beyond my expectations. Instead of a sultry making up that I had in mind when I was planning the whole affair, I felt an urgent need to hurt him badly. Poor Erwin was hit by a truck delivering Budweiser beer and died on the way to a hospital. I wanted him back the next day, when the stupidity of my action became apparent to me, but guess what, I couldn't bring him back. I tried and tried, and some washed-out characters were coming back who looked like Erwin, but the man was gone and I never had him again.*

So, I'm telling you this story because it seems to me that your Jerry is pretty close to the edge of your planet. You are very fond of him, and I am positive you will regret it very much if he dies. The other thing, you yourself are one inch from the cliff's edge. What happens if you fall off, I don't know. I never tried it myself, and you're crazy to do things that you don't know how to control. After all, the whole game is about us controlling our worlds, right?

It crossed my mind that this whole story is actually happening, in the real world. That would be quite outrageous, and I don't think it's true, but if it were—what do I know about the outside world? You're on your own, kid. That brings up a point we discussed in the past; how can you tell if your experience is happening in the outside world or in your head? I think I'm on to something. There are some things that you just cannot bring on, unless you have experienced them in real life. There is no internal image of it that you could recall and use as a model for your own creation.

As you know, I have a bunch of kids, all of them in my head. I took care of them, washed their sweet little butts, made them breakfasts, sent them off to school and so on. But, I couldn't put myself through the actual birth. I could imagine a big belly and an obstetrician and a screaming newborn, but I couldn't feel the pain of labor. Well, how could I? I got sick when I was in my twenties and didn't get around to having babies. The pain of delivery was never imprinted on my brain, and I just couldn't create it from scratch. Never mind birthing, I can't even imagine anymore how it feels to have a good fart; it was such a long time ago. OK, OK, I know you don't like it when I get vulgar, but—frankly— that's the part of the living and pleasure of daily existence that I am deprived of.

SINNERS IN PARADISE

Cat! You are dozing off again, so I will just tell you this—snap out of it and take care of the two of you before it's too late. And if you want to check which world you are in, try to find a sensation that you never had before. Your brain couldn't make it up. If you can feel it, not see or hear, but feel it (because the body is harder to fool than the eye), you are in the material world. And if you are in the material world, you are in deep shit.

CHAPTER 34

The *Javelin* had worked the waters between San Diego and San Francisco for the past twenty years. Captains were changed, crews came and went; the old freighter kept at her trade even though the volume of cargo between California's ports was decreasing, just as the traffic from Asia was increasing. Her profitability had become very doubtful over the past few years, and the decision to send her to a scrap yard was pending. Unexpectedly, she had received the last big voyage to crown her career. She had been chartered by a group of relief organizations to carry their mission and supplies to Hawaii. Despite the media's general preference for pictures filled with the explosions and smoke of the Middle East, enough interest had been created by ex-Hawaiians to spur into action the non-governmental organizations, or NGOs. The *Javelin* had left San Diego carrying a group of volunteer medical personnel, loaded with drugs, instruments, generators and other necessities required to set up a field medical center.

She was chugging south of the Hawaiian island chain hoping to avoid the worst effects of the northern and eastern winds that can be severe in winter. The day was breezy, but the sky was clear and most passengers preferred to stay on deck rather than hide in the cramped quarters. The waves ran in long, regular patterns of the open ocean with white tops here and there breaking the monotony of blue water.

Amanda stood on the lee side, hiding from the wind behind a ship's bridge. Her face felt dry from the wind and sun, so she was quite ready to go to her cabin when a small orange cloud caught her eye. An orange cloud would not be unusual in the western sky, where she gazed—but not at eleven o'clock. She went up to the bridge and asked the officer for binoculars. He smiled and handed her a big marine instrument. She definitely looked cute: a slim, blond girl seriously handling the oversized black tool. The girl looked where the orange cloud was a minute ago. She scanned the horizon for a moment, and then focused on one point. Without a word, she handed the binoculars to the officer and pointed. The man studied the ocean for a minute, and the smile left his face. "Change course to 225, full power."

A rubber boat bobbed up and down, sometimes on top of a wave, more often hidden in a valley. There were no occupants to be seen. Perhaps it was empty, but maybe someone was slumped on the floor. The news spread through the ship, and within a few minutes, off-duty crewmen and medical volunteers gathered on the deck. No facts were known yet, but a tiny boat in the open ocean hardly ever carried a happy explanation. Twenty minutes passed before the dinghy could be inspected from the height of the ship's deck. There were two bodies slumped on its floor. They did not move, even when the ship's diesels' deep purr vibrated the rubber walls of the small craft. The launch was lowered and four sailors slid in. "A man and a woman, they are alive!"

Jerry raised his head when a rough hand shook his shoulder and he looked in disbelief into the wide face of master mariner Shawn Daniels. The woman, feeling the commotion, opened her eyes and mumbled something that sounded like "Thank you, Ruth," although it was probably "Thank you, Lord."

The two were promptly lifted out of their dinghy; the man quite easily as he was assisting, and the woman with more difficulty, as she was very confused and her lower body seemed limp. Once on deck, the medical crew sprung into action. Intravenous lines were inserted and fluids administered while the man gave a stuttered account of events. The ship was full of medical supplies and carried specialists in major medical fields. In all of the Pacific Ocean, Jerry and Cat could not have found a better spot to be rescued—as though a higher force had decided that the trials and punishments they had suffered were sufficient.

Jerry recovered quickly once saline filled his veins, and a few hours later he sat beside Cat who had intravenous lines stuck into both arms and broad-spectrum antibiotics quickly saturating her body. Sometimes she seemed to sleep for ten or fifteen minutes, only to open her eyes with a start and a panicked squeeze of Jerry's hand, but a moment later, a slight smile came to her thin face, only to change into an expression of extreme exhaustion.

The girl who had spotted the orange cloud approached Jerry reclining next to Cat. "Professor Roberts, is that you?"

"What are you doing here, Amanda, in the middle of the semester?" Miss Ambitious, the girl who had been flunking his economics class, grinned under the brim of a big hat.

"I've been looking at you for a couple of hours. You looked familiar, but I couldn't believe it was really you."

That was not surprising, because the new Jerry had a bushy beard and long, dirty hair showing a generous amount of silver at his temples. His face was sunburned, and he was thin as a scarecrow.

"You remember me! You saved me from the horrors of Economics. Now, I am a logistics officer for the relief group. Let me tell you, I owe you big time. I am happy now. Come to think of it, I still could be killing myself trying to be an economist, if you hadn't told me to think for myself. Thank you, thank you, thank you!"

"Well, Amanda, I've quit the University as well, and never looked back."

"Who is she, your friend?" Amanda could not restrain her curiosity. The whole mission was going crazy about the mystery that looked incredibly romantic.

"She is my wife; her name is Cat."

"Cat? The Radio Cat?" Amanda's eyes rounded and bulged.

"You know her, Amanda?"

"Are you kidding? The whole country knows her, the whole world. Her radio speeches were transmitted by hundreds of stations."

"No, we didn't know that she had such a big audience."

Amanda regained control of her face. "They were saying in the papers that, if she wanted, she could win any election she might choose. And we find her in a rubber boat in the middle of the Pacific; this is crazy! I found you, you know." She could resist claiming credit for spotting Jerry, but to find Cat, the famous Cat—that was absolutely unbelievable!

Cat's survival hung in balance for twenty-four hours; she was kept on board the *Javelin* even after the ship arrived at the Kewalo basin in Honolulu. The overcrowded hospitals of the island could not offer anything beyond the treatment she was already receiving. She recovered quickly and three days later Jerry pushed her wheelchair down the gangplank. Cat was still weak and taking medications, but could not stand the inactivity of staying on board.

Army trucks carrying supplies, construction equipment and uniformed personnel— all that she had been begging for—had appeared suddenly two days ago and dominated the roads. They burst out from the Kaneohe Marine Corps base, the Army's Schofield Barracks, the Navy's Pearl Harbor and other military establishments as though the floodgates had opened and released a torrent of food, fuels, medical supplies and construction equipment. For some reason, it all coincided with the arrival of the President. Prominent members of the press arrived on Air Force One while ordinary journalists arrived on chartered planes or hitched their rides on cargo aircraft. The whole country watched in awe as military landing craft stormed the beaches of Kailua, carrying food, medicine and security. Many patriotic eyes became wet at this display of great

American compassion, solidarity and power. It took a week to remove a rockslide blocking the road to the Windward side and to stabilize the mountain. Cellular phone service went up a few days later. The island was united again.

Cat did not have an opportunity to watch these developments. An hour after she went ashore, Men in Black grabbed her wheelchair, pushing Jerry away, and put her into an unmarked car. A few hours later, an extremely apologetic gentleman assured her that her civil rights and freedom were of the utmost importance, and she was a free person. However, she was requested to attend a meeting with Mr. President. The whole idea of a forceful abduction was ludicrous; the transportation had been arranged solely for her comfort and convenience.

* * *

Transcript of a conversation, Washington, D.C.

Speaker 1: *So, how did the meeting go? I mean, Cat versus the Prez.*

Speaker 2: *It was rather funny. The Big Man was so sure that she was a cunning politician that it took him fifteen minutes to figure out that she was, really, a country bumpkin. So he listened for a while to her tirade, which was nothing new if you heard her radio talks. Then he tried to sound out what it was that she wanted out of the deal. And she would not let him in on it, which made him believe that she was a very shrewd player. At the end, he asked her directly. She looked at him without any understanding in her eyes and—listen to this—she said that all she wanted was to go back to her husband.*

311

ALEX Z. MODZELEWSKI

Speaker 1: *You think that's really it? Or is she playing stupid and will spring something on us when we least suspect it?*

Speaker 2: *Well, what counts is what the President thinks of it. He let her go and laughed to himself for five minutes after she left.*

* * *

Jerry stood in the middle of Ala Moana, a big man blocking his way, while two other dark suits hustled Cat to the car. They would not even let him say good-bye. He felt as much enraged as helpless. He had kept her alive during the starvation days and in the dinghy lost at sea, and now three beefy bastards, who looked like they were fed a few pounds of fresh meat every day, had taken her away. He could only curse at his government in action. The men had flashed their badges, and Jerry believed they were federal agents. Only the government would have a car running in Honolulu. He was not worried that she would disappear forever; after all, they had left him as a witness. It just made him very angry to lose control of his life again, because the price of gaining it had been so high.

He went to the Ala Wai marina, a short walk away. Someone might have heard about Abe. He assumed that his friend had survived the stranding. A strong and resourceful man like Abe would not perish a few hundred yards from shore. He walked along Magic Island, the harbor's western bank, towards the wave break. Sunken boats filled the basin, numerous dinghies busy around them, and people seemed to be hard at work wherever the hulls remained above water. They had no power equipment; all work was done with hammers, wrenches, pliers and whatever implements might be found in home workshops. He came to the end of the island, where the port's channel opened into the ocean and stopped, with his heart pounding.

A blue-hulled boat was gracefully set off against a tangled clump of white and gray wrecks. *Lady Luck!* And she has a mast! Jerry struggled to believe his eyes. What's next? John coming out to tell me that the impeller needs to be cleaned?

There was no one on board. Jerry sat on the shore watching her through misty eyes and noted that the mast was rather short for her size while the rigging consisted of a mix of steel cables and ropes. Still, she looked like a beauty queen visiting a city dump.

At last, Jerry saw Abe, in the company of two other Hawaiian men. The strangers were both much older than Abraham; the one wearing a red aloha shirt could be sixty, the other, dressed in a blue shirt, might be forty-five. Strange company for Abe, Jerry thought.

Abe listened to the men intently as they walked, and noticed Jerry only when he stood up. "Where is Cat?" Abe asked anxiously when he finally released Jerry from his embrace.

"Cat is fine. A medical mission ship rescued us. Where she is right now, I don't know; she was snatched by some government agents an hour ago."

The man wearing the red aloha shirt nodded his head. "That had to be expected. She could be worth a lot to the government, as much as to us."

ALEX Z. MODZELEWSKI

"Us? And who are you?" Jerry was about to ask. Suddenly everybody was ready to put a claim on Cat. He felt very strongly that his claim was the prime, and he would not share Cat willingly with anyone. At the same time, he realized that nobody could appropriate her; she was very much her own person. She could bestow her friendship, love or dedication, but nobody could own her, not even him.

"This is Roy Kaiwi and this is Bob Reynolds, both from the Executive Committee of Hawaii Freedom. And this is Jerry, Cat's husband," Abe made the formal introductions.

Jerry had never heard of the organization, but obviously much had changed since he last set foot in Honolulu. Abe was very interested in his companions, and they, in turn, paid a lot of attention to him. It looked to Jerry like Abe was getting into politics, a Hawaiian independence movement most likely.

The blue aloha shirt wanted to explore Jerry's views on the formation of a provisional government, but Jerry was in no mood for politics. All he wanted was to hear from Cat then hide her away so that no one would find them, at least for a month.

"Are you coming back to Kailua to see Kalani?" he asked rather abruptly. Cat would send a message there as soon as she could, he thought.

"Yes, of course," Abe sounded a bit offended. He shook hands with both aloha shirts and promised to be in touch.

"Let us speak with Cat when she is back," asked Blue Shirt.

"If she wants to speak with you, I will certainly not try to stop her," Jerry declared. "But let me tell you, she is not a big fan of any government and that would probably extend to yours."

He made a quick good-bye visit to his new friends on the *Javelin*, loaded MREs that Abe had acquired from the government warehouse. They even managed to get some diesel in plastic containers. Twelve hours later *Lady Luck*'s anchors plunged into the water off Kailua Beach, and the sailors went to the Round House.

It was eight o'clock in the morning; Jerry experienced *déjà vu* when they walked through the door. Cat was sitting in her wheelchair with a toddler on her lap and a bunch of other kids hanging around her chair. Next to them, Kalani was putting food into bowls.

"Hope this isn't blubber soup," Abe said from the door. "You might as well serve two more bowls."

Cat and Jerry were not ashamed of their wet faces, their courage proven beyond doubt. They lay in the high grass, locked in each other's arms, sensing the warmth of each other's bodies and smelling jasmine, again. The cataclysm was over, and they had survived.

CHAPTER 35

Once they landed at Newark, Cat and Jerry had the feeling of stepping into an unheated movie theater with an old projector screening a black-and-white film. It felt so different from Hawaii where—no matter how tough life was—masses of red, pink and yellow flowers and the greenery of fresh growth pushed from all sides to cover any evidence of destruction. Cold wind and gray skies replaced the sweet smells propagated in the island's warm air. As his apartment was gone, Jeremy checked them into a hotel. Pam showed her displeasure about their stay in a hotel rather than in her home, but eventually, she understood their need to disappear in order to enjoy each other. Selfish as it sounded, Cat and Jerry did not want anybody else. The two of them, that was just perfect; they had a lot of catching up to do.

Cat was much stronger since her infection had been treated and they ate well. As a matter of fact, they ate like two horses, at first with a sensation of guilt as if their indulgence were depriving someone else.

"Jerry, I feel guilty every time I reach for another helping." Cat brought the third serving spoon of rice soaked with curry to her plate.

"I can check if there are any hungry kids around, Cat,

but everybody looked very well fed when I was downtown this morning." Jerry lifted his plate, asking for more.

They were regaining weight rapidly, and Jerry again started seeing the woman who had saved him at Bird Shit Rock. Her body was toning up quickly, much to Jerry's amazement. The pitiful, skeletal person he had taken as his wife on the beach was not only rounding out, but developing muscles as well. Her breasts were growing fuller every day, and were well under way to being again almost too large for her body.

An explanation for the muscle tone came a week later. They usually lunched together, then she was supposed to have a nap, while Jerry went out to attend to any of the thousand things that needed to be taken care of since they had returned to the world of rules and regulations. One of these was the formal termination of his employment with the university, which he had left rather hastily and in a very irregular manner. Jerry forgot his documents and had to run back to their apartment. Hearing loud music, he cursed silently, thinking that the neighbor was too noisy and could wake up Cat. He opened the door quietly to discover that the music was coming from their bedroom. The doors were ajar, and what he saw made him stop and watch in awe. A naked Cat hung off the bed, her hips pivoting on the mattress and her upper body supported on her arms: she was doing push-ups. Her rump had plumped up nicely, projecting in perfect harmony above the straight line of her back.

One, two, three . . . Jerry counted silently while she pumped up, unaware of his presence. The shoulder and arm muscles were swelling with contractions as she kept pushing up without much effort. This was certainly not her first session. She stopped and, breathing heavily, wiggled up on the bed.

"How many?" Jerry asked when she looked up.

She was not shocked or embarrassed; nakedness came to her most naturally. They slept nude, and she did not hide when dressing during the day. They had been intimate since leaving Kailua, but somehow Jerry felt that she was fragile and weak; therefore, he should be a very gentle lover.

"Thirty," she replied with a coy smile. "Do you think I'm strong enough to love this big, strong man?"

His coat, pants, shirt and all the rest lay in a heap about fifteen seconds later. Jerry dove into the bed where she pinned him on his back like a wrestler, blue eyes less than ten inches from his face, neither smiling nor sad, just hungry. He felt the soft warmness of her breasts flattened on his chest when she put her lips on his eyes, cheeks and mouth. Jerry sensed her wonderful mouth slowly caressing his face while his fingers slid tenderly from her hair to her neck, languorously explored both shoulders and brushed the sides of her breasts. Cat shuddered and moaned quietly. He gently felt her sides until his fingertips met in the small of her back. The body he held rippled, and her groin pressed hard against his pelvis. His cupped hands followed the roundness of her buttocks as though comparing the size, softness and texture of two exotic fruits and his fingers crept into the crease between them. Cat moaned louder, raised her hips and helped him find the way.

They were spent, physically exhausted and happy beyond post-coital contentedness; they were strong again and worthy of physical love. They had won the battle and consumed the victory.

* * *

Cat had not been introduced to her new family yet, and Pam simply could not wait any longer. Jerry had met his sister on the day of their arrival, of course, and they talked daily on the phone, but her curiosity about Cat was unbearable. A formal introduction had been set for Saturday night, giving Cat two days to get ready. It might sound trivial, but Cat had arrived from Hawaii wearing a borrowed cotton *muu muu*, a long, straight dress sporting a large, colorful flowery pattern. A very popular choice among Hawaiian ladies, it could hardly pass as formal wear in New York.

Initially, Cat refused to go shopping for clothes, saying that whatever she would buy would not fit her in two weeks. Fair enough, Jerry thought, we are gaining weight fast. Now, faced with the formal visit to Pat, she had no way out—they went shopping. It soon became apparent that Cat had neither the technique nor experience that shopping required. An hour into their buying spree, at the second store, Jerry's wife declared: "That's it. I cannot do this any more. I don't need any clothes. I will stay in the hotel room forever." For the last three years, she had lived by her window looking out at the beach, working on a computer, kayaking or loitering around her house wearing a pair of shorts and a tee shirt. That was the accepted extent of a wardrobe in Hawaii, and it suited her just fine. Now, for the first time, Jerry saw Cat clueless, and she despised it deeply.

Buying from a catalog might be the solution, but they had no time. However, they were in New York, the place where every need could be fulfilled, if suppliers were properly compensated. So... a personal shopper came to interview Cat, and with the aid of catalogs and measurements a complete wardrobe appeared at their door the next day.

The clothes fit surprisingly well and despite her initial misgivings, Cat very much enjoyed this buying spree. Jerry felt that the morning sell-order call to his stockbroker had been a good idea. Seated in an armchair, he was treated to a fashion show, clapping his hands to applaud the outfits and whistling with appreciation when the model changed in front of him.

"Now, a change of pace," she grinned. "Jerry, go to the kitchen and stay there until I call you back."

A few minutes later he heard his name spoken invitingly. Opening the door he heard the soft clicking of castanets, which drew his eyes to the far corner. There, draped on the side of the armchair sat a haughty Carmen. A long, red dress with a lacey hem, black shoes with high but sturdy heels, a proud bust barely restrained by red fabric— it was Carmen, complete with a black wig.

Cat clicked the castanets again, enjoying the impression she made, then put up a token resistance as Jerry grabbed her off the armchair. Once they landed on the bed, however, she firmly took his head in both hands, turned it and whispered into Jerry's ear: *"Te quiero, Amor, pero ahora— no. Bamos a Pam, recuerdas?"*

"No" came very clearly, the rest of it was somewhat

confusing. Jerry understood "...I want you," and clearly picked up "my love." Unfortunately there was also a reference to their going to Pam's as well. Jerry worried about this evening. Pam would welcome Cat with open arms; he was sure of that. His wife was eager to meet her new family and wanted to be accepted, that was also a given. What made him sweat was the image of Cat and Henry at one table. Cat was firm in her beliefs and would defend them ferociously. Put her in one room with a provocateur like Henry, and the possibility of a small thermonuclear reaction couldn't be discounted.

The table was covered with a snow-white cloth. Silver candlesticks, elegant china precisely placed; it was to be a full gala dinner. Jerry had nightmares about this kind of dining since the first time he was seated at a table without a booster. A tiny drop of cranberry sauce can become a bloody entry wound in the corpse of an elegant table. The hostess graciously assures that there is absolutely no problem, while the offender knows she has spent hours setting this up like a stage for a commercial video shoot. Jerry always dreaded formal dinners, would rather eat blubber soup sitting on grass than turkey at a gala dinner.

Cat exuded an air of confidence sitting on a dining chair, having transferred from her wheelchair to a dining chair to be at the same height as the rest of the company. She looked elegant in a navy blue suit, selected perhaps to prevent anyone gawking at her legs. Jerry knew that Cat was tense, though, by the small amount of food she consumed. She just nibbled this and that; it was not the way they recently had been eating. They were still two famine survivors and nibbling on food was not what they did.

Pam's children were on their best behavior, probably intimidated by the table arrangement, just as her brother was. They kept their eyes on their plates, sneaking quick looks at Cat whenever she looked away. The atmosphere was prim. Everybody was smiling, minding their table manners and making small talk—all the ingredients of a boring family gathering. The next thing Jerry expected was Henry suggesting that they all watch a game of football on the large-screen TV, the children being excused to do something entertaining, before they decided to cut their wrists with the table cutlery.

Pam seemed satisfied with the initial assessment of her sister-in-law, but was not very cordial, which disappointed Jerry, as Pam had been very emotional about Cat previously. Perhaps it's difficult to break the ice, he thought. I had it easy; all I had to do was come close to drowning, so that Cat could fish me out.

"So when did you get married, exactly? And where?" Pam addressed her brother.

"Twenty-second, perhaps twenty-third, no later than twenty-fourth of January, on Kailua Beach," he answered hesitantly. Dates were not that important then: they measured time by their last meal.

"You aren't sure when your wedding ceremony was?" Pamela raised her eyebrows and looked at Cat.

Cat flashed her full smile at Jerry, the first this evening. "There was no ceremony. We just decided we belonged together . . . on the beach, one night."

Pam's face fell and her mouth opened as though she

wanted to say something.

"Free love . . ." a wistful whisper came from the mouth of Cecilia, the oldest child.

Cat turned to her with the same smile and asked, "Do you think there is any other love, Cecilia?"

The girl blushed, "No, I just thought it was so cool . . . no priest or witness or wedding party, just the two of you."

"You might also add the full moon and gentle waves washing over our bodies, for the full picture, if that's not too kitschy. But in the interest of truth, I also have to add that we were both very hungry, and your uncle Jerry smelled like a three-day-old whale carcass."

"Eeew! Uncle Jerry, you smelled like an old carcass!" The kids broke out of their contrived proper behavior. Everyone suddenly relaxed, the aggravation of elegant manners lifted off their shoulders.

Even Pam gave up on her prim gala dinner. "Ha, you did it on a beach, without a ceremony. Kids, I think you're still living in sin, but I'm going to fix that before you escape from New York. But I have to say, it sounds awfully romantic. Henry, maybe we should try it sometime, what do you think?"

"I like the idea of free love on a beach, but the notion of being very hungry in order to reach this level of delight bothers me a lot," Henry smiled coyly.

Cat looked at his portly figure. "The starvation part was an unfortunate ingredient of our romance. I think it's strictly optional and I assure you that love is better with a full belly."

Cecilia was not going to let this delicious subject be switched to anything else, "Auntie, why did you choose Jerry, if he smelled so bad?"

"First of all, Cecilia, even your children will not be allowed to call me auntie. I am Cat for you as for everybody else. As for choosing Jerry, if someone sailed across the ocean, and climbed over the mountains, and did all kinds of crazy things just to be with you—wouldn't you like him just a little bit? And if he were the most wonderful, intelligent and brave man that you ever knew, wouldn't you choose him, too?"

Pam's face was filled with pride and pleasure as she listened to the list of her brother's qualifications for being the chosen one.

"My real worry," added Cat looking at Jerry, "was that he wouldn't want *me*. I was not a very sexy creature. I was so thin I could have been flushed down a water spout like Itsy-Bitsy spider." Now even the younger kids looked at her with admiration.

Way to go, Cat, we're making friends here, Jerry thought.

"Besides, I knew what the smell was, and I was confident I could get rid of it without killing Jerry," finished Cat.

Dessert was a much more pleasant time than the previous courses. They laughed and joked and dripped melted ice cream on the white cloth without worry or formality. The children were excused, and the adults moved to a smaller table where brandy and coffee were served.

"How was your meeting with the President?" Henry asked.

Cat let the golden liquid swirl in her glass. "It was as though the two of us were in the same room, looking at each other, but speaking different languages—without the benefit of an interpreter. He basically had me kidnapped, so I assumed that the meeting would be important. First, he asked me what I thought about the events in Kailua, after the earthquake. I gave him what he asked for: failure at all levels of the government. I proceeded to elaborate on my criticism, but had a feeling he didn't hear a thing. You expect the other person to make some little gestures at appropriate moments, little head movements to acknowledge a point, a sound— something to let you know that he's with you. I got none of these, as if I spoke Chinese or perhaps his hearing aid failed. After ten minutes or so, he became somewhat impatient and started questioning me about my political experience and ambitions. I have none on either count. Eventually, he looked me in the eyes and said, 'What is it that you want?'

"'What do I want? I want to go home. I want to see my husband!' Did I ask for this meeting, apply for an audience with His Excellence? No, I was abducted and delivered. Two minutes later, I was through one set of doors, then another, then a golf cart took me to the helicopter that dropped me off in Kailua. I have to say, I'm grateful they didn't forget my wheelchair."

Henry chuckled softly, "You are a country lassie, Cat."

Jerry found that quite rude and opened his mouth to rebuke his brother-in-law, but Cat put her hand over his fist—let it go, it's my fight. She smiled innocently and asked, "You know much about rural life, Henry?"

"No, not at all, I was referring rather to your political naiveté." Henry was smiling, but not at all apologetic.

"Oh, you consider it important to be knowledgeable about politics, don't you?"

"Yes, I think politics are important. If for no other reason than it's where the laws are being made and the money being spent, your money included." The chess master was lining up his pawns for a simple, frontal assault. Henry would never overcomplicate a simple game with a known outcome.

Pam was fidgeting with her glass. She hated the direction the conversation was taking. It would spoil her dinner for good.

"Henry, do you take any interest in bank fraud, stolen property trafficking or perhaps illegal stock market manipulations?" Cat was curious.

"No." Henry allowed himself a slight patronizing smile. "I leave those things to the police and the SEC."

"But it is quite possible that your money could be affected by any of these activities. Would say that elected representatives are likely to do their job with less integrity than the bankers or stock brokers?"

Henry's smile became more reflective, and he took a long time to answer, as would be expected from a chess player. "That's a good point; perhaps I am more suspicious of the politicians. Besides, their influence is much more important and pervasive, it affects all forms of economic activity."

"I beg to differ." Cat pressed her point along lines that were becoming apparent to the others. "You are quite right saying their influence is more pervasive, and I would add: they'd like you to believe that it's inevitable. You know— death and taxes. But the truth is, the political class is mostly a parasitic organism living on the body of productive society. One could remove ninety percent of their activities without suffering any bad consequences. On the contrary, the economy would flourish if liberated from thousands of unnecessary regulations. We could do without politicians, but they couldn't do without us. They would wither as soon as we cut off the money flow. It wouldn't be easy, since they have all the instruments of oppression in their hands, and create new ones as they see fit. Look at all these unconstitutional laws: The Patriot Act, Military Commissions Act, all new tools that allow snooping, incarcerating, secret courts, kidnapping, without any meaningful legal oversight. It's nothing but a power grab, one step after another towards a goal of unchallenged state dominance. Call it fascism or communism or whatever you want, but it is not a real democracy."

Cat was warming up and straightened in her chair. Her glass was on the table; she needed both hands for gesticulation. "The sad part is that what I'm saying is nothing new. Samuel Adams, one of the fathers of this Republic said that men should be free from any superior power on earth, except for laws of nature, but nowadays he is remembered only for good beer. I guess his idea has been forgotten and needs to be relearned."

Henry was not smiling. "Looks like you're planning a revolution, my dear."

Cat took her glass, sniffed the brandy and took a sip. "Actually, I am not. I don't think military action would accomplish anything. They will always have more guns and I wouldn't want people to be killed. I would rather deprive the government of its magic potion: money. The change will have to start with us. We need to structure our financial affairs in such a way that the beast will starve, then take its tail between its legs and beg for nourishment with its tongue lolling out. Only then will we be able to defang it, and set it to work on a few projects that the state might actually accomplish: protecting the borders, providing police services, maintaining legal system, and so on."

"How can you starve the beast?" Henry looked puzzled. "You have to generate income, so you have to pay taxes or they'll lock you up."

"That's true, we all have to generate income, but only as much as we need for immediate consumption. That's peanuts to the bureaucracy. They have been spending much more than they collect even now, never mind when we put them on a diet. They will keep borrowing money, but at some point, they won't find any more creditors. That doesn't mean that you have to deny yourself gainful work. There are a lot of ways to defer your profits: buy land or gold, accumulate non-dividend paying stocks, buy a villa on the Mediterranean Sea—all legal measures that allow accumulation of wealth for you and your family."

Henry nodded his head with an ambivalent smile, interested but not convinced.

"And you may need that villa in Europe, Henry, because when the government *really* runs out of money, they will come and take everything you have, with full political support. There will be masses of retirees, unemployed (and there will be a lot of them when the economy collapses), civil servants . . . millions of hungry, desperate and unproductive people who will have no interest in preserving the rights to private property. They will want government assistance, and will *demand* that your bank accounts get seized and your lovely home transformed into a public facility. A soup kitchen, perhaps?"

"It's a scary picture that you paint, Cat." Pam was visibly disturbed and looked at her husband, question in her eyes.

Henry shrugged and sighed. "It might be true; this might be coming our way. No country ever had a national debt of the magnitude that America has at present, and it's rapidly getting larger. I am not as sure as Cat about what happens and when, but her scenario is a possibility. The problem is, we are in uncharted waters, and nobody can predict the future because there is no precedent."

Cat smiled sweetly again, "So tell me, Henry, why should I waste my time and energy at politics? The future belongs to country lads and lassies, as long as they are productive."

The chess master raised his glass to Cat and smiled

with respect. "Check and mate."

Pam held a napkin to her mouth, but soon recovered the faculty of speech. "So how are you going to protect your family, if you are so sure that this catastrophe is coming?"

Cat put her hand on Jerry's arm. "First of all, I've married a blue-water captain who will take us wherever we want, without asking for any official permission. Secondly, we are the producers. Wherever we happen to be, we can provide a service of value, generate income and be welcomed by the locals. Jerry came to Kailua when nothing was working, and organized the beginnings of a fishing fleet and the rudiments of a free market economy. I know that he can do similar miracles anywhere else. I feel safe with him." Jerry's heart was melting. "And I, too, have a skill that can be used wherever we end up," Cat concluded.

"Aren't you going back to Hawaii?" Pamela turned to her brother.

"We will, at least for now. We'll try to rebuild our lives there, but will keep our ears to the ground. Hawaii is an exceptional place where people are compassionate and have an easygoing temper, but the problem that Cat described wouldn't be limited by ethnic makeup. It's a systemic disease that will probably hit the whole country, possibly more than just our country." Jerry felt free of the intimidation he had experienced in Henry's presence in the past. "Most of the world seems to be governed by a bureaucracy unrestrained by voters who don't even try to understand national issues. Wars, interest rates, money expansion—these are boring issues if you look at them in any depth. As long as Joe and Jane can afford food and gas, who gives a hoot? The voters are being shamelessly manipulated and bribed with their own money, but prefer to watch *American Idol* rather than C-span."

Pam held up her hand. "Jerry, be realistic—ignorant people are never in short supply."

"I agree, Pam, that's why I can't see how it could change without a major upheaval; only then will people start looking where their money goes. In Kailua, nobody had any interest in their hospital's functioning until the antibiotics ran out, and their families started dying."

The dinner ended on a pleasant note of reconciliation; Pam was relieved. Just when Cat was ready to roll to the car, Henry asked, "How long are you folks going to stay in New York?"

Cat and Jerry looked at each other; they had no tickets and the date of return was not set. "Maybe two weeks?" Jerry offered, and Cat nodded in agreement.

"I have to inspect our plant in Missouri in ten days. Perhaps we could get together again next week?"

"Don't you have your chess tournament next week?" asked Pam with disbelief.

"I might skip this one; there aren't that many opportunities for an interesting conversation," Henry answered.

"I am jealous as hell," muttered Pam in her brother's ear when she kissed him good-bye. "He has never cancelled a chess tournament in the twenty years of our marriage."

They listened to the news in the car: the price of oil was one hundred and twenty dollars per barrel, and the supply of gasoline was spotty throughout the country; the National Guard had been called to suppress civil unrest in Alabama and Georgia.

"Where the heck did you get all this socio-political reasoning from? It can't be part of the computer science curriculum," Jerry asked his wife.

"No, it's not part of my formal education. It's part of growing up with my father. It all started when I was about ten and couldn't sleep. I would toss and turn in bed and make all kinds of noises to entertain myself.

"He'd put his head into my room and ask, 'Can't sleep, baby?' That was rather obvious. 'I'm going to help you right away.' He was full of unorthodox fixes. He'd be back a minute later with one of his books. 'Read a bit and that'll put you to sleep in no time.'

"Once it was a book of Schweitzer's philosophical essays that my father had read recently. I was desperately bored so I started reading. There were some anecdotes from the author's medical practice in the African bush that I found quite interesting. In the morning we had breakfast together and Daddy asked, 'So, how did you like Schweitzer; did you make it through the first page?'

"I told him that I actually liked it, and we talked a bit about it before I had to leave for school, so he knew I wasn't just boasting. Since that day, he treated me like I was a partner in his philosophical adventures, and he had quite a few. I played along because I was pleased that he had such a high opinion of me. I'm sure I missed most of what he said, but some of it stuck, as you saw."

"You never talked about your family, Cat. Maybe you should tell me a bit since we're now getting acquainted with my relatives."

"We've spent very little time together, Jerry. There has always been some major crisis going on during our brief relationship. You are right: you should know about my folks, especially, since you owe them."

Jerry was puzzled, but let her talk.

"The first time we met—no—I mean when you first came to see me at my home, you seemed strangely familiar to me. It took me a while to realize that you had a lot in common with my father. For example, take the circumstances of our first encounter. You had plunged into a potentially dangerous situation without much thought to your safety. He, in his turn, was an enthusiastic canoeist; so he rented a canoe in Cancun and went exploring in a lagoon full of alligators. He came back rather hastily when an eight-foot gator threatened him on a muddy bank."

It's true, Jerry thought. We had an amazingly easy relationship since I stepped over her threshold in Kailua. Cat treated me like an old friend or a family member right from the beginning.

Cat continued. "Then, both my parents started talking to me after you and I had that lovely swim in my pool. That was significant because I had had problems communicating with my folks for a long time."

"Where do they live? Can we meet them?" Jerry was

surprised she had not invited him to meet her parents yet.

"You might think I'm crazy, Jerry, but I talk to them in my head only. They're both gone, killed in a car wreck in Ecuador, during one of their crazy adventures. That was about six years ago, a year before I crashed myself. When I was a teenager, I somehow got estranged from my parents, although we had been very close in my childhood. Then I went to college, married Nick, and I never took any initiative to reconcile. And suddenly, they were both gone; I felt really rotten about it. After my accident, I learned to have relationships with other people in my head. Ruth taught me that, a woman who had progressive paralysis for many years, but lived a very rich life in her mind. I have to tell you that, sometimes, I have problems knowing which things are real in my life and which I manufacture in my imagination.

"I tried to coax my parents into a conversation in my head, but they wouldn't come, until you entered the picture. So, I think they like you, and they encouraged me to be with you. When you came with that silver tea maker that you pulled from the wreckage of my house—it was something they brought from their old country—I thought it was a sign you were stepping right into my family. Jerry, they like you. They were not very thrilled about Nick. They never said anything negative, but I knew that they thought of him as too much flash and not enough substance. Who knows, they might have been right. With you, I'm sure my father would grab you to sail on his boat, and my mother would make you model for her, naked if possible. She was a sculptor, a good one, and a human body spoke to her like nothing else."

Well, a bit of family history goes a long way to explain certain eccentricities that Cat has, Jerry thought. I wish I could meet her parents; they sound like people I would like.

They were pulling into the hotel driveway when the radio announcer delivered a news flash: an armistice had been reached in the Middle East and active hostilities had stopped. "Thank God; maybe things will start calming down. The economy couldn't take oil that expensive for long." Jerry hoped that Cat's predictions would not come true for quite some time.

The next day, Jerry went to see Schumacher, his former boss. Surprisingly, the old professor did not hold any grudge against him. "Jerry, I admire people who take control of their destiny. I am not sure if your direction is right or wrong, but I can only respect your initiative and courage. I never had the guts to restart my life from scratch and look where it took me," he waved around his office: journals cluttering his desk, walls filled with diplomas, citations and awards and a block of mahogany on his desk engraved in golden letters: "Professor Arnold Schumacher, Ph.D., Chairman, Economics Department."

Jerry was not sure if it was a joke or a complaint.

"By the way, you never sent me your assessment of Amanda Kroll; any chance it is still resting under your coffee mug?" Schumacher asked hopefully.

"I have news for you, Arnold. Amanda escaped your clutches. The last time I saw her, she was a logistics officer in Hawaii. Looks like she has chosen the real world."

"Crap!" Schumacher actually got upset. "I'll get a phone call from Chicago and will have to explain to her genius daddy why Amanda is not going to be a world-class economist."

Jerry chuckled, "Good luck, boss, and good-bye."

Cat and Jerry were fully recovered. Cat's face returned to its customary round shape, broken pleasingly by the lush red lips, usually parted in a smile. Her figure seemed a bit fuller than normal, probably due to lack of regular exercise. Jerry felt better than ever. The chronic stress and constant borderline unhappiness that had been his usual condition in New York were replaced by the almost maniacal optimism and joy of being with Cat. The brick wall had fallen and turned into dust.

They were fascinated with each other, like high school lovers, and took full advantage of being well rested, well fed and in love. Pam tried to persuade them into a formal wedding while still in New York. "Cat, don't you want to have a church wedding? I know if you wanted it, Jerry wouldn't refuse."

"Pam, if Jerry wants it, I won't refuse, either. But we're not church-going people. Why make a mockery of something that is important to other people?"

"You don't believe in God? Are you an atheist?" Cecilia was horrified, and asked the question that her mother wouldn't dare.

"I have no way of knowing if there is a God," answered Cat seriously. "That would make me an agnostic rather than an atheist. But I think, if there is a God, he doesn't need all these big or small churches, organ music, 'Praise the Lord' and 'Hallelujah'. I think these things were invented by people who wanted to benefit from being professional middlemen between God and the people."

Jerry was not sure how well that went over with Pam and Henry. To have a brother who skips a church wedding is one thing, but to have the children led away from the Mother Church is quite another.

Cat obviously had similar thoughts as she added, "But I have no problems with others' beliefs. Most people I know feel better with their faith. They get from it some re-assurance or happiness, something that I don't have a need for. I respect that, and I don't let my own convictions spoil my relationships with believers. In fact, sometimes I do need to talk to someone outside of this realm, and I do. I just don't need any middlemen. So you could call me religious in some sense. But it's my own religion."

"Are there any commandments in your religion?" Henry asked with a small, enigmatic smile. He might have wanted a rematch. It was hard to guess if his question was a joke or a serious enquiry.

Cat thought for a moment, "I can think only of one commandment: 'You shall think for yourself.' If you think deep enough and frequently enough, you don't need all the rest. The Commandments, Mortal Sins, etc., are being passed down along the generations as a shorthand, kind of a brief manual on how to behave so that life is easier for everyone. If you're willing to think, you can predict the consequences, and you don't need a cheat sheet."

Pam was uncomfortable with this discussion. The Ten

Commandments being a cheat sheet—that couldn't be too healthy for her children's souls. She tried to send the kids upstairs, but Cecilia resisted and the younger ones wanted to stay if Cecilia did.

Henry was also in favor of them staying. "You might be right on that, but there are not that many people who are willing to think, particularly if you insist on deep thinking. So maybe it's not so bad if they go to church once in a while. But does it really work? Do you think church-going folks are more honest or better behaved?"

Cat shrugged, "You're older, and you've had more time to observe our fellow man, but I can tell you that under conditions of extreme stress, like in Hawaii a few months ago, we were all sinners. We all stole, if we could. There was a lot of mugging, robbery and even murders. Who the perpetrators were I couldn't say, but I don't think there were enough atheists around for them to be blamed for all this mayhem. The great majority of our neighbors were church-going, God-fearing folks."

"Someone once said that if God didn't exist, he would have to be invented; otherwise, running a civil society would be impossible," Henry was clearly egging Cat on.

Cat was happy to oblige. "Maybe so. It is either think or obey. Just like democracy, we can have the real thing only if voters are willing to spend time and effort to understand the issues. Other than that—smoke and mirrors, vote buying and tap dancing every four years is what keeps the Republic going."

"Cecilia, go do the dishes!" Pam had had enough.

Pam drove them to the airport a few days later. They had become a real family during the last month. Cat fell into the family soup like an exotic mushroom and changed the taste of the whole pot. Pam and the kids loved her, but the most remarkable relationship developed between Cat and Henry. It was clear they sought each other's company and entertained the rest of the family with witty discussions that required rematches. Jerry grew a new appreciation for his family and a sense of pride to come from such fine stock.

CHAPTER 36

B road-shouldered men—their heads shaved except-
ing a small patch at the skull's top, raccoon-like
masks of pale skin left by government-issue goggles—occupied most of the seats on the plane to Hawaii.
The troops were coming back to their bases from the Middle East. A few soft-bellied, suit-wearing individuals who
could be journalists, insurance executives or other people
with an urgent business in Hawaii rounded out the mani-
fest. There were no tourists on the plane.

How are the Islands going to survive without tourism,
the most important cash crop of Hawaii? Jerry wondered.
This was not an idle question of an unemployed economist.
How are we going to make a living there? Cat's computer
business won't work until the broadband connections are
available, and that's probably not high on anybody's list.
The first installment of Cat's insurance payment had been
mostly spent in New York; the settlement would not come
any time soon. Her property had been destroyed by a combination of earthquake and tsunami; what was the insured
loss and what was not—it would be a major battle, he suspected.

Jerry's academic career had translated into the New
York apartment, which he had swapped for *Lady Luck*, and

a modest brokerage account, which had been liquidated during their New York visit. Their life together was starting from a financial point close to zero, but they didn't mind. Being alive was a miracle enough. Expectations change dramatically after a close call, and they had had a lot of those.

Commentaries from Hawaii, which were flooding the media now, hinted that unlike people devastated by Hurricane Katrina, Hawaiians were not taking the government's neglect with mere perfunctory bitching. Deep rumblings of a possible secession from the United States were shaking the Hawaiian Islands, like Kilauea Volcano notching up its angry voice. Cat's anger-spiked radio talks reverberated throughout the archipelago. Grassroots Hawaiian organizations had sprung up, discarding the old government-controlled bodies that offered only token representation. The new people were determined, brash and did not care about protocol and relations with the authorities. They wanted changes and no small changes would do.

Relics of the old regime hung onto power by being the sole distributors of relief supplies, which were arriving in increasing quantities from the Mainland. If the citizens wanted their food rations or a few gallons of fuel, they reported to the government office, hat in hand.

Private enterprise exploded in the backyards, on the streets and beaches in a way unprecedented in the Islands' history. Dozens of tiny boat-repair yards set up along the shores, blatantly ignoring zoning laws. A fishing fleet of small craft, defying technical classification, scattered across the waters of the archipelago, sometimes powered by recently available fuel, more often by sails or muscle. Hawaii, once bound by red tape and innumerable restrictions accumulated during a hundred years of dependency, exploded from the waters of the Pacific like a humpback whale—full of confidence and unafraid.

A new fashion or, rather a new lifestyle had emerged. Once a large, gleaming car used to be the symbol of success; now, a simple bicycle had become the proof of one's worth. The people of Hawaii were proud to get by with a minimum of material things. A sense of power started springing from a sense of independence, from freedom to spurn the things that demanded compliance, obedience and submission.

The airport bus stopped in downtown Honolulu. Saigon in the sixties, Jerry thought. The broad streets were filled with thousands of pedestrians and bikes. Someone was mass-producing rickshaws, which could be seen everywhere. Few cars crept through the throng of muscle-powered vehicles; they no longer owned the streets. Why bother? Jerry thought. They're slower than a rickshaw.

The last time he had walked these streets, people were harried and sad. Now laughter was coming from all directions, and people hurried along the streets on foot or wheels, with a sense of purpose. Honolulu was not a defeated city, its inhabitants were survivors who had been hurt badly, but were now drunk on the joy of existence. The downtown buildings still displayed their scars, but many ground-floor stores had reopened, broken windows closed with rough plywood, but decorated with touching displays of primitive art.

The solid structure of the central bus station at Ala

Moana Shopping Center had withstood the earthquake and a few buses sat in their bays. Cat and Jerry were lucky to find seats on the bus leaving for Kailua in thirty minutes, one of only two that covered this route daily. The bus stopped close to the Round House, on its way to Lanikai. The metal gate was open, but there was no one in the yard. The door was locked. Kalani and her flock of children were gone. Jerry did not dare to force his way through the plywood-covered window; the time of emergency and forgiveness was over. He bought sandwiches at a little neighborhood market, then they lay down under a tree, among tall weeds. They were tired and had no other place to go.

"What do you want to do?" Cat asked.

"Like in any wilderness," Jerry shrugged. "First, find shelter, then take care of food. There must be someone in charge of this building, the door's locked, plywood's in the windows. Maybe the owners have returned. Perhaps they'll let us stay here; if not, I'll go and find Kalani."

Their patience was rewarded. Jerry woke up from a nap, a blond head resting on his thigh, when an older man appeared in the yard. He wore covered leather shoes and a straw hat, obviously not a local. Most likely, he was the house's owner from California, checking on his property. Jerry carefully moved Cat's sleeping head from his leg to the knapsack and approached the man.

Jim Crawford was indeed the owner of the Round House. Jim knew Cat and had been told of her war council and orphanage operating in his building. "Can't imagine a better use for my home," he said kindly, but a moment later, added with a crooked smile, "just hope the smell of the dead whale evaporates soon." He wanted to return to his wife on the Mainland as soon as possible, so he was happy to learn that Cat and Jerry would take care of his house. Hawaii was a difficult place to live, especially for temporary residents.

Jerry set out on a reconnaissance to find Kalani. The banging of hammers resounded all along the street. Half-naked men kneeled on the roofs, stood on ladders and dug in the ground; a big push to rebuild was on. Good time to be a carpenter, Jerry smiled. A bunch of teenage boys sporting shirtless, thin chests sat on the concrete bench in front of the pizzeria. Two girls walked by pretending not to notice them whistling. The lethargy was gone—Kailua was full of life again, moving forward.

Jerry stopped at Starbucks, which had reopened a few days ago. An honest cup of real coffee could be bought again. That was where he caught the scent of Kalani's trail. A girl at the counter told Jerry to try Rosen's restaurant. He remembered that Kalani had taken over Rosen's food supplies at one point, so learning that she had commandeered the rest of the establishment as well did not surprise him.

The restaurant was closed but Kalani was indeed in the building. The kids camped in the restaurant's main room, tables and chairs neatly stored at one end. The floors were swept clean, the windows appeared spotless but, on closer inspection, there simply was no glass left in the frames.

"Republic of Hawaii, Kailua Office," said a sign in red felt pen on a piece of white cardboard, and pinned to the wall above the open door. Inside, Kalani was sitting behind a metal desk. Her body, which seemed to belong to a skinny teenager the last time Jerry saw her, had the voluptuous shape of a very attractive adult woman. She was still wearing the same old dress, now much tighter, but there was something new about her—an air of authority.

She jumped up from the desk when Jerry knocked and wrapped her arms around his neck. "Jerry, you came back! Is Cat with you?"

"She sure is, and she's fine. You can see her anytime at the Round House; we are the house sitters there. But look at you! You look fabulous! How is Abe?"

She let him go. "Abe is gone, fishing. He got almost religious about it, must be trying to make up for all those years he was bumming around. Now, he drops in sometimes, spends a night at home, then he's gone again, usually for a few days. He works your boat really hard; hope you don't mind, but he said you let him."

"Oh, that's fine. I hoped he would do that. I intend to become his partner."

"Are you really going to be a fisherman? You're a professor, Jerry!" Kalani eyed him incredulously.

"I was a professor. Now I need to make some money, however I can. We will see what else I can do."

"You could work for us . . ." Kalani proudly pointed her finger at the hand-painted placard leaned against the wall, red letters framed by the red and blue pattern of the Hawaiian flag.

"Republic of Hawaii," Jerry read aloud. "Have you separated from the USA already? I thought it was to be the Kingdom of Hawaii, not the Republic."

Kalani would not be intimidated by technicalities. "The important thing is, we'll have our own government. Kingdom or Republic... we can decide later."

Jerry felt worried, "What about the old government? You know, the State of Hawaii and the federal government in Washington?"

The young woman waved her hand dismissively. "We have people worrying about that in Honolulu. My job is to make sure that we can run Kailua and the windward side."

"That's not a small project, Kalani; who are you working with, are you the boss?"

"Auntie Malia comes every morning, and she frequently brings friends with her. Other people come and go, but would be here if I needed them. I'm here all the time, so I guess I am the boss," and she proudly raised her chin.

"I would love to help you, but I don't think you can pay me, and I do need money. By the way, is Sergeant Yoshida still around? Does he take orders from you?"

"Mike is still at the station, but I haven't seen him in a long time. I never tried to give him any orders so how would I know?"

Right. Good thing Yoshida didn't come to arrest her; maybe the *new Republic* hadn't caught the eye of the *old Republic* yet, Jerry thought.

Kalani looked directly into his eyes. "You think I'm a silly girl, who plays with things that she doesn't understand, don't you?"

Jerry was embarrassed because something close to that had crossed his mind.

Kalani kept him fixed in her sight. "You know, I'm not a very educated person, but I wouldn't call myself stupid either. We have to start somewhere. I'm not going to be a great help negotiating with the federal government or the Governor, but I know pretty well what people in Kailua need. I've learned a lot over the past few months, when we were working with Cat, and later. What I don't know I'm going to learn, and I will try to find good people who can help, like you and Cat."

Jerry recalled the Kalani who cleaned Cat's house: a pretty but simple girl whose biggest dream was to become a nurse. A new Kalani now stood in front of him, imposing, self-confident and determined. This was not a Kalani to dismiss with a joke and a smile.

"I will make you a deal, Kalani. I will do my best to help you with your mission whenever I can. But, I really have to earn a living for Cat and myself. Your organization needs to mature, too, before you can make use of an economist. But when you are ready, I'll do my best, as long as I agree with you and your people on what a proper government is. I certainly will not get involved in replicating the old system. Do we have an agreement, Kalani?"

The girl shook his extended hand firmly, then giggled and gave him a big Hawaiian hug and kiss on the cheek. "I knew you would help us, and Cat, too. Tell her I'll come this evening to see her."

Abe was expected back in two days. He was selling his fish in Honolulu, where a market had opened and commercial freezers were available. He had hired a young boy as a helper, and had become a real skipper, running the boat confidently on her diesel motor. Fuel was available, though very expensive, but business was good, so he could afford it.

"Ah, Jerry—you know, they found that bastard Rosen!" Kalani stopped him in the doorway.

"Really, Rosen got arrested?"

"Nah, someone shot him."

"Abe?"

"No, they found him dead in Honolulu. Abe was with you then, thank God. I'm glad that he's dead. I still feel like throwing myself through a window when somebody gets behind me unexpectedly. The first thing I did when I took over his office was to smash that figurine that he kept on his desk. I couldn't stop myself until it was dust."

Jerry decided to go see what was happening at the market, his personal monument to Adam Smith. A gathering of canvas tents, stalls and plywood huts spilled over from the tennis courts onto the large parking lot next to the baseball field. Jerry strolled among the stands. Vegetables and fruit mostly, but there were a few places with simple industrial products: bicycles, rickshaws, building materials reclaimed from the ruins, construction tools—things that people had to have, but few customers were buying, even though many people milled about.

Jerry understood why business was slow when he checked the prices. A pound of tomatoes was offered for three dollars. He continued inspecting the prices with an increasingly tight feeling in his throat. The ten thousand dollars they still had was supposed to give them six months of cushion, but with prices like these, they would be broke soon. They needed income as soon as possible.

Jerry came to a bicycle stand; he needed basic transportation and a used bike would do just fine. The stall was an example of capitalism in its purest form: a steel-tubing frame covered with a large piece of blue tarp for a roof and a back wall. A metal bike-stand held upright eight or ten vehicles of different sizes. Jerry checked a solid-looking mountain bike with good tires; the attached price tag: two hundred eighty dollars.

Two hundred eighty bucks for a used bike? That's an outrage! I can certainly do better than that! Jerry approached the bored Asian man sitting on a picnic chair in front of his merchandise. "How come your bikes are so expensive? I could get a new one for less at Wal-Mart."

The merchant looked at him scornfully. He wasn't going to engage in this conversation, but after looking around, and seeing no other prospective customers he decided to chat after all.

"You went to Wal-Mart?"

"No, I didn't," Jerry admitted.

"Only rats there. The old merchandise looted long time

ago; the store's closed. At Sears, you can have pots that nobody wants and maybe some clothes. But they have no bikes, no tools—nothing that people really need." Then he looked the other way.

"I really need a bike; can you tell me why they don't sell stuff that people want to buy?"

"Because they can't. The Chinese decided they didn't want to give away their goods for free, after all. The bikes at Sears would be even more expensive than mine, if they came from overseas. People couldn't buy them anyway. Do you know what the price of an ounce of gold is?"

Jerry shook his head "no." The last time he knew gold's price was three months ago, and then it was about six hundred twenty.

"Eleven hundred twenty one bucks this morning, and you can bet it will be more a week from now."

"Inflation!" Jerry felt a punch in his solar plexus. Inflation has hit us like a car running into a flock of chickens lazily pecking on a village road. He recalled his discussion with Cat in December. There was nothing Schumacher with his great computer model of inflation, the Federal Reserve or anybody else could do. The house was falling, and a lot of people would be crushed. No need for a professor of economics; a first-year student could tell you that gold's price doubling in three months indicates horrific inflation. Like a tsunami, it won't stop until the landscape is flat, all traces and memories of prosperity thoroughly erased.

The merchant watched Jerry with satisfaction. "You better buy now, before bikes get even more expensive." He seemed quite happy with the prices he could command, did not understand yet that inflation would sweep him into the same gutter as everyone else.

Jerry knew better. It had happened to many other people before: the Germans after the First World War, then Argentineans, Brazilians. . . . It happened to every nation that chose to believe that prosperity could be achieved by playing tricks with money. Printing new bank notes at no cost gave an illusion of prosperity to all in the short term, but by the time the public caught on to the shell game, the economy was ruined.

"When did it start? I mean the prices growing so fast," Jerry asked.

"All I know is," the merchant answered, "that since I stopped trading bikes for food, and started using money, I couldn't buy anything for the usual price. I had to pay double or triple for my merchandise. Plus my markup and— you see the prices."

Jeremy bought the bike. I was a part of this scam, he thought, riding slowly over cracked asphalt. I taught my students complicated theories, but never mentioned the most ancient law: *If you want to consume, you have to produce.* The technological progress had been so rapid that it seemed impossible to run out of goods, but consumption rose even faster. The ancient truth had never been revoked.

Fat rubber wheels jumped over the potholes overflowing with exuberant weeds. Jerry turned his bike into the open gate of the Round House, but couldn't shake off his anxious thoughts. People came to believe that prosperity is a natural condition. Big mistake—the natural order of life is starvation, fear and an early death. Being smart and working hard can keep this reality away, but it will return, whenever intelligence or diligence fails.

He found the living room decorated with lavender; flowers are so easy to obtain in Hawaii, just a walk out to the garden, regardless of the season. Cat was reclining on the sofa, a mango in her hand. Her body had acquired a softer shape, less athletic but definitely sweeter. Her round face glowed happily as she coaxed him with her outstretched arms. When Jerry sat on the sofa beside her, she wrapped her arms around his neck and kissed him by the ear, did not let go, but whispered, "Congratulations, Jerry, you're going to be a daddy."

Jerry's arms squeezed her body gently against his chest as if she were a fragile porcelain vase. As he lay next to her kissing her eyes and lips, Cat led his hand over her stomach. Jerry whispered, "You know, there is nothing I wouldn't do to protect you both. A few months ago, I was a shallow, bored, thirty-five-year-old boy, and then you helped me break my brick wall. Now, I'm ready to take on the world. You will never be alone as long as I live."

Cat's face was moist. "I feel safe with you, and this baby will have a wonderful father."

The news Jerry brought from the market concerned Cat, but did not surprise her. "Smart people kept predicting this for years. It's just that the timing is really bad. But is there *ever* a good time for a disaster? Still, it would only be fair for us to have an easier life for a while."

Jerry massaged her belly lightly. "Isn't it a shame the baby will come during hard times?"

"The baby knows best," shrugged Cat. "Anyway, considering all that we went through, this is going to be one tough kid. And this coming storm, maybe it's what is needed to clear all this foolishness and garbage that has accumulated over the years. If that's what we have to endure for our child to have blue skies," she put her hand on her swollen abdomen, "I don't mind, so be it." Cat thought for a moment. "Do you think, Jerry, we will stay here? For many years, I mean. I really like Hawaii."

"You know, Cat, I love Hawaii, too. The best things in my life happened here."

She pushed her head under Jerry's arm and onto his lap, so that he could caress her hair.

"I love people like Kalani and Abe," Jerry continued. "We'll help them and make our home here, if treated fairly. On the other hand, if the government, whatever government it is, tries to make us its servants, I would try very hard to persuade you to move somewhere else."

Cat did not move or say anything for a while, then asked quietly, "Where, Jerry?"

"I don't know, Cat. There must be people who think like us; we would find them." During the long hours Jerry had spent in the rubber boat, holding the dying Cat's head, he thought, "If I had another chance . . . how would I run my life, so I wouldn't have to sit helplessly, watching my love dying?"

"I should never remain defenseless," was his answer. "I might not have much, but what we need, I would have under my control. No one would be in charge of my survival, no person or office would decide if I can have my ten gallons of diesel or a tin of sardines." Jerry wanted to talk about his thoughts and plans, but his wife's eyes had closed and she was breathing quietly. Cat was asleep, relaxed and trusting in his arms, at last.

* * *

Ruth, I know you can hear me; you are hiding somewhere in my head. After all, that's where you moved after your pool eventually dried up; that's where you live now. You were wrong; it's real. You've told me what the test of reality was, remember? I needed to feel something I had never felt before, something that my mind couldn't make up, preferably of the visceral kind. Today, I felt my baby kick—how about that? Are you ready to accept it now? And... Ruth, thank you for that wake-up call on the dinghy. If you hadn't told me, I wouldn't have gotten up to find the flare gun on the bottom, and we would have drifted away forever.

Printed in the United States
113536LV00002B/169/P